TOXIC LOVE

A DARK ENEMIES TO LOVERS MAFIA ROMANCE

VENOMOUS GODS
BOOK ONE

JAGGER COLE

 Created with Vellum

PLAYLIST

Toxic - Rain Paris
VILLAIN - Neoni
Therefore I Am - Billie Eilish
Note To Self: Don't Die - Ryan Adams
I Feel Like I'm Drowning - Two Feet
My Way - Frank Sinatra
Erode - TENDER
Style - Ryan Adams
Where the Dark Things Are - Kerli
Born To Die - Lana Del Rey
Movement - Hozier
Dangerous Woman - Ariana Grande
Devil Like Me - Rainbow Kitten Surprise
Walk Through the Fire - Zayde Wølf, Ruelle
BABYDOLL - Ari Abdul
Slow Dancing in a Burning Room - John Mayer
Beloved - Mumford & Sons
I Will Follow You into the Dark - Death Cab for Cutie
Skinny Love - Bon Iver
Doomsday - Ryan Adams

Listen to the playlist on Spotify!

TRIGGER WARNING

This book contains darker themes and graphic depictions of past trauma, including mentions of SA, suicide, and self-harm. While these scenes were written to create a more vivid, in-depth story, they may be triggering to some readers. *Please* know your triggers, and read with that in mind.

1

TEMPEST

"THIS IS BEYOND OBSCENE."

It's Alistair who breaks the silence first, his tone lethal and menacing in the stately living room.

Usually, the honor of breaking the silence would just about always go to me and my big mouth. Because I have a tendency to "speak my mind", as Gabriel puts it, which is... charitable of him.

The more realistic, blunter way of putting it would be that I have lots of opinions, not much of a filter, and little to no impulse control when it comes to *voicing* those opinions. But in this case, I'm too busy staring at Charles with my jaw on the floor to speak. And Gabriel is obviously too busy marshaling his thoughts into neat, organized lines, like mounted cavalry waiting for the choreographed attack on a battlefield.

It's my brother Gabriel's ability to word his arguments and keep his thoughts in those tidy little lines that make him one of the best lawyers in New York. And it's my *other* brother Alistair's ability to scare and intimidate the living shit out of people that makes him equally as formidable a legal presence.

Unfortunately, if my grandfather Charles is intimidated by Alistair and his menacing tone, he hides it well. He merely rolls his eyes as he drums his fingers on the leather armrest of his chair. His other hand raises a crystal tumbler of whiskey to the bored line of his lips. It's barely ten in the morning, but I doubt a pesky thing like an appropriate time of day has ever once come between Charles Black and a drink.

"Precisely how would you categorize this as obsc—"

"How about the fact that she's fucking *eighteen!*"

Me and my mouth finally join the fray. My grandfather's mouth and jaw tighten at my profanity, which just pisses me off even more. It's not the fact that one of his grandchildren has just sworn in front of him—my two brothers do that all the goddamn time. It's the fact that I'm a *woman* and I've just sworn at all, period.

Because in the world of Charles Black, we all still live in 1910. Maybe even earlier. I'm not sure he even thinks women should have the right to vote, for fuck's sakes.

"Tempest—"

"She's *eighteen fucking years*—"

"I'm going to ask you once, and only once," he snaps coldly, "to stop interrupting me."

I almost explode at the irony of him interrupting *me* to tell me to stop interrupting *him*. When my angry eyes dart to the side and meet Gabriel's, though, he gives me just the briefest and faintest shake of his head.

Pick your battles, kiddo, I can almost hear him saying.

Except a battle is clearly what Charles wanted in summoning us all here today. He could have easily told us all of this over the phone, or let us hear it directly from Maeve.

But no. Charles wanted to witness our helpless fury in person. Relish it.

Because he's a prick like that.

"Your aunt is eighteen years old," Charles drones, glaring at me before he sighs and pulls his gaze over first to Gabriel and then Alistair. "And I am well within my rights to make a suitable...*arrangement* for her that benefits both her and the rest of this family."

It's a little Jerry Springer, yes, but Maeve, who is technically our aunt, just turned eighteen, making her a full six years younger than me and seventeen years younger than my brothers. Weird? Yeah. But that's what happens when your at-the-time fifty-seven-year-old grandfather gets remarried to a twenty-year-old gold digger who in the single smartest career move of her life, almost immediately pops out a kid. And now here I am with a seventy-five-year-old grandfather, a thirty-eight-year-old step-grandmother, and an aunt who just finished high school.

Jer-ry. Jer-ry. Jer-ry...

"Might I remind you, Charles," Gabriel murmurs quietly in that way he has. He sometimes comes across as reserved, but his quietness is never soft or weak. It's more like the soft rattle of the wind in the branches right before the thundercloud breaks. He might take his time lining up those argu-

3

ments and thoughts of his in neat little lines. But when they charge, they mean business.

"That we live firmly in twenty-first century America. And you're honestly sitting here talking about arranged marriages."

A small hint of a smile curls the corners of our grandfather's lips and lifts the edges of his silvered mustache and goatee. Most people consider Charles Black a handsome, distinguished man—a man who shakes hands with governors and state senators. A man to whom the heads of the ironworkers' and police unions owe favors. A powerbroker, of sorts.

Then again, most people don't look past the charming mask bought with wealth and power to see the uncaring, heartless ghoul behind it.

The kind of ghoul who's *actually* about to sell his own eighteen-year-old daughter to the fucking mob: probably for something like first dibs on a new development project, or a cut of sanitation contract kickbacks.

Knowing Charles, it could just as easily be for box seats at a Yankees game, if he's feeling particularly evil this week.

Whatever the reason, the reality of what he's just told us feels like a punch to the throat. To be marrying Maeve into the Italian mafia would be horrendous enough on its own to warrant Alistair's "obscene" comment, especially given the age difference between Maeve and her intended.

But it's not just any mafioso he's marrying her off to. It's to *him*: to—

"Dante goddamn Sartorre?! Have you gone fucking senile?!"

Alistair's outburst garners a slight raise of an eyebrow, but not the same stern look that I got for swearing. Jackass.

"He's an ideal—"

"He's a fucking sociopath and a monster," Alistair snarls, shoving a hand through his dirty-blond hair as he paces the floor. "And after what that piece of shit did to Layla, if you had a single fucking ounce of honor or family loyalty, you'd have—"

"What, killed him?" Charles drones in a bored tone.

The room goes quiet, all three of us glaring at our grandfather: two sets of greenish-hazel eyes from Gabriel and I, and one set of icy cold blues from Alistair.

"Tell me, Alistair," Charles says with a sneering smile on his face. "If you've already passed judgment and sentence here, why haven't *you* taken care of Dante yourself?"

"Because I'm a goddamn *attorney*, Charles," Alistair hisses. "Not..."

"Not what?" Our grandfather's lips curl deeper and his tone grows colder, his eyes narrowing.

"Not...*you*," Gabriel mutters.

Our grandfather isn't *technically* mafia; the kind who rigs poker games, or runs drugs and arms, or fights street wars for territory. He's the more dangerous kind of mafioso. He's the kind of criminal people elect, not realizing who they're voting for. The kind who's learned not to fight the system or even hide from it, but to embrace it and *become* "the system."

Charles built his kingdom out of favors, leverage, greased palms, and probably some blackmail here and there. He's friends with politicians, union leaders, and yes, the mafia as well. And it's that last one he's about to cement his relationship to, when he marries young Maeve off.

To the devil himself.

Dante Sartorre *also* isn't technically a "made" man in the mafia. But he might as well be, even more so than Charles. Raised by the *very* powerful Barone mafia family, Dante—like Charles—built himself a nice little empire in the gray area between the dark and the light. Except while my grandfather deals in favors, Dante deals in *hedonism*.

Pleasure. Darkness. *Depravity*.

Dante owns and runs Club Venom—an exclusive, secret, members-only kink club that caters to the city's most powerful, twisted, and dangerous. Honestly, it's a place someone like me shouldn't even *know* about.

Except I do.

But that's beside the point. Owning a sex club for mafiosos to get freaky at is *not* the reason my brothers and I hate Dante Sartorre.

It's because of what he did to our sister fifteen years ago.

"Does she know yet?"

Charles raises a hard glance my way. "Beg pardon?"

"*Maeve*," I hiss. "Does she know you're selling her to a man twice her age for—" My brow furrows. "Sorry, what exactly *are* you getting out of this, anyway?"

Our grandfather lifts his glass and takes another drink. "Stability, Tempest. We *all* get—"

"Why don't you just fuck off already with the savior complex bullshit, Charles," Alistair growls. "Do not include us in this as if you give a fuck about anyone in this room but yourself. You're selling your own flesh and fucking blood to the very monster who had a hand in Layla's death—"

"Oh, step outside your little glass tower and open your goddamn eyes!" Charles roars, lurching to his feet with surprising agility for a man his age. He levels a withering gaze at my brother, then Gabriel, then me.

"The Greeks are in bed with the Irish, who are now *also* in bed with the Bratva. Meanwhile, the Italians are at each other's throats like—"

"Exactly *when*," Gabriel mutters coldly, "is it going to click with you, Charles, that *none of us* is in the business of criminality! Alistair and I run the most prestigious law firm in the goddamn city, and Tempest—"

"And exactly who pulled the strings to *get you* that law firm, hmm?" our grandfather fires back. "And besides, don't try to look me in the eye and tell me your hands are clean, either of you. I know damn well who you happily represent, legally."

He's not exactly wrong. While my brothers might not be involved in any criminal enterprises themselves, their client roster has definitely started to, shall we say, *trend* a certain way in the last few years: the Drakos Greek mafia family. The Kildare Irish mafia. Elements of the Russian Bratva, too.

But still, we ourselves are not criminals. Or even criminally adjacent, like our grandfather. That was always the major rift in our family: that our dad went into law, instead of following Charles into lawlessness.

"This is fucking medieval, Charles," Gabriel says coldly. "She's your *daughter*, for God's sake. And Dante is..." His face clouds with rage and he trails off. He doesn't need to finish the thought. We all know what Dante Sartorre is.

A monster.

A purveyor of sex and hedonism.

One of the last people to have seen our sister alive, when he *married*, out of the blue, on her death bed.

He's the devil that lurks over your shoulder, whispering poison into your ear as he slowly corrupts your soul. Like he did to Layla.

"I know precisely what Dante is," Charles tosses back. "He's connected, but not *too* connected. He's powerful, yet in need of allies, and—"

"*For fuck's sake, Charles!*" Alistair roars, cutting our grandfather off. "How in the *hell* are you overlooking his obvious involvement in Layla's—"

"Well, I don't see him in jail for it, *counselor!*" Charles volleys back, jabbing a finger at my brother. "So unless there's a smoking gun you've had up your ass for the last fifteen—"

"Does she *know!?*"

My shrill scream silences the room for a second. My pulse thuds in my ears, and for a second, as the too-familiar wave of dizziness washes over me, I'm terrified I'm going to faint again. I'm terrified that I'm going to give myself away, and if I do that right here in front of all of them, there'll be no avoiding the question of *why*.

And right now, I don't have time for the why.

I don't have much time for anything at all, actually.

"Maeve is well aware of what her duty to this family entails —Tempest!"

I ignore Charles' blustering as I storm across the room toward the closed double doors out to the main foyer of the house. One, because I need to talk to Maeve, *now*, and reassure her I'm going to get her out of this, even if I have no idea how. And two, because there's a solid chance I'm going to faint unless I get the hell out of this room.

"Tempest, this is happening!" Charles roars at my back as I reach for the doorknobs. "And Maeve is—"

"You can go to hell, Charles," I spit over my shoulder as my fingers curl around the brass knobs. "You and that sick psychopath Dante!"

I fling open the doors and surge through them...

Until I slam directly into something hard, chiseled, and wrapped in three-piece linen and silk. My world goes upside down as I gasp sharply and tumble backward off my heels. Instantly, two strong, powerful, veined hands grab my wrists in their iron grip, yanking me back upright until I crash back into that firm, broad chest again.

My eyes drag up over the crisp, white dress shirt, the faint shine of a black silk tie, the bronzed, Mediterranean skin of a muscular neck and chiseled, perfect cheekbones. The slight cleft in the chin. The insidiously beautiful and kissable lips...

Yet it's the eyes that capture my soul and bind it fast: sharp, icy-blue, and piercingly lethal beneath a shock of perfectly coifed dark hair.

"Speak of the devil..." Dante growls quietly.

My heart lurches into my throat. I flinch as if to move away from him. But Dante's strong grip only tightens on my thin wrists, sending my pulse skyrocketing and my head swimming. His strong fingers clench even tighter, and those eyes of his don't even blink as they zero in on mine.

"...And he shall appear," he murmurs.

His lips curl dangerously into a darkly unsettling quasi-smile, his eyes glinting as they eviscerate me.

"Now: I do hope I haven't missed the surprise?"

2

DANTE

When I step out of the Range Rover, my brow darkens into a scowl as I glare up at the looming stone New Jersey mansion belonging to Charles Black.

Mine's bigger.

Yeah, it's a childish place to go in my head, but at this point, I really don't give a shit. Because despite everything I've built and everything I have despite coming from nothing, it still all boils down to this: do as you're told, or it all gets taken away.

Sure, my place on Long Island might be bigger than Charles Black's old-money, "my ancestors came over on the fucking Mayflower" sprawling Westchester, New York mansion of a home. My pockets may be deeper than his, and my reach and influence *absolutely* go further than his at this point.

But.

There's still a massive difference between us. Charles is truly monarch of his kingdom. I, however, still can't seem to get out from under the...*influence* of others.

Part of me hates myself for feeling angry about it. After all, I really did come from nothing, and though he might be pushing me toward something in which I currently have no interest, almost all of what I have now is thanks to Vito Barone.

My father once worked as the personal tailor to the don of the Barone family, truly living up to our last name of *Sartorre*. But that was decades ago, in another life. And when my parents were killed when my sisters and I were still kids, instead of shoving us out to fend for ourselves in a world that would have certainly devoured us, Vito took in Claudia, Bianca, and me.

Years later, it was Vito again who helped me lay the foundation and the first stones of my empire. It's by Vito's grace, and the grace of the other Italian families, that Club Venom is even allowed to exist, and I am able to run that empire I've built with almost total impunity.

But the thing is, the wheel of karma always comes back around. The pied piper *always* gets paid.

And my bill just came due. With interest.

Honestly, I've known for years that I was walking a fine line. Club Venom, my empire, provides neither a service nor an entertainment. It facilitates desires, fantasies, and hedonism. That's a fancy way of saying "what happens at Venom, between two—or frequently *more* than two—consenting adults, *stays* at Venom." The wealthy, powerful, typically connected and dangerous come to my house of ill repute to play how they like.

But always consensually, and *without* any money changing hands. There's a membership fee, but that's it.

This is important. One, because I'm not, nor have I ever once *wanted* to be, a pimp. Those who come to play at Venom are there because they one hundred per cent want to be—I know this because I personally and thoroughly vet every single member. Venom is *not* a place for escorts, sex-workers, or anyone else who's only there because they have to be.

Because fuck. That.

Aside from my own abhorrence of any situation where someone *has* to participate in sex for money, the mob also shares that loathing. Or at least, a strong intolerance.

The Commission, which is sort of a council table of the five main Italian families in the United States, agreed almost twenty years ago to stop any involvement in the sex trade. As in, the Italians don't pimp anymore. At all.

One, it's morally reprehensible. But more than that, speaking in a pure business sense, it's just not worth the bullshit involved. Drugs, guns, casinos, sports betting, construction rackets, and grifting city services... They all make *way* more money for a fraction of the headache involved.

But that's where the ice has grown thin in places on the surface of my empire.

I of course knew that Marcia Greco, daughter of Angelo Greco, underboss to Don Cesare Marchetti, was a member of Club Venom, because all member applications run through me. Per*haps* there were some red flags in the back of my mind, letting the daughter of the second-in-command of the entire Marchetti family join my house of sin.

But I'm not here to play arbiter. Marcia is a fully grown, twenty-three-year old woman. If she wants to spend her Saturday nights getting gang-banged by Bratva *avtoritets* or giving lap dances to Yakuza *wakagashira*, what the fuck do I care?

No, the problem isn't so much that Angelo found out where his little princess was spending her weekend evenings—okay, yeah, that *is* a problem, given that Angelo now wants my balls on a plate, despite the fact that I personally never once *touched* her. The bigger problem is that Marcia wasn't just screwing dangerous and powerful men at Venom.

She was *charging them.*

Obviously, I wasn't aware that this was happening. I also haven't the slightest clue if it was because Marcia wasn't getting a big enough allowance from daddy dearest, or if the money thing was her kink. Frankly, I don't give a shit.

But suddenly, The Commission's not looking at Venom as my little fiefdom of hedonism for the wealthy and depraved. They're looking at it as a *brothel*.

And that creates a problem.

Luckily, before I could get my favorite appendage removed by a bloodthirsty capo or have my entire empire yanked out from under me, Vito came up with an elegant solution. Elegant, that is, except I want nothing to do with it.

The solution is this: The Commission families have, thankfully, agreed that Marcia acted on her own. But the image problem with Club Venom remains—that I, a single, unmarried man am running what is effectively a "house of ill repute", minus the monetary transactions.

It's that "single and unmarried" part that creates the real issue, apparently. Now they're worried that it looks like I'm operating as some kind of pimp. So it's come down to this: get married, and quickly, and this whole problem goes away.

The drinks keep flowing, the lights stay on, and the rich, powerful, and kinky of New York City can continue to fuck and suck to their filthy little hearts' content at my club.

But now we come back to the million-dollar question: why do I want to marry Maeve Black? A girl half my age whose father is a poisonous fucking spider with his fingers in every single pie in New York?

Simple answer: I fucking *don't*.

Charles Black is an embarrassing, disgusting stain on this city. And I have zero interest in marrying a child. But I've also been playing this game long enough to understand how to maneuver around while staying just inside the lines. In that sense, Maeve Black is the *perfect* match.

She's mafia-adjacent enough, from her father's connections, that The Commission is okay with it. Yet she's not *actually* mafia, which saves me from getting stuck with some needy, clingy little mafia princess with a don of a father breathing down my neck.

Also, it puts Charles squarely in the palm of my fucking hand.

I know *all sorts* of shit about all sorts of people in this city. That, honestly, is what I truly trade in with Club Venom. Not sex. Not fantasies. Not hedonism.

Information.

By that metric, I'm richer than fucking Elon.

Charles has no idea that I know this, but he's in trouble. As he's gotten older, he's failed to secure new relationships with the younger generations as they come up through the ranks of this city. Which means his little kingdom built on nothing but handshakes and understandings and favors is starting to crumble at the foundations.

Charles *needs* his daughter to marry someone like me. And I plan on leveraging that need to the fullest.

Now, he has no idea that *I* need Maeve to marry me as much as he needs *me* to marry *her*. I mean—he'll probably figure it out at some point. But I've seen no need to put all the cards on the table just yet.

Anyway, for all those reasons, marrying Maeve Black is a perfect plan.

...Perfect, except for the fact that Gabriel and Alistair Black and I *hate* each other.

The details don't matter. I know what they *think* I did to their family.

I, however, know the truth.

And now here we are.

Carmy—as in Carmine Barone, Vito's eldest son and one of my closest friends—snickers from behind me. I turn away from the facade of the Black residence to glare at him, still sitting there in the passenger seat with his fucking feet up on the dash.

"Well?" I mutter, glancing at my watch.

He lifts an amused brow. "Well, what?"

"*Well*, I'm not giving you a fucking piggyback, so let's go."

He chuckles, his white teeth flashing as he runs a hand through his dark hair. "Yeah, no, I'm fine right here, actually."

I glare at him, my jaw clenching. Carmy grins wider.

"Sorry, Dante... Did you think I was coming along for emotional support?" He laughs, sprawling back in his seat. "No way, bud. I'm here because this is *highly* amusing to me."

I give him the finger as I turn to glare up at the house again.

"By the way, were you aware that Charles once tried to use his influence to ban all strip clubs in New York?" Carmy clicks his tongue against his teeth. "You and your new father-in-law are going to have *so much fun* together."

I turn to level a withering looking at the friend who's been more like a brother to me since even before his family took me in. "Venom is *not* a strip club, dickhead."

"Just a masked sex club that regularly hosts voyeuristic orgies and kink nights. My deepest apologies for confusing the two."

"Are you done?"

"For now."

I glare at him once more. "So, you're staying here."

"Yep. Can you leave the radio on and crack a window—"

"Don't fucking smoke in my car."

I slam the door shut to the sound of Carmy's snickering, turning to groan at the Black family mansion once more.

Goddammit.

Alistair, Gabriel and I were never "friends" per se. But once upon a time, when we were all at Knightsblood University together, we were at least...cordial. Knightsblood has four student clubs, and the three of us happened to be the presidents of three of them at the same time: Alistair was head of

17

The Reckless, Gabriel ran Para Bellum, and I was at the top of the Ouroboros Society.

Then Layla died, and it all went to shit.

We haven't spoken or seen each other face to face since. Though they're both members of Venom, which means they haven't considered the fact that I vet every single member. Or else they have and they just don't care.

Gabriel and the lovely and formidable Taylor Crown, the third founding partner of Crown and Black, mostly come to Venom for business reasons: to show prospective clients a good time, or to assure the dangerous people they've been representing these days that they can "hang" with the bad guys.

Alistair comes for business reasons, too. But he also comes to play.

Hey, no judgement.

Still, today will be interesting, to say the least. Not only is it the first time we'll be seeing each other live and in person since what happened all those years ago. But also I'll be casually letting them know that, oh, by the way, I'm going to be marrying their eighteen-year-old aunt.

Yeah, this should certainly be an interesting experience for everyone involved.

Two guards at the top of the front steps of the house pat me down and then let me through. Inside, a butler bows silently, then ushers me through the lavish foyer toward a closed set of wooden double doors.

"Does she *know!?*"

I tense, stopping cold at the shrill scream coming from the other side of the doors. It's a woman's voice, but it's too old to be Maeve, and I know for a fact that Charles' gold-digging wife, Caroline, is in Rio right now spending her husband's money on a butt lift.

She's probably also fucking every cabana boy on Ipanema, given that back home, she's chained to Charles' wrinkly old dick. But I digress.

"Maeve is well aware of what her duty to this family entails —Tempest!"

Aaah. Yes. So it's the fourth Black sibling, Tempest, who's raging like…well, a tempest.

She's also the member of the Black family about whom I know the least.

Gabriel and Alistair I've studied like a scientist. I know Alistair isn't really as dark-hearted as he'd like the world to think, and about his adoption when he was three. And I know Gabriel isn't as *good* as *he'd* like the world to think, as well as all about his political aspirations that he won't admit to anyone.

And of course, I knew Layla.

Probably *too* well.

Too well to save her, anyway.

But Tempest? She's an unknown to me. All I know is, she's eleven years younger than her brothers, doesn't work, and by all accounts is just sort of a trust fund kid living off Gabriel and Alistair's dime. She's probably in Charles' pocket, too—

"You can go to hell, Charles!"

My brow cocks.

Okay, maybe NOT on Team Charles...

"You and that sick psychopath Dante!"

I scowl, and just as I'm about to open the door and make my entrance, they fly open in my face. Something small, soft, freckled, wearing thick black eyeliner and with her dark hair piled up on her head, dressed in a vaguely gothy all-black ensemble consisting of a turtleneck, shiny black leggings, and heeled black ankle boots with buckles and pointy toes, comes barreling into my chest.

She gasps sharply, stumbling back from me. As if on instinct, my hands shoot out, my strong fingers curling around her too-thin wrists and latching on tightly. Before I know what I'm doing, I'm yanking her up to stop her from falling, and right into my chest.

Her breath catches. Her big greenish-hazel eyes with the too-thick eyeliner drag up to mine. When they reach their destination, she doesn't quail. She doesn't flinch or look scared.

She looks *angry*. Wrathful. Indignant that I've had the gall to stop her from falling on her fucking ass.

Tempest is indeed well named.

She glares at me, her glowing hazel-green eyes set deep in the sea of black around them. Her face is very pale, and it's not just her wrists that seem too thin. *All* of her seems too thin.

"Speak of the devil..." I growl quietly.

Tempest glares venomously at me and moves as if to yank her arms back. But I just grip her soft wrists a bit tighter.

"And he shall appear."

Her chin juts defiantly. Her mouth purses.

"Now: I do hope I haven't missed the surprise?"

I'm neither an idiot, nor a hothead. The wise move here would be to defuse the tensions of the room as quickly as possible and tackle this like rational adults. Except I'm not thinking rationally. One, because I don't *like* being called a "sick psychopath", especially behind my back. Two, because I really don't appreciate the way Gabriel and Alistair seem to be barely holding themselves back from physically attacking me.

But the third and biggest reason for the implosion of my rational thinking is the one I never saw coming.

It's *her*.

And I don't know why.

I mean the girl is looking at me like she's trying to decide if she'd get more pleasure from stabbing me in the eye or in the dick-hole. She's also dressed like she's about to go on stage and sing backups for The Cure or Morrissey. She's too short and too thin for my tastes. Too gothy. Too...*stabby-looking*.

And yet...

There's a hum that sparks off her skin into my fingertips; a *something* that the nearness of her does to me.

Fuck.

It's attraction.

That's very inconvenient, given that I'm about to marry her *aunt*. Not to mention her obvious interest in putting out cigarettes on my balls or pushing sharp pointy things into the soft parts of my anatomy.

I need whatever this is to get the fuck out of my system *right fucking now—*

"Get your fucking hands off of me, you pedo piece of shit."

And a solution presents itself…

Instantly, the way I'm rapidly drowning in the nearness of her vanishes. My pulse thudding in my ears goes silent. The blood leaves my rapidly swelling dick.

"Excuse me?"

Tempest glares at me, twisting her wrists and finally yanking them free. She takes a step back, then another, crossing her arms over her chest and sneering at me as she sucks her bottom lip between her teeth.

"You heard me."

"Tempest!" Charles snaps, quickly marching over to us. He shoves her aside, shooting her a menacing glare before turning to beam at me ingratiatingly like the oily, self-serving little fuck that he is.

"Mr. Sartorre, welcome to my home." He sticks out a hand, which I reluctantly take. "Let me just say, I think this arrangement is going to be *fantastic* for the both of us, and I'm excited for our families to be—"

"What the fuck did you call me?"

I ignore Charles, leveling a withering look at Tempest behind him. She just shrugs.

"I called you what you are. You're marrying a fucking *child*, aren't you?"

"*Surely*, growing up in the family you did, you are familiar with the concept of an arranged marriage. And your aunt is eighteen years old."

"Been marking the days down on your calendar, have you?" Alistair hisses quietly.

I sigh as I raise my eyes to him. "Lovely to see you again too, Alistair," I say, with all the sincerity of a rich celebrity talking about ending poverty.

"Go fuck yourself, Dante," he throws back.

"Now now now, that's go fuck yourself *Uncle* Dante these days, isn't it?"

A vein pops out on Alistair's forehead. His mouth draws to a vicious line. Miraculously, he holds it together.

"In through the nose, out through the mouth, Alistair," I croon. "In…and out. In…and out. Serenity now. Serenity—"

"If your goal in coming here is to get punched in the face, I can do that right now and save us all a lot of time, Dante," Gabriel growls quietly.

"Nah, his goal in coming here is to fuck young girls who are barely—"

"*ENOUGH.*"

My roar silences Alistair and Gabriel without much of a flinch on either of their faces. More importantly, it makes Tempest shudder from head to toe and momentarily wipes that little Wednesday Addams sneer off her face.

For a split second, she actually looks scared.

I smile to myself, enjoying the win of piercing her sarcastic little armor.

"If you're done insulting me—"

"I could go all night—"

She jolts as I march past her grandfather right into her personal space.

"Touch her," Gabriel growls, "and we'll have a *very* large problem on our hands."

I shoot him an icy smile. "I'm sure the legal motion will be simply *breathtaking*, Gabriel. But I have no intention or indeed the least bit of interest in touching dear sister Hurricane here."

"It's *Tempest*," she hisses.

I relish the tremor she barely chokes back as I turn to level the full weight of my cold blue eyes on her as I loom over her.

"I really don't care. And let's be perfectly clear on something, shall we?" I smile darkly at her. "I don't give one single *fuck* if you like me or not. In fact, I hope you don't, so that you stay away from me with that stabby fucking look on your face. Are we clear?"

Her answer is a silent purse of her lips and a shiver she can't quite hide.

"Wonderful. Now, two things. One," I tick it off on my fingers right in front of her face. "I have no interest in doing *a thing* with your fucking aunt. I'm thirty-four years old, she's eighteen, and, spoiler, I guess it turns out I'm attracted to *women*, not girls. Two, arranged marriages aren't about getting laid, they're for political clout, treaties, or business. That is *all* this is, *capice*?"

"Go fuck—"

She gasps as I stop my outthrust finger from *just* touching her lips.

"*Resist* the urge to always need to have the last word, little Hurricane. Mouths were built to be shut at times, as strange a concept as that may be to you."

Tempest looks at me like she wants to drive her knee into my balls.

"Why are you marrying Maeve, Dante," Gabriel mutters quietly. "You're obviously not in love with her, since you don't even *know* her. And your eloquent speech just now on your lack of physical intentions is...whatever. So, why?"

"Reasons."

He glares at me. "Care to specify?"

"Not especially."

Charles laughs nervously at the ensuing silence and clasps his hands together. "Just ironing out the wrinkles, I suppose, yes?"

Sure.

"Anyway, I'm sure you'd like to meet Maeve—"

I allow myself to enjoy the chaos of all three of his grandchildren sputtering and bellowing about the injustice of it all, what a piece of shit I am, and what a monster Charles is, blah blah blah, for another twenty seconds or so before I hold up a hand.

"Actually, Charles, no. I just wanted to stop by today and meet my new niece and nephews."

The three of them glare pure death at me as I smile beatifically at them.

"I'm sure Maeve and I will have plenty of time later to get to know one another."

Tempest's eyes narrow dangerously at me. Before she can open her mouth again, Charles clears his throat.

"Tempest, why don't you run upstairs to your aunt and tell her all about Mr. Sartorre?"

Tempest shoots me a cold look.

"You know what? That's a great idea. I'd rather be literally anywhere else in the world but in the same room as you."

"The feeling is quite mutual," I smile.

She wrinkles her nose, holding her head up high as she moves to walk past me. But just as she does, I turn to the side, grabbing her wrist tightly in such a way that her brothers can't see.

"Play nice, little cyclone," I murmur quietly into her ear as she stiffens under my touch. "Or I'm sure I could be persuaded to rethink my position on sleeping with eighteen-year-old aunts."

The fire in her eyes when she whips around to face me is scorching enough to burn. Half of me expects her to attack me. But in a frankly stunning show of self-control, she just curls her lips and leans in close.

"If you touch Maeve, I'll fuck you." She smiles sweetly. *"With a claw hammer.* 'Capice'?"

Then she turns and strides out of the room, letting the doors slam shut behind her.

Charles awkwardly clears his throat. "Well, my apologies for—"

"Let's move on, shall we?"

He smiles. "Agreed. And, since we've got the lawyers here, should we look quickly at the premarital contracts?"

I resist the urge to roll my eyes. As if I have *any* interest in taking anything from Charles. But fine, sure; we can go over whatever ridiculous prenuptial bullshit he's concocted. His two grandsons immediately start poring over the paperwork he whips out, while occasionally glaring at me like they want to shove me out a convenient window.

Infuriatingly, a certain black cloud keeps blowing intrusively into my thoughts, distracting me from the meeting. A black cloud with way too much eyeliner, a mouth full of poison, and a toxic tongue.

A black cloud who, unbelievably, has my cock throbbing against the front of my suit pants for the next twenty minutes.

When I finally leave with a greasy fond farewell from Charles and two frosty "go get hit by a fucking car" looks from Alistair and Gabriel, I head back outside to where Carmy is waiting. When I find him leaning against the side of the SUV with a cigarette dangling from his lips, I frown at what I see scratched into the paint next to him.

"If that was you, it's not the least bit amusing, and you're paying to fix it."

"Not me," he exhales slowly, eying me coolly.

"Well?"

"Goth chick in black, about yea big." He holds his hand up, chest height.

My jaw clenches.

Goddamn her.

"She used one of the rocks from the driveway."

I stare at Carmy. "And where the fuck were you?"

"Me?" He shrugs. "I was in the car, buddy."

I blink. "And you just...*let her* do this?"

"I make a point of not getting between scary goth girls with improvised weapons in their hands and the target of their angst. You should try it. You'll live longer."

I pinch the bridge of my nose and glare at the "i like to fuck teenagers" scratched into the side of the SUV.

"She went back inside the house afterward, if you're looking to make a thing out of it."

If by "a thing" he means throttling her with my bare hands while fucking the living shit out of her , then...

I frown.

Whoa, you gotta chill out with that, friend.

"There's some duct tape in the glove compartment," I mutter to Carmy. "Feel like making yourself useful?"

I wince when the roll of tape comes flying over the roof and smacks me in the shoulder.

"Sorry, man," Carmy grins. "I'm the crown prince. I don't make myself useful to anyone. 'Sides, it's *your* car."

I flip him off as I tear a piece of tape from the roll and slap it over the worst of the words scratched into the car.

"They know why it is you're marrying the kid?"

I shake my head. "Figured there wasn't much need to show all the cards."

"Probably smart. They could use it as leverage and try and get more out of the deal." When he clears his throat, I look up to see him finishing his smoke and stomping it out on the gravely driveway. "They, uh...they still hate you for what happened to that girl?"

"Her name was Layla," I growl quietly. "And they most certainly do."

"You know, a simple conversation would clear that up—"

"I gave my word, Carmy," I murmur.

"I know, buddy." He walks around the front of the car and claps me on the shoulder. "I'm just saying, I think it would help, given that you're about to marry into a family that fucking hates you."

"It probably would."

We both get in the duct-taped Range Rover and I rev the engine.

"Alistair and Gabriel are all bark, to be honest," Carmy frowns, glancing out the window up at the house as I start to pull away. "But that one chick...she's gonna be a problem."

"Sure is."

More than you fucking know...

3

TEMPEST

"So... What's he like?"

Maeve sits cross-legged in the reading chair by the window in her room, a big blanket wrapped around her like a cloak. A sketchpad and a drawing pencil lie in her lap as she gives me a wry smile.

One of the consequences of her and my dad having the same father is that she looks *so much* like my dad sometimes: same green eyes and dark hair, same nose, same cheekbones, same slightly elfin chin.

On top of that, on the personality side, she's *so much* like Nina that it almost hurts sometimes: that same innocent inquisitiveness that my best friend had all her life.

Until the night that life was taken from her.

Between looking like my dead dad and behaving like my dead best friend, I've got a soft spot for Maeve. I'm also not *that much* older than her, and especially now that she's almost out of high school, it feels like we're peers more than anything.

Which is, of course, why I decide to be brutally honest with her instead of sugar coating the awful truth.

"He's a pig," I mutter. "A narcissistic asshole with a god complex who thinks the whole world should bow and kiss his feet just because of his genetics." I give Maeve a sour half smile. "Sorry, but you asked."

She swallows, her face paling a little. Then she nods, forcing a small smile to her lips. "Genetics, you say…?"

My face burns as I realize how that sounded.

"No, not…" I scrunch up my face and shake my head impatiently. "*Not* what I meant. I mean, yes, the man *is* classically good-looking, I guess. If you like that bored-with-the-world, filled with ennui, Armani model look."

"So, he's attractive if you like *hot* people."

I roll my eyes and reach behind where I'm sitting on the edge of the bed to grab a pillow off it. Maeve laughs when I chuck it at her.

"Not *hot*, vain. The kind of vain that probably jerks off in front of a mirror."

"Gross! So…a hot asshole, basically."

I make a face. "Focus on that second part more. He's arrogant, rude, and disgusting. I mean the man runs a fucking *sex club*, Maeve. And he's like twice your age."

Her laughter suddenly dies as she drops her eyes to her sketchpad. "You don't have to sell me on not wanting to marry him, you know..." she mumbles quietly, her throat bobbing.

Shit.

I move across the bedroom quickly to hug her close, stroking her hair as her breath hitches.

"I don't understand," she chokes into my shoulder before pulling away with tear-filled eyes to look into mine. "Why is this happening?"

I flinch, my chest constricting sharply.

"Why is this happening? Why are you doing this?"

The heart-wrenching pleas from another time, from another loved one, echo in my memory. My body shudders as I bite back the urge to scream.

Breathe.

I inhale sharply, forcing myself to stay centered and focused on Maeve and not on my own demons. I pull her into a tight hug.

"We're going to figure this out, okay?" I say fiercely. "I promise."

I'm not going to be so naive to suggest she just run away, or point out the fact that she's eighteen and perfectly capable of making her own decisions. I might not have grown up directly under Charles' roof, but I understand how his world works.

Sure, Maeve could leave. But then what? Best case scenario, she somehow could fend for herself despite living the sheltered, privileged life she's lived so far. But Charles or Dante would find her eventually, probably sooner rather than later, and drag her right back to this situation. And again, that's the *best*-case scenario.

The far less optimal scenarios involve the types of predators who are out there prowling around and hunting for *exactly* the kind of girl Maeve is.

Innocent. Inquisitive. Out of their element and looking to prove something.

Like Nina and I were.

There's my brothers, of course. I know they'd give Maeve a place to stay. But the unfortunate reality is that even they aren't immune to Charles. Our grandfather wields a substantial amount of power on the Crown and Black board of directors, much as Gabriel and Alistair hate it. Most of the time, him having that seat on the board is just an annoyance to them. But he could make their lives and their business *hell* if they took Maeve in over all of this.

Which leaves...me? No, I'm not a viable safety net for her. Not just because I don't have a job, or any money of my own, and still live in my dead father's old house. Not even because I'm sort of a mess myself.

No, I can't be a safety net for Maeve because I won't *be here* for very long.

Not that she, or anyone else, knows that.

I lean against the wall next to the windows. Maeve is quiet as she picks up the pencil and idly starts to move it across the page. It takes me a second before I glance down and realize she's sketching a very quick but very gorgeous portrait of *me*.

Somehow, that makes me even angrier for everything she's about to get thrown into.

33

Before he died, our father and grandfather had barely spoken for years. Dad never wanted the life Charles set him up for: one of grifting, skirting the law, and making shady deals with criminals. Instead, Dad got his Juris Doctor degree at Yale and married a Governor's daughter rather than the mafia princess Charles had picked out for him.

Layla, Gabriel, Alistair, and I weren't raised under Charles' mob-like influence. And I hate that I can't say the same thing for Maeve.

She's so much better than all of this. So *good*, and so fucking talented. And all of that is going to be wasted when Charles forces her into a marriage with Mr. Cocky Psychopath who for bonus points runs the city's most notorious *sex club*. I mean fucking seriously.

"Charles didn't mention a timeline—"

"Tomorrow."

I blink in horror, my mouth falling open.

"*What?!*"

"Not..." She shakes her head. "Not the wedding or anything. But I'm supposed to go to Mr. Sartorre's house tomorrow and sign the blood marker."

Fuck you, Charles. Fuck you. Fuck you. Fuck you.

He's not even just marrying the poor girl to that psycho. He's using the mafia-world bond of a blood marker: a bullet-proof, inked-in-literal-fucking-*blood* contract that the criminal underworld uses for iron-clad agreements.

You can divorce, or annul a marriage.

There's no escaping a blood marker, and Charles knows that. It's fittingly medieval.

"Maeve…" I go back over to hug her just as the tears begin to fall down her face.

"I'm really scared, Tempest."

"I know you are," I whisper quietly as I hold her tight. "I know, and I'm going to fix it."

"How?"

I don't know.

I don't know because I'm running out of time. It's one of the reasons this hurts so much: I'm not able to do a damn thing to get Maeve out of this mess, because in six-to-eight months, I won't even *be here*.

My chest constricts as I hold her tightly. But I don't cry, because I've already cried all the tears I have about the injustice of it all, and how unfair life is.

Tears I might not have any more of. But I *do* still have a heart. And drive. And a burning hot, molten spark inside that hasn't gone out yet.

Suddenly, like an icy blade piecing my skin, it hits me with blinding clarity.

There *is* a way I can save Maeve.

I'd normally label the idea forming in my head as completely suicidal. But in my case, it's just fantastically poetic.

Elegantly so.

A final "fuck you" to all the men in the world who think they can control a woman's life just because they're men. It's also the one chance I have of stopping Maeve from having to marry Dante.

My one chance, because of my big secret.

My cruel fate.

Everyone has a story to tell. Mine is short one. A cautionary tale, if you will. A rotten, black bedtime story.

Oh, and I die at the end.

But not before I take that prick down with me.

4

DANTE

"It's just *marriage*, Dante."

A low grumble escapes my throat as I glance across my study to where Carmy's younger brother Nico is sprawled across one of my couches. He shrugs.

"I mean, in this world, it's just what you *do*. It's the next step. I mean, look at what you've built, man." He raises his brows to the high, gilded ceilings, the tastefully elegant furniture, and the frankly eye-popping view of the Long Island Sound past the sandy beach outside.

Yeah, I treated myself a bit when I purchased this place five years ago. I'm a single, thirty-four-year-old man who's never married, had children, or had the slightest desire to do either of those. In a rational world, I would have no use for a ten thousand square foot, six-bedroom house on the ocean that I live in *alone*.

But I also have zero regrets. Nico's right: I've built quite an empire for myself, especially considering I started life in as a tailor's son.

"The next step?," I parrot with a grunt, my mood sour.

It's D-day. Soon, Maeve and her father will be arriving for her and me to jointly sign the blood marker that will cement our engagement. And more importantly, cement my place at the head of my empire.

I've met with all the dons who collectively make up The Commission: Luciano Amato. Michael Genovisi, who runs the Scaliami family. My distant cousin, Massimo, who is now running the Carveli family like the privileged, pampered, psycho little Napoleonic tyrant that he is. Even Cesare Marchetti, who has assured me that his capo, Angelo, won't be coming after my dick with garden shears after all, now that I'm "settling down".

They're all for this marriage, and the "peace, connections, and understanding" it brings.

Too bad I still fucking *hate* the idea with every fiber of my being.

"Yes, the next step," Nico shrugs, taking a sip of the whiskey in his hand, courtesy of my bar cart. "We're *mafia*, Dante. Us by birth, you by circumstance and association. Arranged marriages are to be expected."

"Yeah?" I snap. "Then how about *you* marry the fucking high school kid."

Carmy chuckles from where he's sitting by one of my half-open windows, blowing smoke from his cigarette out into the sea air.

"She's eighteen, Dante."

"*And?*" I mutter.

"And…" He exhales with a huff. "Look I'm not endorsing sleeping with eighteen-year-old girls…"

"*So* glad you're clearing that up for us, bro."

Carmy ignores Nico, flipping him off as he keeps his gaze focused on me.

"I'm just saying, you *could*, and it's not like you'd find yourself on an episode of *To Catch A Predator*."

I roll my eyes. "There are several things I *could* do that I have absolute zero interest in doing, dumbass." I swivel my gaze to Nico. "And if you're so gung-ho on arranged marriages, where the fuck is your fake wife? Either of you?"

Nico spreads his arms. "Privilege of being second born, man. I'm not a priority for dad. And if you'll remember, Carmy *had* a few arranged engagements…"

"Yeah," Carmine grins. "And then their fathers actually *met me*."

I shake my head. "I'm pretty sure your tendency to shove your dick in said arranged fiancées before actually marrying them didn't make for good first impressions with the future in-laws."

Carmine frowns as he drags on his smoke. "What? Like you'd buy a car without test-driving it first? And, might I add, these cars were literally begging yours truly to be test-driven."

"You could always try something novel like, I don't know, restraining yourself," I sigh.

"There are several things I *could* do that I have absolute zero interest in doing, dumbass," he tosses back to me in a goofy-ass voice, parroting what I just said to him.

"It's just business, Dante," Nico shrugs, giving me his best attempt at a sympathetic look. "You know The Commission is old-school. So, you play their game. Marry this chick, get them off your fucking back, and then live your life. Hell, set her up with a place in the city, let her do what she wants… with discretion, duhh…and you do the same. This doesn't have to change a damn thing in your life."

Yeah. It's a nice thought. But I know myself too well.

The difference between my two friends and I is our upbringings. Of course Carmy and Nico have next to zero regard for the gravitas of marriage; their parents, Vito and Giada, were at their happiest when they weren't anywhere near each other. But they were also old-school Catholic, which meant that even as miserable as they made each other, divorce was off the table. Instead, they spent probably ninety percent of their marriage sleeping in separate, and often times *other people's*, beds.

But I was raised in a different kind of home. My parents were crazy in love with each other until the day they were taken from us. Marriage *meant* something to them, and it's— unfortunately, given my present circumstances—a value they instilled in my sisters and me.

I mean, of course I'm going to do what I have to do, because I'm a big boy and I understand how the world in which I operate works.

Doesn't mean I have to fucking like it.

"You'll have to excuse my brother," Carmy sighs. "He has no respect for the sanctity of marriage."

Nico frowns. "That's not what I fucking said."

"I didn't say you said shit. I was talking about your preference for married women. As in, ones married to dudes who aren't *you*."

Nico lifts his shoulders helplessly. "Hey, the heart wants what the heart wants."

"That's heart spelled D-I-C-K—"

They both shut up when I clear my throat and glance significantly at my Rolex.

"'Bout that time, huh?"

I nod at Carmine. Yup, Maeve and her father should be here soon to sign that fucking blood marker.

"Well, we'd love to stick around for emotional support, as in getting you drunk as fuck after it's over, but we have a meeting we need to get to back in the city."

I frown. "Drazen?"

"Yessir," Nico nods.

Drazen Krylov is the Serbian-Russian head of the Krylov Bratva family and a newly minted New Yorker. A few months ago, he managed to make friends with Carmine, and through him, weaseled his way into a guest pass to Venom in a thinly veiled maneuver to meet me and pitch me on him becoming an investor in Club Venom.

Thinly veiled, but as much of a fucking lunatic as Drazen is, he's grown on me. So much so that he *is* an investor in Venom now, too.

I also know he, Carmine and Nico have their own dealings going on together. But whatever they are, I'm smart enough to know I probably want fuck-all to do with them. I know where my line is. My game is Venom and the information trade. Whatever clandestine criminal shit these two and that psycho are up to, I'm sure I don't want to know the details.

After the Barone brothers take off, I pour myself a heavy splash of scotch and sink into my favorite chair by the window of my study, overlooking the ocean. The afternoon is getting late, and I glance at my watch again.

Fuck. It's almost time.

I exhale and turn to look through the window at the waves lapping lazily at the shore. This whole situation is a shit show. And that was *before* the hurricane herself slammed into me. Literally.

Tempest.

Tempest, with the jet black hair and thick, heavy eyeliner. Tempest with the poisonous tongue and defiant energy radiating off her pale skin that makes you not sure if you want to throttle her or fuck her into next Tuesday.

Or both, at the same time. It might *take* both to wipe that smug smirk off her pretty lips. Though I suppose stretching those lips around my cock…for the sake of argument…might have the same effect.

I growl to myself again as I slug back half my glass.

I've crossed paths with plenty of people who make it clear they don't like me.

Not one of them has ever phased me, or even warranted a second thought from me. But when it comes to Tempest, I can't seem to hold to my usual modus operandum of not giving a shit. With her, in fact, it's the opposite.

I can't stop thinking about her.

Not in a moony, sappy way. Fuck no. But I can't stop fantasizing about her—her and those deep hazel-green eyes. The snidely pursed lips. The whole princess-of-darkness, Marilyn Manson groupie vibe dripping off of her shoulders like a toxin.

I haven't the slightest idea why anything about this woman is hitting me like this. Worse, I have no idea how to flush it out of my system.

It's been two days since she stormed out of Charles' office and barreled into my chest.

I've stroked my cock until cum exploded from the swollen head no less than three times since then. And each of those times, it was black eyeliner, sneery, pouty lips, and stabby, angry eyes I was picturing.

Tempest. Otherwise known as the niece of the woman—*girl* —I'm supposed to marry.

This is…highly problematic.

A knock at the study door pulls my attention.

"Yes?"

The door opens, and Lorenzo, my head of security, pokes his head in.

"She's here, Mr. Sartorre."

My lips thin to a grimace.

Perfect timing.

"Okay. You can escort them in."

Lorenzo's brow furrows. "She's actually alone, sir."

Interesting. Part of me wonders for half a second if Charles sending Maeve on her own is some sort of power move. But then I realize I don't really give a shit if it is or not. Maeve's *here*, which means I can sign this fucking blood marker and get it over with.

"Well, then escort—"

"She, uh…" Lorenzo looks unsure if he's worried or amused to tell me. "She won't get out of the car, sir. Point blank refused."

I exhale with a groan, reaching up to pinch the bridge of my nose. Right. I forgot I'm marrying an almost literal child.

"Fuck it," I sigh, rising from my chair and crossing to my desk. I punch in the code for the built-in safe underneath and pull out the blood marker, the Dickensian quill, and the small silver disk with the two wells and two little pinpricks set into it. With Lorenzo watching, I stab my thumb over one side of the disk, spilling my blood into the little well before dipping the quill into it.

I sign quickly, then press my bloody thumbprint to the page.

So be it. My club is everything, and I'll do anything to keep it.

I've got a dark glare etched into my face as I storm out of the front door of my estate. There's a black SUV parked on the white stone driveway, the engine running. My eyes narrow at my own reflection in the tinted black windows. I'm about to bang on the glass with my knuckles so we get this shit over with when the back seat window cracks open just a few inches.

You've got to be fucking kidding me.

"Are we seriously doing it like this?" I mutter through clenched teeth.

No response from inside the car.

"*Maeve*," I growl. "Understand that neither of us wants this, but that doesn't mean it's not happ—"

A small, dainty hand pokes through the crack in the window, palm up. My back teeth grind.

"Look, when we're married, you can hide all you want," I mutter. "So long as you smile and obey me in public, and at the wedding. Do we understand each other?"

Silence from inside interior of the car.

"*Do we understand each—*"

The hand curls into a thumbs-up.

Oh. My. God. This is why no one does arranged marriages anymore. Marriage itself is enough of a cage. *This* kind of marriage? Ridiculous.

But fuck it. If this is the way she wants to do this, so be it.

I hold up the contract, the quill, and the little metal disc. "Do you know how this work—"

Her hand curls into another thumbs-up. With a roll of my eyes, I pass my high school soon-to-be-bride the fucking contract and the apparatus to sign it with her blood. She takes it, slipping her hand back into the shadows of the car as I stand there glaring at my own reflection in the tint of the windows, shaking my head.

I smirk a little when I hear the quick hiss of pain from inside, presumably from pricking her thumb. A second later, the hand slips back out, holding the signed contract, quill, and disc.

"Well, I'm glad we could do this face-to-face like grownups," I mutter sarcastically. "Your father and I will talk, but you and I will meet privately next week to go over the details for the wedding and the…" I clear my throat. "The *provisions* of this arrangem—"

I'm not even finished my sentence when the window rolls back up.

"Really?" I mutter as the SUV shifts into drive and starts to pull away. I stand there glaring at its rear fender, rubbing my sore thumb on the palm of my hand.

Suddenly, I frown as I glance past Maeve's car. There's a silver Bentley town car pulled up at the gate to my estate, the driver leaning out the window to speak with my security. Security nods, the gate opens, and the Bentley starts to roll in. The two cars pass each other, and my brow furrows as the Bentley stops in front of me and cuts the engine.

The back doors open, and Charles Black steps out…

With *Maeve*.

I whirl, firing my gaze down the driveway to where the SUV has suddenly started to speed up. I drop my gaze to the contract in my fist and my heart drops. The signature is sloppy and barely legible, but it sure as *shit* doesn't say "Maeve Black" on the signature line.

Oh, fuck.

"Close the gate!!" I roar, waving my arms in the air at the security guards. "CLOSE THE FUCKING GATE!"

My men are the best of the best. Instantly, they bolt into action, slamming the gate shut and stepping between it and the approaching SUV, guns drawn. The brake lights glow red as the black Escalade comes to a quick halt and my men approach the driver's side.

"What the hell is going on, Dante?!" Charles demands, storming over to me. He jabs an angry finger at the SUV. "Who the fuck is that?!"

He snatches the blood marker out of my hand.

"Who the *hell* signed the fucking—"

The backdoor of the SUV opens, and someone steps out.

Black boots. Black fishnets. A black miniskirt and a striped Freddy-fucking-Kruger sweater, with too-black hair, too-pale skin, and *too much goddamn eyeliner*.

No. Fucking. Way.

Tempest stands tall, proud, and smug next to the SUV, staring right at me with a shit-eating grin on her face.

Our eyes lock, mine stabbing right into hers as my pulse roars in my ears. My thumb throbs from where I just let out the blood to ink my name on an unbreakable oath.

Right next to hers.

A ringing sound fills my ears as the full gravity of the situation hits me.

Slowly, still smirking at me, the little witch raises a black manicured middle finger and flips me off.

Fuck. *Me.*

5

TEMPEST

"You meddling little *bitch*!"

We're back in the city, after Charles all but threw me into his car and hauled me here to the elegant old-money apartment he keeps on 5th Ave and 89th, overlooking Central Park. Under normal circumstances, being called a "meddling little bitch" by your own grandfather would probably be traumatic.

Except it takes more than mean words to actually traumatize me at this point. Furthermore, I could give a shit about what Charles thinks of me, and even less about what he says to my face.

Right now, I don't give a shit about anything aside from the smug sensation throbbing in my veins.

"Do you have any fucking idea what you've just done?!"

I smile benignly at my livid grandfather. His face is suffused red, and the bald dome at the center of the silver ring of his cropped, thinning hair is shiny as he snarls at me.

"Sure."

I have *every* idea of what I've just done. I've just inked myself to *Dante*, in unholy fucking matrimony.

I allow a shiver to drag its nails up my back before I ignore it and steel my nerves. What I've just done and what it will cost me doesn't matter, because it's a cost I can easily afford to pay. My life is already almost over, but at least what I just did stops Maeve from forfeiting *her* young life as well.

All the same, my gut twists as I finally digest the reality of the situation.

I'm marrying Dante.

I tremble.

Dante of the cold, piercing blue eyes and the heart of black ice, who rules his kingdom of sin with an iron fist and a lethal will.

Despite our dad's best efforts, it's kind of impossible not to cross paths with mafia types as a member of the Black family. But while I've never been intimidated by the mafia men I've met before, for some reason, I don't have that same cavalier attitude when it comes to Dante Sartorre.

With him, I feel real fear. I also feel anxiousness, and doubt, and a humming sensation of danger at the back of my neck.

But of all the things I feel when I think of Dante Sartorre, the worst is the one burning like a hot ember in the very center of my chest.

Heat, of the forbidden and horribly wrong variety.

When I think of Dante, what I should be thinking of is the danger that comes with a man like him. I should be focused on the fact that he runs an organization very similar to the clandestine one I've been hunting down. Or the fact that not only am I marrying him, but that I've just *tricked him* into that marriage, by pretending to be Maeve when I drove up to his house to sign that goddamn blood marker.

If he wasn't a fan of me before, he sure as hell isn't now.

That is everything that should come to mind when I think of Dante. And yet instead, all my traitorous and possibly deranged mind seems to be focused on is the chiseled line of his jaw.

The soft but masculine curve of his lips.

The electrifying spark of blue flame in his eyes.

The way a dark power emanates from him in a way that pulls every single trigger within me.

"Answer me, you little fucking bitch—!"

"That's enough!"

My hazy, murky, horrible thoughts about Dante shatter. Whirling, my brows arch in surprise as my brothers come storming into Charles' office.

Gabriel glares at our grandfather with an icy glint in his eyes. "I said that's *enough*, Charles," he seethes.

"Excuse me," our grandfather snaps. "Last I checked, this is *my* home, and we're discussing *my* business, which your little *cunt* of a sister just fucked—"

"Call her something to that effect again, Charles," Alistair snarls quietly in a tone that chills the room, "and we'll have ourselves a problem you are *not* prepared to deal with."

Our grandfather sneers at him disdainfully, but he doesn't push it, either.

"Do you even know what your sweet little sister just did?!"

Alistair's eyes dart to Maeve, who's sitting frightened and wide-eyed, hugging herself in the corner of Charles' office.

So that's why they're here.

I spent the drive back to the city from Dante's estate in Charles' town car, being berated and generally screamed at. I'm guessing that's when Maeve texted my brothers to tell them what was going on.

They *may* be here to make sure Charles doesn't throw me out a window. But it's pretty clear from the frosty glares they shoot me that neither of them is very happy with me after what I just pulled, either.

"Come on, Tempest," Gabriel mutters quietly. "We're going. Now."

"The fuck you are!" Charles snarls, jabbing a finger at me. "We're not through here!"

"Oh, I can assure you," Alistair snaps. "We damn well are."

"If I needed an attorney, *Alistair*," Charles roars, "trust that you would be the very last one I called! Now get the hell out of—"

"That's not happening without Tempest coming with us."

"Don't make me tell you again!!!"

I flinch, the soft touch to my arm jerking my attention away from Charles and my brothers yelling. Maeve is looking at me woefully, her bottom lip caught between her teeth.

"*Why*, Tempest?" she asks quietly. "Why would you do that?"

It's the first time we've been able to talk since Dante's house, what with Charles spending the whole drive back yelling at me.

Because it's a price I can pay, I want to say. But I can't, so instead I force the calmest smile I'm capable of to my lips as I pull her into a bear hug.

"Because you are *not* marrying that man," I hiss fiercely. "Don't worry, it's going to be okay."

"No, it's *not*!" She pulls back, her face ashen and caved. "Tempest, you can't do this for me!"

Oh, believe me, I can.

"It's already done, Maeve," I say quietly. "You are *not* marrying that asshole."

"But *you* are!" she blurts, her eyes welling with tears.

I smile wryly at her. "Just trust me, okay? I've got an ace up my sleeve here."

"But—"

"Tempest…"

I flinch, turning to find Gabriel standing right behind me, leveling one of his chilling, lawyerly looks at me. Gabriel's one of those people who are normally so even-tempered that when they get that sort of "quiet mad" it's twice as terrifying as it would be if they were prone to angry outbursts. In this moment, the "quiet mad" smoldering in his eyes is hot enough to turn me to ash right here on Charles' office rug.

"We're leaving," he snaps coldly. "*Now.*"

I turn to glance at Maeve, who looks just as chilled by my brother's glare as I am.

"It's going to be okay," I say quietly, reaching out to squeeze her hand before I turn to face my brother's wrath.

"Let's go," he growls thinly.

"Don't you dare walk out that door!" Charles roars as Alistair, Gabriel, and I walk toward it.

"Get fucked, Charles," Alistair mutters.

"This isn't over!"

Gabriel's jaw clenches as he reaches for the knob. "Charles—"

"She signed a goddamn *blood marker!*"

Everything goes still. Gabriel's eyes narrow. So do Alistair's before they slowly swivel to lance into me. He raises one brow as if to say "You didn't actually fucking *do* that, did you?"

My throat bobs as I swallow a lump in my throat. When I slowly nod, I watch my brothers' faces pale.

"*Tempest…*" Gabriel hisses under his breath.

Charles laughs coldly as the three of us slowly turn to face him. "Not a contract. Not an agreement," he sneers. "A goddamn *blood marker.* And you might choose not to participate in the world that is governed by those, but believe me, that world won't care."

He levels his eyes at me, his nostrils flaring.

"Tempest *is* marrying Dante Sartorre now, and there is nothing *any* of us can do to change that." His lips curl. "Now, the prudent thing would be to sit down and figure out how this affects the family—"

"You mean how it affects *you* and your personal mafia wheeling and dealing," Alistair hisses. "Which I couldn't give less of a fuck about, Charles."

Gabriel yanks open the office door, and Charles is still roaring as my brother pulls me through and kicks the door shut behind us. No sooner are we all out of Charles' apartment and in the hallway than Gabriel slams me against the wall, his face livid. Alistair looks just as menacing and furious standing behind him.

"You did fucking *what?!*"

"He was going to force Maeve to marry that fucking pig!" I snap. "What the hell else was I supposed to do?!"

"Not go anywhere fucking *near* Dante Sartorre, for a start!" Alistair snaps coldly.

I roll my eyes. "You know, it's slightly insulting that you think I'm dumb enough not to know you're both members of his little sex club."

My brothers glance at each other nervously, and then back to me.

"That's for…business," Gabriel grunts.

"Yeah, *business.*" I pantomime a blowjob motion as Gabriel makes a face.

"Do me a favor and literally *never* do that in front of me again," he groans, looking positively ill.

"Then do *me* a favor and stop insulting my intelligence! I don't know how many times I need to say this, but I had to do something. Maeve is family."

Alistair's eyes narrow. "She's Charles' daughter with—"

"She. Is. *Family*," I hiss viciously. "Period! Full stop!" I glare at them both. "Wow, I guess I'm the only one who understands what that means."

The two of them are silent for a second, sharing a glance before they look back at me.

"Did you *really* sign the blood marker?" Gabriel grunts.

I nod, and he groans as he squeezes his eyes shut.

"I mean, Jesus Christ, Tempest…"

A shiver riffles down my back. There's something about the gravitas with which they're both treating this that has me suddenly feeling the full weight of it, too.

The full fear.

I did what I did because I have a rapidly approaching expiration date. But it's not tomorrow. Or the next day, or even next week or next month. And pretty soon, I'm going to be chained to Dante, for however long I have left.

Suddenly, that sounds way, way more daunting a prospect than it did earlier when I was fueled by bravado and impetuousness.

I swallow weakly as I drag my eyes from my hands up to my brothers' faces.

"I won't apologize for what I did, okay? It would be obscene for her to marry Dante."

Gabriel shoves his fingers through his dark hair. "Neither of us disagrees with you there, Tempest."

"Well," I shrug. "Now she's not. Problem solved."

"Except you've just stepped in front of a bullet."

"Yeah, well..." I chew on my lip and look down again. "After it's official, I'm sure you two can find a way for me to...you know..."

Alistair laughs coldly. "To what, Tempest? This is mafia *oath* shit!" he hisses. "What, you think Gabriel and I can haggle better terms, or add provisions to the contract?"

I smile weakly. "I mean, you...*can*, right?"

When they're both deadly silent, my heart plummets.

"Guys—"

"Tempest, we're not talking marital law or alimony here. In fact, we're not talking *law* at all," Gabriel mutters. "This is above and beyond that. A blood marker is *final*. Period. Full stop. Do not pass go, and *fuck* collecting your two hundred dollars."

My skin prickles as a cold sensation slithers down my spine.

"You just sold your soul to the devil, Tempest," Alistair murmurs darkly. "And there is nothing that Gabriel, or I, or you, or *anyone else* on God's green Earth can do to stop that now."

6

DANTE

"So, you get a *goomar*. Easy."

I groan, shaking my head as Vito chuckles. Lying in the pool lounger next to mine, he grins around his cigar as he deftly lights a wooden match and brings it to the finely cut tip. The cherry catches and glows orange before he drops the match into the ashtray perched on the side table next to him, beside his glass of Fernet Branca. Then he leans back in his lounger to gaze out over the pool and at my back garden.

Vito, aka Don Vito Barone, head of the Barone mafia organization, was always like a second father to me. Well, more like a fun uncle in the beginning, I suppose. But when my real father and mother died when I was barely fifteen, Claudia sixteen, and Bianca only two, that fun uncle very much *did* become a father to all three of us.

Vito took us in and raised us right alongside his two blood sons, Carmine and Nico. He gave us all a good life and used his influence—and his wealth—to get Claudia and I into Knightsblood University, and Bianca into the School of

American Ballet at Lincoln Center when it was clear that she was a very talented dancer.

I grew up fucking around with Carmy and Nico whenever my dad dragged me along to the Barone house when he was doing work as Vito's personal tailor. Given Don Barone's sense of style and love of fashion, my father was over a *lot*. So it never felt odd after my father's death when Carmy and Nico went from being my friends to me and my sisters' unofficial brothers.

When it…happened…they mourned Claudia and wanted vengeance for her death as if she were their own flesh and blood. I know they'd give their lives to protect Bianca just the same. So would Vito, without flinching.

"Seriously, a *goomar*. That's your solution to this bullshit."

Vito grins as he puffs on the Cuban. I glance over at him and resist the urge to chuckle at the sixty-five-year-old man in the tiny black speedo sprawled next to me.

The older Barone is a tanning junkie, even if Carmine, Nico, Bianca, and I have all tried to impress upon him the concept of skin cancer. Whenever we do, though, Vito just starts waxing eloquent about the glory of Rome and superior Italian genes.

For years, Vito was quite happy sunning himself on the over-sized patio of his luxury midtown penthouse—with or *without* a comically small speedo like the one he's currently wearing. That is, until New York continued to grow around him, and his newer neighbors started to complain about the naked Italian guy sipping Montepulciano and bronzing his ballsack for them all to see.

Apparently, even highly connected and lethally dangerous mafia dons bow to the pressures of multi-million-dollar co-op boards. Who knew.

Anyway, Vito's go-to spot for sunning himself these days is my pool.

...I've made the speedo mandatory.

It being barely spring and not, in my opinion, nearly warm enough to be sunbathing, I'm dressed in white linen pants, Italian loafers, and a pressed black polo shirt.

This is about as casual as I get.

Jeans are for riding a motorcycle. Sneakers and t-shirts are for the gym. I absolutely do not *own* a fucking hoodie.

My predilection for style and fine fashion certainly stemmed from growing up as master tailor Bruno Sartorre's son. But it was honed under Vito's fashionable eye and taste for luxury. I mean, you only get so many turns around the sun. Dress for the occasion.

"Well, okay, not a solution. But getting a side piece might certainly make your life a little happier." He smirks. "Not to mention your dick."

I'm always slightly amused at the differences between my birth father and my adoptive one. Bruno prided himself on good manners and didn't approve of crude language and swearing. Meanwhile, I can't imagine Vito not talking like a sailor about fucking, genitals, and other similar topics that would have given my father a stroke.

"Well," I lift a brow. "I'll consider it."

"Do. It saved my marriage, Dante."

I roll my eyes, suppressing a grin. I already have a pretty good understanding of the…I suppose you could say *gray areas*…of Vito and Giada's marriage.

While Giada was still alive, my adoptive parents were *famously* at each other's throats half of the time and locking themselves in their bedroom to hate-fuck each other's brains out the other half of the time. I don't know—and can't imagine a world where I'd *need* to know—the details of whatever their "arrangement" was. But I do know Vito had plenty of *goomars* in and out of the house—and I would suspect Giada did as well, she was just a hell of a lot more discreet about it.

"And your dearly departed wife? What did she think of a side piece 'saving your marriage'?"

Vito puffs on his cigar and shrugs. "I doubt she thought about it very much at all. She was too busy fucking the gardener for the last ten years of our marriage."

I snort a laugh.

"Dick like a fuckin' donkey, or so I'm told," Vito continues, holding his hands easily a foot apart from each other. "I'm amazed she could walk at all after we hired him."

I grin. "Well, maybe I'll need to hire a gardener, too."

The second I say it, a strange sensation ripples over my skin: a feeling somewhere between anger and revulsion that I'm not quite able to pin down before it slithers away.

"Maybe." Vito turns to me and lowers his sunglasses, his brow furrowed. "Listen. I obviously don't know her that well, but even I can tell it takes a special sort of man to handle a woman like Tempest Black, my friend."

"I don't need to *handle* anything," I grunt. "She and I understand what this is."

"Of course, of course," Vito sighs, waving his cigar. "But only a very foolish man would walk into this thinking he'd never have to handle his wife. And you, Dante, are not foolish."

My brows draw together as I lean back in my lounger. "She can do whatever the fuck she wants, for all I care. There'll be no *handling* of any kind."

"Ha! Spoken like a man who's never lived with a woman," Vito grins.

I sigh. "Amused by all of this, Vito?"

"Hugely," he chuckles, stretching as he leans back in his chair. "Oh, did she ever acknowledge your gift, by the way?"

I roll my eyes. "My gift" wasn't from *me* at all. It was all Vito's idea, and when I nixed it, he had one of his people send the fucking package over to Tempest anyway on my behalf. This was a week ago, right after Tempest signed that goddamn blood marker.

When I don't respond, Vito turns to me and lowers his shades again.

"You're still sore about that?"

I turn to glare at him. "I just don't like people putting words in my mouth or speaking for me," I mutter.

This time he's the one who rolls his eyes, shoving his cigar back between his lips as he waves me off.

"Listen to *signore* Drama Queen over here. No one was putting words in your mouth, Dante. It's simply customary to gift a ring at a time like this, regardless of whether it's 'real' or not. You might not like Ms. Black—"

"She's a fucking witch with a mouth like a sailor who dresses like she's fronting a grunge band," I grunt. "*Not liking her* is an understatement."

Yes, Vito sent a goddamn *engagement ring* to Tempest. From me. Which she promptly sent back, to my house, in a much larger box.

…because it came back to me together with a claw hammer and a bottle of lube.

Point taken.

"She's a pretty girl, no?"

"No, she's not."

Vito snorts. "What, you prefer the sort of woman who frequents your club?"

"I prefer the sort of woman who doesn't trick me into fucking *marrying* them," I grunt. "And besides, you know damn well I don't play at Venom."

It's one of my firm rules: I don't shit where I eat. Club Venom is my business and my empire, not my playground.

"The man sits on a mountain of cake and complains about being hungry," Vito says to the air, shaking his head.

I glare at him. "I'm not complaining."

"That's all you've done since I arrived."

"Well you are *welcome* to go sun your wrinkly nuts back at your penthouse and risk the wrath of the 5th Avenue co-op boards," I mutter.

Vito laughs loudly and takes a sip of his Fernet Branca before turning to eye me. "It could be much worse than Tempest Black, my friend." His brow darkens. "Like one of those goddamn Greeks."

I bite back a smirk. Vito *hates* the Drakos family, which is fair. Their youngest son, Deimos—a fucking psychopath with...*interesting* kinks—scared the ever-living fuck out of Vito's niece Francesca one night at Club Venom. Granted, she only got in because the men working the door that night knew her uncle and were scared of the name. Later, I made them far more scared of *me* if they ever considered letting her in again. I also booted that little psycho Deimos from Venom and revoked his membership permanently.

"You know, when I mentioned hiring a stripper for your bachelor party, I wasn't picturing my own father."

Carmy steps out of the house and onto the back patio. He makes a face as he nods his chin at Vito.

"For fuck's sake, Pop, put on some goddamn pants."

Vito snorts, patting his belly contentedly. He's still got the imposing physique he had as a younger man. But, I mean, the guy is sixty-five, and he *does* love his wine and pasta.

"Does the peak male form intimidate you, son of mine?" Vito grins, tossing back his Fernet and then cupping his package through the speedo.

Carmy rolls his eyes. "No, but your *peak male form* in that fuckin' banana hammock is going to put me in therapy."

"Which would probably be a good thing for everyone in your life that has to interact with you on the regular."

Carmy flips me off before he frowns and tilts his head, noticing the Sinatra playing softly over the outdoor speakers. His eyes roll.

"Jesus, Dante. He's even got you listening to this old timey shit on these little playdates of yours? I'm gonna walk out here one of these days and find *you* in a cute little G-string too, aren't I?"

"Aww, you fantasizing about me, Carmy?"

Vito laughs heartily before he wags a finger at his son. "This *old timey shit* is solid gold Sinatra. You should get some musical taste, like Dante. Anyway, I'm gonna go hit the head."

Carmy grins at me as his father gets to his feet. "Yeah, I'll work on that, Pop."

Carmine and I repress our laughter as we watch his father amble inside, ass hanging out of his speedo.

"I mean, to be fair, you gotta have balls to wear one of those things," Carmine sighs, sitting in his dad's vacated lounger.

"Yeah, well those balls have just been all over that chair, Carm."

He makes a face as he scoots to the far end of the lounger. "So, anything?"

I shake my head sadly. Carmy swears under his breath.

When I was going to be marrying *Maeve* Black, Carmine, Nico and I had a fuckton of ideas lined up for ways to basically take Charles Black for everything we could. Yes, I need to get married to hold on to Venom and my empire. But *his* empire is crumbling around him, and I'm the only one offering cement and rebar. He needed that match more than I did.

However, given that I'm now marrying the queen of the damned herself, the plans we had set up with Charles are no longer viable. I've been looking at angles for putting the squeeze on him anyway—I mean, I'm just marrying his granddaughter instead of his daughter. But I'm hitting a roadblock.

The nice version is: Tempest hates Charles. The not so nice version of that uses much more colorful language. So the odds of using my marriage to Tempest to gain any sort of leverage over Charles is looking bleak as fuck.

Before, it was *me* doing Maeve—Charles, really— a favor by marrying her. Now that it's Tempest's name on that blood marker, though?

She's doing *me* the favor. *She* has the leverage and the power.

Not, of course, that she needs to know that. *At all.*

He exhales heavily. "Well, shit. This sucks—" Carmine winces as his eyes snap to mine. "I mean, you know, relatively speaking. Not sucks like—"

"Like having to marry Tempest fucking Black?"

He shrugs. "Hey, she's…"

"Batshit crazy?"

"Headstrong," he grins. "*Tempestuous*, if you will."

"She's a brat with authority issues and a terrible sense of style."

Carmine sighs. "Dude, by your standards, even I have bad style."

I arch a quizzical brow at his black suit, no tie, fitted, with the top two buttons of his dress shirt undone. I clear my throat. "I mean…"

"Dude, it's *Armani*. Even you can't say shit about Arma—"

"That jacket cut is at least eight years old, the inseam on the trousers should be tightened up a half inch, and there is absolutely *no* reason you should be wearing French cuffs without a tie. I don't care what Tom Ford is doing."

Carmine is silent as he slowly shakes his head at me.

"You're a fuckin' snob, bro."

"Hey, you asked."

"I…didn't, actually?" He rolls his eyes. "You know, I was all set to commiserate with you about having to tie the knot with Tempest. But shit, I think I feel worse for *her* now."

"Yes, that's the support in these trying times I was looking for. Thanks, Carmy."

He sighs heavily. "You used to be fun, you know? And I don't know why you're so bent out of shape about Tempest. I mean, yeah, she's…rough around the edges. But, bonus! She doesn't come with all the baggage and psycho family drama of a mafia princess."

"No, just the psycho family drama of her brothers being Alistair and Gabriel fucking Black. Who would happily stab me in the neck if they thought they could argue their way into—."

"Again, one conversation would—"

"Carmine."

He holds his hands up. "All right, all right, I'm done." He clears his throat. "Hey, at least she's hot."

I scowl. "Excuse me?"

"Your fiancée. Great legs. Cute face. Fantastic ass."

"Well then, *you* marry her."

"And what exactly would that accomplish?"

"Me *not* having to marry her?" I grunt.

Carmine grins widely. "Well, maybe after you two are officially hitched and you tell her she can do whatever she wants because it's all for show, I could be *her* side piece, you know?"

My jaw grits, and a feeling not all that different from the one I felt at the idea of me "hiring a gardener" creeps over my skin, turning my nerves raw and my blood hot.

"I mean she's got crazy written all over her, and man, crazy chicks?" Carmy whistles wolfishly. "Those bitches will fuck your dick raw—Dante?"

I blink and snap out of my daze, realizing I've been glaring a laser hole right through Carmine. He frowns, cocking one brow.

"You, uh, you good, man?"

"Yeah," I shake my head. "Yeah, fine. Just a lot on my mind."

He smirks at me. "Well, I do have a cure for that. It starts with a B...then an A..."

"If it's *bachelor party*, my answer is no."

"It *is* bachelor party!" he crows. "And your answer is hell yes." He reaches over, clapping me on the shoulder. "I mean," he winks. "Throw as many hissy fits about it as you want. But you're getting married, Dante."

7

TEMPEST

I FUCKING HATE HOSPITALS.

I mean, it's not like most people *like* them. But ever since that night of blurred horrors and silent tears—the night Nina died—when I was brought to one, stunned, numb, naked, and wrapped in a paramedic's jacket, I've fucking *loathed* them.

I think it's the antiseptic smell that gets me, as if the building itself is trying to destroy anything living within its walls. That chemical smell of bleach and rubbing alcohol that leaves your nostrils singed and your skin raw.

To me, it's the scent of probing, invasive tests, of swabs rubbing against sore, torn, and vandalized flesh. A scent that says life is never, ever going to be the same again.

The scent of death.

The smell diminishes a little when Dr. Han shuts the door to his office behind me. But there's no blocking it out entirely. Maybe it's psychosomatic. Or maybe the chemical toxicity is so deeply ingrained in the floors and walls of this place that there's simply no escaping it.

Dr. Han clears his throat in that professorial manner that he has and walks around his desk to sit facing me. He frowns, thumbing a file folder full of my tests in his hands.

I'm not sure why he looks so defeated today. It's not like either of us have had any illusions that this current round of examinations and tests would change anything about what's wrong with me.

Dying sucks. The only thing worse is dying *slowly*.

It's not going to be today. Or tomorrow. Or even the day after that. It won't be next week or next month, either. But it's an odd, empty, bizarre sensation knowing your last Christmas has already passed you by.

I discovered all this two months ago, when my GP couldn't figure out what was going on to explain my lethargy, lack of appetite, and, sometimes, general confusion. I figured it was some fucked up manifestation of my trauma seeping back into my life, or maybe insomnia or something. But Dr. Han, the specialist I was referred to, found something else.

It's called severe late-onset methylmalonic acidemia, and it's a rare liver disorder usually found in infants. What it means is that my body has stopped being able to break down fats and proteins effectively, which creates a buildup of something called methylmalonic acid in my blood.

The lethargy and lack of appetite are going to get worse. So is the brain fuzziness, and there's a good chance I'm going to start having random seizures sooner rather than later. In the next few months, I'll probably need to go on dialysis as the toxicity in my blood begins to shut down my kidneys.

And then, after all that, to add insult to injury, it's going to kill me.

That's why I did what I did. *That's* why I put myself in front of that Dante-shaped bullet. Because Maeve's got her whole life ahead of her.

I've got…eight months, at best. And they're not going to be pretty.

"So," I lift the corners of my mouth as I shrug. "Guess I'm still on the hunt for a miracle?"

Dr. Han smiles weakly before taking a deep breath and exhaling slowly. His eyes drag from the folder in his hands up to mine.

"On the plus side, your levels are consistent."

He means consistently *shitty*. But, consistency is good. At least I'm right on schedule for dying at the age of twenty-four.

"The renal protein blockers you've been taking have slowed the toxicity in your kidneys, which is good. It means we're not having to start talking dialysis yet, so long as you maintain the diet we discussed." He frowns. "I'm a little concerned about your weight…"

My eyebrows shoot up. "Excuse me?"

"Are you skipping meals, Tempest?"

I *know* I'm too thin. At first, everyone around me just figured I was getting in shape or hitting the gym more than I used to. But now, even my brothers are clearly trying to bite their tongues at the weight I've dropped.

But "are you skipping meals" makes it sound like I'm trying to slim down for prom or something stupid. The reality is, I'm literally almost never hungry. Frequently, the very idea of putting food into my mouth is nauseating.

"No..."

Sort of. Sometimes.

He gives me a stern look. "Is it nausea?"

I shrug and look down at my hands. I hate this. More invasive questions in a building filled with the stench of rubbing alcohol and death.

"Because if it is, Tempest," he continues, "I can prescribe you something. And I would also recommend cannabis for an appetite boost and a nausea suppressant."

I manage a grin. "Are you saying the munchies are going to save me?"

Dr. Han gives me a wry smile. "I'd welcome you to visit the oncology ward and talk to some of the stage four cancer patients up there. They'll swear by it, I can assure you."

I nod, picking idly at my cuticles and the remnants of black polish on my nails. I smirk inside when I flash back to the other day in my grandfather's study...

When I bumped into the Devil himself.

My fiancé dearest.

I remember the way he grabbed my wrists, and then how his eyes lasered in on my hands and nails. I replay the wrinkled nose look of...something...on his face when he took in the chipped black instead of the manicured French tips I'm *sure* he's used to seeing on the women of his harem at his little club.

I make a note to repaint them extra black and shiny, maybe with some skull nail art for extra fuck-you points before our next meeting. Which—crap—is *tonight*, at our engagement party.

Okay, it's not *really* an engagement party. It's worse. Instead of a celebration of this nauseatingly fake arrangement, it's more like showing off a pony to a panel of judges.

And guess who's expected to trot, trot, trot.

Yuuup.

Tonight, Dante is going to "present me" to a who's-who of the city's most connected, influential and dangerous mafiosos, including at least three heads of families belonging to The Commission.

So yes, black with white skulls, for sure. Maybe I'll even chip them up a bit for a little extra shock value.

Dr. Han takes a deep breath. "Tempest, have you—"

"No."

I'm so tired of this question. But he doesn't tire of asking it.

"I really do urge you to speak to—"

"I'm fine."

Dr. Han wants me to *start talking to the people in my life about what's happening with me*. Because, well, I...haven't yet.

At all.

No one, and I mean no one, knows about the toxic blood poisoning my body from the inside out. Not Gabriel, not Alistair, not Maeve; *no one*.

And I'm fucking going to keep it that way.

Losing Layla was hard. For all of us, of course, but I was only eleven when it happened. Meanwhile my brothers were twenty-two. I vaguely remember losing my sister. But I'll never forget the way it scarred and ripped open Alistair and Gabriel.

They've been through enough already. They don't need to spend the next six-to-eight months of their lives worrying about me dropping dead in the street.

"Tempest, it's often helpful to open up about your fears or how you're feeling to family and loved ones. Not just for them, but for you, too."

"I said I'm *fine*, Dr. Han," I say quietly, my voice thin but hard as my brows knit. "And if you say a word—"

He stops me with a raised hand. "There are ethical codes, you know that. And even if there weren't, I would never in a million years go behind a patient's back like that, okay?" He smiles, but it's the smile of a man looking at a wilting flower. "It wasn't a threat, just..." He shrugs. "It can help—talking to loved ones, I mean."

It wasn't a threat...

I *do* have a tendency to take everything as one, I'll admit. I have to: it's part of the armor I've worn since I was seventeen. I'd say I should work on that, but...

Yeah. That.

Dr. Han clears his throat. "Well, is there anything new going on in your life?"

"I've been making a short list of places to have my thirtieth birthday."

Dr. Han looks worried for a second. When I grin, his shoulders relax and he clears his throat awkwardly.

"Just a little gallows humor, Doc."

"Yeah, uh, hilarious." He smiles. "Though, humor in general *can* be helpful." He sighs as he rearranges my tests into a neat pile in front of him. "Well, unless there's anything else, I'll see you in three weeks—"

"Also, I'm getting married."

It flies out of me, I have absolutely no idea why. Or worse, why I fucking *blush* when I say it.

Dr. Han's brows shoot up. "Oh?" He smiles warmly. "Well, congratulations, Tempest! I didn't realize you had a partner."

"It's pretty new." I shrug. "He's in the mafia and runs a sex club."

Dr. Han's brows knit for a second, then he smiles wryly. "More gallows humor, huh?"

Nope, that one's real.

"Tempest."

I flinch at the touch on my arm, whipping my head around to gape at Taylor.

Her fiery auburn brows knit. "Sorry, I didn't mean to startle you."

Generally, I *am* somewhat skittish, especially if someone comes up behind me without me hearing it. But Taylor didn't exactly sneak up on me. I mean, it's the middle of the afternoon, I'm standing in the middle of my bedroom, and the door to the room is wide open behind me.

Taylor's been like a big sister to me since I was a kid, when she and my brothers met at Knightsblood University. As far as I know, there's never been anything romantic between her and either of them—or between her and *anyone*, given that she's married to her job. They're just three good friends who went on to law school together after college, and eventually started Crown and Black, building it into the powerhouse legal firm it is today.

"I was just…"

I trail off, my face reddening.

I'd been staring at the clothes strewn across my bed. And while I'd love to claim I was thinking of ways to skip the event tonight, or to make it blow up in Dante's face, that wouldn't be the truth.

The truth is, I wasn't thinking about the event at all.

I was thinking about *him*.

It's been made abundantly clear to me in my twenty-four years on this planet that life is simply not fair. Good guys frequently lose, and bad guys have a depressingly horrible tendency to win most of the time. Life does *not* play nice, it *is* out to screw you, and it cheats whenever it can.

Case in point: my current situation with Dante.

I mean the man is a mafia thug, runs an actual, *literal* sex club, was totally fine with marrying and probably screwing my eighteen-year-old relative, and almost definitely hates me at this point for throwing a monkey wrench into his life plans.

But hey, at least he's *got* a life to live ahead of him. Like, cry me a fucking river.

The man *should* repulse me to my core. He *should* be one of those intrusive thoughts that you shove to the back of your mind the second it crawls its way into your consciousness, like remembering that parking ticket you never paid, or the memory of saying something horrendously stupid in front of your crush in the seventh grade.

If only.

Because instead of being a bleak thought I can shove to the corners of my head or bury underneath distractions, he's the opposite. Vile, arrogant, corrupt, and brutish as he may be, Dante Sartorre has managed to slither his way into the very front of my cerebral cortex and establish a permanent settlement there. And try as I might, I *cannot* evict him.

If the world were remotely fair, all of his utterly toxic character traits would translate into Dante being a hunchbacked, scowling, filthy, knuckle-dragging troll of a man. Instead, he looks like a fucking Armani model, with a ludicrously perfect jawline, eyes that make your pulse skip, and the build of a Marvel superhero.

Not to mention his smell. I mean it's honestly insane how good he smells, like this clean, slightly spicy *good* scent. Which makes no sense, considering he's a purveyor of sin and the Devil himself. The man should smell like sulfur, brimstone, and the burned-out souls of his enemies, not fresh soap, morning dew, and clean linen.

And it's all of *those* reasons why I've been standing here staring at the bed and imagining Dante Sartorre lying on it, naked, beckoning me with two fingers, like some Fabio lookalike on the cover of a cheesy romance novel, instead of picturing creative ways I might murder him if he even tries to *touch* me once we're married.

"Pam let me in," Taylor says, by way of explaining how she got into the house that I share with Gabriel. She doesn't really have any family of her own, so Taylor's spent just about every holiday here with us since she and my brothers met.

Gabriel still lives here in the West Village townhouse where we all grew up because one, it's gorgeous. But two, he detests change, not to mention likes every aspect of his life neat, ordered, and routine. *I* still live here because, well, I don't have a job, money, or anywhere else to live.

That all said, I *do* love living here. It reminds me of our parents, it really is a stunning home, and I actually kind of enjoy living with Gabriel, even though he is a total neat freak at a slightly psycho serial-killer level.

Which is *exactly* why our other brother does not still live with us, by the way.

Alistair also likes things neat, organized, and precise. But neat, organized, and precise on his own terms, not Gabriel's. Not to mention, they do also work together probably eighty hours or more a week. Living together on top of that would result in one of them killing the other, I'm sure.

For a while, it was just Gabriel and I here. But then about six months ago, he hired Pam as a full-time housekeeper and cook. At first, I was skeptical. Or maybe I was worried that some outside person was going to throw off the vibe my brother and I had established living here just the two of us. But I gotta say, she's really grown on me.

Pam's one of those woman who's embracing her later years with class. She clearly takes care of herself, but she's also not super obsessed with hiding the fact that she's in her late sixties. She doesn't overdo it with the makeup, doesn't dye her silver hair, and somehow looks classy all the time, even when she's working around the house.

Maybe that's why I like her. There's something comforting seeing someone embracing the inevitability of life and its end when you're staring down the barrel of your own mortality.

Right on cue, there's a knock on the open bedroom door. I grin when Pam waltzes through with a big milkshake glass filled with a creamy, green smoothie.

"Here you go, hon."

Pam *majorly* won me over when she first started working for us with her on point smoothie game. She's even tailored some of my previous favorite combinations of hers to suit the diet Dr. Han has me on. Of course, she doesn't know it's a doctor-mandated thing. She just thinks I'm being healthy.

"Avocado, blueberries, vanilla yogurt, chia seeds, hemp seeds, spinach, and almond milk."

I still get a tiny wave of nausea when I take the glass from her. But for some reason, smoothies I can tolerate a little easier, and they don't seem to trigger my gag reflex.

"You seriously pamper me, Pam."

She nods in the curt way she has before turning to Maeve. "Would you like one too, Ms. Crown?"

Taylor glances at the gloppy green drink. "I'm…good, thank you."

When Pam leaves, Taylor eyes my smoothie again suspiciously. I grin.

"I know, it looks like vomit. But it's actually delicious. Well, delicious for something on the Keto diet."

"Remind me again *why* it is you thought you had to go on a diet?" Taylor's gaze slides up and down my frame. "It's not something some douchebag guy said, is it? I mean, Tempest, you're in fantastic shape. I'd even say—" Her mouth snaps shut.

I'd even say you're TOO thin.

I can see the unspoken words in her eyes.

"Look, I don't have an eating disorder or anything, Taylor."

"I wasn't—"

"I'm just trying different elimination diets for food sensitivities, that's all."

I ignore Dr. Han's voice in my head, encouraging me to tell family and friends about what's happening with me.

Taylor clears her throat, turning to nod her chin at my bed with all the clothes strewn across it.

"I was trying to pick out what to wear tonight."

She frowns. "You want me to come with you?"

Yep, there's the big sister vibes. My brothers are fiercely protective of me. But "protective" to them means putting on armor and dueling with anyone who'd try to hurt me using swords or battle axes. With Taylor, it's a sweeter, human touch.

She was instrumental in helping my brothers deal with everything when Layla died. And she was my biggest lifeline after what happened to me, when I couldn't be around men, not even my brothers. She's the sole reason I can be out in the world these days instead of staying the shut-in I was for about six months afterward.

Still, I shoot her a look.

"You don't want to come to this shitshow."

"The *hell* I don't! You need backup in there."

I grin. "You mean besides Alistair and Gabriel?"

"Let me restate," she sighs. "You need backup who isn't drowning in testosterone *and* who can think further ahead than one swung punch. Besides, Dante *is* my client."

Considering the...*history* between my family and Dante, it's crazy that he uses Crown and Black at all for his personal and business legal needs. That said, she's really the only one he interacts with, according to Gabriel.

It *is* a tempting offer. My brothers are, obviously, coming tonight. But having Taylor there would definitely give me a bit more comfort. Maybe it's a girl thing, or maybe she's right: she can have my back rationally without immediately going to the thrown fists place like Gabriel and Alistair would if things went sideways.

But it's not that I don't *want* her there. It's that I can't *have* her there.

I need space tonight when I go to Dante's house. Not because I want to impress his guests.

Marrying the head of New York's most secretive kink club might not have ever been on my bucket list. But ever since the day I pricked my finger and signed my blood across that page, I've started to consider some of the potential upsides to getting inside Dante's world.

Upsides like *access*.

At first, after what happened to me when I was seventeen, I wallowed in the "random bad luck" of what had been done to me and to Nina. But slowly, with therapy, and in the survivors' groups I went to, I started to realize what had been done to us maybe wasn't so random after all.

It was the rings that clinched it for me.

That's one of those weird, horrible details I'll never forget about that night. Even if the rest of it is a terrifying blur, what I do remember with utter clarity is the gold ring with the lion's head carved into it, with two little gems for the eyes and "AC" engraved on the band.

The man who hurt me wore one. I'll never forget the feel of its weight as his fingers tightened around my wrist, pinning me down. And he wasn't the only one.

…The men who raped and killed my best friend not three feet from me wore them, too.

To most people, these would be insignificant little details in a horrible, painful story. But to me, they're clues. Breadcrumbs. And I can't stop following the trail, even if I dread thinking what I might find at the end of it.

I don't know who they all are. But I know the matching rings aren't coincidence. It means those men were connected, and organized: a club, or maybe a fraternity of some kind. And while I know Club Venom is its own thing, and doesn't involve lion head rings, it *is* also a secretive, clandestine club that attracts men with certain tastes and desires.

What I'm looking for is overlap. Connections. *Anything* that might lead me to members of Club Venom who perhaps also enjoy wearing lion rings and hurting young women against their will.

Marrying Dante Sartorre might be signing my soul over to the devil. But it might also give me access to clues—club registries, member details—that would allow me to track down the men who took my friend's life, before mine runs out.

"Tempest?"

I blink as I pull my thoughts back to the present.

"Sorry, Taylor, my head's all over the place today." I exhale. "Look, I'd love you to come, but wouldn't it be a conflict of interest, with Dante being your client?"

She frowns. "It wouldn't *have* to be."

"Tay," I sigh, smiling to cover the twinge of guilt I feel with semi-lying to her. "It'll be a who's-who of New York mafia. That's not exactly a good look, is it?"

She snorts. "You do realize who half our clients are, yes?" Then she exhales. "Fine, if you don't want me there—"

"Taylor…"

She grins, reaching over to squeeze my arm. "I'm *kidding*, girl. You're probably right. This is a family thing, and I'm not that."

I roll my eyes. "The hell you aren't."

She chuckles. "All the same, I didn't receive an invite. And in Dante Sartorre's world, that means you're not invited. Period."

I scowl. "Is he always such a dick?"

"He's..." Her brow furrows as she folds her arms across her suit jacket. I'm sure she just came from the office. "*Efficient.* Sometimes brutally so. He's the type of man who doesn't see any reason to use several words if one will do, if that makes sense."

"So he's a neanderthal."

Taylor shakes her head, frowning. "All I will say is that if I'd ever had any suspicion that he was the type of man who'd try and marry a fucking eighteen-year-old, or *you*, I'd have fired him as a client a long time ago."

My mouth twists. "Thanks," I mumble quietly.

"This whole thing..." She looks away angrily. "I'm so sorry this is—"

"We don't have to talk about it," I murmur.

Taylor nods before walking over and giving me a much-needed hug. When she pulls back, we both wordlessly agree to exhale the Dante from our lungs.

"So..." She nods at the pile of clothes on my bed. "Do you know yet what you're wearing?"

"Hell, yes."

I pluck a few garments from the pile and lay them out: black ripped skinny jeans, a black Joy Division t-shirt, and heeled boots that go up to my knee.

Taylor makes a face.

"You can't be serious."

"Oh, and I'm painting my nails, too. Black with skulls," I laugh.

Taylor says nothing. I frown as I glance at her.

"Okay, what is it."

"It's just…" She sucks on her teeth. "You know how Gabriel is always saying to pick your battles?"

"Yeah, but that's easy for him to say. He literally *does* pick his battles, and he only picks the ones he knows he's ninety-five percent or higher likely to win in court."

She grins. "And is dressing to shock or piss Dante off tonight the battle you want to pick?"

"Yyyes?"

She chuckles, pushing an errant lock of red hair behind her ear. "Well, it's your call."

I purse my lips.

Goddammit. She has a point.

If I walk in there tonight dressed to piss off Dante, who did imply via text yesterday to dress to impress, it's going to put him on edge and keep his attention on me, waiting for me to do something else to stir shit up. And that's not ideal, given that my plans for the evening include slipping *away* from this stupid party and snooping around Dante's house for any clues or connections between Venom and the men with the rings.

Shit.

"Okay, okay," I concede. "Fine. Maybe I could be persuaded to elevate the look a little."

"May I suggest something that isn't black?"

I sigh heavily. "*Maybe.* But I'm still painting my nails black and doing the little skulls thing."

I *am* marrying the devil, after all.

8

TEMPEST

"You look nice, Tempest."

From the back seat, I look into the rearview mirror, meeting Gabriel's eyes.

"Thanks. You sound surprised."

His lips curl slightly at the corners. "If I were a betting man, I'd have put money on you showing up tonight in a gorilla costume or like you were going to a death metal show."

"Shit, am I that predictable?"

He chuckles. "I'm just saying, you look nice."

I glance down at the shimmery silver, sleeveless, ankle-length dress with the tastefully teasing neckline, plunging back, and the slit up the side to mid-thigh.

Not-really-a-spoiler: it's Taylor's, not mine. After she offered to help me find an appropriate outfit for this debacle, we both realized exactly how much *in*appropriate shit was in my wardrobe. The strappy silver heels are also hers, for the same reason. But I will admit, even if I feel like I'm cosplaying a European princess in this ridiculous thing, it *does* go with the tuxedos my brothers are wearing a bit better than that Joy Division t-shirt.

We're long past the point where I press them on ways to get me out of this situation, or where they ask me for the millionth time what the fuck I was thinking. Instead, we sit in silence as we drive through the night to Dante's Hamptons estate where I snuck my signature onto that blood marker two weeks ago.

Alistair clears his throat, his eyes flicking from the road ahead to my mine in the rearview mirror.

"Why were you at Mount Sinai earlier today?"

My spine stiffens, my heart dropping for a second. Dr. Han's office is at Mount Sinai. I will myself to keep cool as I frown at him in the mirror.

"Were you spying on me?"

He rolls his eyes. "Obviously not. Katerina's grandmother has her dialysis sessions there. Katerina took the morning off today to be with her, and when she came in later, she mentioned she saw you in the lobby of the nephrology center."

Katerina is Alistair's secretary, a sweet, quiet young thing who somehow works happily under my brother's iron-fisted rule. I did know she had a grandmother going through dialysis for Lupus-related kidney issues.

...I just never realized grandma was getting dialysis in the same *department* of the same *building* where I go to see Dr. Han.

Fuck.

"Well?"

I blink, glancing up and meeting my brother's gaze in the rearview mirror again. "Well what?"

"*Well*, what were you doing at a dialysis center?"

I shrug. "Nothing."

"Tempest—"

"Alistair, forget it."

Ugh, totally wrong thing to say. Both of my brothers are like sharks around drops of blood in the ocean when it comes to sniffing out lies or strings to pull on. Telling Alistair in particular to "forget it" or "don't worry about it" is a surefire way to get him to zero in with lethal precision on that private thing you don't want to talk about.

"Tempest, if there's something we need to know, I'd like to hear it."

"I'm pretty sure asking someone about their medical history is illegal, Mr. Lawyer."

"*Disclosing* someone's medical history without their consent is," Gabriel mutters. "Asking them about it is not."

"Potato, po-tah-to. Mind your own—"

"*For fuck's sake, Tempest!*" Alistair hisses. "I'm just asking if—"

"Oh my *God*," I sigh with exasperation. "If you *must* know, my OB-GYN is in the same building."

Not even a little bit true.

"And, since you're *so* interested in my personal medical shit, I was seeing her because I was…concerned."

Both my brothers tense, their eyes snapping to mine in the mirror.

"Concerned about what?" Gabriel says quietly.

"Well, what with all the anonymous gloryholes I've been visiting all over the city…I mean, that's a *lot* of random dicks to be sucking and fucking without protection. Who knows what I might have picked up?"

The car goes quiet. I bite back my grin, relishing the looks of disgust on my brothers' faces. Gabriel swivels around to give me a look.

"That's not funny."

My grin breaks free as I hold my thumb and finger up an inch apart. "It's a *little* funny."

It is, and it isn't. There are women who've gone through what I have who do turn to hyper-sexual activity as a coping mechanism. And no shade or judgment there, but that isn't me.

I'm the opposite. I've barely been able to sit through a dinner date with anyone since that night. Forget screwing them.

I smirk as I spot the sour look on Alistair's face.

"Just dick after dick after—"

"Yeah, okay, point taken. Thanks, Tempest," he mutters.

"So, class, what did we learn tonight about prying into people's personal lives?"

"I said point *taken*. You can lose the moral superiority."

89

I laugh. "I was just in for my annual checkup. Chill. And for what it's worth to the two judge-y little shits sitting up front, *I'm* not the one in this car who frequents a sex club."

Gabriel sighs as the car pulls off the main road and stops at the huge metal gate to Dante's estate, the one that shut on me when I was attempting my getaway before.

"I go there for business, Tempest. We've been through this."

"Alistair doesn't."

The conversation pauses while Alistair shows his ID to the guards at the gate, who wave us through.

"What I do or don't do in my private life is…"

Alistair trails off when he spots the shit-eating grin on my face in the backseat. My smile widens as I smack my lips and rub my stomach happily.

"Num-num-*num*! I'll take another helping of that delicious irony with a side of double standards, please!"

When the car stops, Gabriel helps me out, and both of them offer me an arm as I teeter my way up the steps to Dante's sprawling mansion. I haven't worn spike heels since I was a teenager, and it shows. Hope my new fiancé wasn't expecting grace and elegance. After tonight, he won't be seeing me in anything but boots or sneakers.

We're ushered from the front foyer of the home down a gilded hallway and into a huge, stunning ballroom. A *ballroom*. I mean, I didn't exactly grow up poor, and my brothers are killing it, but this?

This is next-level. It also feels utterly ridiculous to be putting this much effort into "celebrating" what is clearly a steaming pile of bullshit. Between the string quartet and waiters passing around trays of champagne to what must be over two hundred guests, it feels like I just walked into Jay Gatsby's house, complete with a who's-who guest list of gangsters.

Even I recognize some of the dangerous and powerful faces milling around the party. Michael Genovisi, head of the Scaliami mafia family, is a client of Alistair's, and when we walk in, he makes a point of nodding at my brother. As I scan the room, my gaze lingers on a weirdly familiar-looking pretty blonde girl with a look somewhere between boredom and fear on her face.

"Eloise LeBlanc," Gabriel murmurs under his breath. "You might have seen her at the office. Her father, André, uses us for his US-based legal needs. She's been in with him a couple of times."

My gaze wanders back to Eloise, and I frown when a handsome but malicious looking Italian man with dark hair and a grimace on his face moves close to her. Instantly, her whole body tenses and she recoils. Then his hand comes up to wrap around the back of her neck roughly, turning her face even paler as he leans close to snarl something in her ear.

When I glance at Alistair to ask who the hell that creep is, I freeze. My brother's face is darkened and tense, a lethal look in his gaze as it stabs across the room to the pair.

"Massimo Carveli," Gabriel mutters, his eyes darting toward Alistair. Our brother's jaw is clenched like iron, with a vein popping out on his forehead. "Rumored to have killed his father last year to take over the Carveli throne." Gabriel's face sours. "He's Eloise's husband."

My stomach clenches as I see him lean closer to the poor woman, hissing something into her ear that makes her flinch. His hand visibly tightens on the back of her neck.

"He's hurting—"

"Tempest."

I glance at Gabriel, who soberly shakes his head side to side. "Leave it. Seriously. Massimo is a fucking lunatic."

"But he's—"

I turn toward Alistair, blinking in surprise when I see him already storming away to the bar at the side of the ballroom with plodding, furious steps.

"Okay, what's his—"

"Tempest."

I turn back to Gabriel, who shakes his head again. "Just… leave it. Trust me."

Suddenly, I shiver as the scent of clean linen and spice invades my senses. My back straightens, a tingle sliding over my skin as the dark, malevolent energy of him billows over me like a poisonous black cloud.

I turn, and my heart skips as my eyes lock with his.

Dante.

He completely ignores me as he glances at my brother.

"Gabriel."

"*Dante,*" Gabriel mutters back through clenched teeth.

"Welcome to my humble—"

"Let's skip the fucking gracious host and formalities routine," Gabriel spits. "We both know what you are."

Dante's lips curl devilishly at the corners. He's still not looking at me. Asshole.

"Ah, but what we are, old friend, is *family*, now. Thanks to your dear sister…"

My breath catches in my throat as Dante's icy blue eyes finally swivel to pierce mine. His lips are still curled into a smile, but it's hollow.

Empty.

Devoid of warmth or sincerity.

All I see is cold, dark malice.

"We'll see about that."

"Yes, well, if you find a way to cancel a fucking *blood marker*, Gabriel," Dante says coldly, "*do* let me know. In the meantime, if you'll excuse us…"

I gasp, my eyes flying wide as Dante's arm suddenly encircles my waist and yanks me to his side. A shiver drags its nails down my spine as the heat and hardness of his body electrify my skin.

"And *before* you put on your cape to play superhero and tell me to take my hands off her," Dante growls quietly, turning back to Gabriel, "let's not forget that the entire reason for this celebration tonight is *our engagement*." He smiles icily. "Enjoy the party, Gabriel."

I shudder as his arm tightens around me, whisking me away and off into the crowd.

"What the *fuck* do you—!"

"What I'm doing is a tour of the room to show off my new fiancée, *dear*," Dante hisses. "That's the entire fucking point of this entire evening, thanks to you."

"Well, you can do it without putting your fucking hands on—"

I gasp again as he grabs my hand and spins me in time to the waltz music the string quartet is playing in the corner of the ballroom.

"Exactly *what* are you doing?!" I hiss, shivering as he pulls me right against his chest and starts to dance with me, one hand holding mine, the other firmly gripping my waist.

"Dancing with my fiancée."

I try and pull away, but his iron grip only tightens on my hand and my hip, pulling me against his body even harder.

"*Stop it*," I mutter, glaring up at him. "And don't try and tell me this is for appearances." My eyes dart side to side, taking in the smiling, slightly drunk faces of the various guests watching us dance. "As if any of these people legitimately think we're a couple."

"They can think what they want. But let me explain to you how this world you've bamboozled your way into works," Dante growls testily. "Behind closed doors is one thing. In public, however, you will *be my fucking wife*."

I'm not prepared for the jolt in my belly when he says it.

You will be my fucking wife.

It's raw, brutally honest, and unapologetically possessive.

…And *skin-tinglingly hot* when he growls it into my ear.

"At the moment," Dante murmurs, "that entails dancing with me, playing the fucking part, and smiling when you should, like a good girl."

Something electric and throbbing pulses in my core.

Damn him.

My stomach flutters as Dante spins me again and dips me expertly before pulling me back into his arms.

"I must say, I'm shocked."

"Oh?" I spit.

"Yes. You came here dressed like a grownup. I assumed your entire wardrobe was concert t-shirts and ripped jeans."

"Oh, I'm saving my best burlap sack for the wedding, *honey*," I drawl.

"Well, anyway, the gown looks better on you than on Ms. Crown."

I tense, trying to swallow the bitter twinge deep inside, my eyes snapping to his, which glint with amusement.

I am *not* jealous. I do *not* care if Taylor and Dante have...or had...*more* than a professional relationship. I mean, I've wondered about it before. He's—well, just look at him. And Taylor is hot, successful, stylish, and confident. Not to mention, she's a member of Club Venom.

She's always *said* she goes purely for business reasons, same as Gabriel. But...who knows what happens with her and Dante behind closed doors?

Or open ones, given the nature of that place...

I don't realize I'm still scowling until Dante's lips brush my ear, jerking me back to reality with a gasp, sending another heated shiver down my spine.

"*Go ahead*," he whispers darkly. "Ask."

I glare at him. "Ask *what*."

"If I've fucked her."

I start to open my mouth, but he shakes his head.

"Don't play stupid, because I know you're not. You want to know if Ms. Crown and I are, shall we say, *more* than a client and legal counsel."

I swallow back the fresh wave of bile rising in my throat.

"I don't care."

He grins. "Oh, I'm sure."

"No, you're right, I do care," I smile acidly. "Only because it would make me concerned for her well-being, making awful life choices like fucking *you* of all people. Or that you'd give her something gross."

Dante chuckles. "You have a very low opinion of me, Ms. Black."

"Gee, I wonder why."

"Taylor is my *attorney*, Tempest. You may be surprised to hear that I'm also not screwing my dentist or the pleasant old man who does my taxes. So for the record, no, I haven't fucked her," he murmurs sinfully in my ear, the scent of him enveloping me like a drug.

"I already told you, I don't—"

Dante suddenly spins me again, causing my heart to leap into my throat. A thrill I'm not really prepared for or interested in acknowledging explodes deep in my core, making me bite down hard on my lip.

"Hmm."

The fluttery feeling instantly evaporates as I glare at him. "*What.*"

"You're not as terrible a ballroom dancer as I would have expected. I figured mosh pits were more your speed."

I've grown up being trotted around at enough Crown and Black functions, galas, and shareholder parties that I can waltz my way across a room.

The arrogance of him assuming I *can't* pisses me off, though. So on the next turn, as he spins me again, I do the only thing I can: I make a point of stepping down *hard* on his foot with my strappy heel.

Dante's teeth grind as he swallows a grunt.

"*Oopsie!*" I giggle like an airhead. "I'm *so* clumsy! It's probably because I'm just a silly widdle girl and I've never been to a big fancy party with real dancing like this one!!"

Dante levels a cold, dark glare at me.

"Having fun yet?"

"Loads," I grin saccharinely. "What a *swell* party."

Dante twirls me again, and this time, as I'm once more aiming my heel for his foot, I jolt when his hand suddenly slides from my hip. It skims deftly over my bare skin where the dress splits, his touch leaving throbbing, electrified shivers in its wake before his large fingers tense like an iron vice around my thigh, stopping me from stamping my foot on his.

His mouth suddenly dips to brush against my ear and the crook of my neck.

"You made this bed, little hurricane," he rasps darkly. "So now you'll fucking sleep in it."

I try to twist out of his grip, but it's like fighting concrete. He doesn't budge one eighth of an inch.

"You will swallow your terminal need to pee in the punchbowl and *behave*," Dante growls quietly. My core turns to molten lead as he yanks my thigh up to his hip, whirling and dipping me as the quartet slips from Tchaikovsky into a tango.

I shift abruptly, my knee jerking toward his balls. But *again*, his iron hands wrench me back into place, my knee up on his hip, my breasts squashed against his rock-hard chest, my entire body pressed right against him.

"I said *behave*," he growls.

"Or?" I snap back.

"Or I will *teach you to*."

Sweet Jesus.

The fact that the more forceful, overbearing, and domineering he is to me, the *warmer* I get deep in my core is so very, very fucking unfair.

Fuck you, trauma. You too, issues.

I try to ignore the tingling sensation creeping over my skin and attempt to twirl out of his grip. Predictably, that gets me nowhere but tighter against his body.

"I won't warn you again, *dear*," Dante mutters.

"Well, marriage is sure going to be fun," I spit. "Threatening me already, Ike Turner?"

He smiles coldly. "*I'm* not the threat." He drags his gaze past me and around the room. "These are not good men. Not most of them. And if you think *I'm* not happy with your last-minute changes involving marriage deals and blood markers..."

"Gee, I'm so sorry you don't get to screw a teenager anymore. That must be a real bummer for a creep like you—"

I gasp sharply as his fingers dig like iron into the bare skin of my hip. When his hand suddenly slips a few inches higher, my blood turns to fire.

God. Fucking. *Damnit.* What is it about his touch that sends me into a spiral? I'm overlooking that this is the most intimate I've been with a man since I was seventeen.

Dante's touch is...something else. Something forbidden, yet alluring. Something sizzling and dangerous that scares the shit out of me while keeping me biting my lip for more.

"Once again," Dante growls. "The marriage to your aunt had everything to do with business arrangements and *nothing* to do with sleeping arrangements, and for the very last time, I had and continue to have *zero* interest in fucking her."

"Let's hope not," I snap back with a venomous glint in my eyes. "I doubt any of these mafia creeps would be too happy to find you sticking your dick into other girls after you're married."

Dante comes perilously close to laughing. My brows furrow.

"What?"

"Easily half of these *mafia creeps* have at least two *goomars* warming their beds each."

"I'm sorry, they have what now?"

Dante's eyes roll. "*Goomars*. Mistresses. Side pieces."

I shiver.

"So, *if I were so inclined,*" he growls, "don't for a moment think that Maeve would be off the table."

My temper flares, and my arm jerks as if to hit him. But of course, there's no breaking free from Dante's iron grip. I grit my teeth as he pulls me harder against his body.

"But again, I have no interest in your young aunt," he murmurs, his eyes sizzling into mine.

"Well, better find yourself a *goomar*, then," I spit. "Because your nights are going to be pretty fucking lonely with me as your wife."

His lips curl with dark amusement. "And why is that?"

"Because they'll be spent *alone?*"

Dante's lips stay curled at the corners, like he finds this funny. His brow cocks. "On the contrary, I'll be having you any time I want."

I bark a cold laugh. "That isn't happening in a million years, creep. I'm quite fine in my own bed."

"It's not a discussion, it's a deal-point."

"The fuck it is—"

"Dante."

The boiling tension bubbling and frothing between us drops back to a low simmer as the man steps next to us and clears his throat. Dante turns, his hands suddenly dropping from me as he steps back.

It's *bullshit* that what I feel when he does so isn't relief.

It's the total opposite.

"What is it?"

The man is just as tall and broad-shouldered as Dante; he's a little rough around the edges, but still immensely handsome. After a second I recognize him as the man who came out to meet my car when I was pretending to be Maeve the day of the signing.

"There's something you might want to address." The man coughs and lowers his voice. "Silvio is here."

Dante's jaw clenches as he nods. "Okay. Thanks, Lorenzo." He swivels his gaze back to me, his eyes simmering. "To be continued."

"Or *not—*"

He's already marching off with his goon, leaving me undecided if I'm more pissed at *him* for being such an arrogant tyrant, or at *myself* for attaching myself to him.

…Not to mention, the physical sensations being near said tyrant brings out in me.

I glare at Dante's back as he strides through the crowd with Lorenzo.

Then I whirl and march across the room, flashing zero-effort smiles at people I don't know when they congratulate me on an engagement I don't give a shit about. I don't usually drink much. But tonight, I'm gladly making an exception. I order a gin and tonic at the bar and take a large sip as I turn to survey the room.

Gabriel is, of course, being Gabriel, glad-handing his way through the crowd. Granted, a lot of these people are clients of Crown and Black. But it also wouldn't shock me if Gabriel leaves here tonight with one or two *new* clients.

Alistair, however, is nowhere to be seen. I'm about to go try and find him, since he looked like a ticking time bomb earlier, when suddenly, I feel a presence next to me.

"I suppose congratulations are in order."

I turn with a jolting sensation. Massimo Carveli. My mind flashes back to earlier when we first walked in and Gabriel pointed him out to me. I also remember my brother calling this man a "fucking lunatic".

He's standing next to the same blonde girl from before—his wife, Eloise LeBlanc. Pretty, but scared-looking. His hand is still wrapped around the back of her neck in a really menacing way.

And now that I'm closer to her, I can see the darkness around her left eye, with concealer caked over it to hide the bruising.

My hand tightens around my gin and tonic. My teeth clench hard.

You motherfucker.

"My wife," Massimo laughs easily, clearly seeing where my gaze is lingering. "She's so clumsy sometimes. Aren't you, sweetheart?"

Eloise smiles wanly. "Yes indeed," she says in a musical French accent. "So very clumsy."

I swear, I'm half a second away from throwing my drink in this fucker's face when he clears his throat.

"But as I was saying, congratulations are in order." He grins. "For marrying my cousin."

My brow arches. Massimo's grin widens.

"Well, only a distant cousin. But still, I consider Dante family, and now this makes *you* family, too."

Jesus. Of *course* Dante is "family" with creeps like this. Wonderful.

"Although," Massimo continues, stroking his strong jaw meditatively, "I suppose the bigger congratulations are owed to my cousin, since he gets to keep his lovely club now."

Wait, what?

"Oh...yes, of course," I feign a knowledgeable nod. "Yes, that's...good."

Massimo, who already looks pretty drunk, knocks back the champagne in his hand. "You know, I was *sure* they were going to take it from him. These puritanical old men on The Commission who somehow still find the idea of a single man running a club of that nature distasteful..." He shakes his head. "I say who gives a fuck if he's married or not. But then, I'm not an old man."

Well now.

This is interesting.

My gaze slides past Massimo. Across the ballroom, through a set of gorgeous French doors open to a balcony overlooking the ocean, I can see Dante heatedly speaking with a younger man. My eyes stab into his back, my jaw tightening.

You. Mother. Fucker.

This whole time, he's been framing this marriage thing as if he's doing *Charles* a favor. Or like he was going to marry Maeve to get something from him.

Now, I see the truth.

He needs me *way more* than I need him.

I smile darkly inside.

I'm going to use that to my utmost advantage.

"Welcome to the family, Ms. Black," Massimo mutters, yanking Eloise away with him as he disappears back into the crowd of laughing, drunk mafiosos.

I'm ready to get the *hell* out of here. I put my drink on the bar and turn to go find my brothers. But just as I do so, cold liquid splashes down my side, soaking the dress.

"Oh my *God*!"

The girl looks around Maeve's age, with her dark hair up in an elegant bun and piercing blue eyes that are currently as round as the "O" her heart-shaped lips are making. Her gaze snaps to mine in horror.

"I am *so* sorry!" she blurts, her face scarlet as she grabs a handful of cocktail napkins off the bar and starts to blot at my dress awkwardly.

"No, it's totally fine—"

"Seriously, Tempest, I'm *so* sorry! I'm the world's biggest klutz—"

She stops as I tense, my eyes narrowing. "Have we...?"

The girl blushes even more, her nose wrinkling. "God, worst first impression ever. I'm sorry, hi…" She sticks her hand out. "Bianca." She smiles weakly. "I'm, uh, Dante's sister."

Oh.

"I *swear*, drenching you was not in the plan! And it's just ice water, I promise! But if it screws up your dress, *please* let me know. I'm happy to cover the dry-cleaning."

There's not a single ounce of malice on her face. In fact, this girl is so sweet and exudes so much innocence that I'm struggling to accept the reality that she's *Dante's* sister. But when I stop and really look at her…yeah, there's no question she is.

The same nose, same cheekbones, even the same eyes, to an almost freakish degree.

She smiles apologetically. "Seriously, I'm so sorry. I was just coming over to say hi, but then you turned so fast—" she stammers. "I mean, not *at all* to imply it's your fault, I just—"

I cut her off with a grin, taking her hand and shaking it warmly. "Tempest, hi. Seriously, don't worry about it at all."

Bianca visibly relaxes.

"So…" I mumble. "We're going to be sisters, I guess."

"Yeah. I'm just sorry for you that it entails marrying my brother."

I chuckle as she blushes.

"I mean, don't get me wrong! I love him and all, but… Yeah, no, I can't imagine being married to him."

"Well, that makes two of us."

She laughs, biting her lip a little shyly as she eyes me. "By the way, I heard what you did with the whole blood marker thing." She dips her chin. "That was pretty badass."

I spread my arms. "It's a gift."

Bianca laughs again. "Can I get you another drink or something?"

I shake my head, nodding to the gin and tonic on the bar that I've barely touched. "Thanks, but I don't really drink much."

"Me neither," she shrugs. "I'm a dancer. Body is a temple and all that."

Somewhere in the back of my mind, I remember Gabriel mentioning this.

"Oh yeah, ballet, right?"

She nods. "Yeah. SAB."

Her eyes dart past me, and I catch the way her breath catches and her body tenses a little.

"*Shit.*"

I frown as she ducks down, moving closer to me as if trying to hide behind me. I glance over my shoulder, shivering slightly when Dante's eyes catch mine from out on the balcony. But the younger man standing next to him is also looking our way with a dark expression. I'm guessing that's who Bianca is trying to avoid.

"Come on," I say quietly, taking her arm. "Let's get out of here."

Her nose wrinkles. "I think Dante would prefer it if I stay. I'm supposed to make the rounds of the room and—"

"Bianca. He's your brother, not your boss." I glance out to the balcony again. Dante and the other man are still talking heatedly. When I turn back to her, Bianca's still chewing on her lip uncertainly.

"Okay," she finally blurts with a shy grin. "But first..." She turns and smiles at the bartender. "I'll have one of whatever she's having."

"Your brother is going to kill me for being a bad influence, isn't he?"

"Well, it *would* get you out of marrying him."

I laugh as she takes a sip of her drink and then grins.

"Come on, I know a place we can hide out."

9

DANTE

"This is fucking insulting, Dante!"

I resist the urge to tell Silvio that what is *actually* insulting is showing up to my engagement party uninvited, especially after being told in no uncertain terms to stay the fuck away from my sister.

I haven't the slightest fucking clue how a second-rate dumb-fuck like Silvio Bonpensiero managed to convince Bianca to go out with him in the first place. It's actually so difficult to imagine at times I've worried that coercion or drugs were involved, except for the fact that my sister doesn't do drugs and has never done a thing in her life that could be held over her head as blackmail.

In any event, Silvio and Bianca dated casually for a little bit about a month ago before she came to her senses and called it off.

Silvio, however, is having a *really* hard time getting the message about that.

Since my sister ended things, the fucker has showed up looking for her at her school, her apartment, my own house *and* the place I keep in the city, and even Club Venom—as if I would ever in a million years let Bianca go there—where he made a scene at the door until I finally came down and told him to go get fucked.

Usually, I'd have done *far* worse by now than use strong language with Silvio for continuing to creep after my sister. Except unfortunately the little shit is the son of Frank Bonpensiero, the head of one of the top tributary families of the Amato family. His mother also happens to be Luciana Amato's *niece*.

That makes mailing Silvio to various points around the globe in separate little boxes a no-no.

Lucky little douchebag.

"You *know* who my father is," he whines in my face. "And yet here you are, treating me like—"

"Like *what*, Silvio?" I hiss. "Like an intruder? Like a *pest?*"

His face turns bright red. "How *dare* you! How *dare*—"

"Yes, Silvio, I'm quite aware of who your father is." He gasps as I grab his collar in my fist. "But I need *you* to be equally aware that that is the only reason I haven't cut off your balls and *choked you* with them," I snarl right in his face.

I release his collar and step back. The second I do, his head swivels to the ballroom inside, and when I follow his gaze, my jaw clenches.

Not *just* because he's eyeballing my sister *again*. It's because when I follow his gaze to Bianca, I also catch a flash of a glimmering silver gown, black hair, and soft, pale skin.

Tempest.

Tempest, at whom I should be glaring with as much malice as I was at Silvio. Except when I look at the meddling little sneak who just royally fucked up my plans, it's not malice I feel.

It's something darker. Illicit.

I'm not looking at Tempest Black and fantasizing about putting her in a hole in the ground. The fantasy is more like me putting her *on her knees* with those sassy, vitriolic lips of hers wide open and waiting for my cock as I tangle that hair in my fist.

I suddenly realize I'm staring at her. Worse, she's staring right back.

Fuck.

I shake myself back into reality, grabbing Silvio's collar again and yanking his head away from staring at Bianca.

"Out of respect for your father, and who he answers to, I'm inviting you to leave on your own accord. This offer has a time limit, though, Silvio. In one minute, the invitation to walk out on your own two legs turns into Lorenzo *throwing* you out. And for every minute you overstay your non-welcome, I'll tell him to go up another flight of stairs in my home *before* tossing you out of it."

Silvio glares death at me. But there's not a real "tough guy" bone in his body. Silvio is pure spoiled mafia princeling, through and through.

"Do we understand each other?"

His lips curl. "My father will be hearing about this disrespect."

Oh my God.

"Forty seconds, dipshit."

"You can't order me around, Dante. I'm not one of your whores from your little club—"

"Thirty seconds."

Silvio swallows heavily. His eyes dart past me to Lorenzo.

"This isn't over," Silvio mutters. "Your sister and I have unfinished—"

"My sister and you, much like my tolerance for your presence in my home, are over. Fifteen…no, ten seconds."

Silvio starts to open his mouth. Then he's got the good sense to close it before giving me one last glare and storming away through the ballroom toward the exit.

Probably the smartest thing the idiot's done all day.

"Have him tailed after he leaves," I growl to Lorenzo.

"You got it, boss."

Lorenzo disappears back into the crowd inside as I wait in the shadows of the balcony, surveying this whole debacle.

An engagement party.

Give me a fucking break.

It's not that I actively never wanted to get married. I mean if we want to get technical with things, I was once married, for about eight minutes.

…To Tempest's sister Layla, right before she died.

These days, the lack of any motivation or urge to get married is because I already *am*. To my job. To the club. To the webs of information I weave.

And that's not even counting my *other* job. My…crusade, if you will. My hunt.

But that's another story entirely.

My gaze darts to the bar before I can stop myself. She's not standing there anymore. I actually don't see Tempest *anywhere*, actually. But before I can chide myself for looking for the little agent of fucking chaos, a heavy hand lands on my shoulder.

"Congratulations, my friend."

The heavy Serbian accent is a dead giveaway before I even turn toward him. I'm not a small man by any standard. But fucking hell, it's hard for even me not to feel small next to Drazen Krylov.

The man is just *big*—tall, broad-shouldered, and built like Henry Cavill's Superman. He's a good-looking guy, and he's taken to wealth with style. I mean, I don't know if Drazen was ever *poor*, per se. But the mercenary-turned-Bratva kingpin came into *billions* about a year ago with the discovery of a long-lost treasure of Tsarina Alexandra's royal jewels, which she'd bequeathed to Drazen's great-great-grandfather a century ago, when the Romanov family fell.

Now, he calls New York home as he works to build the Krylov Bratva family into a formidable empire. He's also become a friend of sorts, now that he and Carmy and Nico are pals and business partners. And, of course, now that he's an investor in Club Venom.

I roll my eyes. "Let's skip the congratulations."

Drazen grins. "Well, whatever the circumstances, she's beautiful. So there's that."

"She's crass, mouthy, and a royal pain in the fucking ass."

He chuckles as I sigh.

"So where are your partners in crime?"

"Carmine and Nico?" He snorts, nodding his chin at the crowd inside. "Playing with fire."

AKA, hitting on anything with a pair of a tits and a pulse, regardless of which of the dangerous mafiosos here they might be married to.

"I'm surprised you're not out there hunting with them, Drazen," I eye him. "Although I haven't seen you at Venom much recently, so perhaps...?"

He spreads his arms. "No, work has become my new mistress. Empires don't build themselves. But also," he makes a face, "I find it distasteful to chase pussy at the celebration of someone else's engagement."

"Yes, we wouldn't want to sully the sanctity of my arranged— and stolen, I might add—betrothal to a woman I want nothing to do with."

Drazen chuckles to himself. "You amuse me, Dante. You've grown up in this world seeing marriages exactly like this time and time again. And yet you're shocked and outraged when it happens to you. Surely you considered the possibility of a marriage that might benefit—"

"I was content to never consider the possibility of marriage *at all*," I growl. "As you say, empires don't build themselves, and some of us are coming up a little short in the Romanov diamonds department."

Drazen chuckles a deep, rumbling laugh. "Touche." He glances my way with a furrow to his brow. "Tell me, though. What is this animosity between her brothers and you? I thought you were a client of their firm."

My tongue runs over my teeth. "I am, but I work with Ms. Crown. Gabriel and Alistair and I just went to university together."

"What did you do, fuck their girlfriends?"

Wouldn't that have made things simpler...

"No. They believe I..." I shake my head slowly, looking at the middle distance. "It's complicated," I growl quietly.

Drazen opens his mouth to say something else. But just then Lorenzo suddenly strides toward me with a dark look on his face.

"Dante..." He glances at Drazen. When I nod for him to continue, he clears his throat. "I'm sorry, boss. We lost track of Silvio."

Shit.

"The fuck do you mean?"

"I mean I think he picked up on the fact that we were tailing him and lost us somewhere in the house. My guys are going through all the camera feeds now, but, well..."

It's a big house.

There's a *lot* of fucking cameras.

"Fuck," I mutter. "He's definitely still on the grounds?"

"Unless he pole-vaulted the fences. His Ferrari's still here, and the men on the gate never saw him leave with anyone else."

"*Find him*," I hiss. My pulse suddenly lurches afresh. "Shit, and find Bianca, *now*."

He grimaces stonily. "We're on it, boss."

He mutters into his radio and dives back into the party. Drazen clears his throat.

"What can I do to help? I have five of my men outside with cars."

"I'll take you up on that, thanks," I growl. "We're looking for Silvio Bonpensiero. I'll text you his picture. He's probably looking for my sister—"

A scream rips through the night. I whirl, lurching to the balcony railing: that didn't come from inside the party, it came from out here. I tense, my gaze stabbing into the darkness of the gardens surrounding the house.

"You fucking *bitch*!"

Drazen and I both whirl and look up at the same time.

Fuck me. It's not coming from the yard. It's coming from the fucking *roof*.

I dive back into the ballroom with Drazen right behind me, make a beeline for the side door, and crash through it. We tear down a hallway, up the main stairs, down another hall, and then up the staircase to the rooftop patio.

My gun is already out, and I can hear Drazen chambering a round in his behind me as I slam the door to the roof open.

"Don't you fucking *touch her*!"

Across the patio from us, Tempest is standing tall and furious between my sister and Silvio like some kind of shimmering avenging angel. Bianca's eyes are wide and her face pale as she cowers behind Tempest. Silvio, meanwhile, is snarling in rage, holding his hand to his bleeding cheek. Fuck me, are those *scratch marks*?

"You little *cunt—*"

It happens in a millisecond. Silvio goes to shove Tempest aside. But the second he takes one step toward her, she winds up and then absolutely *crushes* the highball glass in her hand against the other side of his face.

Silvio screams in agony, instantly dropping to his knees as shattered glass and blood explodes everywhere. Tempest shrieks too, dropping the smashed glass and clutching at her hand as Drazen and I bolt across the patio.

I knee Silvio hard, smashing him to the ground and sinking my toe into his soft belly.

"*Watch him,*" I snarl at Drazen. The Serbian grins with pleasure as he puts the heel of his wingtip dress shoe to the back of Silvio's neck and points the gun at the snivelling asshole's head. I rush over to Bianca, but she shakes her head.

"I'm fine! Help her!!"

I whirl and my eyes lock on Tempest, kneeling on the ground, wincing as she holds the hem of her dress to her bleeding hand.

Fuck.

"I'M FINE, DANTE. SERIOUSLY."

Bianca pushes past me, and walks over to where Tempest is sitting on the kitchen counter nursing the hand Lorenzo has just finished bandaging. It's nothing serious: no stitches needed. Still, I'm not exactly stoked for the inevitable shit-storm that's going to hit the fan when Gabriel and Alistair find out what happened.

Apparently, Silvio blundered his way up there, found my sister and Tempest having a drink, and tried to start some shit with Bianca. But then Tempest got between them, shoved him away, and scratched him when he tried to hit her. Drazen and I barged in just in time to see her smash her gin and tonic against the side of his head, cutting him up pretty badly and her only *sort of* badly in the process.

There's going to be fallout from this. Luckily, I've got security footage of the roof showing Silvio as the instigator. Drazen and his men are currently bringing him to a superb Russian doctor Drazen knows who's apparently a real pro. He'll be fine.

But it's also not like Frank Bonpensiero is an old buddy of mine, and he does love his moron of a son. This will take some special handling.

I'll deal with that later. More importantly, and mercifully, Bianca is fine, aside from being a little shaken up.

"You shouldn't have done that."

Tempest gives her a wry smile. "Why not? I mean, screw that asshole. He can't talk to you like that."

My sister turns and smiles at me. "She's a total badass, dude. Congrats."

I just nod quietly. "Lorenzo, would you make sure my sister gets home okay?"

Bianca's smile drops as she glares at me. "Really? Is this you sending me to my room? I mean what the *fuck*, Dante?!"

I shake my head as I walk up to her and hug her tightly.

"No, B. This is me getting you as safe as I can right now."

Her scowl softens as I pull back to lock my eyes with hers.

"My house is currently crawling with mafia from four different families with fuck knows how many different dramas lurking beneath the surface. *Your place*, meanwhile, is mafioso-free, and is a goddamn fortress."

I know this because I paid a small fortune to make it one.

"Plus, you'll have Lorenzo and his men there making sure there's no blowback from this. Okay?"

Lorenzo's been my head of security for years and has watched Bianca grow up. He'd step on a landmine for her without hesitation.

"*Okay?*"

Bianca sighs, puffing air through her lips. "Okay, okay. Fine." She frowns and turns back to Tempest. "Do you want to ride back with me? I mean, not to be weird, but you can totally come hang at my place—"

"No. Ms. Black and I need to talk."

Bianca turns to frown at me. "Dante—"

"I'll swing by your place as soon as I can wrap up the party," I murmur softly, hugging her again. "Okay?"

Her lips twist as she nods. "Okay." She frowns at me. "*Be nice to her*," she mutters before turning and hugging Tempest. "Thank you. Seriously."

"No prob," Tempest smiles, hugging her back.

After Lorenzo ushers my sister out of the kitchen, leaving Tempest and I alone, the kitchen goes silent. I rake my nails down my jaw, and our eyes lock.

"*What*," she mutters testily.

"Do you have any idea who that was that you almost blinded with your cocktail glass?"

She stares at me. "No. I just knew he was some asshole who was trying to put his hands on your sister. Are you seriously *mad* at me for stopping him?!"

I roll my eyes. "No, and you know I'm not. I'm honestly thankful you were there."

"Coulda fooled me," she mutters.

I glare at her. "What I'm *pissed* about is that I never asked for tropical storm Tempest to come smash up my shit!"

She jumps off the counter and marches over to me with a lethal glare on her face. She's ditched the heels by now, and she's even shorter than me than she was before.

"That fucker was going to *hurt her*, Dante. Don't you dare try and somehow blame *me* for him getting past security and being here at this stupid party in the first—"

"The stupid party we're only throwing because *you* fucking waltzed in and signed that fucking—"

I stop when her eyes glaze over. One of them starts to roll back in her head, and her mouth falls open.

What the fuck.

"Tempest—"

Her face goes chalk white as both eyes roll in different directions. Her legs give out, and I stick out my arms just before she topples to the ground, catching her full weight against my chest.

Fuck me, she's so light in my arms. Like a barely-there rag doll collapsed against me.

I kneel, lowering her in my arms and hovering over her. Tempest flinches. Her eyes flutter closed, then open, then closed again. Then they open again, with clarity this time. Her brow furrows in confusion, and as our eyes lock, my face leaned down close to hers and my arms wrapped around her small frame, I'm almost compelled to kiss her.

Mercifully, reason takes over. And by that, I mean Tempest flinches again, shoves me away from her, and lurches up.

"What the fuck are you doing?" she blurts, unsteady on her feet as she backs rapidly away from me.

"What the fuck am *I* doing? Tempest, you just collapsed. I think you blacked out."

Her eyes dart around the room, as if slowly refreshing her memory of her surroundings.

"I'm calling a doctor. I think you lost more blood than—"

"I'm fine."

I arch a stern brow. "The fuck you are. You just blacked—"

"I'm *fine*."

She rolls her shoulders as she pushes her hair back.

"Where are my shoes?"

Wordlessly, I nod my chin to where her heels are sitting by the fridge. She's still unsteady as she shuffles over and slips them on, tightening the straps and taking slow, deep breaths as she stands. Without another word, she walks—wobbles—to the door. There she pauses, turning back to look at me, her mouth pursed.

"I'd like to propose a deal."

I fold my arms over my chest. "Exactly what sort of deal?"

"You don't tell my brothers that I passed out. And I won't tell them that a deranged maniac managed to get past your security and hurt me while I was here tonight."

She's got balls, I'll give her that.

"Interesting proposal," I growl quietly.

She looks around vaguely. "I need to find my phone. I'm going to get my own ride back to the city. I'll call an Uber and text my brothers that I left. I don't think they'll have a hard time believing I skipped out on this party."

"I can call my helicopter."

"Yes, because that would be *way* easier to explain."

I smirk. So does she.

"And the hand? You don't think Gabriel and Alistair will possibly have a question or thirty about what the fuck happened to you?"

"My hand is fine," Tempest murmurs. "In a day or two, I'll just take the bandages off and tell them I slipped on the stairs or whatever. But you—"

"Don't mention your little collapsing routine."

"Exactly."

"Why not?"

"Because those are the terms of our deal."

I draw in a slow breath, walking toward her. Tempest shivers, but she doesn't move away.

"What are you—"

"I'm amending the terms."

Tempest scowls. "You can't do that."

"Watch me."

She chews on her lip, eyeing me. "Well?"

"I'll play this game and accept your terms. But I'm adding one more of my own."

"Which is?"

"No more surprises or bullshit. And you know what I mean."

Tempest looks like she's getting ready to throw something biting back in my face. But then she nods swiftly and sticks out a hand. "Okay, fine. Let's shake on it."

I smirk, rolling my eyes. "Fine."

I take her small hand in mine, almost enveloping it.

...I *refuse* to acknowledge the burst of heat that lances through my chest when our hands connect. I also refuse to dwell on the tingling sensation where her skin touches mine, or the way her eyes flicker with something forbidden when our gazes lock.

Then the moment's over.

Tempest pulls away, nods at me with her lip still caught in her teeth, and turns. I watch from the kitchen doorway as she walks down the hall. Once, she stumbles, her hand shooting out to steady herself against the wall.

"Just the fucking heels," she mutters over her shoulder. "I'm fine."

Maybe it was the heels just now. But that doesn't explain what happened before. That was certainly *not* her goddamn shoes.

It wasn't blood loss, either: she's right, her hand isn't that badly cut at all. It could be shock, I suppose.

My mind replays the way her eyes rolled back. The way her body just went limp in my arms, like a rag doll.

…who weighs, frankly, not enough.

Could *that* be it? An eating disorder? Tempest is *tiny*, and not just thin, either. She's gaunt, as if she purposefully doesn't eat. Fuck, like some of Bianca's dancer friends.

Whatever it is, I'll find out. Whatever she's hiding, I'll uncover. Whatever she's trying to keep buried, I'll dig up.

I'll discover every fucking secret you have, little hurricane...

10

TEMPEST

JUST AS I THOUGHT, Gabriel and Alistair require *zero* convincing to believe that I dipped out of my own engagement party. I think they're even a little amused.

The amusement fades a little when Gabriel realizes I put twelve hundred dollars for a two-and-a-half-hour Uber back to Manhattan from Dante's Hamptons estate on my "strictly emergency use only" Crown and Black credit card.

Damn surge pricing.

My hand really *is* fine. And after hiding from them for a few days, I'm able to ditch the bandage and explain the cuts with a bullshit story of tripping down some subway steps. Gabriel and Alistair buy it. But every time I look at the little cuts on my hand, I'm reminded of that engagement party.

I mean, yes, throwing myself between Bianca and that asshole ex-boyfriend of hers was dumb. Smashing the glass against his head was insane.

But the part that I keep returning to is the moment I came to after that dizzy spell where it felt like I was going to pass out for a hot second.

…in Dante's arms.

I'm choosing to forget how awkwardly I explained, or rather *didn't* explain, my little attack. How I brushed it aside instead of casually explaining that my kidneys are slowly shutting down and that frequently even the *idea* of food makes me retch.

Dante probably thinks I'm anorexic or bulimic or something. Whatever. He can think what he wants.

Doesn't stop me from replaying that moment when I opened my eyes and looked up into his, over and over again.

I have no idea why.

A week after the engagement party, I have to get back into character as Dante's fiancée for two events. The first, almost tongue-in-cheek thing, is that Taylor is insisting on taking me out for a "bachelorette party" along with Elsa and Fumi, two of the top lawyers at Crown and Black who I'm pretty chummy with.

The idea of going out to "celebrate" my arranged marriage to the devil himself is actually nauseating to me. So even though Taylor won't take no for an answer to her idea, she's agreed to my stipulation that we all wear black.

Like a funeral. Cute, right?

The second event is a "ladies' bridal luncheon", which sounds fucking awful. I'd skip it, except, well, *I'm* the bride, so…yeah.

On the plus side, though, Bianca is coming too. She ends up picking me up at Gabriel's and my place in her car, driven by

Dante's head of security, Lorenzo. Then we drive out into the Bronx to Arthur Avenue, home to dozens of super old-school Italian restaurants and bakeries.

The luncheon itself is at this somewhat dated but cute place called Da Pietro's, in their private dining room on the second floor. Bianca's told me no less than three times that the cannoli here are "to die for" and has been coaching me on the way here about what to expect, but I can still feel my nerves jangling as we get out of the car.

"You're not at all Italian, right?"

I shake my head. "Nope."

"Did you ever go to a Feast of the Seven Fishes, or one of the saint's days?"

"Negative."

Bianca chews on her bottom lip. "No big family or anything, either?"

"I don't see how this is supposed to help my nerves."

She makes a face. "Sorry. Just trying to prepare you. These ladies can be..."

She trails off, and I wince as I glance up at the facade of the restaurant. Already, I can see a dozen or so older Italian women gawping at me from the second-floor dining room window and murmuring with each other.

"Cold, nasty bitches?"

"Well," Bianca's mouth twists. "*Yeah*. Some of them, at least. A lot of them are married to seriously powerful heads of families, and some of them basically *are* the heads of families behind the scenes. It's all very Game of Thrones. Some of these women are friends, meanwhile others want to kill each other through their smiles."

"So, play nice, or one of these ladies will have me whacked before dessert?"

Bianca giggles. "It's not *that* bad. Just… Yeah, play nice."

"Hey, I did wear my bestest black jeans."

It's the one piece of my outfit I've kept as "me"—my own little act of defiance for this dumb luncheon. Gabriel already hinted pretty heavily I shouldn't come dressed like I'm going to a punk show.

So, I've paired the black skinny jeans with a silky dark maroon top that comes down to my mid thighs, and a pair of black chunky heels borrowed from Bianca. Which *I* think looks pretty sharp until we walk in, and I'm the only woman in the entire place not wearing a dress.

Great.

But pretty soon, I'm just lost in the blur of new faces. Bianca introduces me to a Mrs. D'Amico, who's first cousins with Vito Barone and who organized this entire thing. She warmly welcomes me with a big smile, embraces me, pats my thin waist, and tells me to order two entrees.

And honestly, the luncheon ends up being not *too* terrible. I end up sitting with Bianca and a few other women who are genuinely nice. The only weird thing is that they insist on gushing over Dante's and I "relationship" and wanting to know the details of our "courtship".

I end up making up a story involving both of us walking around a corner at the same time and spilling coffee and orange juice on each other, which I one hundred percent stole from *Notting Hill*, but whatever. My table full of new lunch friends buy it and think it's the sweetest story ever.

I'm taking a break from lying my ass off to worry down sweet potato gnocchi when Bianca leans close with a low snicker in my ear.

"So, should I call you Julia from now on?"

"Shut *up*. I had to think fast!" I hiss back. "I didn't expect all of these people to seriously think I was *in love* with your brother!"

Bianca snickers. "I mean, they do and they don't. *Most* of these women married for arrangements, so they get it. But there's also this weird element of group denial, and they all want you to play along."

"That's…fucked up."

"Tell me about it—"

"Why don't *you* tell me what exactly happened to my son's face, you sleazy little bitch?"

We whirl at the sharp words. Behind us, backed by a sneering little crowd of women who were giving me the stink eye earlier, is a stern dark-haired woman in an aggressive shade of teal. She glares at us down the bridge of her nose like we're dirt on her carpet.

I went to an all-girls' private school. I also grew up hanging around the Crown and Black offices, watching female interns, paralegals, and junior partners *eat each other alive* for coveted promotions.

I can smell mean girl energy a mile away. This woman *reeks* of it.

I'm about to ask her what the hell her problem is, when I notice the scared look on Bianca's face. Then what this woman just said really clicks. I smile sweetly as I stand to look her dead in the eye.

"Oh, you mean the little creep who doesn't realize no means no?"

The woman sneers at me. "Ahh yes, the blushing bride." She drags her gaze up and down my outfit with a look of utter distain on her face before she turns to glare at Bianca again.

"My Silvio was sweet enough to feed me a white lie about falling through a window after too many drinks."

I roll my eyes. More like Silvio was *pussy enough* to lie about a girl smashing a glass into his face when he was being a creep.

"You'd have been lucky to get Silvio, you little bitch," she spits venomously at Bianca.

The mean girl posse behind her murmurs and mutters, nodding in agreement. I mean Jesus, have any of them even *met* this woman's prolapsed asshole of a son?

"Mrs. Bonpensiero," Bianca mumbles, now looking white-faced and scared. "I—I'm sorry, I just...your son and I..."

"She doesn't want to be with your son because he's a gigantic douchecanoe with all the personality of a hemorrhoid."

Dead silence. Silvio's mother narrows her eyes at me.

"*I beg your pardon?*"

"Here's an idea," I mutter. "How about teaching your son to treat women as human beings instead of objects, and maybe he won't get highball glasses smashed into his face anymore."

Her eyes go wide. "How do you know about—"

"It was *my glass.*"

Silvio's mother stares at me in pure horror as the gaggle of witches behind her gasp and murmur to each other like a Greek chorus.

"I would have *hoped,*" she finally hisses quietly, "that Dante would have ended up with a woman with some class."

I smile. "And *I'd* hoped to eat lunch today without having to deal with a cunt like you."

Mic. Drop. Silvio's mother looks caught somewhere between shocked and livid as she stares at me, mouth agape. Finally, without a word, her mouth closes. Her eyes narrow to lethal slits before she turns on her heel and marches out the door, head held high, her little mean girl crew scurrying after her.

"You know how I said it wasn't that bad when you worried about someone having you whacked before dessert?" Bianca murmurs quietly to me as the rest of the room pretends they weren't totally watching all of that go down.

"Yeah?"

She swallows. "It…may have just gotten that bad."

No one says anything at first when I sit back down. But I get more than a few grins and winks from some of the other ladies at the table. And pretty soon, we've all moved on to discussing whose offspring is betrothed to whose, whose son is in jail or out on parole, and having a *lengthy* gossip about some new Serbian-Russian Bratva bigshot who's recently made New York his home that the ladies I'm eating with breathlessly assure me is God's gift to the female gaze.

"What about you, Angelica?" one of the ladies at the table grins to another. "I think you're due to add to your collection soon, aren't you?"

The table, including Angelica, erupts into laughter. Bianca turns to me and holds up five fingers.

"*On her fifth husband,*" she mouths with an arched brow.

"I'd sooner collect husbands than cats, Teresa."

Teresa clearly gets that it's a joke as she pantomimes looking offended. "Don't you dare talk ill about my kitties."

"How about you, Tempest?" Angelica smiles. "Collect anything?"

I'm shaking my head no when Bianca giggles next to me.

"Dante does. He collects rings," she blurts, and then immediately covers her mouth. "Oh, God," she glances at me. "Please don't ever repeat that. He's super weird and secretive about it. He even keeps them hidden, no idea why."

"Any particular designer?" Teresa asks.

Bianca shakes her head. "I don't think they're *from* a known designer. They're not exactly the same, but they're similar. Big chunky gold things with lion heads engraved on them."

A cold sensation slices into the nape of my neck and drags down over every vertebra in my spine. The rest of the table keeps going on about rings and jewelry, and then moves on to other topics. I'm still gripping the tablecloth by my lap with white knuckles as the past jumps out of the darkness at me with a snarl.

The man who pinned me down, the gold band of his ring digging into my flesh. The men who did the same to Nina right next to me, knuckles glinting with the jeweled-eyed glare of golden lions.

"Tempest?"

I blink back to reality as I slowly turn to stare at Bianca. She frowns with worry.

"Are…are you okay?"

"Sure," I mumble, swallowing the bitter lump in my throat. "Yes," I force out with slightly more conviction.

She smiles. "The cannoli are here." Her chins nods, and I look down in front of me, realizing the dessert has been brought out.

Dante collects rings.

Specifically, Dante collects the rings I see in my nightmares. And I'm not sure if that makes me more curious, or more completely fucking terrified.

When the whole thing is over, I walk over to Mrs. D'Amico and apologize for my language and for disturbing the peace earlier. She just smiles and shakes her head.

"First, just call me Maria, hon. Second, it's no trouble at all. I've met Silvio a number of times…" She winks. "'Hemorrhoid' is a compliment compared to what I'd call him."

Then she insists I take the box of to-go food she's taken the liberty of ordering for me, because "if I'm too thin, I'll snap when I walk down the aisle".

I'm outside with Bianca and she's calling Lorenzo for a pickup when I suddenly think of something.

"Hey—what are you doing tonight?"

She shrugs. "I've got rehearsal in an hour until six, but nothing after that."

I'm not exactly great with friends. I mean you don't need to be a therapist to get that I purposefully don't encourage interpersonal relationships after what happened to Nina, probably as some sort of self-defense mechanism. Now, knowing that my timeline is shorter than anyone would imagine, it feels even more of a waste of time to attempt to make friends, because what's the point?

But I don't know. I *like* Bianca. She reminds me of Nina, or maybe of myself, when I was younger.

"You, uh, wanna come to my bachelorette party?"

Bianca's brows shoot up. Her lips curl into a grin. "Whoa, seriously?"

"Yeah, I mean, don't feel like you have to," I shrug, my mouth twisting. "It's not a fancy thing, just some girlfriends taking me out—"

"I would *love* to!"

I smile. "Yeah?"

"Definitely!"

"I mean..." I snort. "When I say *girlfriends*, I mean my brothers' business partner and two of her employees." I give Bianca a weak smile. "I'm not great with friends..."

"I would *love* to come," she beams at me.

A happy spark—the kind that's been pretty damn quiet since my diagnosis—flickers inside of me as I grin back at her.

Maybe I could use some more friends.

Even if they're only temporary.

11

DANTE

She's insane.

She's certifiably *insane*.

It's not like I've ever once thought of Tempest in the brief time I've known her as rational, cautious or anywhere *near* someone who, oh, I don't know, thinks literally anything through, *ever*. I mean she's fucking chaos personified, despite being so tiny.

But this is too much.

Club music pounds through my chest, the dazzling blue and pink lights of the place flickering in time to the beat as I prowl through the crowd. I know they're here because Lorenzo rarely *doesn't* know where my sister is, and Bianca was a last-minute invitee to Tempest's bachelorette party.

I ignore two club girls who throw themselves at me, grinning with drug-fueled energy and powdery noses. Pushing past them with a low growl and my jaw set, I shove my way through more sweaty dancers until I get to the staircase that leads up to the VIP booths and rooms that ring the perimeter of the top floor.

It's no Club Venom, but Doomsday, the Cold War-themed clubI'm barging my way through does have pretty tight security, being that it's a popular celebrity hangout.

That said, the two bouncers at the bottom of the stairs nod when they see me and instantly step aside.

So sue me: I know the owner and called ahead.

Upstairs, I immediately catch sight of the group I'm after, dancing around in a glass room overlooking the DJ booth: Tempest, Bianca, Fumi Yamaguchi, who's one of Crown and Black's top lawyers, and Elsa Guin, another of their top attorneys, who happens to be married to Hades Drakos, of the Drakos Greek mafia family.

They're all in head-to-toe black.

Like a fucking funeral.

How cute.

Trust Tempest to throw up a middling finger at every conceivable opportunity. And there's the blushing bride herself, dancing to the music thudding through the club, her bare arms up in the air and the skin-tight black dress clinging to every single...

Fuck.

I don't realize I've stopped walking and that I'm just standing there outside the room staring at Tempest until it's been... longer than it should have been. My eyes wander over her gyrating hips, the swell of her breasts in the tight dress. The way her dark hair tumbles down her back, and the way her ass…

Yeah, this has to stop *now*.

I'm marrying her to save my empire, to keep my club, and because that little fucking hurricane in there *tricked me into it*.

Not because I want to watch her gyrate exactly like this while my cock is buried to the hilt in her tight little cunt.

"Dante."

I flinch, thoughts of Tempest scattering as I turn, locking eyes with Taylor Crown.

Contrary to what I let Tempest wonder about, no, I've never once slept with my attorney. Nor have I ever wanted to. Not because powerful, intelligent women scare me.

Because you don't *fuck* your goddamn attorney.

She's also simply not my type, and plus, we've got a good relationship professionally…and as friends of a sort, I suppose.

"What the fuck were you thinking getting into this with that girl?"

I arch a brow. I *also* like Taylor because she's completely fine throwing my shit in my face. And that's not something I get much of.

"Don't pretend for a second that Alistair and Gabriel haven't filled you in on every single detail," I mutter. "You know damn well how it happened."

Taylor eyes me, shaking her head as she shoves her fingers through her long red hair. "I know, but honestly, Dante. She's twenty-four."

"Yes. And for the last time, *counselor*," I hiss, "if you've got a magic cheat code for breaking fucking blood markers, I am all ears."

She frowns, glancing past me. I turn, my jaw clenching as I watch Tempest dance, her eyes closed and her hips swaying.

"If you mistreat her—"

"Taylor—"

"*If you mistreat her,*" she repeats, "you won't have to worry about Alistair or Gabriel coming after you. Because *I* will first. That girl is like a little sister to me, Dante. That supersedes any professional relationship you and I have."

"Yeah, well to me she's a fucking *pest*. I won't be laying a finger on her."

Taylor's eyes narrow. "See that you don't. Also, why are you even here, anyway?"

I roll my eyes. "Miss Hurricane and I need to—"

"What the fuck are you doing here?"

I turn, immediately locking eyes with a particularly sassy-looking Tempest. Her cheeks are flushed, too, and not just from dancing. I glance past her to where the girls are dancing, spotting the bottle of vodka on ice with numerous glasses around it.

Interesting, considering I know for a fact that Tempest doesn't drink much at all.

"You and I need to talk."

"No," she shrugs, smirking. "I don't think we do."

The sassy little attitude drops as I surge right into her, looming over her as she presses her back against the glass wall behind her.

"*Dante...*" Taylor warns behind me. But I ignore her as I lean down, putting my lips right by Tempest's ear.

"You and I need to talk," I growl quietly. "Alone, right now. You can come willingly, or I can hoist you over my fucking shoulder right here in front of all of your little friends and make it happen myself."

When I pull back, the pink is flooding her cheeks even more.

"You wouldn't dare."

My lips curl. "I would ask yourself exactly how well you know me before you choose to start calling my bluffs, little hurricane."

Her lips purse. "It's *Tempest*," she mutters. "Stop calling me hurricane or cyclone or whatever, it's bullshit." She fidgets in front of me another five seconds, but then clears her throat. "*Fine.* What do you want to talk about?"

"This way."

I grab her hand, ignoring Taylor's wrathful glare as I pull Tempest after me. Another bouncer nods as I approach, opening the door to a *non*-glass VIP room. The second we're inside, I whirl and slam Tempest against the door behind her. She gasps.

"*Fuck you*, you—"

"*Stop*," I snarl, silencing her with a dark look and a firm grip on her upper arms, pinning her to the door.

I refuse to acknowledge the sultry mood of the room. The low lighting and deep sofas behind me. The way the club music thuds like a pulse in the air.

Or the glint in Tempest's eyes.

The way her tongue slips out to deftly wet her lips.

Get your shit together.

"Do you have a death wish?"

She frowns. "What?"

"You do understand the world you've chosen to insert yourself into is the fucking *mafia*, right?!" I hiss. "Not the sanitized Hollywood version, not the musical *Chicago*. The real, actual, *dangerous* fucking mafia."

"Thanks, I'm not nine, dickhead," she spits back.

"Good to know," I smile coldly. "Then maybe there's another perfectly good explanation why you would call Renata fucking Bonpensiero a *cunt* to her fucking face?!"

Tempest raises a single brow. "Uh, because she *is* one."

Jesus fucking Christ.

"She's also Frank Bonpensiero's wife!"

"And?"

"Oh, *and* the small little detail that she's also Luciano Amato's niece!"

"Great," Tempest groans in a bored tone. "So make me a family tree or a flow chart thing so I can ignore it and tell you I studied—"

"You need to know these things," I hiss.

"I don't think that's part of the—"

"If you shit on this, Tempest..." I shake my head. My fingers tighten on her arms, feeling the thud of her pulse beneath her soft, warm skin. I inhale the scent of her—jasmine and citrus, mixed with something floral and slightly spicy.

I close my eyes, taking a deep breath to try to calm my roaring pulse. But all I get is more of her scent—more of the heat of her body, so close to mine.

"If you shit on this," I growl quietly, "then this whole thing falls apart."

"I'm not *shitting* on anything," she snaps back.

"The fuck you're not!"

It comes out much more forcefully than I intended. Tempest's eyes go wide, her mouth falling open as a little gasp tumbles from her lips.

That gasp has no business being so fucking sexy.

Focus.

"If this falls apart, there are forces at play that could destroy us both," I continue. "And I don't mean ruining our credit scores, in case that needs to be made clear. As I said before..." My eyes lock with hers. "You made this bed, and now you're going to fucking lie in it."

Tempest doesn't say anything.

"Take this fucking seriously. I know that's a foreign concept to you."

I ignore the "asshole" that falls from her mouth as I push her aside and storm out of the VIP room.

Not because I'm angry.

Because if I stay in there another fucking second with her, neither of us will be leaving until I have taken her in every single way a man can take a woman.

12

DANTE

It's two in the morning when I get the alert on my phone.

Since I left Tempest the temptation in that VIP room at Doomsday, I've holed up in my office at Venom.

Contrary to popular assumptions, my work *does not* involve hunching over an array of screens jerking off while I watch people fuck on camera.

Although yes, my job certainly *does* entail walking around the club, shaking hands or having a drink with various people. And while I'm doing that, there could be twenty or forty people fucking literally five feet away—all masked, all wearing bracelets indicating their preferred kinks and roles.

But I don't join in. I've *never* joined in.

Like I said, I don't shit where I eat.

When the alert on my phone goes off, I've just stepped back into my office after having a quick drink out on the floor with Konstantin Reznikov and his wife, Mara. Konstantin runs the immensely powerful Reznikov Bratva together with his brother, and recently moved back to New York after the birth of his twin daughters about a year ago.

Knowing Konstantin's *notorious* overprotectiveness and jealousy concerning Mara, I was a little surprised when he reached out about them both becoming members. But they come to have a drink now and then, and yes, maybe watch whatever "group show" is being put on in the main rooms while they're here. But it's watching only.

Fine by me. Besides, Konstantin is a powerful ally to have.

I glare at my phone, lifting it from my desk. I mostly commute to my Hamptons house after work. But I do keep a penthouse here in the city that I occasionally stay in if it's been an exceptionally late night. And right now, my phone's just told me that someone's just *entered* said penthouse.

They've inputted the correct security code, but it took them three fucking tries, which seems...off. I scowl as I open the app to check the security cameras, hoping it's just Bianca. She occasionally crashes at my penthouse if she's had a long rehearsal that gets out late, instead of trekking all the way uptown to her place.

I flip to the cameras and start thumbing through them. Instantly, the hairs on the back of my neck go up.

Fuck.

It's Bianca all right, sprawled on one of the couches in my living room, utterly motionless. And when I switch to a different camera angle, a figure in all black darts across the screen and then disappears.

Motherfucker.

IT'S a strange line that I straddle. On the one hand, I mingle with the darkness: the mafiosos, the bratva kingpins, Italian and Greek mafia, and Japanese Yakuza. They all come to Club Venom.

But darkness, depravity, and deviance aren't just for those who operate outside the law. Venom also has its fair share of those very much inside the law, or at least those who know how to bend it. Politicians, lawyers, captains of industry. It's one of the reasons Venom is an anonymous club, where all members wear masks *everywhere*.

So I exist somewhere between light and dark. I'm not a mafia thug, but I'm not exactly a good man, either. It's because of that gray area I live in that I can't just barge into my penthouse guns blazing.

I mean, I have neighbors to consider.

So I slip in through an emergency door in the pantry of my kitchen that unlocks with my thumbprint. I make sure the silencer on my gun is fitted tight as I creep through the darkness. In the living room, I clear the corners before bolting silently to where Bianca is still slumped motionless on the couch.

If she's hurt, this is where my restraint will end, and an entire city block will know the wrath I dole out on whoever is still in my penthouse.

But even before I touch her neck to find a pulse, my jaw clenches.

Goddammit.

She's not hurt or knocked out.

She's *wasted*.

I can smell the booze on her a foot away, and when my eyes adjust to the darkness of the living room, it's clear she's sleeping off one hell of a night, not an attack.

So who the *fuck* else is here?

The sound of shuffling rips my attention from my sister to the doorway. The gun raises in my hand as I walk silently, following the rustling sound upstairs, and then down the hallway to the office. The door is ajar, the desk light is on, and I use the silencer to gently and quietly push the door open a little wider.

A figure in black, a hood up, is hunched over my desk, rummaging through the drawers.

Not today, motherfucker.

I could shoot them right now and end this. But fuck that. I want to know who dragged my sister back here half-unconscious, and possibly used her to unlock the front door. And I *really* want to know what the fuck they're looking for.

I move like a wraith, crossing the distance between me and the intruder in seconds. Then I slam into him, pinning him to the desk with a snarl on my lips, my hand wrapped around his fucking throat, and my gun pressed to his temple.

"Who the *fuck*—"

"Get your hands off of me!"

I freeze.

Tempest.

I instantly draw the gun away, thumbing on the safety and jamming it into the waist of my pants at the back. I violently twist her around and keep her pinned to the desk as I grab a handful of the front of her hoodie and leer down into her glaring eyes.

"My, my, my," I growl quietly. "What the *fuck* do we have here?"

"Take. Your. Hands—"

"As soon as you tell me what the fuck you're doing in here."

My eyes slide past her to the mess of papers on my desk and the open drawers.

She was snooping. Looking for something.

Spying.

It's not the first time the thought has crossed my mind. And in this moment, with her caught red-handed, the idea is suddenly rammed into the front of my brain again.

…The idea that Tempest Black inking her name on that blood maker was *not* simply because she's an impetuous agent of chaos, but because somebody *wants her* to be ushered into my inner circle, so she has access to things she might not otherwise have.

Somebody like her grandfather.

"What were you looking for?" I growl.

Tempest raises her chin defiantly, her eyes locking with mine.

"Nothing."

"Bullshit."

"A stamp. I need to mail a letter."

My lips pull to a hooked, barbed smile. "We're going to play it like that, are we?"

It suddenly hits me that Tempest is still probably wearing her club dress and heels under the oversized black hoodie.

"Play it like—"

"Take off your sweatshirt."

Her cheeks flush.

"*Excuse me?* Dante, I'm here because Bianca *brought me* here. Jesus. She had a bit too much—"

"More than a *bit*," I snap. "She's shitfaced. She doesn't get like that."

Tempest glares at me. "So, now I'm a bad influence?"

"Your words."

She rolls her eyes. "I barely drink myself. And we only came here because she said it was closer than her place and I didn't want her to go home alone."

"I see," I smile thinly. "And at which point in this noble endeavor did you decide to paw through my office?"

I can see the wheels turning in her head. She shrugs casually, but I know people. I can read them like books. This girl is hiding something.

"I already told you, I was looking for a—"

"Yes, a stamp. For all those letters that desperately need to be mailed at two-thirty in the fucking morning."

Tempest sucks on her teeth.

"I didn't find any," she mutters quietly, squirming a little in my iron grasp.

"Then prove it. Empty your pockets."

She blinks quickly. "The fuck, dude—"

"Empty. Your. Pockets."

She does, turning out the pockets in her hoodie to show that they're empty.

"Take off your fucking hoodie."

"*What?*"

"Take off your hoodie, or I'll do it for you."

The room goes silent.

"Fine," she hisses. She unzips the hoodie, her eyes avoiding mine as she opens it and spreads it wide. "See? No stamp —hey!"

She gasps when I grab the hoodie out of her hands and shove it wide open and then down over her arms.

My blood thuds in my ears and scorches under my skin like napalm. My eyes drag over her skin-tight black club dress— strapless, short, and...*tempting*.

Too tempting. Too provocative.

Too alluring.

"*See?*" She mutters. "No stamp—"

"What were you really looking for."

Her eyes snap to mine. I can see those wheels turning again, looking for an out. An excuse. A *lie*.

"Don't even try, little hurricane," I growl quietly, shaking my head as I grab her wrists and pin them to the edge of the desk behind her. Tempest's breath catches as our bodies press tight.

"Don't lie, because I will see right through it."

"I wasn't—"

"You're doing it *right now*."

Her face flushes, her eyes flickering with a fire behind them. "Let go of me."

"Was it Charles?" I growl. "Is that who you're doing this for?"

Her brows knit. "What? Fuck, no!"

"Then who?"

"*No one!*" She hurls back at me. "Dante, I didn't take anything, okay!?"

"Let's find out."

I don't think, though I probably should. I don't slow down, though I definitely should. And I don't stop myself, though it'll be my fucking ruin. I just spin her, pin her to the desk with the weight of my body, and grab the zipper in the middle of her shoulderblades with two fingers.

"*Dante—!*"

The way she chokes out my name, it's not fear. It's not shock, or horror. And it's *not* a warning.

It's an invitation.

A fucking *dare*.

I can feel her body shiver as I tug the zipper down, letting the dress peel away from her soft skin. I move unhurriedly; slowly, patiently.

Methodically.

I let the zipper bump over each individual tooth, letting inch after inch of her pale, soft skin come under my gaze in the dim light. I watch the goosebumps flutter over her back. I hear the way her breath catches, feel the way her body shivers.

…The way her ass subtly presses into me and tenses when she feels how fucking hard I am.

When I bring the zipper to the small of her back, the front of the strapless dress falls away. My eyes raise to the reflection of the room in the window, my gaze locking on her sweet, soft tits.

This isn't about fucking thievery anymore. It's not about whatever the fuck I'm still vainly trying to tell myself I'm looking for—what, *documents*? As if she's a spy out of *Mission Impossible*?

The dress unzips all the way and drops to the floor, much like the lies I've still been trying to tell myself. Suddenly, I'm not hunting for stolen documents on a would-be thief or looking for her lies.

I'm just a man with his hands on a woman he wants.

And the woman is *stunning*.

It's clear that Tempest doesn't eat enough. Her ribs are far too visible, her arms much too thin. But neither of those things does *shit* to diminish her beauty and allure. Even having seen her in something other than her usual punk-rock princess attire, like the flirty club dress, or the gown she wore to the party the other night...none of it has prepared me for seeing Tempest like this.

...Bare to me except for a tiny little black thong tight between the taut globes of her ass.

Waifish and breakable, and yet so fucking womanly it takes everything I have not to groan. There's something disturbingly sexy about the way she shivers as her breath catches in her throat. The way her light pink, almost ghostly pale nipples harden to points in her reflection before me.

The way she whimpers when I grab a fistful of her hair.

"*Show me where it is, little hurricane,*" I rasp into her ear as my control begins to shatter like broken glass. "Show me where you've hidden it."

"*I...I haven't...*"

She's shaking. But it's not fear doing that.

It's *me*.

I can tell by the way her body subtly pushes back into me. The way her back arches, and her ass moves against the bulge in my pants.

Her arms are taut as steel bands, her nails digging into the edge of the desk. I slide my hands up them, relishing the shiver that ripples through her body.

"Is it *here*?"

She whimpers again as I brush her hair aside and trace the backs of my knuckles over the soft skin of her neck.

"*No...*" she whispers in a throaty, aching tone.

She shudders when my hand circles her neck, my fingers wrapping gently but firmly around her throat and jaw as I twist her head toward me. Her eyes are hooded, almost closed. Then slowly, they open to stab right into mine with greenish-hazel fire.

My other hand slides to her hip, making her mewl softly as her teeth quickly bite down on her bottom lip. My hand slips higher, tracing over her ribs and then over her sternum, a single finger teasing up between her breasts.

"How about *here*…" I murmur darkly.

Tempest shivers, shaking her head. *"No..."*

"I'll find it, little hurricane," I growl quietly.

"I didn't—"

"I'll find *every* little thing you've ever hidden. Every stolen thought. Every buried secret."

Tempest whimpers so deeply it's almost a moan. Her body shudders against mine, her chest rising and falling as my finger teases just underneath her breasts.

Then my hand slips lower.

And lower.

And *lower*, teasing over the soft skin of her stomach as it caves under my touch.

"Where is it, Tempest," I murmur.

Her eyes bulge wide, her jaw dropping and falling open as my fingertips brush the lacy edge of her panties. I swear to fuck, I can feel the heat of her pussy even from here. Feel the way her body clenches and tenses, and the way her skin hums beneath my touch.

"If you don't want to tell me," I murmur, my mouth inches from her lips, "then I suppose I'll be forced to fucking *find it myself.*"

Tempest *moans*, loud, when my hand crosses the final barrier between us and slips into her lacy panties. My fingers delve deep between her legs, and I growl when I feel exactly how fucking *soaked* she is.

Silky-soft petal lips open at my touch. Slickness coats my fingers as I drag them up through her seam and roll one over her throbbing clit.

"Where have you hidden it, little thief," I murmur an inch from her quivering mouth. "Maybe it's in *here…*"

I sink two fingers into her in one thrust, gritting my teeth and feeling my dick throb at the insane tightness of her. Her silky walls and sticky heat envelop me and suck my fingers deeper, greedily. Her eyes fly open as the moan she's fucking powerless to stop comes pouring out of her mouth.

My fingers curl deep, stroking in and out against her g-spot as my palm grinds against her needy clit. I push against her, pinning her to the desk, caught between my hand and my throbbing cock against her ass.

"I'll find it, Tempest," I growl, my fingers stroking in and out over and over. Her legs begin to tremble, and when her mouth falls open in a wail of pleasure, I start to finger her even harder and faster.

"…And if I don't, I'll take your fucking *cum* all over my fingers as collateral until I do."

Her legs buckle and her eyes roll back in her head as she clings to the desk with white knuckles, her nails digging into the wood. Her stomach clenches and ripples, her cunt greedily clamping tighter around my fingers as I fuck her with them.

"*Oh my fucking God...*"

"You can call me whatever you want, little hurricane," I rasp right at her lips. "But you *will* fucking come all over my hand right the fuck now."

Her body goes rigid, her legs clamping tight together as a moan of pure release explodes from her mouth.

...Right as I slam mine to hers and swallow every decibel of it.

There's no walking back from this edge now.

13

TEMPEST

WHAT EXACTLY ARE you supposed to feel on your wedding day? I have zero idea.

I was never one of those girls that thought about that—dreaming of Ken or Prince Charming, and poofy white princess weddings, even when I was little. Maybe it started with losing our parents. Maybe it got worse when Layla died.

Or maybe I was just born without that gene that yearns for a fairytale.

As of a few months ago, I *definitely* stopped believing in fairytales. That included dreaming about a wedding day I knew was never going to come.

And yet, here I am, and it's the whole fucking shebang.

The ridiculously huge white dress. The church. The guests. The white flowers fucking *everywhere*.

It's all so real.

Except it isn't.

What *is* real, though, is the dark, murky, throbbing mess of thoughts swirling through my head. And at the very epicenter is the skin-tingling memory of what happened two nights ago at Dante's penthouse.

I shiver in spite of myself, my face turning pink in the dressing room vanity mirror in front of me.

The idea really *did* start as getting Bianca home. She wasn't the only one who'd had too much. Even the three glasses of champagne I had were way more than my usual intake. Taylor and Fumi were definitely feeling the vodka, and Elsa was *comically* drunk, to the point that her husband Hades had to come get her as we were all leaving the club and throw her, giggling, over his broad shoulder before carrying her to quite possibly the world's coolest vintage muscle car.

But since I was the least drunk of the whole crew, I got in a taxi with Bianca. That's when she mentioned in between hiccups that Dante kept a penthouse in the city, which was half the distance compared to her apartment on the Upper West Side. So after fumbling her way through the key code… finally…that's where we ended up.

The plan initially was to put her to bed and leave. But then she crashed hard on the couch while I was peeing. And after that, the little worm of an idea buried deep in my head came to life as I flashed back to what she'd told me at the ladies' luncheon.

Dante collects rings.

Part of me was terrified to even go looking, for fear of what I might find. Which ended up being nothing, because there were no rings in his office—at least, none that I found.

But I did find something else.

Heat. Pleasure. Excitement.

Intimacy, when I was sure that part of me was long dead and buried.

I haven't let anyone come *close* to touching me like that since that awful night. There's even been times where I had to stop things when it was just me and my own fingers, because the resulting sensation brought back terror. When Dante first grabbed me, it was pure fear that exploded through my system.

And then it melted away, leaving only fire and need.

Want and desire.

A hunger I thought I'd lost.

When he touched me, I didn't go cold. I didn't retreat in on myself.

I came alive. I craved more; ached for it. He could have told me to do anything in that moment—*anything*—and I'd have done it, willingly.

…Thank God it was just making me explode all over his fingers.

Everything after that thunderous orgasm is a blur. I vaguely remember realizing I was kissing him. I remember tasting his lips and wanting more and more before he pulled away. Then I have hazy, embarrassing memories of putting my dress back on and blushing fiercely as he licked his fingers clean.

The next thing I knew, I was in a cab heading home, the window down and my head hung halfway out of it, positively *inhaling* the night around me.

I felt like I was finally living again that night. And I'm not sure what to make of that, or how it fits into my plan for the short remainder of my life.

I stand, smoothing down the supremely overdone white wedding gown. The sound of people pulls me to the window of Dante's Hamptons estate, where the wedding is being held today. It's not a huge crowd gathering in the rows of white chairs outside in the gardens, but it's not small, either. I spot my brothers. Maeve isn't here, for obvious reasons, and although I think he was invited, Charles isn't coming either.

I spot Taylor, Fumi, Elsa and Hades, and Elsa's little sister Nora. Bianca is sitting with an older man I recognize as Vito Barone, who I've now heard via my brothers sort of raised Dante and his sisters.

Guess I'm not the only one who lost their parents young.

The string quartet outside continues to play as more guests take their seats. And suddenly, this whole thing becomes very, very real.

Holy-fuck-I'm-getting-MARRIED-today.

It might not be real, but it is happening. And it might have an expiration date, but it's not tomorrow. Suddenly, the realization that for the foreseeable future, I will be *MRS.* Dante Sartorre, and that I will be living with him, hits me like a brick to the face.

I stagger back from the window, my throat closing as I claw at the bodice of my gown.

I need to breathe.

I yank the door open and go tumbling into the hallway. One of Dante's men is right outside, and he frowns as he jumps to his feet.

"Ms. Black—"

"I need some air."

I shove past him, ignoring him blurting something about the ceremony starting soon. I plow down one giant, gilded hallway of Dante's massive estate after another. I almost trip on my train and my heels when I go rushing down a curved staircase, when suddenly, a wall of a man steps quietly in front of me.

Lorenzo, Dante's head of security.

He frowns deeply. "Ms. Black, is everything—"

"I just...I...I need—" My head starts to spin, my breath becoming ragged as my eyes dart around. "I just...I need to—"

"Come with me," he says gently. He doesn't touch me at all, just sort of gestures, and herds me down a side hallway and through a door into a large, room full of bookcases with a vaulted ceiling and big, airy windows.

Okay, it's not outside, but it's pretty close. It's so airy and bright in here that it feels like the noose around my neck is loosening.

I turn to smile weakly at Lorenzo. *"Thank you,"* I murmur quietly.

He nods with a small, understanding smile. "Not a problem, ma'am. The ceremony will be starting soon, but I'll let Mr. Sartorre know that you need a minute."

After he exits and closes the door behind him, I look around. Then it hits me: I'm in Dante's office. My eyes slide across the very masculine and tastefully decorated room—a mix of old money wealth, midcentury rat-pack style complete with framed pictures of Sammy Davis Junior and Frank Sinatra on the walls, and modern chic.

I mean, the man has killer taste, that's for sure.

I prowl the perimeter of the room, tracing my fingers over the pristine shelves of leather books and trinkets. Suddenly, I stop cold when my eyes land on something sitting on the shelf.

A small, sad smile creeps over my lips as I take in the pack of American Spirit cigarettes.

"I knew you'd come."

I'm not religious, and not very spiritual, either. But sometimes, I like to think I see signs from Nina. A bluebird—her favorite—outside my window on my birthday. Her favorite song, Velvet Guillotine's *Exorcise My Love*, playing on the radio when I'm having a bad day.

Or this: the pack of American Spirits—light blues, of course —on my wedding day.

Nina wasn't even really a smoker. But sometimes when we were together she'd have one, probably just because she thought she looked cool. And I mean, *she did*. And sometimes, I'd take a puff or two, probably also to look cool, even though I'm sure I didn't.

I grin as I pick the pack up off Dante's shelf, curious about why this is even here. He doesn't smoke, does he? It's open, and I take one out and bring it to my nose.

Holy shit, even though these are a little stale, sometimes I *love* the smell of tobacco. I bite my lip, thinking it over for a second before I shrug.

Fuck it.

I slip the cigarette between my lips with a giggle. "This is for you, Nina."

Then I frown. Crap, I don't have anything to light this dumb thing with. I glance around the shelves, but there's nothing. The bar cart is the same, not even matches.

I am *not* asking Lorenzo for a light. Frowning, I head over to Dante's desk and start pawing around. The top of it, like his desk in the city, is *immaculately* neat and tidy. It's also devoid of a lighter. So I start poking around in the drawers.

File folders. Legal documents. An ancient, dead iPhone. Suddenly, I pause as I push aside a stack of papers and see a wooden box. It looks like the kind of thing you'd keep cigars in, and cigars mean a lighter, or at least matches. I haul it out and lay it on the desk.

Grinning with anticipation, I flip the lid open.

…And my whole universe stills.

Oh God.

My skin turns to ice as my heart crawls in on itself and the bile rises in my throat. There, on individual holders in neat little rows, is the collection Bianca mentioned at lunch.

Rings.

Five of them. Little golden rings with carved lions' faces in them, set with blueish-white diamonds for eyes. And right there in the middle of the row is the worst of them: the ring I watched from barely two feet away as the hand wearing it tightened around Nina's neck. As it squeezed and squeezed as she tried to get him off her.

My whole body goes cold as I lift it from the case and stare at it, transfixed. This one is slightly different from the others from that night. Maybe that's why I remember it the sharpest. Instead of two blueish-white diamond eyes, one eye of this ring is a blood red ruby, as if its owner lost one of the eyes and decided to replace it with something sinister.

Part of me wants to scream until my throat bleeds. Part of me wants to hit something until I feel nothing at all.

But then, the biggest part of me turns to stone.

Dante rubs shoulders with dangerous men daily, and has the criminal underworld at his fingertips. His entire circle is men who are used to getting what they want regardless of who says no. Or who screams at them to stop.

I've been an idiot. I was hoping for access when I inserted myself into Dante's world, but now that I'm in…

…I might be in a hell of a lot deeper than I ever wanted to be.

A knock on the door has me leaping out of my skin and dropping the ring onto the closed lid of the box.

"Ms. Black?" Lorenzo calls through the door. "It's time."

My heart hammers against my chest as I back away from the box.

"Ms. Black?"

"One second!"

Holy shit.

Dante is connected to the men who hurt me and killed my best friend. Fucking hell, he may even be the *leader* of those men, given how many of these fucking rings he's got in this box. And now, I'm about to *marry* the motherfucker? I'm about to spend what little time I have left *chained* to one of the monsters who destroyed me?

I'm going to be sick.

"Ms. Black, I'm sorry, but—"

"Be right there."

My voice is cold and sharp, my eyes laser focused on something sitting on Dante's desk: a display case with a wooden base and a crystal clear, domed glass lid.

...And an ancient-looking metal dagger carved with runic letters sitting on a stand under that lid, labeled "Norse, 1107 AD" on a small brass plaque beneath it.

The door to the office starts to creak open. And by the time Lorenzo steps inside, the glass case is empty, and there's something cold and metallic hidden in the folds of my wedding dress.

Lorenzo smiles a small smile at me. "Time to go, Ms. Black."

All I can do is nod, numb, as I follow him out.

Alistair and Gabriel floated walking me down the aisle in lieu of our father. But I opted for a solo walk. My heart thuds with every step as I move down the aisle on autopilot. I don't even see the faces of friends and families. All I can do is stare straight ahead, my eyes locked ono the man waiting for me.

The devil who I've just realized is even more a demon than I ever imagined.

But there's an out here. There's one play I, and I alone, can make.

Because I have nothing to lose.

I'm numb as I stand facing Dante, listening to the priest drone on. The man in front of me with the lethal blue eyes and the sharp jaw frowns slightly at my silence. The priest has him recite his vows. Somehow I manage to recite my own, in a fog, the fingers of my right hand curling around the hilt of the dagger in my gown.

"And now, by the power vested in me by God and the State of New York, I now pronounce you husband and wife."

There are polite golf claps as the crowd rises from their chairs.

Time to play the last card I have.

For what was taken from me.

For what was done to me.

For *Nina*.

"You may kiss the bride!"

We never discussed this part. If we had, I'd have laughed in his face and told him it wasn't going to happen. Maybe I'd have changed my mind after the other night. Maybe I *did*, in a dark, secret part of me.

But that was before I found that box just now.

Before I learned the truth.

I jolt when his one hand lands on my waist, and the other cups my face. His piercing blue eyes stab into me, flickering with venomous fire as I feel the etched cool hilt of the dagger solid and comforting in my palm.

Dante leans in as the cameras flash and the crowd applauds.

…And my arm stabs forward.

But just as it does, the hand on my waist grabs my wrist with frightening speed, yanking and wrenching it aside. I hear him grunt as the blade slips past his hip, but he's not groaning in pain. He's not falling to his knees with his life bleeding out of him.

He's still kissing me.

"*Smile for the fucking cameras,*" he hisses against my lips, nipping at the bottom one so hard that I yelp when the taste of copper explodes in my mouth. "*Dear.*"

14

DANTE

SOME OF THE women present blush and giggle amongst themselves when I grab my new bride and yank her off the garden stage toward the house. Alistair and Gabriel Black shoot me venomous stares.

Carmy gives me a thumbs up, and Vito...of course...grins and makes a crude gesture with two pointed fingers of one hand, and looped fingers of his other.

But I'm not dragging Tempest away to consummate a goddamn thing. In fact, if she doesn't have some *very* illuminating things to say right now, I might fucking *bury* her.

She was in a daze as I yanked her through the gardens, away from the wedding. But the second we tumble in through one of the side garden doors to my house, she comes alive again.

Alive, animated, and *very* angry.

"GET YOUR HANDS OFF OF ME!"

It's not just anger in her voice, or malice in her eyes, though. There's pain there, and horror. Fear, and disbelief.

Christ, it's like she's just walked in on her *actual* husband balls-deep in her sister or something.

I drag her into the study, slamming and locking the door shut behind us before I let her go. Tempest flings herself from me like she might catch on fire, backing away with hatred and horror in her eyes.

"Stay the fuck away from me!!"

"What the *fuck*!!" I roar back. I yank the blade out of my jacket pocket where I've hidden it, catching sight of a splash of red slowly staining my dress shirt. Wow, she *did* actually cut me a little.

At least she didn't jam this fucking thing through my heart, like she was trying to do.

I glare at the blade, just now realizing I'm looking at the twelfth-century Viking blade given to me by the Prince of Denmark.

What? He's a voracious member of Venom.

"Well?!" I bark, wincing as I open my jacket and shirt to glance briefly at my cut. It's superficial, but it still hurts like a motherfucker. I angrily move toward her. Tempest flinches, but then she's the one lurching at me with fists flying.

"Enough!" I hiss, catching her wrists and yanking her tight to my chest. Her knee jabs up as if to catch me in the balls. But I knock it aside easily with my own thigh. In one move, I'm throwing her over my shoulder, dodging her hammering fists and feet, and tossing her down on the couch.

"*STOP IT*," I roar, momentarily making her go still. "What the actual *fuck* was all of that about?!"

"You son of a bitch!"

I wince again as I glance down at my side. Then I raise the blade and shake it. "Next time you try and fucking stab me," I snarl, "use something from this goddamn century!" I whirl toward my desk to put the dagger back in its case when suddenly I freeze.

My gaze lands on the little wooden box, closed and lying on my desk.

My trophies.

And right on top of it lies *his* fucking ring: the one with blue and red eyes.

I hear Tempest bolt toward me. I turn, catch her mid-swing, and yank her hard against my chest. My hands pin hers tight behind her back, rendering her helpless in my grasp as I glare down into her furious face.

"I'm only going to ask you this once," I hiss coldly, my pulse thudding.

I think I know. This is about the rings. She saw them, she knows what they are. And then she tried to fucking kill me.

I am suddenly not at all worried that Tempest is a plant from Charles to try and steal something from me. I'm worried that she's with *them*.

The ones who took Claudia from me.

The ones I *hunt*.

"Once, Tempest, and only once," I rasp. "What do these rings mean to you."

Fire smolders behind her eyes as she remains tight-lipped.

"I would start answering if I were you," I hiss through clenched teeth.

"Or what?!" she chokes. "You'll kill me too?! Like you killed Nina?!"

What?

"I have no fucking idea who the hell that—"

"You bastard!"

She almost gets her hands free, but I tighten my grip and whirl, pinning her back against a bookcase.

"The owners of those rings," I snarl, leering close to her. "Specifically, the owner of the one you left on top—blue and red eyes."

I lower my face even closer to hers.

"Who. Is. He. To. You."

Tears bead in her eyes. *"Fuck you—"*

"Because I *killed* the man who wore that fucking ring."

Tempest freezes. I smile coldly.

"Does that pain you to hear?" I leer closer. "Trust me, he didn't die well, either. It was slow, and painful, and—"

"Is that the God's honest truth?"

Her voice is papery and thin, her pulse thudding in the soft hollow of her neck.

"Yes," I growl. "It is."

"Then *good.*"

When a dam bursts, it's not all of a sudden. At least, the build-up isn't. First there are small tremors. Then there are warnings, like the foundations cracking, or the mechanics stopping. And then, right before it gives way, it's as if the

Earth itself knows it's about to unleash hell upon its surface. The birds and animals leave. The air goes still.

Then—only then—does the wall holding back the water give way, with an explosion of violence and urgency.

That's what this is—this thing between Tempest and I.

There were tremors weeks ago. The foundations cracked two nights ago. And there hasn't been a bird in the sky ever since.

And in this exact moment, locked eye-to-eye with each other, our blood roaring hot, our breaths coming hard, and our bodies slammed together with the scent of my blood and her fury swirling in the air, it's like the final calm before it all gives way.

My eyes drop to her lips, and for the first time, I realize she's bleeding a little, from where I bit her at the altar.

It's that little drop of blood on the lips of the woman I married about three and a half minutes ago that's the final straw.

The last stroke.

The release.

When I grab her face and slam my mouth to hers, tasting her moans, her blood, and her pain, it's like the whole fucking dam gives way.

And God help whoever's downstream.

15

TEMPEST

There's a chance I might be crazy. Like, legit psycho. Because five minutes ago, I literally tried to stab this man at the altar. And now I'm moaning sinfully into his lips as he pins me to the bookshelf and kisses the ever-living fuck out of me.

Which part of that scenario makes me *more* psycho? I don't know.

All I know is, it feels like I'm coming alive when his lips crush to mine.

I whimper as his teeth sink into my lip again. I can feel him suck, tasting my blood as I cling to him and mash my lips to his. His hands slide over my hips, pinning me against the shelves, then slide up my ribs and forcibly grab my wrists before shoving them high above my head.

This should be hitting every single trigger in the world for me. This should be pushing me back into that black hole in my head from seven years ago.

Instead, Dante's touch makes me *ache*. It makes me crave more of him.

…and it makes me very, very wet.

Deep down, I know that's screwed up: that after what I've experienced, it's precisely the roughness in his touch and the forceful way he's capturing me and caging me against the wall that has me melting for him and aching for more more *more*.

That has me dripping wet.

But I just don't care.

Dante keeps my wrists pinned above my head with one hand. He uses the other one to capture my jaw as his tongue dances with mine. The possessiveness of the touch makes my knees weak as I eagerly suck his tongue deeper into my mouth.

His hand drops to the laced bodice of my wedding gown, yanking the ties loose and pulling it open. Heat pools between my thighs and my breasts spill free, and when his strong hand cups one of them, I shiver against him.

Dante groans as his fingers twist and pinch my aching nipples, sending electric shocks zapping through my core that have my thighs clenching tight. His hand slides lower, grabs the hem of the dress, and bunches it up to my waist.

His mouth drops to my neck, his teeth raking over the delicate skin there as his hand slips between my thighs. His hand cups my throbbing pussy through my slick panties, and my eyes roll back in ecstasy as something dark and volatile sparks inside me.

Oh fuck...

"Now, which part made this little pussy so fucking messy, dear wife of mine," Dante snarls savagely into my ear. It's that roughness and savagery that ratchets up the heat and the ache for him even more.

"Was it stabbing me?"

I gasp sharply as he nips hard at my neck.

"Or was it knowing that now I'm going to *fuck* that stabbiness right out of you."

I shudder, pleasure humming through me as his finger drags along my seam through my drenched panties.

"Or *maybe*, little hurricane," Dante rasps into my ear, "that's exactly what you were hoping for when you tried to hurt me. Is that it?" he growls. "Were you trying to *provoke me* into pinning you to the wall like a bad girl and *taking* this pussy for the first time?"

I gasp as his fingers slip under the lace of my panties. He sinks into me, and when two of his fingers slide deep and curl against my g-spot, there's no stopping the whine of pleasure from tumbling from my lips.

"Next time you want me to fuck you," Dante murmurs thickly against the shell of my ear. "You'll ask me nicely. And when you do…"

I cry out as he starts to thrust his fingers in and out of me roughly, sending explosive heat and pleasure sparking like wildfire through my body.

"When you do, little hurricane," he hisses. *"You'll fucking say please."*

He suddenly hooks his other hand under my ass and lifts me up. I whimper, my arms and legs wrapping around him instinctively as he holds me against his body with one hand, keeping the other between my thighs and fingering my dripping pussy with deep, rhythmic thrusts.

His mouth slams to mine in a bruising kiss as he turns and storms across the room. My heart lurches into my throat when he lets go and gravity takes over. The second I land on the couch, he's on me again.

Dante's lips crush to mine, hungrily tasting my mouth and sucking my tongue into his. He moves lower, nipping at my neck, then my breasts, finally wrapping his lips around a soft pink nipple.

I hiss in pleasure, my hands sliding into his hair and gripping hard as he bites down and then slips his mouth lower.

And lower.

My eyes fly open as he shoves my dress up to my waist and yanks my panties off. Suddenly, his mouth dives between my thighs, and when I feel his tongue drag up my slit, it's like sticking my finger into an electrical socket.

Holy. FUCK.

My hips jerk off the couch, and I slam a hand over my mouth to muffle the humiliatingly loud whine of pleasure that's only overshadowed by how embarrassingly *wet* I am. I feel this insane need to apologize for the mess I'm making of his furniture, but before I can even open my mouth, Dante's burying his between my legs and tonguing me deeply.

Sweet Jesus.

It's like nothing I've ever known. My fingers can't hold a candle to his tongue and lips. All I can do is writhe and moan, my vision blurring as he wraps his lips around my aching clit and swirls his tongue over it. He sinks two fingers back into my greedy pussy, stroking them against that rough spot inside as he sucks on my clit.

When I feel the first spank of his palm on my ass, it's like someone's poured napalm on the fire roaring inside of me. When he does it again, the spark catches in a whooshing roar. And when his tongue bats over my throbbing clit, the whole thing explodes.

I bury my face in the crook of my arm as I scream my release. It's the single most explosive orgasm of my life, and his mouth stays right where it is through every rolling, thunderous wave. My hips buck and grind shamelessly, my vision blurs at the edges, and my pulse roars in my ears as I come hard against Dante's tongue.

There's still a ringing in my ears as Dante stands and shrugs off his suit jacket. My eyes drop to the bloodstain on his shirt as he unbuttons it and drops it to the floor, baring his ridiculously chiseled chest and abs.

When I realize what's happening, my pulse quickens. But there's no apprehension, and there's no part of me that feels I should tell him to stop, that I don't want this to go further.

Because I *do*.

I've never been able to even sit through an entire dinner date with someone. But there's something so volatile and unapologetically possessive and forward about this man that it's not that I *can't* say no.

It's that I don't want to.

His pants open and slide down, and when he peels his briefs down over the grooved lines of his hips...

Holy fuck.

I stare at Dante's very large, very *thick* cock as he wraps his hand around it and strokes leisurely. His thighs push mine open as he moves between them, and when he eases the fat head of his dick against my swollen pussy, my breath catches in my throat.

I could say no. I could tell him to stop, right now. He might be cold, and he might be the devil. But I've known rapists, and Dante isn't one.

But I'm not going to say no. Because for the first time ever, I fucking *want this.*

Dante leans over me as I shiver at the feel of his cock dragging up and down my slick pussy, still wet and glistening from my orgasm. His hand moves up, cupping my jaw before two fingers brush over my lips.

They're wet.

From *me.*

"Open your mouth," he murmurs darkly.

I do, and when his fingers slip inside, I close my lips around them.

"*Good girl,*" Dante growls, making my eyes bulge as his mouth teases over my neck all the way up to my ear. "Now *suck.*"

I whimper, my cheeks hollowing as I do as he says. My tongue wraps around his fingers, tasting myself on them.

I taste sweet.

I'm still moaning around his fingers when I feel his cock sink between my pussy lips. My eyes widen, my pulse skips.

My whole body quivers and shudders as he pushes into me.

Holy fucking shit.

He's so fucking big, it feels like he's ripping me open. But then the pain turns into something molten and throbbing—something all-consuming and wild as he sinks deeper and deeper into my tightness.

It takes me a moment to realize the whining sound I'm hearing is *me* and the whimpered, panted moans around his fingers are mine.

He keeps going, burying inch after inch into me as the pressure builds and builds and builds. As he groans and drives the last inch into me, it's like I'm breaking apart.

Because suddenly, I'm coming.

I scream, my hips bucking off the couch and my legs wrapping tight around his muscled hips. My body shudders and wrenches as the orgasm explodes through me.

…I just came from *one thrust*.

"*Good girl,*" Dante murmurs low in my ear as I gasp for air. "Making my cock extra wet so that I can *fuck you better.*" I shiver as his finger slips from my lips, his hand cupping my jaw at my throat. "Imagine what I'm going to do to you when I *actually* start to take you."

His mouth slams to mine as he pulls out and thrusts right back in. My face caves, and I whine into his lips as I cling to him.

Then, Dante truly starts to fuck me.

He's not gentle, and he's not tender. His coiled muscles clench and flex against me as his swollen cock pounds deep.

His mouth devours mine, and his hands are everywhere as I cling to him and moan.

And it's *so. Fucking. Good.*

It's fast and wild. It's a blissful agony I've never known, and I find myself trying to memorize every moment.

Every groan from his lips.

Every ripple of his muscles.

Every thrust of his thick cock, touching me in places I didn't know could be touched.

There's a frenzied madness to the way our hips slam together and the way my nails rake down his shoulders and biceps. The way his hand wraps around my throat as he bites down on my lip and buries himself deep inside.

I've done everything I can to forget the one other time I've felt this sensation, but it wasn't even *this* sensation at all. That time was just violence and pain; humiliation and shutting my mind off from the rest of me.

This time, I let it all wash over me. Every sensation. Every nerve buzzing and exploding.

Dante Sartorre's no knight in shining armor, but I was never looking for one anyway. What he *is*, though, is the man who's taking my virginity.

For real this time.

And Prince Charming or not, and even though this whole marriage is fake, and we're not really a couple...I want *this* to be what I remember.

This is what I'm going to consider my first time.

For years, the mere idea of having sex with someone made me feel dirty. And even if I ever did get the slightest flicker of desire for physical intimacy with another person, it would be extinguished by my self-loathing and anger.

But right now, here with Dante, I don't feel bad about this at all.

I feel *freed*.

The pulsing, throbbing wave inside me crests higher and higher. My vision blurs, and I lose myself in the sensation of his body pressing to mine, being so deep inside of me, being as close to me as another human can be.

In the sound of his groans and his grunts of pleasure mixing with the whimpered moans of my own. In the feel of his skin against mine, and the intoxicating scent of him invading my senses. One of his hands pins both of mine above my head, and the other clenches possessively on my hip, driving me to his pace.

The tingling throb in my core surges hotter and hotter, until there's no stopping it.

"Oh fuck…"

I choke as the orgasm hits me like a train, slamming into me and wrenching my body hard. I feel myself clamp down around his thrusting cock, my thighs squeezing tight around his grooved, muscled hips.

The release explodes out of my mouth with a cry of pleasure, just as Dante slams his lips to mine. He swallows my moans, his tongue dancing with mine as he pounds as deep as he can into me. I can feel him throbbing and pulsing, the heat of his cum flooding into me as I drown in the madness of it all.

Then, it's over.

Every inch of my skin tingles. Every nerve ending thrums and buzzes with an electricity that leaves me shaking. Dante lingers for a moments, his lips brushing against mine as our eyes lock.

Holy shit.

I mean holy. Fucking. *Shit.*

Slowly, he slides out of me, and I wince slightly at the delicious soreness between my legs. His gaze drops, frowning, and I tense, glancing down as well.

Shit.

There's some blood on his dick, and a little on my thigh.

"It's fine," I blurt quickly, before he can say anything.

Dante slowly raises his eyes to mine. For a second, I think he's angry. But then I realize it's more a look of concern.

"Are you hurt?"

"No," I shake my head. "No, you're just..." My face heats. *"Big."*

He doesn't respond. But his brow slowly furrows deeper and his sharp blue eyes lock on mine. "Are you on birth control?"

I consider lying for a second. I mean, in a way, I am. The combination of the protein blockers and some of the other meds Dr. Han has me on has made it, in his words, "extremely unlikely, to a near-certain degree" that I could become pregnant. I never pushed for specifics because, well, *not having sex* is also a great way to avoid pregnancy.

"No."

The second I say it, something dark flickers in his eyes.

"*Shit*," he hisses.

"It's fine," I mumble.

"No, Tempest, it's *not*," he growls. "I can do fake marriage." His eyes narrow on me. "I'm not doing fake parenting."

"Well, me neither!" I spit.

It's his insinuation that I for whatever insane reason *would* want to have a kid with him that pisses me off the most. I awkwardly get to my feet and turn away, my face red as I pull my panties back up, shivering when I feel them cling to the wetness from us both. I shove my skirts back down and start to retie the bodice.

"You should have told me you weren't on birth control," Dante mutters.

I whirl on him. "I can't get pregnant anyway, asshole, so it's a moot point!"

"Why?"

I ignore him as I turn on my heel and march to the door, wincing a little at the soreness between my legs.

"Tempest."

"Fuck you, it's none of your—"

"Thirty minutes ago when I fucking *married you*," he snaps at my back. "It very much became my business!"

A roaring sound fills my ears as I angrily fumble at the lock on the door.

"Tempest—"

"Fuck you!"

"Why can't you get—"

I snap, and I turn on him, all the rage at the unfairness of everything that I've been trying to hold back for so long finally erupting out of me.

"Because I'm fucking dying, okay?!"

16

DANTE

For what feels like a solid minute, I stare silently at her, trying to convince myself that I heard her wrong. But we both know I didn't.

Her face turns red, as if she's embarrassed.

"*What?*" I growl quietly.

Tempest looks away, turning to fuss with the lock again. "Nothing," she mumbles. "I…I didn't mean that."

I cross the distance between us, grabbing her by the chin and turning her to face me.

"Yes. You. Did." My pulse thuds as I peer into her face.

There's not a single trace of lie.

Holy fuck.

"*Jesus*, Tempest…"

"I shouldn't have said anything," she blurts, looking away. "Look, it's nothing, just forget—"

She jumps as my hand on her jaw pulls her face and her gaze back to me. "Tell me."

"Dante, forget—"

"No," I growl. "*Tell me.*"

Her gaze drops, her teeth worrying her bottom lip.

"Short answer, it's this liver thing, and usually only babies get it, but..." A shadowed, wry look crosses her face. "Well, lucky me."

Fuck.

I'm not expecting or prepared for the wave of emotions that hits me. Anger, for one. I want to tell myself it's anger at her for not disclosing this before. But it's not. It's that I'm angry at the unfairness of someone as young as her having something like this.

"My body doesn't effectively break down fats and proteins, which creates a buildup of something called methylmalonic acid in my blood." She raises her eyes to me, a dry smile on her twisting lips. "So, I'm *literally* toxic. My blood is, at least."

I don't immediately say anything because how the hell do I respond to that.

"No one knows about this," Tempest blurts into the silence. "I mean *no one*. And I want to keep it that way."

"Your brothers, though—"

She shakes her head. "Not even them."

I bring my hand back up to cup her jaw again, and raise her gaze to mine.

"Why are you telling me this?"

"I actually have no idea..." She looks away. "I guess you caught me a *sharing mood*," she mutters sarcastically.

My head slowly shakes side to side, still not quite comprehending.

"You're..."

"Dying, Dante," Tempest says quietly. "Ceasing to live."

"How soon?"

She doesn't answer.

"Tempest..."

"To be determined. But...six months, maybe?"

What the fuck.

The pain in my chest is sharper than the blade she tried to stab me with earlier. It also cuts much deeper. I'm trying to wrap my head around that.

I mean this is Tempest fucking *Black*—aka the pain in my fucking ass who weaseled her way into a blood marker marriage to me. She's not my *actual* wife. She's not my girlfriend.

We don't even fucking *like* each other.

So why the hell does learning all this make me want to destroy something?

I slowly shake my head. "Tempest..."

"*Don't*," she mumbles. "Don't say you're sorry or something else stupid and make me regret saying anything even more than I already do." She exhales heavily, looking away. "God, I can't believe I told you that."

"Why the hell haven't you told anyone else?"

"My own reasons."

"Like?"

"They're *my* reasons, Dante," she says tiredly.

"That's why you took Maeve's place."

"Bingo," she says dryly.

"It's a little easier to dive onto a grenade when you're already bleeding out," I growl.

"Basically." She exhales again. "Look, I know what I signed up for. And I'll play the part when I have to." Her eyes lock on mine. "I'll be your wife."

She blushes the second she says it, looking away quickly.

"And…after?"

"Well," her lips twist in a sardonic smile. "*After*, I'm afraid I'll have to retire the role."

I frown deeply. Tempest smirks.

"You're gonna have to be cool with gallows humor, Dante."

This is surreal. And again, this is not the reaction I would have pictured myself having. Not because I'm a heartless monster who doesn't give a shit that this woman is on a countdown. But again…we're not *really* a thing. We're virtually strangers, and it's clear that all we have in common is the *white hot* sexual chemistry between us.

"Look, you don't have to worry, Dante. I'm not telling anyone, like I said. And when I go…" she shrugs. "You'll be golden."

I frown. "What?"

"You'll never have to marry again to appease them."

"What are you talking about?"

"I went to lunch the other day on Arthur Avenue—"

"I know."

"And I met a lot of mafia women, and you know what I noticed? The ones who were married were…okay. Meanwhile the *un*married ones had this look like there was a clock ticking down the seconds until they were married themselves. But the ones who were free, sitting pretty, and doing just fine?" She shrugs. "The widows. They'd already proven themselves to your world. They did it: they got married, and then some higher power or karma or whatever took it away. They'd gotten their participation trophy, you know? They didn't *have* to play the game anymore."

I arch a brow. "You're saying I'll be like an old Italian widow."

She grins. "Something like that."

I suck on my teeth. Tempest clears her throat.

"Anyway…" She trails off, looking down at her hands. "I guess we should probably get back to the reception before—"

"I'm going to bring in a doctor I know."

Her gaze lifts to mine, a look on her face I can't quite read before she rolls her eyes.

"Dante, I'm done looking for a miracle."

"So you're *fine* with dying by the age of twenty-five?" I growl. "That's okay with you?"

"I mean, it wouldn't be my first pick," she snaps back. "But what am I going to do? Cry for the next six months?"

So it's not that she's okay with it, or at peace with it. It's that she's *unafraid* of it, and she's facing it on *her* terms.

It's...foolish. But admirable, in a way.

Tempest starts to fix herself up a little more, turning to mess with her hair in a mirror. I start to get dressed again too, but as I'm tucking myself back into my pants, my gaze lands on the bit of blood on my dick.

I'm not *bothered* by it. But still...

"Tempest, what I want from you for the next six months is honesty. I mean it."

She looks puzzled, but she nods. "Okay?"

"Just now, when I fucked you." I walk over to where she's standing by the door. I reach out and cup her jaw, my eyes burning hotly down into hers. "Was that your first time?"

Tempest is silent for a moment. Then she reaches up and tucks a lock of hair behind her ear, and it's like she brushes a sly smile to her face at the same time. Her hand reaches behind her, opening the door to my office.

"It is now."

She slips out the door without another word, shutting it behind her.

17

DANTE

TWO NIGHTS AFTER THE WEDDING, Tempest moves in. I know she was stalling on that, and I'd have been fine with delaying too, except for the image problem of my new wife living ninety miles away.

The dons, the capos...they're not stupid. They understand what this is. But the whole point of me getting married was to showcase an image, so I intend to uphold that image.

But there's another reason I've put my foot down about Tempest moving in with me: the fact that I know her dark secret now.

I'm not even really prepared to ask myself what it is about that makes me possessive of her in a way I haven't been up till now. Makes me want to *keep her safe*—to lock her in a box, like some sort of overprotective psycho. Outside of Bianca, that's never something I've ever been before.

So what the fuck changed?

Tempest isn't wrong: sad as it is, her...*passing* would slap a neat little bow on this whole situation. I'd no longer be fake married, and, come on. What's better than a nice married man running Club Venom?

A *widower*, that's what. It's neat, it's efficient, and it's bulletproof.

...It also makes me feel like a sociopath, because that "neat little bow" entails this woman *dying*.

So I suppose that's a major contributing factor to me overriding her excuses and demanding that she move in: I want to protect her, in some weird way.

However, Tempest, as anyone who's known her for longer than forty seconds would understand, has a certain...bullheaded willfulness to her. In other words, she's a headstrong fucking terror when she wants to be. And she is clearly *not* down with moving all the way from Manhattan out to the Hamptons.

I mean, I get it. It's ninety miles from her brothers, and she's not exactly a Hamptons gal. So in the end, a compromise is reached: we'll *both* move, to my penthouse in the West Village.

I mean, it *is* closer to Venom. And, as Tempest was all too eager—and smug—to point out, the ability to compromise is a "cornerstone of any strong marriage."

I'm also pretty sure that strong marriages involve sleeping in the same bed, but in our case, we'll be skipping that. Which I'm more than okay with. I've never once spent the entire night with a woman, and I see no reason to start now.

...Even if I was her first.

At least, I think I was. I'm still not quite sure what the fuck she meant by "it is now", when I asked her if that time in my office at the wedding was her first time.

There's a part of me that's more than a little pissed about *not* being told that the girl I fucked so roughly in my office, still wearing her wedding dress, was possibly a virgin. Again, I'm not a monster, and taking a virginity in that manner wasn't really ever on my bucket list.

But that said...the idea that I *was* her first is more than slightly intoxicating. Even if we haven't so much as looked at each other since.

Tempest has been moved into my penthouse for all of three hours when I find myself standing outside her bedroom door. I knock, and when there's no answer, I simply open the door and walk in.

"Um, *hello*?!"

Her voice comes from the ensuite bathroom. The door isn't shut all the way, so I march over and rap my knuckles on the doorframe.

"You decent?"

"No?"

I walk in anyway.

"Are you fucking serious!?" Tempest is quickly buttoning up her pants as she stands from the toilet. She glares daggers at me. "What the *hell*, Dante!"

"Did I interrupt something fun?"

She rolls her eyes and glances back at the toilet. "Only if you're into pee," she mutters.

Spoiler: I'm not.

"And if I was?"

She wrinkles her nose. "Ew?"

"We don't kink shame in this house."

She rolls her eyes. "Well, it's still in the toilet if you want to like, I don't know…whatever you do with people's pee?" She makes a grossed out face.

"This is what I do with it."

She shivers as I walk past her and flush the toilet. Tempest's face burns as she moves over to the sink to wash her hands.

"What do you want, Dante?"

This is how it's been since the wedding. And I don't need to be a psychologist to understand that what she's doing is overcompensating.

She thinks she shared too much. She opened up too much, made herself too vulnerable. And now, she's yanking things back in the other direction by being her usual smart-mouth, smug little brat of a persona.

As if that's going to make me forget what she told me, or the way her cunt felt when she came all over my cock.

"I need you to dress up."

She's not the bait, but I *am* going hunting in a week or so.

Ostensibly, the dinner I'm holding is to meet and greet some potential new investors in Venom. Some mafia types will be attending, as well as mafia-adjacent finance guys. But it's all a cover. What I'm really doing is hunting.

When my older sister Claudia was first taken from us, we all thought it was just random violence. That she'd been out on the wrong night, and crossed the wrong guy, who drugged her drink, raped her, and then killed her to cover his crimes.

At least, that's what the police report says.

But I have a way of digging, and prodding, and ripping at the edges of things until I've peeked behind the curtain and I'm satisfied that I know the truth. And nothing about that report made me think we had reached the truth, so I dug deeper.

That's when I uncovered them.

They call themselves the Apex Club. They're mostly very connected, very rich, and from very prominent, untouchable families. They're the type of men who think the world belongs to them.

There's plenty of private "old boys" clubs out there where rich, entitled douchebags can drink together and congratulate each other on *being* rich, entitled douchebags.

Apex Club is next level.

To those "men" who wear the golden lion signet ring, being rich, powerful, and untouchable isn't enough. They need dominion over others—namely young women and girls.

That's who killed my sister. That's who I hunt, and whose rings I keep as trophies in the box in my office. The crown jewel in that collection is the one with blue and red eyes, that belonged to the man who murdered my sister: a waste of skin named Alan Codrey, heir to the Codrey family oil fortune.

It will be my eternal regret that after I tracked Alan down, in his attempt to escape me, he shattered his jaw falling off a fire escape. He lived—at least for another three days of what I hope was truly *agonizing* pain and misery while I tortured him. But he wasn't able to tell me anything more about the Apex Club.

I've killed five of them so far. Later this week, I'm going to see if there's a sixth on the horizon.

Tempest arches a brow as she turns to lean against the white marble bathroom vanity. Her arms fold over her chest.

"Excuse me?"

"I need you to dress up."

"Yeah, that's not happening."

"It's not a request."

Our eyes lock, and I relish the pink flush that heats her face. We may not have even touched each other since the other day, but that doesn't mean she doesn't get all flustered around me now. Especially when she's cornered like this.

"I'm your wife, right?" she mutters.

"It would appear so."

"Not your servant? Or your slave?"

I smile thinly. "I think that could be up for interpretation."

"Think again, asshole."

"Hmm. I'll get right on that. In the meantime," I level a stern glare at her. "*Dress up.*"

Tempest follows me out of the bathroom and into her walk-in closet, where I start rifling through her clothes.

"I'm sorry, can I *help you* with something?" she snaps. "What exactly am I dressing up for, anyway?"

"Ah, I knew you'd come around."

She glares at me. "I meant what *would I*, potentially, be dressing up for?"

"Dinner, with guests."

"What sort of guests?"

I exhale heavily, turning back to her. "How about you just do as you're told for once?"

Her face heats.

"Tempest, I just need you to put something nice on. Something sexy."

Okay, I lied. She's *kind of* the bait.

"*Wow*," she says flatly. "What are you, my pimp? Who are these guests?"

"Nuns, schoolteachers, the PTA board." I smirk at her. "Who do you think?"

"Mafiosos? Investors in your little club?"

"*Potential* investors."

"*Ahhh*, I see," she mutters. "So I'm dressing sexy to make a bunch of pricks more willing to give you money."

"Something like that."

I turn back to her wall of black clothes, scowling as I paw through the hangers.

"Is this seriously all you have?"

"I didn't realize being your fake wife had a fucking dress code," Tempest snaps.

"Well, it does And none of this will do."

Tempest glares at me as I pull out my phone and call Ginevra.

Ginevra was always the *one* tailor that my father considered his better. And even though she's pushing eighty by now, Ginevra is still the best tailor and seamstress in all of New York, probably one of the best in the world.

She's also a good friend.

She greets me warmly, and pretty soon we're playing a quick game of catch up in Italian. I glance over, smirking to myself as I see the confused look on Tempest's face.

Then I tell Ginevra what I need, thank her profusely, and hang up.

She glares at me. "Who was that?"

"A friend who's going to help you look fantastic."

Tempest gives me a suspicious look. "For the dinner for a bunch of sleazy potential investors in your club, where you, what, fuck around in orgies all day?"

"I don't participate at the club."

"So it's more of a you sitting in a dark room watching security cameras and jerking off kind of situation?"

"I'm sorry, remind me what you do for work?"

Tempest gives me a frosty look. I give her a hard stare right back and try and pretend that I can't see the hard points of her nipples through her Black Sabbath t-shirt.

"*This* is what you signed up for, little hurricane," I growl.

"I didn't *sign up* for—"

"You *literally* did," I mutter. "In blood, I might add."

Her lips purse. I smile.

"This is your new reality, Tempest." She shivers as I lean down to let my lips brush her ear, and she sucks in her breath sharply. *"I'd get used to it."*

18

TEMPEST

By any standard, Dante's penthouse is *huge*.

That said, it's not big enough that two people could live in it together and not cross paths with each other. But five days in, that's what it feels like, because I've barely seen him.

It's starting to feel deliberate. And his absence is so noticeable that by this point I'm actually wondering if he even *is* coming home. After all, we do sleep in separate rooms. We're even on two different *floors*—my guest room is on the first, and he's upstairs next to the home office that I snooped through the night I brought Bianca here. Also known as, the same home office where he pinned me to the desk and made me explode with his fingers.

Finally, though, I decide to find out for sure about Dante's nocturnal habits. And I go to sleep on that fifth night with a plan in place.

…Which pays off about an hour later.

I'm wakened by someone pounding on my bedroom door, and I'm still shaking off sleep when it flies open, and a drenched, furious Dante storms in.

"What the *fuck*!?"

The initial burst of him storming into my room has my pulse racing, and, shamefully, a throb aching in my core. But then, when he flicks the lights on, and I drink in the sight of him standing there in the doorway, dripping wet, I grin.

"Oh, so you *do* live here."

It's not—or at least, I've *told myself* as much—that he's not here enough. It's the principle of the thing. If I damn well have to be stuck here "living with" my husband, then he fucking should be, too.

So my idea tonight was to prop his bedroom door open and balance a paper cup full of milk on top of it, so when...or if... he opened it, he'd get drenched.

Looks like it worked.

"*Milk*?!" he seethes, looking disgusted.

In the five days I've been living here, I've noticed something: Dante doesn't keep milk in the house. Or any dairy product, actually, except for butter. No milk, cheese, yogurt, nada. I actually had to go out and buy some from the bodega down the street to set my trap.

Why milk? Because getting drenched with water is an easy fix. You dry off and go on with your life. But getting drenched with milk, even if you *like* dairy, is objectively disgusting.

"Uh oh, are we going to need a lactose pill or something?" I grin smugly.

Dante glares at me. "I'm not lactose intolerant, Tempest. I just think dairy is fucking gross."

I'm about to open my mouth to make some crude joke when he starts to yank off his shirt. My lip retreats between my teeth and my face flushes as I watch him peel his dress shirt off his insanely toned, muscled and grooved body.

There's a chance my juvenile antics are at least half fueled by sexual frustration. And I *hate* admitting that, even to myself.

I've gone years without even having the slightest desire to have sex or do anything sexual, with anyone, anywhere. I've been *fine* using my own fingers and the occasional battery-operated assistance.

But then *he* shows up, pins me to the wall, rips my wedding dress off, and shows me what a *real* orgasm could feel like.

And now, fingers won't do. But the *real* pisser is, in the seven days since I came harder than I've ever come in my life, Dante hasn't made the slightest move to touch me again.

And now I feel like a junkie being denied her fix.

"Are you bored?" he grunts, glaring at me. "Is this fucking cabin fever? You're not a prisoner here, Tempest. You can leave and do whatever you want."

I shrug. "I know. But if I have to sleep here and live here, so do you."

"Club Venom is open until *six in the morning*," he seethes. "I keep late hours. That doesn't give you the right to douse me in fucking milk!"

I swallow as he storms toward me. My pulse quickens, and my whole body tightens with need and anticipation.

But he still doesn't touch me. He just grabs my favorite t-shirt—black, with a photoshopped picture of Dolly Parton wearing KISS makeup—off the bed.

"Hey!!"

Dante ignores me as he blots the milk out of his hair.

"That's my favorite shirt!"

"Aww, really?" He hurls it back onto the bed. "*Good*. Now if you'll excuse me, I need to shower."

He turns and storms back to the doorway, where he pauses and glances back at me.

"No more fucking pranks, Tempest."

"Fine."

"Say it."

"Nah. You need to go shower, you reek of milk."

His eyes narrow dangerously at me. A thrill teases through my body.

Okay, I'm goading him now.

Sex withdrawal is *real*.

"Courtesy of Pam."

I grin as Alistair sets a large cooler down on the desk between us, already knowing what's inside.

"Oh my God, *yessss*." I groan as I pop the cooler open to reveal the half dozen Tupperware juice containers filled with the creamy, greenish smoothies Pam makes for me.

She's given me the recipe before. But they always turn out like crap when I've tried to make them myself, no idea why. Making them at Dante's house has proven to be impossible anyway, what with his carpet ban on dairy products. The French vanilla yogurt in Pam's recipe is crucial, and the tyrant king control freak I live with now threw out both containers of the stuff that I stuck in his fridge before I could even use them.

Asshole.

"Want one?"

Alistair makes a face as I pop one open right there in his office and take a big gulp. "Absolutely not."

This morning, in a fit of, well, homesickness I guess, I texted both of my brothers about meeting up for lunch. Gabriel was in court all day, but Alistair said yes, as long as lunch could be delivered to the office.

People have often asked me why both of my brothers, with their looks and success, are still single. I'm sure most people assume it's because they like playing the field. The reality is, they're both married to their work.

Alistair opens the take-out containers from Wo Hop, aka the best Chinese food spot in all of New York City, and slides my pork fried rice toward me.

"So—"

"I'm fine, Alistair."

He scowls. He hates when I cut him off like that, especially when it's obviously he's about to launch into a big speech.

That's another thing people have asked me a lot over the years: if my relationship with Alistair is different from the one I have with Gabriel, because Alistair is adopted.

The answer to that *asinine* question is a quick and easy "no." Well, quick and easy aside from the time I got suspended in the seventh grade for kicking Chrissy Klein in the shin for saying Alistair wasn't my "real brother".

I mean, my parents adopted him two years before I was even born. He's literally always been my brother.

He watches me not touching my lunch—which I only ordered to avoid a lecture—as he absent-mindedly chews on a dumpling.

"I've been looking into the contract situation."

He means the blood marker.

"Oh?"

The black look on his face tells me all I need to know about where this conversation is going.

"I made my choice, Alistair," I say quietly, sipping my smoothie.

"We didn't exactly have a course on mafia blood markers at school," he grunts. "But I've reached out to a few of the more...*colorful* types I might know who know more about the politics and traditions of the mafia world."

"And?"

Alistair just grunts again as he deftly plucks up another dumpling with his chopsticks and pops it into his mouth.

"You *could* annul the marriage provided the original intended bride stepped up to take your—"

"Not fucking happening."

Alistair cracks a wry smile. "Didn't think so." He frowns. "How's fuck-face?"

I shrug. "He's...Dante. We mostly avoid each other."

Aside from that one time a week ago when he fucked me in ways I've never even known were possible, and now I'm fantasizing about him and craving it again, even though I know how fucked up and wrong that is.

My brows knit as I glance up at my brother. "Can I ask you something?"

He nods. "Sure."

"It's about Layla."

Alistair stops chewing abruptly. *Shit.*

"We don't have to—"

He shakes his head. "No no, go ahead," he murmurs darkly.

I take a small sip of my smoothie. "Why do you think she did it?"

A silence settles over the office as Alistair turns to gaze out the windows.

I was eleven when my sister died at Greenwich Hospital, near the Knightsblood University campus. There are three question marks surrounding that night.

One: despite never doing drugs in her life, the official cause of death was listed as a heroin overdose.

Two: *Dante* is the one who brought her to the hospital.

And of course, three: even though they weren't even friends...and as far as I know, didn't even know each other... Dante and my sister *got married* in that hospital, during the brief half-hour window where she regained consciousness before she died.

After that, of course, Dante lawyered up, sealed her medical records, and stonewalled the rest of us.

Over the years, my imagination has run wild speculating about what might have happened that night. I'm sure Alistair's and Gabriel's have, too; wondering how their straight-A, non-drug-using sister found herself overdosing on heroin and marrying Dante.

"Which 'it' do you mean: the drugs, or *him*."

"Him," I murmur.

Alistair exhales slowly. "I don't know, Tempest," he growls quietly. "I've looked at all the potential angles: financial gain would be the big one. But..."

"But he never tried to use the marriage to get anything from us," I finish. "Did you ever think that...I mean...he had something to do with it?"

My brother's jaw clenches.

I know we all had, maybe still have, hunches about Dante and his involvement with Layla's death. Maybe it's part of our grieving process, but we've never voiced those hunches out loud to each other, though.

"Sorry," I mumble. "We don't have to—"

"No, we *should*," he grunts. "I mean, you're living with the guy now." He exhales slowly. "Honestly? Please, don't ever repeat this to Gabriel, but...I doubt it."

I frown. "Really? But you hate him."

"I hate him because he's a conniving fuck who hides behind the Barone family and the rest of his mafia buddies. I hate him because he fucking wouldn't talk to any of us about *any of it* after Layla—"

Alistair stops and collects himself.

"Look: I've known men who are capable of things like that—I mean *really* bad, evil motherfuckers. If you look, you can see the monster in them—it's right there in their eyes." Alistair lifts his shoulders as he gazes at nothing on the desk in front of him. "As much as I don't like the guy, I don't see that evil in Dante. Nor do I see him being a heroin user. But even if he had nothing to do with whatever happened that night, the fact that he so pointedly shut us out and sealed her records looks suspicious as fuck, and honestly, yeah, it makes me fucking hate him."

He frowns, leaning across the desk to peer at me. "Where is this coming from, T? Is Dante doing or saying anything—"

"No, nothing like that." I shrug and laugh dryly. "He basically just ignores and avoids me."

Alistair's lips thin. "*Good*. Best case scenario, honestly."

We both exhale in the ensuing silence before he nods at my to-go container. "You gonna eat that fried rice, or...?"

The man is built like a movie superhero and still manages to eat like a total pig.

"All yours." I slide it his way. "I filled up on smoothie."

Alistair looks like he's going to say something, but he takes a bite of my fried rice instead. As he's chewing, his eyes land on my hand. He squints.

"Did you get your nails done?"

My face heats. "I...yes?"

"*Pink?*"

"Please. It's rosé blush." My face gets pinker than my nails. "Is that a problem?"

"No, just...confusing. I haven't seen you wear anything except black nail polish, much less *rosé blush*, since you were in high school." His eyes snap to mine. "Is this Dante? Did he make you—"

"Did he make me..." I gasp dramatically, clutching my hand to a string of imaginary pearls. "*Get a manicure?!*"

My brother gives me a cool stare. "It's just completely unlike you. I'm worried, Tempest."

"Well, I'm fine, Alistair. You don't have to be worried. I can *guarantee* it."

"And why is that, exactly?"

I take a beat before breaking out in a smug grin. "Because Dante needs me. He wasn't just going after Maeve because of whatever business dealings he and Charles were cooking up. He needed a wife to appease the dons over his ownership of Club Venom."

Alistair raises a brow. "Single guy running a sex club," he grins. "I was wondering when they were going to start getting iffy about that." He smiles darkly at me. "Dante knows you know about all this?"

"Oh-yes-he-does."

He chuckles. "I know I've said it before, and I'll say it again: you'd make one hell of a lawyer, Tempest. I mean, if you *ever* decide to take Columbia up on that deferred enrollment in their pre-law program, I can make sure—"

"Thanks, Alistair," I blurt sharply. "I'll let you know."

He smiles, nodding. "Only when you're ready. You've got all the time in the world to conquer it, T."

All the time in the world.

Something like that…

19

TEMPEST

"I'LL BE RIGHT OUT HERE when you're finished, Mrs. Sartorre."

I sigh heavily as my eyes raise to Lorenzo's in the rearview mirror. "Can we *please* just stick with Tempest?"

"'Fraid not, Mrs. Sartorre."

His face stays utterly neutral. In the few times I've interacted with Dante's head of security slash right-hand man, it's become clear that he's a man of few words. Not exactly big on showing emotions, either.

Honestly, the guy's a brick wall.

"Okay, but, *Mrs. Sartorre* isn't my name. It's Tempest Black. So if you're dead set on formality, can you use Ms. Black?"

Lorenzo doesn't reply verbally, but the look on his face speaks volumes.

I step out of the Range Rover and look up at the unassuming narrow building on West Seventy-Third Street: Ginevra's shop and showroom, where apparently I'm getting fitted for new clothes I don't need or want.

Whatever. Dante's paying for it. At least, he'd better be.

"Mio Dio! Sei così bella!"

The voice surprises me as I step into the small but elegant front room. I spin to see an older Italian woman probably in her late seventies with silvered hair come bustling out of a side room. A tape measure hangs around her neck, as well as a pair of shears in a little holder dangling from a thin chain. She smiles warmly at me, and before I know it, she's coming over and throwing her arms around me.

Okay?

I awkwardly hug her back before she pulls back to beam at me.

"I...I'm sorry," I say slowly. "I don't speak Italian—"

"Honey, I've lived in New York for sixty years," she chuckles in an almost-cliche Brooklyn accent. "I think I did okay picking up the language. What do you think?"

I look down. "Sorry."

"Don't be. "She grins widely, stepping back to let her eyes drag up and down my frame. "Such a beauty!"

I blush even deeper as she chuckles and shakes her head.

"If only Dante's father had lived to see the day his boy married a girl like you." She makes a clucking sound with her teeth. "He'd be pleased as punch."

I smile weakly back. "Thank you. But—"

210

"C'mon, sweetheart," Ginevra chuckles. "I'm not blind or stupid. I know why you're married to him." She winks. "I even heard *how* you married him." She swings open a doorway to a much larger room and ushers me inside. "I've worked with made men my entire life, dear. I know how that world works. Still, even if it *is* just business, Dante's a lucky man to have you at his side."

"Thank you," I mumble awkwardly.

She leads me into the larger room that has a small platform surrounded on three sides with walls of mirrors.

"Now, the yoga pants you can keep on. But I'll need you to lose the sweatshirt."

I nod, blushing slightly as I turn away and pull off my hoodie. I only have a bra on underneath.

"Here, hon."

Ginevra hands me a thin tank top. I blush as I take it. "Sorry, I get…shy."

She smiles warmly and genuinely as I slip on the top. "No problem, dear. Now, let's get you up there and I'll start measuring you. Or maybe coffee first?"

Turns out Ginevra is *awesome*. We do end up having an espresso before doing the measurements. While she takes them, she chats away to me about Dante's father, Bruno, who she apparently knew for years and years.

"Lovely man, and a fantastic tailor. Almost as good as me," she winks with a grin.

"So you've known Dante for a long time?"

"Since he was born. Which is why I can say, even though he's lucky to have you on his arm, you're not so hard up yourself to be on his."

My brows furrow, but she ignores my look. "Oh, I know it's just pretend, hon. But he's a good boy. Always was. And after all he's been through? Can't have been easy. First his parents when they were all so young, then poor Claudia when he was still a teenager?"

"His older sister?"

She nods. "Terrible, that was."

My brow furrows slightly. I knew that Dante and Bianca had an older sister who died young. I just never heard how.

Now feels like *not* the time to ask, though.

After she's got my measurements, Ginevra brings out an array of *stunning* gowns and dresses. They might not be my usual somewhat gothy style. But still, they're gorgeous.

"These are close to your size. Try a few on, see which ones you like. And if there are even *aspects* you like, a neckline, a color, let me know that, too. Sound good?"

I nod.

"Good," she grins. "I have to run down the street to the bank. You stay here and take your time."

When she's gone, I strip off my yoga pants and the borrowed tank top. Most of the dresses are definitely not meant to be worn with a bra, so that goes, too.

Ginevra's right: there are some things about some of the dresses I like, and others I don't. But they're all equally stunning. Finally I shimmy my way into a light blue gown with especially tight quarter sleeves and very narrow shoulders. As I'm trying to get out of it again, I tense.

Oh shit.

It's *stuck.*

"*Damn it!*" I hiss, trying to move my arms and shoulders in ways they don't usually go, attempting to slip the dress up over my shoulders. I peel it up even higher, but all that does is trap it even tighter, and now my arms are up and stuck like that.

Crap. At least Ginevra will be back at some—

The door opens behind me. I laugh awkwardly. "Well, this is embarrassing, I think I'm stuck—"

"Personally, I like the look."

I jolt, whirling with my hands up in the air and the gown bunched up at my armpits. I gasp sharply when I see Dante standing in the doorway with a hungry, wolfish smile on his face.

Oh my God.

I'm only wearing panties, and with my arms over my head like this, I'm giving him a fucking *show.*

"What the *fuck!*" I blurt, turning.

"Oh, yeah, much more modest now."

I groan. I might have pulled my tits away from his gaze. But now my bare back is to him, with just a thong splitting my ass. I squirm and shimmy, trying to get my arms and the dress back down, but it's not budging.

"Can you please find Ginevra?!" I blurt.

"I could, but I'd hate to interrupt her lunch."

I scowl. "What lunch? She said she was going to the bank—"

"Which is exactly where I bumped into her. And I thought, that woman works *so* hard, she deserves some 'her' time. So I bundled her into a cab and sent her off to Jean Georges for a lunch on me."

"*What?!*"

"I wouldn't expect her back soon. I called and ordered her the full Chef's tasting menu with wine pairings."

"*Dante—*"

"I think you need some help with that."

My face explodes with heat as I hear him walk up behind me.

But here's the terrible part. What I *should* be feeling—trapped, exposed, vulnerable, and now alone with this man—is terror. I should be having a goddamn panic attack.

Instead, my pulse turns to liquid fire. My skin tingles as I feel his eyes drag over my bare back and ass. And I tremble when I inhale the clean, spicy scent of him.

"I—I can do it myself—"

"*Sure,* you can."

My gasp hangs in the air as his hands wrap around my wrists above my head. He shoves, and my heart lurches as I bend at the waist, my hands flattening against the mirrors in front of me.

With my history, this should be the very *last* scenario that turns me on. But apparently, my body never got the memo from corporate. Because it does. Horribly so. When I feel him pin my hands to the glass, and feel the hard, muscled heat of his body at my back and against my ass, my legs tremble.

My pulse sizzles through my veins.

Desire pools between my thighs, dampening my panties.

One of his big hands keeps mine pinned to the mirror. The other slips down my arm, his knuckles brushing my cheek on the way. His hand drops lower over the bunched-up dress until I feel his fingertips against my bare skin at the middle of my back.

A shiver ripples up my spine, followed by his hand. His fingers slip underneath the bunched fabric, sliding it higher…

And then abruptly stopping, just as the gown binds me even tighter, and now blinding my vision.

"If…if you keep tugging, it'll come off."

"Yes, probably."

I whimper as he growls the word right into my ear.

"But where's the fun in that?"

"Dante—"

"Is this why you've been acting like such a brat?"

My entire core begins to melt as his rumbling voice purrs in my ear.

"Because you just need to get fucked?"

His palm smacks one ass cheek, hard, as he says it. I yelp, biting back a whimpered moan as desire explodes over my skin and floods my panties.

Holy shit.

He does the same thing to the other cheek, and this time, I can't stop the moan from tumbling from my lips. Instantly, my face turns red-hot.

This is…new. It's not something I've ever explored before, either with porn or in my imagination. But I like it.

A lot.

"Dante," I mumble, my voice shaking. "I… Let me go—"

"*No.*"

I gasp sharply as his hand spanks me again, sending bolts of fire and lightning exploding through me.

"Because the thing is, my little hurricane," he growls. "I think you *like* being bound like this. I think you *like* having your bratty ass smacked to teach you some fucking manners."

I moan, my fingers clawing at the glass as he spanks me again.

"N-no," I stammer, shaking my head. "No, I don't. So take your hands off me and let me—"

"Let's find out."

I don't even realize he's yanking them down until my panties are at my knees. His hand slides up my inner thigh and then boldly cups my slick, swollen pussy from behind.

Dante chuckles quietly in my ear.

"For someone who doesn't like this, you are *awfully* fucking wet."

My face fills with heat, and my body jerks as his fingertip drags lazily through my lips, spreading my wetness all over my pussy.

"You're coating my fucking hand, you greedy little thing," he growls. "Making a fucking mess of your thighs with your eager, drippy cunt."

I gasp sharply as his teeth graze my earlobe through the bunched gown.

"You *do* like it when I make a mess of you like this."

Shame, desire, and pure heat explodes through me.

He's right.

It's not just the way he's touching me and growling dirty things into my ear. It's the utter loss of control. It's being pinned down with the promise of being used. Which, again, *should* be sending me into a panic attack, or worse.

Instead, I'm so turned on that I'm shaking, and it's taking everything I have not to shamelessly and wantonly beg him to fuck me.

Because I *like* this loss of control. I like how he makes me helpless and at his mercy. And I'm sure that's a red flag for any therapist in the world. But that's another concern for another day.

Right now, all I want is this.

Him, his touch.

My release.

His palm slaps my ass again, making me whimper eagerly. Then he suddenly grabs the gown, yanks it off over my head, and tosses it away. Before I can even move or turn, he grabs my wrists and yanks them behind my back.

"*Grab your ass*, little hurricane," Dante rasps into my ear.

I look up into the mirror, and our eyes lock.

"Spread yourself wide for me."

I watch in real time as my pupils dilate. As my face suffuses red as it presses against the mirror. My hands grip my ass, lewdly spreading myself open as Dante suddenly drops to his knees behind me.

Oh fuck…

The second his tongue touches me, I jolt as if I've been electrocuted. Dante groans into my pussy, pushing his tongue deep as I cry out in pleasure. The mirror fogs with my breath as he drags his tongue up and down my pussy lips, curling it around my clit and sucking as I start to shake.

His hands skim up and down the inside and backs of my thighs, teasing me higher and higher as he tongue-fucks my eager pussy. He drags his tongue up further, and when the tip swirls over my asshole, I choke out a whine of ecstasy.

"Something *else* for me to claim," he growls. "Another tight little hole for me to take for the first time."

My eyes start from my head, my breath becoming ragged as he tongues my ass and then brings his mouth back to my clit. His fingers sink into my pussy, curling against my g-spot as he sucks on my button. My nails dig into my skin, bruising my own ass as I moan wildly against the mirror.

I'm so close. Then, with no warning, Dante suddenly pulls back and stands. I'm about to whine in frustration when I hear the jangle of his belt and the sound of his zipper yanking down. His thick, swollen cock slips between my thighs, his knee pushing my legs wider apart. My eyes hood as the thick head eases between my lips and his hand grasps my hip.

"Keep your hands right where they are," he growls against my neck. *"Don't fucking move."*

Again, this really should be a trigger that sends me spiraling. Instead, it's like detonating a bomb. The second he says it, he rams into me hard. My eyes stare as every inch of his thick cock sinks deep into my slippery heat.

And suddenly, I'm coming. *Hard.*

I cry out, choking against the mirror as Dante thrusts into me. The orgasm explodes through me as he slides out and then back in, fucking me hard and deep. The wet sounds of my pussy clinging to his thick dick fill the room, and the fog of my breath against the mirror clouds my vision as I moan desperately.

Dante grabs my hands away from my ass, pinning them both to the small of my back. His other hand grabs a fistful of my hair, tugging it hard, making my back arch as I scream for more.

He fucks me relentlessly, sending me reeling as his grooved abs smack against my ass over and over.

"Don't stop now, little hurricane," he groans, nipping my ear as I whine for more. He lets go of my wrists to spank my ass as he fucks me. "I want more of that sweet pussy coating my cock. I want your wetness dripping down my balls before I'm done with you."

I cry out as he fucks into me harder, pinning my whole body to the mirror, my panties still around my knees as his

219

gorgeous cock fills me to the hilt. His hand keeps spanking me, and his god-like dick keeps fucking me, until suddenly, everything explodes.

With loud, guttural moan, I shatter for him, screaming my release as my entire body shudders and quivers. Dante groans, ramming his cock deep inside of me as I feel it swell and pulse. His hot cum spills into me, making my vision go blurry as the aftershocks ripple through me.

He stays like that, still pinning me to the mirror. His hand in my hair twists my head around, and before I know it, his mouth is on mine and stealing my very breath away.

I whimper when he slowly pulls out. He reaches down and pulls my panties up tight against my well-fucked pussy. I flush, squirming as I feel his cum dripping out of me and filling them.

Fuck, why is that so hot?

My throat bobs as I try to catch my breath and slow my pulse.

Why was *any* of that so hot?

"I'm excited to see what Ginevra ends up putting together for you."

But before I can form a response, he's grabbed my jaw, pulled me close, and is searing his mouth to mine again.

Then, leaving me blinking and gasping for air, he turns and strides for the door. His hand is already on the knob when I think of what I want to say. Or rather, what I want to ask him, even if I know it's not the appropriate time by a mile.

"Why did you marry her?"

Dante stiffens instantly, his hand still on the doorknob. His head twists slightly.

"Excuse me?"

"Layla. At the hospital that night. You weren't together or anything."

His mouth thins. His eyes narrow.

"Weren't we?"

Something vicious and thorny twists in my chest as I glare back at the man who just fucked me like an animal until I exploded for him.

"No. She'd have told me."

"Maybe."

My brow furrows even deeper.

Asshole.

"I've told you the most private secret I have," I hiss. "The least you can do is tell me why you married my sister on her fucking deathbed!"

The room goes silent. Dante draws in a slow breath.

"No, little hurricane," he finally grunts quietly. "The *least* I can do is leave. Which is what I'm doing. We're done here." He yanks open the door. "Lorenzo will drive you home when you're finished."

"You took a girl you weren't even friends with to the hospital and then *married her* ten fucking minutes before she died from an overdose of a drug she'd never taken before!" I blurt. "And then you threw up the Great Wall of China between you and her whole family and told us jack shit about what the *fuck* happened!"

He pauses halfway out the door, his back to me. Slowly, his head swivels, and those piercing blue eyes bore right into me.

"What we do in the shadows of the past rarely looks the same in the light of the present."

Then he's gone.

20

TEMPEST

A week and a half later, my first "outing" as Dante's wife is not, in fact, the disaster I thought it would be.

It's *twice* the disaster I thought it would be.

In my defense, my mental fog was especially bad that evening. Also, cigar lounges are *gross*, and Dante's three "potential investors" were piggish older douches who were all but straight up asking Dante if investing in Venom directly equaled free sexual favors from "the girls". And that was right in front of their wives, which I'd feel badly about if they weren't just as gross as their husbands.

"I'm not doing that again."

I make a face as I sniff, still smelling the overwhelmingly stinky scent of cigar smoke on my skin.

"Yeah, but, the thing is," Dante mutters, walking past me and flicking on one of the lights in the penthouse living room, "you are."

"No fucking way. That was terrible."

He turns to level a look at me. "Well, it might have helped to be *present* at the table."

There's a chance I snuck off to the bathroom a few times during dinner. Okay, ten times. Not because of any medical issue, I just couldn't stand to sit there pretending I couldn't hear the men's awful conversation while simultaneously pretending I gave a shit about the Kardashians and *The Real Housewives of Duluth* or whatever the hell the wives were talking about.

"I was *there*," I mutter back at him as he shrugs off his jacket. "I never said I'd be the life of the party. And those women were *awful*. One of them sent her entree back three fucking times. I mean tell me that's not just a shitty power play."

Dante frowns. "Who cares if it is?"

"I do! And another of them asked me if I had cocaine on me as casually as if she was asking me the fucking time!" I scowl. "I mean, are you kidding me?"

Dante folds his arms over his chest, leaning against the banister at the bottom of the curved steps that lead up to the second floor.

"Did you?"

I stare at him. "Excuse me?"

"Did you have coke on you?"

"*What*? Why the hell would you think I have cocaine?"

"Gee, I dunno, Tempest," he growls, his brow furrowing and his jaw clenching in a way that is *way* too hot. "Maybe it's the fact that you literally had zero bites of dinner, went to the bathroom a thousand times, and were talking a mile a minute when you did deign to join the conversation."

I glare at him. "I wasn't hungry. The cigar smoke killed my appetite. And I was nervous. I babble when I'm nervous."

"Do you need to see a doctor about your bathroom usage?"

I roll my eyes. "I was *escaping*. Chill."

He shoots me a look before he starts to take off his shirt.

"*Ummm*, what are you doing?" I blurt, my face flushing a little as he shrugs off the white linen, giving me an eyeful of his firm chest, chiseled abs, and those goddamn v-lines delving into the waist of his pants.

"I have to change and then get to Venom for a thing, but I'm showering first." His brow arches, a smirk creeping over his lips. "Care to join me?"

I know it's not a real invitation. He's saying it to ruffle my feathers, to see if I'll pathetically say yes.

And, yeah, if we're being honest, there's a very large part of me that *does* want to say yes to joining Dante in a shower. Because again, I've been given a hit of the dragon now, so to speak, and seen what this man can do sexually. And now almost two weeks later, without him so much as touching me, I'm quite honestly climbing the goddamn walls out of frustration.

But there is no way in *hell* I'm going to be Dante's little "piece" sitting at home waiting to give him his release when he wants it.

I might be dying, but it's not from a complete lack of self-respect.

"I'll pass."

He shrugs. "Suit yourself." He turns and starts to climb the staircase. "Don't wait up, *dear*."

Two HOURS after Dante leaves to go back to Club Venom, at one in the morning, I'm still wide awake in the huge, glass-walled living room when Jeff calls.

They say the past is best left there. But when your past fucked you up as much as mine did, that's easier said than done. I can't just let the past stay there, because those monsters still haunt me, even if two of them are dead now.

I'm know there's more of them out there, but there have always been three that live rent-free in my head, even seven years later. The first—the man who held me down even though I couldn't even move from the drugs I'd been given—is gone.

I've spent the last few years hunting for the other two men—the ones who killed Nina. For justice. For revenge. For *her*.

The day of our wedding, Dante told me one of those two was also dead: the one who held her throat, the one who wore the lion ring on his finger with one blue and one red eye. The ring that now sits in a box in Dante's office, that he called a trophy.

But the last of them is still out there. That's where Jeff comes in.

"Tempest, hi. I hope I'm not waking you."

"Not at all."

Jeff works as an investigator for Crown and Black. He digs shit up for them that they might need for cases. But Jeff *also* has a habit of staring at my tits, a lot, which is how I ended up asking for his help a year ago.

Basically, I pay him a retainer, and he uses his network of informants to keep an ear out for a man with a gold lion ring. It's a long shot, but you never know.

"I think I might have something for you, Tempest."

I go still, sitting bolt upright on the couch.

"Seriously?"

"Yeah. A woman who's done some work for me in the past and owes me some favors works concierge for this super exclusive club."

My brows knit. "And?"

"*And*, I've had her keeping an eye out for your lion ring, and she just texted me to say a rich dude wearing one exactly like you described just walked in."

Holy shit.

"Jeff, that's *amazing*. Thank you! What's the—"

"Don't thank me yet," he grunts. "I just did a drive by to scope it out. It's a dead end."

Fuck. "Why?"

"Because the place is as exclusive as it gets. It's all hush-hush, invite, members only. I've heard of this place, Tempest. It's like one of those Eyes Wide Shut kinky-ass sex clubs."

I blink.

No. Fucking. Way.

"It's called Venom. Club Venom. And listen, I can pull strings, but there's no strings in the city you can pull to get you into that place—"

"She's sure?" I blurt. "This woman you know?"

"She says she's positive."

"Thanks, Jeff."

I hang up and take a deep breath.

Time to hunt monsters.

———

I COULD SAY that the ends justify the means. I could blame the period approaching at the end of my sentence. Still, neither of those makes this okay.

I straighten my black cocktail dress and my mask before I take a deep breath and walk through the unassuming front doors of Club Venom.

It's not my first time here.

It's my *fourth*.

I'm not a member. At least, Tempest Black isn't a member. But I'm not Tempest Black tonight.

I smile as I approach the concierge desk, where a pretty young woman with dark hair—Jeff's contact, I suppose—smiles at me.

"Good evening, ma'am."

"Good evening." I slip the membership card out of my clutch and pass it across the desk to her. She looks at it, then me, teetering in the tallest heels I own, as I tuck a lock of the red wig behind my ear.

She smiles at me. "Welcome back, Ms. Crown. Please, right this way."

To quote Dwight Schrute, "Identity theft is not a joke, Jim". But tonight, same as the last three times I've been here, it's necessary, even if it makes me a terrible friend.

Taylor keeps her Club Venom membership card in her desk at Crown and Black, probably because she never comes here unless it's for a work-related thing, and plus I'll bet she doesn't want anyone in the know to spot it in her wallet or something.

Discovering this is how I was able to start coming here, prowling for monsters. I know Club Venom is not the club-house for the men who attacked Nina and me that night. But it's a place that might *appeal* to men like that: rich, powerful men who don't fear consequences, and might like the sexual dynamics that places like Venom allow its members to enact.

So tonight, same as before, I used Gabriel's code to get into Crown and Black after hours, let myself into Taylor's office, and snagged her membership card from her desk. Then I put on the tallest heels I could to get close to her height, donned a black cocktail dress and a redheaded wig, and took a taxi here.

The last three times were just me aimlessly looking for clues. This time, thanks to Jeff's contact, I've got a solid target.

I just have to find him without anyone realizing I'm a fraud— namely the grumpy jerk who runs this place, that I happen to be married to.

…I'm guessing he would be, shall we say, *less than pleased* to find me here.

I follow the concierge into the next room, past two security guys in black suits with gold and black carnival masks covering the top halves of their faces. My mask is already on, but I still instinctively reach up to make sure it's secure.

Another door opens, and a stunning blonde in essentially nothing but a mask and the world's most see-through golden mesh cocktail dress—with nothing on beneath it—slips into the room, holding a wooden box. She lifts the lid wordlessly, revealing an array of bracelets in gold, green, blue, white, and other colors, accented with gold and black in various combinations.

It's the club's kink signifiers, so that potential playmates can look for a suitable partner. Red, for example, means you're into sadomasochism. Red with black lines across it indicates you're a Dom; gold lines, a submissive.

In my previous visits, I've always chosen white with gold, showing I'm just here as an observer. But tonight, I pick something different: light blue with gold.

It means I'm *open to persuasion*.

"Enjoy your evening, Ms. Crown."

I follow the gorgeous girl in the see-through cocktail dress down a dark hallway with matte-black walls and gold sconces. Sultry club music thuds through the floor as we enter one of the smaller side rooms.

There's no stopping the blush that spreads across my face.

On a small couch, a naked brunette with bronzed skin and gorgeous tattoos running down both arms bounces on the lap of a muscled, even more tattooed man. It's almost impossible not to stare at where they join, her pink pussy stretched around his girth as she rides every impressive inch, her breasts swaying.

Next to them, a dark-skinned girl has her face buried between the thighs of a blonde, making the girl squeal and moan around the thick cock fucking her throat.

Yeah…welcome to Club Venom.

The blonde looks up and catches me watching before I can look away. She grins a sultry smile as she slides her mouth from the man's glistening cock, giving it a cheeky lick before she beckons me to join them with one finger.

My face explodes with heat as I awkwardly look away and quickly bolt after my guide into the main room.

If that appetizer in the first room is enough to make me blush, the main course spread out in the central room of Club Venom is enough to turn me into a puddle. I've seen it before, but holy hell, I don't know how anyone could get used to seeing this without leaving their jaw on the floor.

The scene in front of me can only be described as an orgy.

There are smaller surrounding rooms, like the one I walked through a second ago. And there are private rooms elsewhere in the building. But it's this main room where the true hedonism of Club Venom is on full display.

"Enjoy your night, ma'am."

The guide leaves me with a wink that I barely register, given that I'm staring dumbfounded at the scene in front of me.

The room is done in the same matte-black walls and gilded gold sconces and light fixtures as the hallway, accented with dark red, and has a vibe somewhere between *Eyes Wide Shut* and a 1920's speakeasy. There are two bars along two sides, with gorgeous, scantily clad male and female staff passing trays of champagne and cocktails.

The main focus, without question, is the very center of the room.

Because there, spread out across a couple of couches and a huge bed approximately twice the size of a king, is almost every combination of couples, throuples, and groups you could imagine.

Every hair color. Every skin tone. Every combination of orifice to appendage, and every pitch and tenor of moans and groans. The men's bodies are gorgeous, the women's are stunning, and you can spot the different criminal connections from the different tattoo ink on show: Italian Mafia, Russian Bratva, Japanese Yakuza, and some I don't even recognize.

A slender woman with ginger hair and surgically enhanced breasts chokes out an intense moan of pleasure as two muscled guys with Bratva ink on their chests and arms hold her tight and slowly push their thick cocks into her—one underneath her, sliding up into her pussy, the other crouched over her, feeding his cock up her ass.

It takes *a lot* to keep my jaw from slamming to the floor. I mean, holy *fuck*.

Next to them on another couch, a stunning man with Irish knots tattooed all the way down both arms is fucking the absolute *shit* out of a blonde girl who looks like she's in outer space from the look of bliss in her eyes through her mask. The man groans, pounding into her bare, swollen, pink pussy with one hand wrapped around her throat as the other brutally pinches her nipples. He gives each of her breasts a firm slap, then does the same to her clit as she shrieks in pleasure.

I notice his bracelet is red and black; hers is red and gold.

So their thing is sadomasochism; him a Dom, her a sub.

I'd never admit it to anyone, but I could stand here all night watching the erotic, raw, sensual display in front of me. But I'm not here to watch, squeezing my thighs together as my panties turn to a soaked mess under my cocktail dress.

I'm here to hunt.

So I pull my eyes away from the orgy and start to slowly make my way around the room. I pluck a glass of champagne from a passing waiter, taking a small sip as my gaze drifts over the various male fingers.

For a moment, I think I've spotted what I'm looking for. But it turns out to be brass, not gold. Another ring is gold and chunky, but as I get closer, I realize the man wearing it is in his fifties, which makes him too old to be who I'm looking for. Plus, it's not a lion ring at all.

Fuck.

I'm beginning to think the woman at the front desk was mistaken when I suddenly feel a presence behind me.

"It appears you're looking for something in particular."

Sweet Jesus, no.

It takes everything I have not to whirl around and destroy him with my bare hands right here in front of all of these people, and I physically choke back a gagging sensation.

It's him.

I know even before I turn around, from the slight French accent, and a tone I couldn't forget if I tried.

It's the man who, along with his buddy, killed Nina, not three feet from where a piece of my soul was being ripped out.

I take a shaky breath as I force myself to turn around. I do my best not to, but I still physically wince and recoil a little when I see it: his hand, wrapped around a glass of scotch, with the golden lion's head ring with two blueish-white diamond eyes looking right at me.

"Have you found it yet?"

I blink, nausea rolling over me as I stare at the lion's face.

"Miss? Hello??"

I blink again, flinching. It's like someone's just snapped their fingers to bring me out of a trance. I drag my eyes up to his, steeling myself as I force myself not to gag.

"Not yet," I smile.

The man is a little older, of course, and wearing a mask. But I'd know him anywhere. He grins a toothy smile, his eyes dropping to my cleavage.

"Maybe I can help you find what you seek."

I stiffen as he moves closer to me and he chuckles, tsking with his teeth.

"You don't need to be frightened, *mon petite.*"

My blood turns to ice when his hand wanders over my hip, and I really do almost throw up.

"What is it you're looking for tonight?"

"I...I'm not sure. I—"

"Ah, then maybe you need to be *shown*."

I start to close myself off. I have to. I need to put up walls between my soul—the real "me"—and the rest of my brain.

I fight back the nausea as I reach out and trace one of my fingers over his hand holding the glass.

"I like your ring," I smile.

The man grins. "You like danger, then." His eyes raise curiously to mine, peering at me from behind his matte black and gold mask. "You've seen a ring like this before?"

I'm not sure how to answer. Yes? And risk him cluing into my motives? Or no?

I throw caution to the wind.

"*Yes*," I croak, trying to sound shy.

His lips curl. "Ahh, then you *do* like to have fun."

I lift a shoulder coquettishly. "Maybe." I nod at the ring again. "What does it mean?"

He chuckles, a salacious edge to his laugh. "What do I get if I tell you?"

God, I feel sick. I want to throw up. Or scream. Or snap the stem of my champagne flute and stab him in the eye with it.

"My...gratitude?" I say hopefully, batting my eyes under my mask and flashing a coy grin.

His smile darkens, and for the first time, I notice that he's wearing a red and black band on his wrist.

"And how will you *demonstrate* that gratitude?"

It takes everything I have not to scream right here and now. My blood turns to ice and bile rises in my throat when he touches my wrist and leans close.

"Perhaps we should go somewhere and discuss it in private."

Before I can even answer, he grabs my hand tightly and all but drags me behind him as he marches out of the main room. He hauls me down a dark hallway, a loud, whining sound filling my ears.

I've pictured this scenario a thousand times from the safety of my own bed. I've imagined hunting down the pieces of shit who killed Nina and killing them in ways that would make Quentin Tarantino blush.

But fantasies are one thing. Reality is another. And suddenly, I'm being forced to ask myself: *do I* have it in me to do this?

"Tell me," the man growls as we come to a stop in front of a blood-red door with the black Club Venom emblem of a viper on it. "Will you scream for me?"

My stomach heaves.

"Depends," I manage to choke out in what I hope is a sexy voice. "Will you make me scream?"

His eyes level with mine. "Oh, definitely."

He opens the door, pulling me roughly inside before shutting it behind us.

I've made three other visits to Venom, but this is the first time I've been in one of the opulent private rooms. All matte black, blood red, and gold. No windows. Dark leather furniture, a roaring fireplace taking up an entire wall, a bar, and a huge four-poster bed draped with a red duvet emblazoned with a gold viper.

And a table.

It's laid out with what I can only describe as instruments of *torture.*

Fear rakes its nails down my back and I glance nervously toward the bar.

"Maybe we should have another drink—"

I choke as the man grabs me by the neck and slams me into a wall.

"How about instead you *get on your fucking knees,*" he snarls. "So I—"

"Let me…" it takes everything I have to smile coquettishly at him. "Let me go *freshen up*. Get out of all these clothes?"

"Yes," he purrs. "Yes, go do that. Take it *all* off. I want the full canvas of your skin to mark."

Fuck you, you motherfucker.

I manage one last smile as I slip out from between him and the wall and cross the room toward the ensuite bathroom next to the fireplace. Just before I walk in, my eyes drop to the iron fire-poker sitting in its little stand next to the flickering flames.

The bathroom door is barely shut before I sink against it, shaking.

What the fuck am I doing?

I hug myself, trying to take slow, steadying breaths. But I'm shaking so hard my teeth are chattering.

My mind wanders back to the poker sitting right outside the door.

There's no doubt in my mind that the man out there is one of the two motherfuckers who killed my best friend in the world.

I could do it…

And what the hell do I have to lose? I could walk back out there and smash that fucking predator over the head with the fire poker. Then I could leave, and when Venom discovers the body and *maybe* launches an investigation…yeah, it'll trace back to Taylor, which I feel terrible about. But she'll obviously be able to prove she wasn't here tonight. If they keep looking, it could take months, or years.

And within six months, the killer will be dead anyway.

My pulse skips as I stare at myself in the mirror. I mean I've dreamed and fantasized about avenging Nina a million times from the comfort of my own bed. But now, here, alone with one of her killers in the flesh, I start to wonder if I seriously have this in me.

You can do this.

For Nina.

Except the thing is, if I just run out there swinging a fire poker around, I *might* catch him by surprise. But I have no idea if I could overpower him. And I only get one shot.

I'll have to distract him.

I blanch as I slip off my dress, leaving on my panties and heels. I *hate* that he'll see me like this. But fuck it.

It'll be the last thing he ever sees.

I reach for the doorknob. My chest rises and falls as I set my jaw and my resolve.

Do it for Nina.

I open the door and step out.

…And then stutter to a stop. The room is empty.

He's gone.

"Slight change in plans."

I scream, whirling at the sound of the deep baritone, at the clean scent of linen and spice.

Dante emerges from the shadows by the bathroom door, dressed in a dark suit, a white shirt open at the collar. No mask.

The light from the fireplace flickers in his eyes as they burn right into mine, drinking in my nakedness and my fear. His face is half furious, and half smiling, like he's savoring my panic.

He moves toward me, his lips curling as I scramble back until my ass hits the back of one of the sofas.

"Now, little hurricane," he murmurs. "You're going to tell me *exactly* what the fuck you're doing here, and *exactly* how you got in."

21

DANTE

RAGE. Jealousy. A primal pull to assert dominance over what is *mine*.

The rational part of me, or at least what's left of it, isn't really functioning at the moment. All I can focus on, all I can *see* is Tempest, sauntering basically naked out of the bathroom *looking for another man*.

Not just any man.

I've been tracking Robert Mouret for a year. Usually, he rarely leaves his estate in the English countryside, and he's got a twenty-four-hour personal security detail that watches his every step.

When he popped up on my radar as shopping for penthouses in New York, and then applied for a membership at Venom a few months ago, I started to pay attention.

He only knows me as the charming proprietor of the club. I know him as a *predator*.

Tonight started off badly, when Mr. Mouret cancelled on my dinner invitation, leaving me to entertain the three other couples Tempest and I went out with, none of whom I have any interest in.

However, despite a rocky start, tonight has turned out splendidly. Because while Robert might not have been hungry for cigars and a Michelin starred dinner, he *does* seem to have an appetite for pussy tonight.

Rich and powerful as Mr. Mouret is, being the son of an actual duke and worth north of two billion from his family's mineral mines in South Africa, he's embarrassed about his sexual needs, and to be here at Venom. So tonight, he threw off his own security, giving them the slip and letting them follow a town car he wasn't in all over Manhattan. Meanwhile, he hired a *second* car to bring him here for an evening of acting on his carnal urges.

That was his first mistake.

The bigger one, though, was laying hands on Tempest.

It's a jealousy I wasn't aware I was capable of feeling.

Venom has about eight-hundred current members, and a third of those are here maybe twice a year at most. So it's not as if I recognize *everyone*, but something about the particularly thin, waifish redhead that Robert was talking to tickled my brain.

So I had one of my people walk past them and discreetly scan her wristband to find out who it was. Imagine my surprise when the system told me *Taylor Crown* was having a conversation with Mr. Mouret.

One, I'd literally just spoken to Taylor on the phone an hour previously, from her office. And two, that girl was *not* Taylor

Crown. It wasn't until the redhead happened to look squarely at one of my hidden security cameras that I realized the truth.

Tempest.

Here, pretending to be Taylor and going with *that* mother-fucker to a private room.

The dent in the wall next to my office door will linger as a testament to my wrath.

Meanwhile, Robert's been *relocated* elsewhere. And if I'm being honest, he'll never leave that place. But that is *not* what I'm focused on right now.

Tempest shivers, her eyes fearful behind her mask. Her hands suddenly fly up to cover herself, like she's just remembered that she's virtually naked.

I stop that with a shake of my head.

"*Uh-uh,*" I growl, closing the distance between us and yanking her arm down, revealing her soft breasts with those mouthwateringly pale pink nipples to me.

"You don't get to do that, little hurricane," I growl darkly. "If *he* was going to get to enjoy the view, *I* damn well will."

"Dante—"

"You will not fucking *speak* until I tell you to."

Tempest's nipples tighten to points as she shivers under my fierce gaze.

Furious as this situation has me, the sight of her has me rock fucking hard.

"What were you going to do with him?"

Her eyes widen. "N-nothing, I—"

"Just some light conversation?" I snap coldly. "Maybe call the front desk for a fucking Monopoly board and play a quick game?"

She quails under my wrathful gaze, shrinking against the back of the couch.

"*Nothing.* I wasn't going to *touch* him," she chokes, a sour look on her face.

"No?" I murmur darkly. "Then why the *fuck* are you in a private fucking room with him, dressed. Like. *That.*"

Tempest says nothing, and her eyes narrow behind the mask as her lips purse.

"I'm waiting...*Taylor.*"

The color drains from her face, her greenish-hazel eyes sparking as they lock with mine in the low, sultry light of the room.

Her lips curl into a sneer.

"As someone pointed out earlier, I'm not a prisoner, am I?"

"*Careful*, little hurricane."

"So what I do with my time, and where I spend it, and *with whom,* is none of your business—"

"We are literally standing *in* my business," I snap, surging into her and wrapping my fingers around her throat. Tempest's eyes go wide, and her pulse throbs. Her entire body trembles, and I bite back a groan as I feel the hard pebbles of her nipples against my chest through my shirt.

"In case it's slipped your mind," I growl, "you're my fucking *wife*. So you can drop the bullshit attitude."

Tempest snorts, knocking my hand away from her.

"Oh, is that what I am?!"

My voice is a snarl. *"Careful.* Don't go there. I can only tell you so many times that you made this bed yourself—"

"Dante," she continues, looking triumphant. "I don't have to be careful at all. *You're* the one who needs *me* in order to keep this place."

I chuckle darkly. "That's not the mic drop you think it is. It's not exactly a state secret. What I fucking want right now is an answer from my fucking *wife*. Why the fuck are you pretending to be Taylor and coming back here to private fucking rooms with—"

"I'm not your wife."

Jesus, this woman's *constant* need to sass back. There's a burning desire in me to put her on her knees right now and fill that mouth with something other than her need to have the last word.

"Our marriage certificate suggests otherwise."

"I'm not talking about a piece of paper, Dante," Tempest spits back. "I'm talking *really* being married, the way two people usually are. That isn't us by a fucking mile."

"Why, because I haven't bought you flowers?" I snap. "Are you wanting breakfast in fucking bed?!"

She glares coldly at me.

"Elaborate for me, Tempest. Should we get a fucking dog together? Is there a lack of back rubs in your life?!"

"*Please,*" she laughs coldly, rolling her eyes. "You barely touch me."

The room goes silent. Tempest's back snaps tight, her eyes widening and her face turning pink as the full weight of what she's just said hits her. My lips curl dangerously as I move closer to her. She shivers, her breath hitching as I reach up and take her jaw, tilting her face up to mine.

"Is *that* what this is about?"

"Get away from me—"

She whimpers as I hook two fingers from my other hand into the front waist of her lacy black panties, pulling them toward me.

"Is that it, Tempest?" I growl quietly. I lower my mouth to hers, darting to the side at the last second and relishing the way she bites her bottom lip as I hover by her ear. "Do you just need to get *fucked*?"

A soft whimper half escapes her mouth before she tries to bite it back. Her body trembles under my touch, and I grit my teeth.

'Is that what you wanted from *him*?"

"Why?" she sneers quietly, pulling her face back and levelling her eyes with mine. "*Jealous*, Dante?"

I chuckle darkly. "*No*, little hurricane," I murmur. "Not jealous."

She moans as I suddenly grab a fistful of her hair and tug, forcing her face to look up at mine at the exact moment my hand slips into her panties. My fingers sink between her slick, velvety lips, and curl deep in her hot, messy little cunt.

"*In charge*," I rasp into her ear. "You're in *my house* here, and you'll play by the house rules, because they're *my fucking rules*. And I'll have your obedience, *wife*—either standing proud and tall, or on your knees, or over mine."

She shivers, her breath coming ragged as I roughly thrust my two fingers in and out of her eager little pussy. Her slickness coats my hand, the wet squelching sounds music to my ears as I bite down hard on her earlobe.

"In this case, Tempest," I growl. "I'm going to make the choice for you. And since you can't seem to stop with that fucking *mouth* of yours, I'm going to have to fill it with something."

Her legs start to shake as I finger her faster and grind my palm harder against her throbbing clit.

"So get on your fucking *knees*, baby girl," I murmur. "And then look up, open those pretty lips, and say *please*, unless you want me to spank your ass until you can't sit for a fucking week. Are. We. Clear?"

She whimpers, panting and trembling as I finger her pussy toward release. I slide my other hand down her back, hooking a finger under the tiny little triangle of lace at the back of her thong and letting it slide down between the tight globes of her ass. Tempest stiffens, her breath catching. When she moans as my fingers tease over her tight little puckered hole, I groan to myself.

"Answer me, little hurricane."

There's no way she can. Her eyes roll back in her head and her mouth falls open as I start to swirl my fingertip around her asshole as my two other fingers curl deep against her g-spot. My palm rubs against her throbbing clit, and my cock swells to iron as I feel her body quiver and tense.

"Are you going to be a good girl for me?"

A raw, broken moan rips from her throat.

"Please…" she chokes.

"That's a good rehearsal. But for the actual performance, you'll be on your knees with your pretty lips wrapped around my dick when you say your line. Now, stop trying to fight it and come on my fucking fingers like the greedy little girl you are."

My finger sinks into her ass just as I stroke against her g-spot and grind her clit mercilessly. With a cry, Tempest suddenly grips my wrist, her nails digging into me. A moan rips from her lips as she drops her head back, her body twisting and shuddering, her legs almost buckling as she sags against me.

My hand slips into her hair, tangling it in a fist. I let her down slowly, her shaky legs giving way as she drops to her knees, looking up at me with fire in her eyes.

"You want to play husband and wife, little hurricane?" I growl darkly, undoing my belt. "Start by showing me what a good little wife you can be."

22

TEMPEST

THE SPARK EXPLODES through my body when he opens his pants and pulls out his cock.

Holy. *Fuck*.

I mean, I've seen him before. And I've certainly *felt* him. But somehow, being on my knees, in the opulent private room, with the lights low and the flames flickering in the firelight, it's something different. When Dante pulls his swollen dick out of his pants, my jaw almost hits the carpet right next to my knees.

The man is *huge*.

Muscled abs lead to the hard grooves of his hips and those "V" lines that point directly down to his thick shaft. His cock hangs heavy and swollen between his legs—already massive but clearly not even fully hard yet. I swallow and my eyes lock on the clear drop of precum at the thick head.

Dante reaches down, slips the mask from my face, and lets it drop behind me.

"I thought wearing it was in the rules—" I whisper hoarsely, my pulse racing.

"Yes, because you're *so* concerned with rules," he murmurs, pulling the wig off and tossing that aside too as my dark hair tumbles free. My skin throbs when he grabs my jaw and tilts my eyes up to his. "Well?"

Fuck.

It's like the other day at Ginevra's shop all over again: the loss of control, being helpless and at his mercy. Being dominated by him and being so eager to be used by him.

All of this should send me spiraling. But when Dante looks at me like this, and talks to me like this, and *touches* me like this, I don't get shoved back into that black place in my mind I went all those years ago.

I get freed from it.

The growl in his tone, the possessive way he grabs me and wrestles all control from me, is one of the biggest reasons I've been craving sex with him since that first time. It's the release and the mind-blowing orgasms, too. But it also runs deeper than that.

He's not just freeing my dopamine and inhibitions. He's freeing my past from the claws that hold it there.

So when he lifts my chin and locks his eyes with mine and says "Well?", I know exactly what he means, and it sends a zap of desire exploding through my core.

"So get on your fucking knees and say please..."

"Please," I whimper in a choked voice, looking up at him.

"Please, *what.*"

Desire pools between my thighs.

"Please let me suck your cock!"

Fuck me. Saying it gets me even more turned on. I can feel the heat and the slickness coating my thighs as his cock thickens right in front of my face. I reach for him, shivering when my fingers curl around his shaft. It feels like silk covering steel, and my skin tingles as I stroke him.

I lean in and swipe my tongue over the swollen head, tasting his salty sweetness.

"Open your mouth, little hurricane," he groans. "Take me deep. Let me feel your tongue and your lips on me. Let me feel your fucking *throat* wrap around my dick."

I moan as I suck him into my mouth, my lips slipping wetly over the ridge of his crown. My tongue dances over the tip, teasing the little hole as he groans and clenches his jaw. When I swallow him a little deeper, his hand slips into my hair and wraps a handful of it in his fist.

"I'm going to fuck your mouth now."

Fuck.

It's so crude, so dirty, so…I don't know, *porn-ish*…that, again, it feels like it should repulse me. I shouldn't *want* him or anyone to use me like a sex toy of some kind.

So why *do* I?

"Wider, baby girl."

I moan as I open my jaw and he thrusts into my mouth. His hips rock, his abs rippling as he starts to fuck in and out of my lips, over my tongue.

I look up at him, feeling so slutty but so fucking turned on, kneeling in front of him with my hair in his fist and his cock pushing into my throat. Dante uses his other hand to yank off his jacket and then unbutton his shirt. He shrugs it off, his chiseled body etched in the flickering shadows from the fireplace as his eyes lock with mine.

He groans, pushing himself the deepest down my throat he's been yet. I almost gag, but right before I do, he pulls out, leaving me gasping and panting, spit and precum dripping down my chin and onto my breasts.

I gasp when he pulls me to my feet, effortlessly lifting me. A squeal escapes my lips as my legs wrap around his torso, his hands cupping my ass as he carries me across the room. My pulse skips when he drops me onto the bed draped with the red duvet emblazoned with the gold viper.

Dante crawls onto the bed and looms over me, his eyes blazing.

"My turn."

His lips crush to mine, stealing the breath from my lungs as his tongue invades my mouth. The idea dimly echoes in my mind that no guy ever wants to kiss you after you've had their dick in your mouth, especially if you've got precum all over your lips.

But apparently, Dante never got that memo. He kisses me with all the force of an invading army. Of a conquering king taking his birthright.

His mouth slips from mine, his teeth nipping my bottom lip for a moment before releasing it. I tremble, sucking in a shaky breath as his lips tease down my neck to my collarbone. He bites, making me yelp as his hands skim down my sides to slip beneath my ass.

I moan, arching my back as his mouth sucks, bites, and mauls its way down my chest until he captures a nipple between his lips.

I've always been self-conscious about my nipples. I mean, I'm not very big on top, which I've made peace with. But my nipples are this super pale light pink that almost blend in with my skin, making them ghostly in appearance.

"I...they..." I swallow thickly, trying to find the right words. "I thought about having them surgically colored once, but—"

I yelp when he bites down on my nipple, sucking until something electric and toe-curling zaps right into my core. My thighs clench, and my back arches as I cry out.

"There isn't a single fucking inch of your body I don't want to devour, exactly how it is," Dante growls, his eyes on mine as he moves his mouth to the other breast. I'm prepared this time, or at least, I should be. But I still convulse and jolt with pleasure when that same zap buzzes through me again.

His mouth drops lower, teasing and licking down my stomach as it caves under his tongue. His big, powerful hands grab my thighs, shoving them wide apart and pushing my knees up to my chest.

"Oh FUCK..."

His tongue drags slowly through my lips, spreading them open like petals before bumping over my throbbing clit.

I've seriously never been this turned on before. I've never been this *eager* and desperate for release before. And it's almost like he knows it, because the fucking man *takes. His. Time.*

I couldn't tell you how long I lie there writhing on the bed as Dante devours my pussy, my thighs, my hipbones, and my ass. The tip of his tongue traces all over me, his fingers making my skin come alive as they tease as well.

He licks slowly, then fast—lightly toying with me before sucking my clit between his lips and punishing it with his tongue and teeth until I'm screaming and my hips are rocking off the bed.

I'm teetering on the edge of release when he drags his tongue slowly through my lips and then over my clit. He keeps going, dragging higher over my quivering stomach, then up to my sternum. His shoulder muscles bunch and coil as he slides up between my legs, his lips teasing one nipple and then the other.

I feel his swollen cock notch against my opening as he drags his tongue up my neck before leaving it hovering an inch from my lips.

Time stops for an instant.

Then, in one motion, he slams his mouth to mine and buries his cock deep in my pussy. I moan into his lips, my arms and legs wrapping around his hips. I can taste myself on his tongue as it invades my mouth, my nails dragging down his muscled back as he slams into me.

Dante pins my wrists above my head. His body ripples and thrusts as he fucks into me, his eyes locked on mine.

"Is this why you really came here tonight, little hurricane?" he rasps darkly as starts to fuck me even harder. "Did my wife just need to get *fucked* like a greedy little slut?"

Something primal rips from my throat as I whine in pleasure, panting and shivering, my hips rising to meet his thrusts.

"*N-no*, I—"

My eyes roll back as he pounds hard into me.

"Your pussy gets even tighter when you lie to me, baby girl."

He suddenly pulls out and flips me over like a rag doll. His hands keep mine pinned over my head as his cock slips between my thighs, his own on either side of them. We both moan when he sinks in, the pressure of his knees on the outsides of my thighs making me even tighter as he squeezes his dick into my dripping wet pussy.

"Tell me again how you haven't been soaking your little panties all night, hoping to get *fucked* like this. Hoping to be pinned down like a whore and used like my personal little fuck toy. Like my greedy, needy, submissive little cock slave."

His words are unbelievably crude, and dirty, and fucked up almost to the point of being demeaning. I fucking love it. I want more.

It's making me want to come, hard.

"Squeeze my cock, little hurricane," Dante groans, his teeth biting the lobe of my ear. He spanks my ass, making me squeal as my pussy clenches tight around his huge dick. "Squeeze me with that pretty little pussy and milk every single drop of cum out of my balls."

His rock-hard, god-like body pins mine to the bed. I can feel his muscles rippling against my back as he holds my hands down, spanks my ass until it's red, grabs another fist of my hair, and starts to pound me into the bed.

It's hard, and rough, and merciless.

I'm going to come.

So fucking hard.

And *right fucking now.*

"Dante…"

"Come for me, Tempest," he growls into my ear, sucking on the lobe. "Come all over my dick, *wife.*"

All I know is white-hot light. I go blind from it, gasping for air and writhing as my body spasms and wrenches. The orgasm explodes through my core, my feet kicking and my toes curling against the duvet as Dante fucks me into the bed.

His cock throbs as his cum spills into me. Then he's pulling out, and I moan as I feel him stroke against my ass, spraying more cum all over my skin, hot and sticky as it drips over my swollen, well-fucked pussy. Dante groans as he eases back into me, using his own cum for lubricant as he starts to fuck into me again.

His palm spanks my ass, and my eyes roll back as his rock-hard cock and its swollen head hit a certain spot deep inside me over and over and over.

And suddenly, I'm coming again.

I come so hard I see stars, and my entire body eventually goes limp on the bed.

Dante slowly slides out and gently rolls me onto my back. My chest is rising and falling with my breath as I look down in shock when he slips between my legs. He lowers his mouth, his eyes locked on mine as his tongue drags through my tender folds.

Oh FUCK, is that hot.

He's just come in me, and on me, but he *clearly doesn't care* as he tongues my clit and swollen pussy until I'm buzzing all over.

He slides up, and I moan when I taste his cum as his tongue swirls with mine.

"*Holy shit...*" I murmur, shaking and dazed as he pulls back.

"Proud of yourself for sneaking in, little hurricane?"

I grin a lazy smile up at him. "Maybe a little. Glad I did, that's for sure," I giggle.

He smirks. "Good." I gasp when he suddenly flips me over and gives me a hard swat on my tender ass. "Because this is the last fucking time you'll ever come here."

I grin as I roll over to face him. "We'll see about that."

Dante's brow cocks with a warning look. "That *constant* need to test me..." he growls darkly. "It's going to get you in fucking trouble."

"Is that a promise?"

Spoiler: it totally is.

23

DANTE

WHAT THE FUCK is wrong with me?

It's close to four-thirty in the morning, and I'm sitting on the edge of Tempest's bed, in her room, watching her sleep.

It gets worse.

After fucking each other's brains out at Venom, Tempest crashed hard in the private room. I took her home, and I've just tucked her in. Now I'm just watching her sleep, and *I can't seem to stop.*

I push a lock of hair out of her face, and my jaw sets.

This wasn't supposed to get this deep. This big.

This...*real.*

It can't. Not just because our worlds are not compatible, but also, and worse...

...she comes with an expiration date.

I don't get to keep her, no matter how much I want to. And all the rage and fury at the injustice of that isn't something I'm prepared to deal with.

So instead, I stand, and go deal with something else. Something that I *have* been prepared for, for a long, long time...

"THANKS FOR THIS."

Carmine shrugs casually as we descend into the sub-basement of a restaurant in the Meatpacking District that he owns. Beneath the basement prep-kitchen, the walk-in, and the kegs of beer, this last staircase takes us deeper and darker into the bowels of the building, to a place from which most of its visitors don't return.

I've been down here with Carmy before. Mostly only as an observer. But one of the trophy rings I have in the box in my office came from a night down here much like tonight.

"Hey, no worries, brother," Carmine grins when we reach the bottom of the metal stairs. "I mean, I haven't gotten you a wedding gift yet, so..." He chuckles darkly. "You're welcome."

"I'll take this over matching china or a toaster oven any day."

He grins. "What we do for the women we care about, huh?" Then he turns to arch a brow at me as he hands me the key to the padlock. "You want a hand?"

"No," I shake my head. "No, this is mine."

"Well, restaurant's closed today, so no prep crew coming in. Take your time."

I nod.

"I plan on it."

When Carmine disappears back up the staircase, I insert the key into the padlock. The heavy door of the refrigerated room that was probably once used to butcher and cure meat swings open noisily on old, rusty hinges.

My eyes land on the blindfolded man inside as he lifts his chin from his blood and sweat-soaked shirt, moaning pitifully.

"Hello, Mr. Mouret."

The man screams through the gag in his mouth, thrashing at the chains and ropes binding him to the metal chair bolted to the floor.

Good. *Let* him try to get free. Let him taste hope and think even for a second that maybe—*maybe*—he'll be spared. Let him get one tiny inkling of the horrors the girls he's hurt felt, wondering if perhaps they'd be let go.

I step into the room and close the door behind me. Then I yank the filthy gag out of his mouth.

"PLEASE!" he blurts, abject fear lacing his tone.

It's always like this with predators like him. They prey on the weak and helpless. They use money, power, alcohol, and drugs to reel in their victims and render them incapable of fighting back before they dig their fangs in.

Put those same fuckers face-to-face with someone who actually *can* fight back, and they crumble like the pathetic pieces of shit they are.

Every. Single. Time.

There was a time, back when I first started this dark crusade, that I worried what it said about myself. Before that first taste of vengeance, I was afraid that maybe this was a symptom of something far worse, far darker. That maybe I was insane, or psychotic, or a killer my whole life, and was just now realizing it.

But then I slit that first throat, the one belonging to the man who killed my sister with a nine-iron golf club to her head after drugging and raping her.

And after that, it became clear. I'm not psychotic. I don't seek out murder and I don't rejoice at ending a life.

But I will put animals like this piece of shit down *all day every day* if it means stopping them from doing to someone else what they did to Claudia.

Reaching out, I yank off the blindfold.

I want him to see it all.

He blinks under the glare of the single overhead bulb, and when his bleary eyes focus on me, they go wide.

"*Mr. Sartorre?!*"

I don't say a word as I reach into my jacket and pull out the twelve-inch blade of folded Japanese steel.

"*Non*! *NON!*" Robert screeches, squirming and yanking against binds. "Please! Whatever you want, it's yours, *oui?!* Money?! I have lots of—"

"*That.*"

He goes quiet at my response. I use the tip of the knife to point at his finger.

"I don't want your money, Mr. Mouret. I have plenty of my own, thanks. But I'll take that ring."

He blinks, panting as sweat drips down his face. His eyes drop to his hand, then yank back up to me.

"Yes!" he screams, nodding frantically. "Yes! Yes, of course! Please! It's yours!"

I smile widely.

"That's *very* kind of you, Mr. Mouret."

The wet CHUNK sound fills the room. Robert blinks, staring at his hand for a full two seconds before his brain realizes that I've just lopped off his fucking finger.

Then he starts to scream, and bawl, and plead for mercy. I ignore him as I pluck the finger off the floor, slip the ring off, and drop the digit back to the ground.

"How many more are there, Mr. Mouret."

He's still sobbing and shrieking, staring at his bloody hand.

So, naturally, I punch him in the face.

I mean, I'm trying have a conversation here. The shrieking is just plain rude.

"Stay with me, Mr. Mouret," I say flatly. "We're just getting started. How many *more* fuck-faces with these fuck-face rings are there."

"W-w-wha—!"

He's hyperventilating, so I punch him again to center him.

"How. Fucking. Many."

"I—I don't know what you're t-talking about!"

261

I roll my eyes. "I know all about your little club, fucker. Apex. The lion rings. Your penchant for drugging and raping young women."

Whatever color. was left in his face drains as he realizes A, I'm not fucking around, B, I'm not here to rob him, and C, we're barely scratching the surface of what I'm capable of doing to him.

"Surely you've noticed a few of your rapey pals missing from recent nights out?"

His eyes widen. *"You—"* He chokes and flinches, a scream gurgling in his throat as I bring the point of my knife against his cheek, just beneath his eye.

"I'm going to hunt you all down, Mr. Mouret," I say in a bored tone. "Every single one of you. I'd just like to know how many more times I'll be coming down here to cut one of you into pieces. I'm a busy man. I'm sure you understand."

This time, when he starts to sob and beg and piss himself and lose his shit, there's no bringing him back. I punch him a few more times just to try, but it's useless.

I push the tip of the knife against his side, between the costal cartilage of his eighth and ninth ribs. Robert stiffens as he goes white.

"Well?"

He's crying as he shakes his head. "It's just a few friends, j-just…having fun."

I push the tip into him, sinking the blade into his blubbery side. He screams bloody murder, coughing and sputtering like he's going to puke.

"You were saying?"

"*Seven!*" He chokes. "There are—*were*—seven of us! We were in the same fraternity and then business school. It was—"

He screams when I twist the knife again.

Seven. I've taken five. He's six.

Only one more.

Robert drags in a ragged breath as I slip the knife out of his side. Blood soaks his shirt.

"You like to penetrate people who don't want to be penetrated, Mr. Mouret."

This time, I press the lethal, razor-sharp tip of the knife against his belly.

"Allow me to demonstrate what that feels like."

Two hours later, he's short five more fingers, two toes, his tongue, and *obviously*, his dick and his balls.

Eventually, his life.

I know his screams of misery won't bring Claudia back. But somewhere up there, I hope she enjoys the show.

24

TEMPEST

My first outing as Mrs. Sartorre may have been a bit of a disaster. But again, I'm choosing to blame the disgusting cigar bar, not to mention dinner with the Mafia versions of the Stepford wives for that one.

It's going to be tough to blame the setting the second time around, though, considering that the venue tonight is the stunning Metropolitan Museum of Art.

I mean, I've been to some pretty swanky parties and galas thrown by Crown and Black over the years. But when Dante pulls the black Mercedes G-Wagon up to the front of the museum, my jaw drops when I stare out through the tinted windows.

Holy. Shit.

The event tonight is a fundraising gala for the New York City Fallen Firemen's Fund, a group that helps the families of firemen killed in the line of duty receive benefits and financial support. But you'd swear we'd just pulled up to the Oscars.

Paparazzi cameras flash. There's a red carpet. Limos full of minor celebrities, the mayor, and more. Dante opens my door and helps me out, even catching me when a photographer who probably thinks I'm someone important blinds me with their camera.

Inside, he arches a brow at my hesitation when we stop by the coat check. The implication isn't lost on me.

At that awful dinner, I kept my coat on for most of the meal. One, because it had been spared the stench of smoke, since it was coat-checked at the cigar bar. And two, because one of the Mafia Stepford wives—the one who asked me if I had cocaine—made a comment about my "perky little titties" when we were leaving the cigar bar. She even made a comment to her gross husband about it, who then made a point of staring at my chest for the rest of the evening.

So, yeah, I'm keeping the coat on this time.

"What?" I shrug at Dante. "I'm cold."

"Lose. The. Jacket."

"Why? Trying to show me off? Using me as bait to lure in—"

"No, you just look fucking *beautiful*, and I think you should embrace that for once."

We both stiffen the second he says it. My cheeks flush, and a tingle zaps through my core.

"I mean...the dress looks beautiful, on you," he grunts, frowning. "Ginevra does amazing work."

"That she does," I say distractedly, looking down at the gorgeous black and gold strapless number she made for me that feels very vintage Audrey Hepburn. The dress arrived complete with black heels, thigh-highs, and matching lacy black lingerie that's about one thousand times sexier than any underwear I've ever owned.

"Did Genevra pick the heels, too?"

He nods. "She does it all."

"Well, she's got fantastic taste in lingerie."

"That part was me."

My eyes lift back up, faltering before they even get to Dante's when they lock onto his lips.

…His perfect, masculine and yet supremely sensual lips.

Okay, we seriously need to stop doing what we did last night at Club Venom. And then again, against the inside of the front door of his penthouse the second we got home.

Or…*do we?*

It's something I've been wrestling with. A huge part of me feels like we're not supposed to be crossing this line physically. But I mean, the clock is ticking for me, and there are worse ways to spend the last few months of your life than screwing a man with divine, God-like dick that he knows how to use.

Like, even if the relationship and the marriage are pretend, the orgasms are totally fucking real.

But now, the way he's looking at me, and the tingle that creeps through my chest when he calls me beautiful…I don't know. It does feel like crossing a line we're not supposed to cross. I think we both realize that.

Hence him downplaying it immediately afterward.

I tremble when I let Dante take my coat and give it to the attendant. Then I shiver again when he slips his arm through mine and leads me into the gala itself.

It's not from the cold.

I spot the mayor, and a late-night TV host who's here with his B-list actress girlfriend. I also see two stars from the Knicks, the point guard from the Nets, and a Yankees pitcher. Also in attendance are celebrities of a far more notorious kind: Gavan Tsarenko, co-head of the Reznikov Bratva, along with his wife, Eilish, of the Kildare Irish mafia family. They're in a group mingling with Eilish's older sister, Neve, and her husband, Ares Drakos, head of the Drakos Greek mafia family.

I clear my throat, ignoring the tingle on my skin where Dante's arm is touching mine.

"So, who exactly are we here to charm tonight?"

"As many people as possible."

My brow furrows. "Is Venom that hard-up for money?"

He turns to smirk at me. "Hardly. You've seen the homes I own. Tonight is not just about the club."

My brow arches as he sweeps me onto the dance floor. "What else is it about, then?"

Dante just cocks his brow a little, his mouth pointedly closed.

I roll my eyes. "Oh, come *on*. Who am I going to tell?" I tap a finger against my temple. "This is a steel trap." I grin wryly. "Actually, it's a steel trap with a self-destruct button. Even better!"

He frowns.

I sigh, shrugging. "Gallows humor, remember?"

"I'm not sure I'm a fan."

"Well, get on board."

He shoots me a funny sort of dark look, but then shrugs it off. "I mean it's not just about money or new investors. Venom also trades in favors, influence, information."

I smirk. "You mean *you* trade in favors, influence, and information."

"Well." He flashes a grin. "I *am* Venom."

"And here I was thinking I'd have to spend the whole evening suffering bad dick jokes from your brothers."

Both of us turn to the deep baritone voice. I blink, looking up at an insanely handsome man who towers over even Dante. He grins a gleaming, shark-like smile as he shakes Dante's hand firmly.

"Good to see you, my friend," the man purrs in an Eastern European accent before turning his piercing gaze to me. He fixes me with a hunter's smile as he takes my hand in his. I blush when he raises it, as if to kiss it. "And you must be—"

"*My wife.*" Dante plucks my hand away forcefully from the other man, even if he's still smiling. "Tempest."

The other man chuckles and claps Dante on the back. "Indeed." He turns to smile a much less wolfish grin at me, this time *not* reaching for my hand. "A pleasure to meet you, Ms. Black. Or is it Mrs. Sartorre?"

"Ms. Black," I say.

"Mrs. Sartorre," Dante says at the exact same time.

"Tempest," Dante grunts. "This is Drazen Krylov, head of the Krylov Bratva, and a recently new resident of New York."

I flash back to that luncheon, when the ladies I was sitting with were gabbing about the new-to-New-York Russian-Serbian Bratva kingpin whom they described as "God's gift to the female gaze." I gotta say…

They weren't exactly wrong.

"Nice to meet you," I smile, ignoring the granite look in Dante's eyes as I reach out to shake Drazen's hand.

Then I twist my gaze to Dante, frowning. "Wait, you have brothers?"

He makes a face. "*No*. I have two idiots who at times feel like brothers. But they're not blood relatives. Carmine and Nico Barone, Don Vito's sons."

I remember Gabriel telling me about Dante's background weeks ago, how he and his sisters lost their parents young and were basically raised by Vito Barone, for whom their father worked as his personal tailor. I guess we've never really had an in-depth talk about our families and all that.

Or even a *not* so in-depth talk on the subject.

…Which is weird, considering we're, A, married. B, sleeping together. And C, standing like a couple at a fancy gala with his hand firmly on the small of my back.

Dante's brow furrows. "I didn't realize Carmy and Nico had secured invitations to the event tonight."

Drazen smiles coolly. "I believe their invitations involve the back service entrance and dodging security." He looks past us momentarily, and his smile fades. "My apologies. I suddenly have to be elsewhere."

Dante looks intrigued. "Why is that?"

"Because I *loathe* Renata Bonpensiero and she's walking right this way." He turns and bows crisply to me in his even crisper tux. "Again, a pleasure to meet you, *Mrs. Sartorre.*"

"*It's Ms. Black,*" I mutter at his back just as Dante turns us around. Sure enough, here comes the miserable hag herself.

Renata comes to a halt in front of us, shooting me a sour look before she smiles imperiously at Dante. She offers her hand for him to kiss it.

Dante pointedly ignores it.

"*Renata,*" he grunts with all the warmth of a coal mine. "How are things?"

"Just lovely, Dante," she responds in an equally chilly voice. "How's the *brothel* business?"

"I wouldn't know. What can I do for you?"

Her lips purse. "Your *wife*, if we're even calling her that—"

"We are."

She grits her teeth at the interruption. I bite back a grin.

"*Well*, not only did she assault my son—"

"Allegedly."

A vein pops out on Renata's forehead. "She admitted it!"

"I don't think I did any such thing," I shrug.

She shoots a cold glare at me. "*Not only* did she injure my dear Silvio," she barrels on, still looking at me while addressing Dante, "but this little gold-digging whore—"

"Don't *ever* speak of my wife like that again." Dante's growl is quiet but carries all the lethal sharpness of a samurai blade.

Renata huffs. "The things this little bitch said to me—!"

"—Were, I am sure, well deserved," he snaps back. "And I already told you once not to speak to her like that. I won't say it again."

Her face goes purple.

"Before you say whatever you're *dying* to say next," Dante murmurs, leaning closer to Renata and dropping his voice. "We both know the *side business* your husband is involved in, don't we?"

Her face pales so fast it's as if he's flipped a switch.

"I—I don't know what you're implying…"

"I'm *implying* that your husband has been selling arms on the side to the Croatians, not to mention taking kickbacks from Kratos Drakos not to bid on certain construction projects that your family might otherwise have bid on."

Renata looks like she might throw up. "I—that's…those are both *grossly* untrue—"

"Maybe we should see what your uncle, Don Amato, has to say." Dante finishes smoothly. "I'm sure he could sort out fact from fiction quite easily."

Her eyes go wide and her mouth flaps open and closed for another few seconds like a fish on land. Then without another word, she spins and scurries away, shoving her way through the crowd.

I don't realize I'm grinning widely until I turn to shake my head at Dante.

"What was that about?"

He shrugs. "You weren't wrong. Renata *is* a cunt."

My lips split into a grin. "Well, thank you—"

In one motion, he pulls me close, cups my cheek gently in his powerful hand, and sears his lips to mine.

Leaving. Me. *Floating.*

A camera flashes right next to us, startling me back to reality. I flinch, but Dante holds the kiss for another half second before letting me go. We both turn, and he smiles at the professional event photographer before she wanders off to shoot more attendees.

"Image is everything," Dante murmurs quietly.

"Yeah, no, of course…" I smile weakly. "Image. All these people and everything."

We stand another second or two in silence before I blush and clear my throat. "*I* am going to go find the bar."

Dante gives me a quiet smile. "And I, unfortunately," he nods with his chin to a group of old men who nod back and raises their glasses to us, "have to go talk to creepy old Italian men who've spent more time in brothels and basement gambling dens than in their own bedrooms."

"Well, you should be right at home."

He arches a sarcastic, stern brow at me as I grin at him. "My my, Mrs. Sartorre—"

"Yeah, no, it's still Ms. Black."

"You should pay more attention to legal documents you sign at wedding altars, *dear*."

I grin as I roll my eyes. "Which—oopsie—I never mailed in. So, you know, checkmate."

"That's an oversight we'll have to correct quickly."

"I don't think so."

We both pause, both of us grinning.

Jesus Christ, am I FLIRTING with him?

Yeah, I am.

It feels pretty good.

"Enjoy your creepy old men."

"Enjoy your cocktail."

I'm grinning from ear to ear and floating as I make my way to the bar. I daresay, I might have a little crush on my husband.

I order a glass of white wine, and I've just taken a sip when a young woman slips out of the crowd and stops right in front of me.

"Oh my God—Tempest?"

My brows tighten. "Yes?"

Shit, I have no idea who this brunette is. She looks to be a couple of years older than me.

"Oh, we've never met, don't worry!" She smiles as she thrusts out a hand. "I'm Michelle. I knew your brothers at Knights-blood. I was in Para Bellum with Gabriel." Her smile fades. "I...I was actually friends with your sister, too."

My mind flashes back for a second to my conversation with Alistair the other day about Dante's involvement with that. I glance around looking for him, but I can't see him in the crowd. I shake those thoughts away as I smile back at Michelle.

"Nice to meet you!" I shake her hand.

"I was going to ask you if I could buy you a drink, but..." She nods at the full glass of wine in my hand. Then she grins mischievously at me, reaches into her cleavage, and pulls out a joint.

"Would you...." She waggles her brows. "Care to join me?"

"Thanks, but no," I smile and shake my head. "It's just not my thing."

"No worries," Michelle shrugs.

I glance over my shoulder, looking for Dante again as the dark, intrusive thoughts involving my sister start to filter back in.

He was there the night she died. The night she overdosed on a drug she'd never taken before.

And Dante married her, sealed her medical records, and stonewalled our family.

I swallow weakly as I smile at Michelle. "You know what? I won't have any, but if you're going outside...I could use some air."

She grins. "Awesome! Come on, I know a spot."

She leads me out of the crowded main hall of MOMA and down a side hallway. There's a security guard at the end of it, but he seems to know her, and waves us through with a knowing wink.

Part of me is beyond *shocked* that I'm following a literal stranger someplace random where she's going to smoke weed. But Michelle seems nice, and she does know my brothers.

We round a corner and get to a big glass door that leads out to a dimly lit, beautifully landscaped little courtyard. Michelle slips the joint between her lips as she holds the door open for me.

"It's a little chilly, sorry," she mumbles as I step out.

I laugh lightly. "We'll see how long I last—"

I turn to see her suddenly yanking the door shut and hear the click of a lock turning: her still inside, me outside in the cold.

"What are you doing?!"

My heart climbs into my throat as Michelle leers at me and lights the joint, slowly taking a puff and exhaling a thin stream of smoke against the glass toward my face.

What the fuck?

My mouth opens as if to voice that very question out loud, when a man's voice breaks the silence from behind me.

"Don't mind Michelle."

I gasp, whirling to see Renata's son Silvio Bonpensiero. My face pales as he shuffles out of the shadows. Bandages still cover one side of his face.

"My older sister is a tiny bit overprotective of me," he grins darkly, moving toward me. I try to move backward, but I'm stopped by the cold glass of the door.

"Funny, she doesn't like it when people smash fucking *cocktail glasses* over my head," Silvio growls, his face contorting with rage. "And *neither. Do. I...*"

25

DANTE

"You're going soft in your old age, Dante," Carmine sighs, taking a sip of his scotch.

Nico snorts as I give them both a sour look.

"The fucking *mayor* is here, in case you two geniuses missed that," I growl.

"And?"

"And typically, leaders of major cities come with a massive security presence, the members of which tend to frown on gala attendees *without* invitations. Especially when said attendees happen to share a last name with a fairly well-known mafia don."

Nico grins at me and then glances at his brother. "Yep, nailed it. Dante's going soft."

I roll my eyes. "Fine, just don't come crying to me when the NYPD throws you out on your asses."

He grins. "I mean, Dante, I know you're a married man now and everything, but will you open your eyes and look around? Have you *seen* the women here? We needed in!"

I smirk, shaking my head. "You do understand, dipshit, that the single women at a *firemen's* gala are typically looking for —wait for it—*firemen*, right?"

Nico sighs and glances at Carmy again. "As if we said a thing about the *single* women. Absolutely going soft in his old age. Or maybe it's a symptom of marriage."

"Definitely." Carmy claps me on the shoulder. "Relax, buddy. We'll make sure not to go near the wives of all your potential investors or spies or informants or whatever the hell you're fishing for tonight."

"And they say chivalry is dead," I mutter dryly.

Carmine chuckles. "Speaking of marriage making you soft in the head, where *is* your lovely bride?"

I frown as I glance past him toward the bar. I spotted Tempest over there a few minutes ago, drinking a glass of wine. But she seems to have disappeared since. Probably found a quiet corner somewhere to hide and avoid this entire evening.

Part of me completely gets that. The other part of me wants to find her and punish her for her bratty attitude—over my knee, for example.

Or *on* hers.

I push the thought away as my cock throbs and thickens in my tux pants.

This game the two of us have started to play is…dangerous. Mainly because this whole thing is just supposed to be a facade to appease the dons who took exception to my single status.

Second, I don't *do* relationships, not even casual ones. And marriage? As in the real kind? Never once on my radar.

Neither was the concept of having a woman constantly on my mind, invading my every thought.

And yet here we are.

Of course, there's the other, darker element to all of this: Tempest's medical condition. If I actually were a soulless, heartless bastard, the situation would be ideal. She wasn't wrong with her theory about The Commission all but canonizing me after her death. A widower? I'd be untouchable and unimpeachable in my operation of Club Venom.

And yet, despite general public opinion, and my own suspicions, it would appear I *do* in fact have a soul, and at least the shadow of a heart.

Maybe more than a shadow. Because the idea of Tempest being taken away from me is...

Intolerable.

Unacceptable.

Enraging, in a way that shocks me.

Perhaps making things physical was a mistake. It would be so easy to put the blame on her, and to chalk this up to me being her first, and her in her naïveté confusing physical lust with emotions and feelings.

But that would be cheap.

And grossly untrue.

Because if Tempest is confusing physical closeness with emotional intimacy?

Well, she's not the only one. And that is a bigger problem than I'm willing to admit to myself.

"Dante?"

I blink back to reality. "I have no idea," I shrug. "Maybe she went for a walk?"

Nico smirks. "Careful, brother."

"Of?"

"Carmy and I aren't the only sharks prowling around this gala looking for unattended women."

Something hot and vicious flashes within me like oil splashed into a searing hot pan. But just then, Drazen joins our little circle.

My hackles raise at the dark look on his face when he turns to me.

"Where's your wife?"

I sigh. "The three of you do realize that we're at MOMA, complete with a mayoral security detail, and not Mogadishu after dark, yes? What the hell is the deal about Tempest not being glued to my goddamn side—"

"Silvio Bonpensiero is here."

Something cold and sharp drags up my spine. My face hardens as I turn to scan the crowd. I don't see Tempest.

I don't see Silvio, either.

And *I don't like that one fucking bit.*

"I'll check the front," Carmine growls, all the goofy playfulness of his earlier tone gone in an instant.

"I'll take the upstairs galleries. I know a few of the guys on security tonight," Nico adds, also now completely serious.

This is one of the reasons I love these two. They might act like absolute muppets at times. But when shit gets real, there's no one else I'd rather have in my corner.

"I have two men here with me tonight," Drazen mutters, pulling out his phone. "We'll secure the main floor."

I nod my thanks before I storm over to the bar and instantly catch the bartender's attention. I flash him a picture of Tempest on my phone and ask if he saw her, and he nods.

"Yes, sir. She and another dark-haired girl were talking. They, uh…" He coughs delicately. "I think they may have gone to smoke a joint together." He nods toward the back of the gala.

Goddammit, Tempest.

At the far end of the main function room, I glance down a hallway and spot a guard standing at the end. The fact that he yanks out a cellphone and starts texting someone madly the second he sees me tips me off. The nervous look in his eyes as I storm toward him pushes me over the edge.

"Sir," he begins. "This area is off—"

"You know who the fuck I'm looking for," I snarl, grabbing him by the collar and slamming him to the wall. "And I have a feeling you know *who I am*, too."

He swallows. "Mr. Sartorre—"

"You have two seconds to tell me where the fuck my wife is."

He pales and jams a finger behind him. "Courtyard!"

I leave him shaking as I stalk around the corner and down one dark hallway, then another. It's when I round the last corner that I freeze.

The first thing I see is a girl standing inside the hallway, snickering to herself as she puffs on a joint, her face pressed to the glass door. But it's what I see on the other side of the door that has me charging like a predator.

The girl shrieks and drops the joint as I wrestle her to the side and yank the door open. I barrel out into the chilly courtyard to where Silvio Bonpensiero is snarling down at Tempest on her knees, one hand holding a fistful of her hair and the other one raised as if to strike her again.

Again, because the terrified look in her eyes and the pink mark on her cheek tell me he already *has* struck her once.

That makes him a dead man.

I slam into him like a train, knocking him off his feet so hard that one of his shoes actually flies off. I'm vaguely aware of the girl I shoved aside a second ago screaming as I straddle Silvio's chest and start to hit him.

And hit him.

And fucking *hit him*.

I pound his face until I feel the bridge of his nose and a few teeth break. Until I feel his orbital crack under my fist. Until blood is pouring from the pulpy, swollen mass that used to be his mouth and nose.

Until I feel, see, and know nothing but the satisfaction of inflicting pain on this piece of shit for touching Tempest. I ignore the cold, the raw throbbing in my hands, the screaming of the girl inside. I ignore it all…

Until a soft, gentle hand lands on my arm.

"Dante."

I go still, my nostrils flaring and my blood roaring as I glance to the side. Tempest is kneeling beside me, her eyes locked with mine, filled with concern and yet also understanding as she touches my arm.

"You're going to kill him."

"I know. Tell me to do it," I rasp thickly, my eyes locked with hers, "and I will."

The girl behind me screams over and over even as I ignore her.

"Just say the word, and he's fucking—"

"*Don't kill him,*" Tempest says quietly, shaking her head. "Please."

I glare down at Silvio, who's completely unconscious now. Standing, I kick him hard in the side of the ribs one last time, still ignoring the screams of the girl behind me.

My hand slips into Tempest's and grips it tight.

"We're leaving. *Now.*"

———

THE NEAR-LETHAL COCKTAIL of emotions still roaring through my system when we get home is equal parts vengeance and fury, shaken with half a teaspoon of fear.

I don't know what that motherfucker was prepared to do, or how badly he was prepared to hurt her. That's where the vengeance and the fury come from. But Silvio isn't the only one I'm angry at, and I know damn well that my wife knows it.

Tempest was silent the whole drive home from the gala. She remained quiet in the elevator, and when I opened the door to the penthouse.

She's still mute now, looking almost meek as she stands in the front entryway, wearing her coat and looking scared as I storm across the living room to the bar cart. I pour myself a heavy splash of bourbon and knock it back before pouring another and whirling on her.

"What the *fuck* was that?"

When I glance back at her, Tempest's eyes are narrowed. "Excuse me?"

"You heard me."

She barks a laugh. "I'm sorry, am *I* the one on trial for that prick ambushing me and fucking slapping me?!"

"Wanna tell me how you managed to get yourself out to that courtyard in the first place?"

Her mouth purses.

"By following a complete stranger out there to smoke weed, right?" I snap.

Her lower lip quivers. "Fuck you, that's not fair—"

"No, but it's the *truth*!" I hiss.

"Why the hell do you even care?!"

"Because you're my *wife*!"

"Only when it suits you!" she fires back.

I storm over to her, sneering. "*Don't*," I seethe. "Don't even *try* to play that card. You're reckless, and we both know it!" I yell loud enough for her to tremble. "You have no fucking clue about the consequences of your choices and actions!"

Her eyes gleam. "You are *way* out of fucking line, asshole."

"Your impetuousness is fucking *dangerous*, Tempest!" I fire back. "You have zero impulse control! You just *do* things, and you act without once thinking of what might happen!"

She's so angry she's shaking, but I can't stop. I'm not trying to be an asshole. But this woman has wormed her way so fucking deep under my skin and I care so fucking much that it's impossible to brush this off anymore.

"Are we talking about that psycho bitch at the party pretending to be my friend so she could lead me to Silvio's little ambush?" she snaps. "Or is it jealousy about Venom the other—"

"*Careful*, little hurricane," I hiss dangerously.

"What I do with *my* free time, asshole, is none of your fucking—"

"The fuck it's not!" I roar. "You are my fucking *wife*. So tell me one more goddamn time how you slinking off to private rooms at Club Venom isn't any of my business. I'm all ears."

She swallows. "We never talked about exclusivity—"

"We're talking about it *right now*," I snarl, lurching into her and lifting her face to mine, watching the hazel-green fire

285

flicker in her eyes. I slowly shake my head. "I'm through believing in coincidences."

"Meaning?"

My lips curl. "I want to know how you know about Apex."

Her brow furrows. *"What?"*

"The rings, Tempest."

She pales, and I know I've hit a nerve.

"I want answers. *Now.* You followed that fucker back to the private room for a reason."

She sneers. "Maybe I just wanted to fuck him—"

She gasps sharply as I kiss her hard enough to bruise, making her yelp and whimper when I bite down on her plump bottom lip until I taste copper.

"No, you didn't," I hiss.

Her eyes narrow. "What makes you so damn sure—"

"Because *I* fuck you better than anyone else every could," I snarl. "And I *know* you know that."

She sucks on her lip, her chest heaving.

"You went with him because of the rings. You tried to fucking stab me at our *wedding* because of the rings."

She whimpers as I twist her face up to mine, looming over her.

"So I'm telling you for the last fucking time. I. Want. *Answers.*"

At first, I think it's just something in her eye. But suddenly, she's crumpling.

Fuck.

I catch her as she falls, gently holding her against me. She doesn't just start to cry. It's like she's ripping her entire soul open in front of me.

And then, she tells me everything.

Every horrible, nightmarish detail.

Every secret from the darkest parts of her past, that rips my heart in two as they fall from her lips.

Holy fucking God.

She tells me about Nina, and how when they were seventeen, they went out and got into this exclusive dance club with fake IDs. How they met a bunch of cool, rich guys a few years older than them who invited them into their VIP booth for drinks.

How her memory goes fuzzy right after that.

Tempest tells me about being vaguely aware of being brought to some fancy apartment. How she remembers saying "no" when one of those motherfuckers brought her into a bedroom, and *two* of them pulled in her friend Nina.

How her first time was nothing but pain and shame as that piece of excrement hurt her while she couldn't even move from whatever they'd given her. How she could only watch powerlessly as the two fucks raped her best friend right next to her, choking Nina until the light went out of her eyes.

…And how *all three of them* wore golden lion's head rings.

Just like the fucks who killed Claudia.

After she's done sobbing every awful detail of that horrible night into my chest, and we're sitting on the floor at my place, she raises her red-rimmed eyes to mine, and the pain on her face is enough to break my heart.

Or make me want to kill.

To slay her demons.

To burn the fucking world for her.

"Dante…"

She reaches up and grabs my collar, and before I can say or do a thing, she's pulling me down and crushing her mouth to mine. I kiss her back, groaning, my blood turning to fire as she whimpers and slowly starts to crawl into my lap. Her hand snakes down between us, and I growl deeply when her small fingers find my swelling bulge.

"Tempest…"

It's not that I don't want her, and it's not that I don't want to rip her dress off and *feast* on her until she sees God. It's that this woman has just ripped out her soul to me and shown me the worst of her scars and her trauma.

"*Please*," she whimpers, yanking off my shirt. Her mouth falls to my neck, and I groan as she starts to kiss her way up it to my ear. "*Please fuck me…*"

"Jesus, Tempest," I groan as my hands slide over her torso, gripping her thin waist as I pull her against the throb in my pants.

"I'm not asking you to fall in love with me," she chokes. "I'm not even asking you to care. All I know is, when you and I had sex that first time, I finally stopped hating myself, hating the very whole of sex and intimacy." She pulls back and I can see the tears roll down her cheeks, her eyes locked on mine.

"I stopped jumping at every shadow. I can't go back to feeling those things again, so I *need* you to fuck me."

My jaw clenches.

"Please," she whispers, stroking my face, her eyes pleading. "I just want to feel something else. I *want* darkness. I want to be *fucked*, Dante. Not made love to. Not coddled. Not pitied. I want—I *need*—to be *fucked*, until I forget every—"

She moans as I slam my mouth to hers.

"I won't hold back, little hurricane."

"*Don't*," she whimpers.

"And I'm not going to stop."

"*I don't want you to*," she whimpers into my lips as I scoop her into my arms, her legs wrapping around my waist.

"I'm going to push you past every single boundary you have until you're *mine*."

"*I already am.*"

26

TEMPEST

THERE ARE moments in life that feel like you're teetering on the edge of a cliff. One little breeze—one touch, one gasp—will have you falling into the abyss.

And when you *do* fall, it's like your mind focuses on individual senses. The sound of the air whooshing past your ears. The taste of the dust from the cliff wall behind you collecting on your tongue. The scent of your own fear as the adrenaline takes hold.

I might not literally be falling from a cliff when Dante scoops me into his arms and strides into the bedroom as he devours my lips. But try telling that to my senses as my reality splits into pieces.

The feel of his hands on my ass as my legs wrap around his hips. The thudding sound of my own pulse in my ears, mixed with the low baritone of his groans.

The taste of his mouth.

The scent of his body.

There's no sight, at first because the bedroom is dark. Then, before my vision can adjust, it's because he's slipping something silky over my eyes, blindfolding me.

For a moment, my adrenaline spikes. My heart misses a beat, and the desire pooling between my thighs evaporates as a vicious darkness takes hold.

"You're not there, little hurricane," Dante growls in my ear, his weight shifting on the four-poster bed behind me as I perch on the edge. His hands tighten the blindfold a little more, sending my heart rate through the roof.

"You are *not. There,*" he rasps against my neck. The mix of muscle memory panic swirling with the intense physical desire even smelling this man evokes in me is both breathtaking and unnerving at the same time.

Hot and cold.

Yin and yang.

Order and chaos.

"You're here, with me," he growls quietly.

I flinch, whimpering as his teeth nip at my earlobe. His hands take fistfuls of my dress, and I shiver as I feel him pull it up over my hips, my ass raising as the garment slips up my spine. He lifts my arms in slow, sensual, unhurried motions, slipping the dress off me. I hear it being tossed aside, feel his hands slide slowly back down my raised arms.

"*Do. You. Trust. Me.*"

Each word brushes against my ear like a painter flicking paint. Like a whispered prayer, or an incantation.

I can still feel the fear rippling inside of me, threatening to flay me alive. But the nearness of him and the rasp of his voice right in my ear keep me from flying away on the wind.

"*Yes*," I choke through panted breaths.

"I told you I was going to push you, Tempest," he growls quietly. "I warned you I was going to break down your boundaries. Are you sure you trust me?"

I nod again. "*Yes*."

"*Good girl.*"

He lifts one of my arms, his hands sensually teasing up and down the inside of my forearm and wrist, so gently that I can feel the tension leaving my body as my eyes close under the blindfold.

And then something metallic clamps around that wrist with a sharp click.

Oh fuck.

"It's still me," Dante murmurs into my ear, stroking the other arm. "It's just me, and it's just you. And you know you trust me."

He lifts the other arm, and even though I'm expecting it this time, I still jerk when I feel it clamp around my wrist.

"Stay with me, little hurricane," he growls softly. "Stay right here with me."

His hands slide down my arms, over my shoulders, and then slip down to the sides of my ribcage. It's only then that I realize my arms are both up, totally immobilized.

Just like that other night long ago.

The fear begins to flood my core, my breath coming in short, staccato gasps as I start to shake. But slowly, his warm, strong hands slide over my skin until his fingertips tease over my breasts. Even through there's fear, the feel of his touch and the scent of him have my nipples tightening to points against his palm as he cups my breasts, lifting and squeezing until his fingers pinch the aching buds.

Oh fuck.

I'm shaking from the mix of adrenaline and fear. But this is different than the night I was helpless to say no, or to fight back. And it's not just that I know I can speak up this time and end this whole thing.

It's that this time, it's Dante.

Whom I *trust*.

"I'm not bringing you back to that place in your mind to scare or hurt you," he growls. I gasp as his fingers tease and roll my nipples, sending electric sparks zipping through my core. "I'm bringing you back there so I can *destroy* that place in your head. When you feel the pull of being restrained, or find yourself in the darkness, or sense that you're being pushed to the bleeding edges of your boundaries, you won't feel afraid anymore, little hurricane."

His hand slips slowly down my stomach, sending rippling sparks spiraling out like waves from his touch. His fingertips slip under the lace edge of my panties, and when they slide wetly through my lips and roll over my clit, my eyes roll back and my jaw falls open in ecstasy.

"Because you'll feel *me*."

Two thick fingers sink deep into my pussy. I moan, shuddering against the cuffs holding my arms up and trembling when I feel the heat of his body envelop mine. His fingers slide back out, rubbing my clit in slow circles before they sink back in, *deep*. I cry out, my back arching and my arms straining against the bonds on my wrists. Dante strokes his fingers in and out of my soaking pussy, his palm grinding against my clit until I'm gasping.

Which is exactly when he pulls away. Suddenly, his fingers are tracing my lips.

Wet. Slick. Tasting of me.

"*Suck*."

I groan, opening my mouth and letting my lips close around the fingers he was just teasing my pussy with.

I taste *good*.

His fingers leave my mouth, and I hear him slide off the bed to stand right in front of me. His hands grip my hips and my ass, lifting me up slightly before he slides me back on the bed.

"We're only just starting, baby girl."

His hands skim up my thighs, making my hips rise on their own accord as his fingers slip into the waistband of my panties. The lace slips down my legs before I feel his hands wrap around one ankle. He lifts that foot, placing it on the bed and pushing it out to the side. I almost expect it this time when a cuff clicks shut around it, but I still burn with heat.

"If it's too much, tell me," he growls, his hands sliding up my thighs until they stop *just* short of touching my pussy.

"Will you stop if I do?" I whisper.

"Maybe."

Fuck, that shouldn't be so hot.

He lifts and clamps my other ankle, making my face heat at the lewd, vulnerable position that has me sitting on the edge of the bed with my legs spread as wide as they can go.

His hand cups my pussy, a finger dragging up through my slick lips as I gasp sharply. It's insane how fucking wet I always get for him: I can feel it dripping out of me and coating his fingers, and my face throbs with embarrassment at just how *much* there is.

"Don't get shy," Dante growls quietly. "Do you have any fucking idea how much I like how drippy and messy your sweet pussy gets for me?"

I jolt when I feel his breath hot on one thigh, then the other, then back, all the while inching closer and closer, until suddenly, his tongue drags through my lips, and I cry out loudly.

"*Good girl,*" he growls, licking me again. "Let me hear how much you want my tongue on this pretty pussy."

"*Please,*" I choke. "*Don't stop—oh, fuuuuck…*"

His tongue plunges deep into me, like he's trying get every drop of me or taste me from the inside out. My eyes roll back again under the blindfold, my whole body spasming and jolting as Dante devours my pussy.

I moan when his tongue drags up to my clit, his lips wrapping around the throbbing nub, his tongue swirling over it. He does it again and again, adding pressure as he sucks until my body begins to shake and clench.

Slowly, he sinks two fingers into me, stroking them in and out against my g-spot as he tongues my clit. His thumb dips lower, and when it *just* brushes over my puckered back hole, electric sparks explode throughout my core.

"Oh my fucking God—"

"If you're going to pray to someone, little hurricane," he rasps against my pussy, "It'd better be me, because I don't see God down here with his tongue buried deep in your messy little cunt."

The breath explodes from my lungs with a whine of pleasure as he attacks my pussy again. His tongue is everywhere: licking, teasing, tasting, swirling. His lips hum and suck, and his fingers push deep, stroking my most intimate places. My muscles contract and pull tight, straining against the cuffs on my wrists and ankles as I drown in the pleasure of his mouth.

When I come, it's like the whole world goes white and explodes into flames. My head drops back, my entire body arching shamelessly against Dante's tongue.

His mouth stays where it is, still sucking my hypersensitive clit and sending aftershocks thrumming through my core. When he pulls away, he leaves his fingers inside me. I feel him stand, and when he slides between my spread thighs, I realize he's naked.

I whimper as I feel his throbbing hard, swollen cock press hotly against my breasts. The fingers of one hand stroke in and out of me as his other hand cups my cheek. His mouth slams to mine, sending my pulse skyrocketing. His tongue dances with mine, and I suck it hungrily into my mouth, tasting myself in his kiss.

"Are you scared yet, little hurricane?"

I shake my head.

"How about now."

I gasp as he pushes me back, a metallic sliding sound accompanying the feel of the arm restraints sliding back a little on some sort of track. When they come to a stop, I'm leaned halfway back down to the bed, with my arms still over my head and my legs still spread wide.

"Scared?"

I shake my head again. *"No."*

Dante makes a tsking sound. "How about *now.*"

Adrenaline redlines through my system as his hand suddenly wraps tight around my throat. He squeezes a little, making it feel like every nerve ending in my body is exploding into flames simultaneously.

"And now?" He growls, a menace to his voice. "Are you scared yet?"

"Do whatever you want to me," I gasp, shuddering with pleasure as my pussy tightens around his fingers. "You're not going to scare me."

I feel him stiffen and pause, his lips an inch from mine.

"No?"

I shake my head. *"No,"* I choke. "Because I want you to do anything you want to me."

"Careful what you wish for, little hurricane," he growls.

"Please—"

"Let's start with seeing how well you can take every inch of my cock."

It happens so fast it takes my breath away. His fingers slip from between my legs. And suddenly, the huge head of his cock is pushing into me. Fuck, he always feels big, but it's like he's even harder than usual this time, if that's even possible. Like he's extra eager to fuck me.

Which is exactly what he does.

I moan when Dante rams his cock deep into my needy pussy. His thickness stretches me to my limit, knocking the air from my lungs before he slams his lips to mine. I moan into his mouth, desperate to wrap my legs around him before remembering that my ankles are held fast.

Knowing that I'm bound and wide open for him to use as he pleases, I've literally never been so turned on.

It's the loss of control that puts me in charge.

It's the immobilization that sets me free.

It's facing the past and telling it to go fuck itself because I'm not afraid of it anymore that breaks whatever hold it still has on me.

When I cry out into Dante's mouth, it's a scream of freedom. A sob of release and a plea for more. His hand tightens on my throat, his tongue dancing with mine as his other hand fists my hair. The hand on my neck drops to my breasts, pinching and rolling my nipples as he fucks me hard.

The hand in my hair yanks my head back, exposing my neck as his lips drag from mine to bite and suck at the tender flesh. His hand drops between my legs, and when he starts to rub my clit as he fucks the living hell out of me, I come completely undone.

"Dante!"

"*Louder*," he growls into my neck. "I want you to scream it."

"*Dante!!*"

"LOUDER. I want the neighbors a goddamn *block* away to know who's fucking you, and taking you, and *owning you.*"

"*DANTE!!!*" I cry out, choking on my breath as my entire body spasms and tightens into a white-hot ball. "*Fuuuucckk meee!*"

I came harder than I've ever come before earlier on his tongue.

This orgasm is even stronger.

It's like the molecules of my mind and body break apart and shatter into the cosmos. My entire soul swells to ten times its size, exploding from my pores and mouth and fingertips. My pussy ripples and clenches around his cock over and over as he keeps fucking me from one orgasm into another, until it feels like I might black out.

With a groan, Dante pulls out, his breath ragged. I moan as the hot spray of his cum splatters in thick ropes over my stomach, my breasts, and my neck. It drips sticky and hot from my nipples as more sprays against my pussy and my thighs, covering me in his cum before he plunges back into me.

I'm shaking as we come to a stop—literally, like my entire body is about to give out. I'm only dimly aware of him undoing my ankles, still between my legs with his cock still hard inside me. My arms are next, and he pauses after undoing the first cuff to hook it around his neck before removing the second.

I cling to him with all four limbs, limp and shaking as he picks me up gently and carries me into the bathroom. He sets my ass on the edge of the vanity as he uses his foot to kick on the tub. It fills with steam and bubbles as we stay like that, my legs around him, his cock still inside of me.

His mouth gently kissing mine as I come back to earth.

And that's exactly how we stay once the tub is filled and he carries me over and sinks into it: with me still impaled on his cock, and my lips locked with his.

27

TEMPEST

"Whatever happened to him?"

It's a strange thought, given that I'm lying naked in Dante's bed with my cheek against his chest and his arms around me.

My entire body is still tingling and buzzing, as if my fingertips are touching live wires. My wrists and ankles are sore—actually, a *lot* of me is sore. But it's a delicious, toe-curling, pulse-quickening kind of sore.

It's an ache that makes me feel free of the demons and the darkness of my past.

And yet, this one intrusive thought keeps wriggling its way inside.

"Who?" Dante murmurs.

I look up into his face, debating even saying it.

"Tempest…"

"The man from Venom."

Dante's face darkens.

"Is he dead?"

No answer.

"Dante—"

"Yes," he finally says quietly. His eyes lock with mine. "He's dead."

My throat bobs heavily, and I don't realize my fingers are curling to claws against his chest until his hand lands gently on mine.

"Talk to me, Tempest," Dante murmurs, tilting my chin up so my eyes meet his.

"I'm…" My lips curl into a surprised smile. "I'm okay."

The second I say it, I realize exactly how true it is. I'm not merely okay. I'm *free*—free of that nightmare of a night. Free of the past still clawing at my heels.

What happened still happened.

But now, the monsters are all gone.

Dante's just slain the last of them for me.

Dante's brow furrows a little, and I already know the question hovering on his lips.

It still blows my mind that I told him about what happened to me. I've never told anyone about that night, aside from my brothers and Taylor. I never imagined I *would* tell anyone else.

Shame. Fear of being judged. Fear of reliving it by talking about it. But with Dante, it just sort of…fell out.

It wasn't forced. It wasn't something I felt I *had* to do. And, weirdly, telling him didn't shove me back into that darkness. It opened the blinds and let the light in, banishing the shadows.

Letting him into the worst parts of my past felt like opening my soul for him to wrap his hands around it. Which should terrify me. And yet, it doesn't. Instead, it's like a weight's been lifted from my chest.

Dante's brow creases. "Was he..."

I whisper it out. "He was the second of the two who killed Nina."

And Dante already has the other ring, the one with mismatched eyes, from the guy who choked her life away. I allow it to truly sink in: all three of the monsters from that night are dead now.

My lip retreats between my teeth as I glance up at him again, my brows furrowing. "Can I ask you something?"

He nods, pushing a lock of dark hair back from my face.

"Why did you do it?" I say softly.

"What, kill him?"

"Yeah."

He frowns. "You're my *wife*, Tempest," he murmurs darkly, his eyes flashing.

Heat sizzles in my core.

"Well, yeah, but..." I look away. "C'mon, Dante. It's...I mean, *I'm* a temporary prop—"

He pulls me up, clasping my face in his hands, his eyes burning hotly into my own. "Is that what you still think this is?"

Before I can answer, I'm moaning softly as his lips bruise mine.

"Do you really think I'd just kill for anyone, little hurricane?" He growls. "For a *prop*?"

I smile against his lips, shaking my head before I start to kiss him again. When I pull away, a second question hangs on my lips.

"What is it?" Dante murmurs, clearly seeing through my silence.

"How do *you* know them?" I run my lip over my teeth. "The men with the lion rings."

He's silent for a few seconds that drag on too long as he turns to look away with a sad, faraway expression.

"They took my sister Claudia from me."

My face falls. "*Jesus*, Dante—"

"The *authorities*," he spits acidly, "said she was just a statistic— wrong place, wrong dress, wrong guy." He grits his teeth. "But I dug deeper, because that's what I do. And that's how I found them."

"You called them Apex, before?"

He nods. "Yeah. Apex Club. As in 'apex predators'."

My stomach twists and knots, sour bile creeping up my throat.

"They're a bunch of sadistic rich douchebags who were in the same frat together and went to the same business school. And they…" His gaze stabs violently into the wall. "That's how they get their kicks. They hurt women."

Part of me wants to throw up. There's a fucking *club* of them?

"From what I can tell," Dante spits, "there were seven of them." He turns his head and lets his gaze hold mine. "I killed five."

My heart clenches. *Holy shit.*

"Well, six, now," Dante grunts. "But there's one I've never been able to track down. A man named Brett—"

"Sinclair." I spit the name like a curse. "Brett Sinclair."

What happened to me never made the news, mostly due to a court gag order Brett's lawyers rammed through. But my brothers agreed to it, not because they gave a fuck about "sullying" the Sinclair name. But because they were worried about it ripping me apart if the media got wind of the story.

I nod numbly. ""Yeah, he's dead. He…" My eyes squeeze shut, and I turn away.

"You don't need to tell me, Tempest," Dante murmurs.

"No, I want to." I swallow, tasting bile. "They never knew I was awake. I think they thought I was totally out, like Nina was. So afterward…" I shudder. "Afterward, they just *left me* on the side of the street in Chelsea."

Dante lets out a deep, lethal growl and whirls, and I gasp when he grabs the bedside table lamp, yanks it out of the plug, and viciously hurls it at the wall.

Everything goes silent except for the thud of my pulse in my ears.

"I'm sorry, Tempest," he finally says quietly.

"Don't be," I whisper, kissing his chest again. "I still couldn't really move when they dropped me off. But I was able to scrape my nails down his forearm before they dumped me on the side of the road. So when the paramedics took me to the hospital, they were able to get a DNA sample."

I can still remember the disbelief on the faces of my brothers and Taylor when the word came back that the man who'd done this to me was Brett Sinclair, of *the* Sinclair family.

"He posted bail, obviously," I spit. "But then he was caught trying to leave the country and got thrown in lockup." I grimace. "He hanged himself in his cell using the string from his hoodie."

"*Good*," Dante grunts through tightly clenched teeth, his rage palpable as his body clenches against me.

"His family covered it up, but..." I shake my head. "There's your seventh guy you've been looking for."

We're both silent a minute before I slowly lift my head from his chest, my brows lined with worry.

"What if there are more?" I murmur.

"Then I'll destroy them," he murmurs back, his quiet tone belying the look of sheer malice and savagery on his face.

He slides me onto his lap, kissing me slowly before I pull back a little.

"Why?"

His brow furrows. "Why what?"

"Why destroy them? I mean, why risk anything, especially your empire, to go hunting for *my* shadows and ghosts—"

"Because you're my *wife*," Dante spits viciously. He's so matter of fact about it that it forces a ripple of heat down my spine.

His hands tighten on my waist, pinning me to his lap as his eyes lock with mine. My lips curl slightly as I chew on them.

"Don't," I whisper, shaking my head.

"Don't?" he grunts.

"Don't...say anything more," I croak, my face twisting sadly. "This *ends*, Dante. Remember that."

He smiles a wry, bitter smile. "So... No falling in love with you."

My face heats as my lips curl. "No," I whisper softly.

"How about crushes?"

I grin, my cheeks turning pink. "*Stop* it."

Dante just grins back as he kisses me slowly and deeply. "Until this...ends," he says quietly, "you're my wife, Tempest. You're *mine*." His eyes lock boldly with my own. "And I'll kill for what's mine."

28

DANTE

"HAVE A SEAT."

Vito looks tired as I sink into the couch facing the one he's sitting in.

It's funny how the more things change, the more they stay the same. When I was a kid, Vito used to bring Carmy, Nico, and I up here to visit him at work. Back then the office was above Lickety Splits, quite possibly the most fantastically named strip club ever.

These days, the first two floors are no longer all mirrored VIP champagne rooms and stripper poles. Now the ground floor is a two Michelin star French restaurant, and there's a tech startup above it. But Vito's office on the third floor still looks *exactly* the same.

Same desk. Same ancient leather Chesterfield sofas. Same tobacco-laced air from when he still smoked. And the same neon Lickety Splits sign up on the wall.

"Can I assume you've got an idea of why I called you in here today? You're a smart kid, Dante."

I doubt I'm going to be surprised. I'm almost definitely in here to talk with Vito about Silvio, and to be reminded that his mother's uncle is Don Luciano Amato, who sits on the Commission alongside Vito.

"You put the kid in a fuckin' coma, Dante."

Yeah. Currently, Silvio's in a hospital room hooked up to about a half dozen machines, including one that's breathing for him.

He's having a hard time doing that for himself.

My eyes narrow coldly. "He assaulted my *wife*, Vito. I'm not exactly sure how else I was expected to fucking react!"

Vito's mouth twists. "Look, I can appreciate your passion, Dante. Of course I can. But Jesus fucking Christ, kid! You know things have been tense at the Commission table recently, especially with Massimo now running things."

Christ, this daytime soap opera drama. The quick version is, while The Commission exists to keep the peace between the most powerful Italian families, not everything is rainbows and unicorns under the shiny surface. Don Amato has been wondering aloud why the Commission is even necessary for years. And since Massimo "relieved" his father as head of the Carveli family—*allegedly* relieved—he's been singing the same tune.

In short, putting Silvio in the hospital is somewhat akin to walking up to the dividing line between two tense armies and pissing over that line onto their boots.

"Luciano is calling for blood, Dante. There's even rumors he's going to use this to push for a vote to remove you from Venom."

"That little shit Silvio attacked my fucking *wife*!" I roar, lurching toward Vito and slamming my fists down onto the coffee table. "I won't ever apologize for responding accordingly! Not to you, not to Don Amato, and sure as *fuck* not to Silvio!"

The office goes quiet. Vito strokes his jaw, leaning back as he eyes me cooly.

"The Commission pushed for this, Vito. They wanted me to marry—"

"To keep your club!"

"Which I'm doing!" I snap. "And now I'm following through with the rest of it!"

Except that's not all, and I fucking know it. Everything changed the second I fell for Tempest.

The second I knew I'd kill for her.

Yes, this whole marriage thing has gone further than I ever intended. And I fucking *hate* that I'm going to lose her, far too soon. So until then, there's nothing "fake" about this to me. Not anymore.

I'm about to say as much to Vito when I see his mouth curl into a grin. His brow arches as he starts to chuckle quietly to himself.

"I suppose this means you won't be needing that goomar after all, huh?"

Some of the steam rumbling under the surface of my skin lets up. I exhale slowly, shaking my head.

"No. I won't."

He leans over the coffee table to pat my knee before he leans back again.

"You and your in-laws," Vito sighs. "Your relationship is...*prickly*, to say the least."

I scowl. "Alistair and Gabriel aren't exactly my biggest fans, no."

"Well," Vito sighs. "We both know why, and we *also* both know you could clear that up with a simple conversation—"

Not him as well. "That isn't happening," I hiss quietly with finality.

"Tempest's brothers are one thing," he presses. "Her grandfather is another story."

My brow furrows. "I don't follow."

He sighs. "Look, I don't like Charles Black any more than you do. He's no don, even though he acts like one. He's just a glad-handing, self-serving prick. But the balance is shifting."

Sometimes Vito forgets that I make knowing everyone else's business *my* business.

"You mean that he's getting very cozy doing business with Luciano and Massimo."

Vito nods. "Exactly."

I don't usually pay much attention to the workings of the Commission. But even I can see that Massimo is a walking hand grenade that's missing a pin. Luciano is far more level-headed—the guy's been in this game for forty-plus years—but he's power-hungry, and it's never enough.

"Dante, you know I don't like to push you to get involved with family politics…"

He really doesn't. I've always appreciated that about Vito. He's got every right to call in every favor he wants from me, given the life he set me up for. But he never goes there. So the fact that he's asking right now speaks volumes.

"But I *need* Charles to stop working with Massimo and Luciano. Not just me. Michael Genovisi and Cesare Marchetti feel the same. Charles working with those guys is dangerous for all of us, and I need it shut down."

I do owe this man almost everything I have, after all.

"Let me see what I can do."

He smiles as he stands and shakes my hand. "Thank you."

I nod. "Of course. But seriously, if Luciano or his fuckhead great-nephew say a goddamn *thing* about Tempest, or try and come after her again," I snarl, "I'm done playing diplomat."

Vito smirks as he walks around the table and claps me on the shoulder.

"I think the entire city is clear on the consequences of laying a hand on your wife, my friend."

TEMPEST IS asleep by the time I get home much later, after checking in at Venom.

…In *my* bed.

I grin as I close the bedroom door behind me and walk to the foot of the bed, watching her sleep. I don't even remember the exact day when she switched from sleeping in "her" room to sleeping in mine.

It just happened.

I brush my teeth, shed my clothes quietly, and slip in behind her, wrapping her in my arms. Tempest murmurs quietly in her sleep, her lips curling into a lazy smile as she snuggles back into me.

Fuck.

This started as fake.

Now I've never felt anything more real.

The more things change…

The more I want them to stay the same.

The more I want this moment to last forever.

29

TEMPEST

"Tempest."

Someone's calling my name, but it sounds as if it's being spoken underwater. Why do I feel so sluggish?

I frown and glance down.

Why the hell am I sitting on the floor next to the toilet in Dante's bathroom?

Blinking to try to clear the fog in my head, I force myself to stand.

"Tempest, are you okay?"

My brow furrows as my hand comes up to push the hair back from my face. I turn, frowning again at the vomit in the toilet, tinged with red.

Oh. That can't be good.

Slowly, the events of the last five minutes come back to me. I was getting dressed for dinner and suddenly felt both light-headed and nauseous, so I ran into the bathroom. I'm not sure how I ended up on the floor, but I'm starting to think it was after I realized I was throwing up blood.

"I'm fine!" I call to Dante through the closed bathroom door. "Be right out."

I flush the toilet and walk on slightly unsteady feet to the sink, where I splash cold water on my face and rinse my mouth out with mouthwash.

I'm getting sicker.

Deep down, I know it's true, even if I keep coming up with every excuse in the book to explain my worsening symptoms. That I slept badly. That I need to eat more than Pam's smoothies, which she's been amazing enough to keep sending to Dante's house.

The central air in the penthouse.

The *weather*.

Basically anything I can blame instead of the increasingly obvious reality: that I'm *dying*.

The sand in my hourglass is running out.

Taking a deep breath, I open the bathroom door to find Dante standing right there. But it's not anger or suspicion on his face as I exit the bathroom.

It's concern.

"Sorry, I was zoned out on my phone," I lie. "Ready to go?"

His hand comes up to touch my chin gently, lifting my eyes to his.

"Are you okay?" he rumbles quietly, sending a bolt of...I don't know what...deep into my chest.

Something's changed with us. I could say it happened the night of the firemen's ball, when Silvio attacked me. I could say it was when we let our pain bleed out together—me telling him about what happened to me, and him telling me about Claudia.

But not so very deep down, I know it started much earlier than that, even if I can't pinpoint exactly when. I don't even think there was a "moment" when things flipped like a switch. It's like reading a good book and getting so lost in it that when you finally look up, day has turned to night.

It's changed. *We've* changed.

…Just in time for the tragic ending.

"Yeah," I lean my cheek into his palm as my eyes get lost in his. I inhale his familiar scent, and feel the way his closeness makes my core tighten, my skin tingle, and my heart race a little faster.

"I'm great."

No falling in love.

No falling in love.

…Except I've already broken that rule.

30

DANTE

GABRIEL'S LIVING room is silent. No background music. No conversation. Just the occasional cleared throat and the distant sounds of Pam cooking in the kitchen down the hall.

To say that this dinner with Tempest, her brothers, Charles, and Maeve is going to be frosty is the understatement of the fucking millennium.

Charles isn't even here, not that I really expected him to come. But that's fine. The main reason for this dinner was, yes, to be Vito's ambassador and to make sure Charles doesn't do business anymore with Massimo Carveli or Luciano Amato. But I had other motives as well.

I don't know if the Cold War between Alistair and Gabriel and me will ever end. But if it could be put on hold for a while, that would be nice. Tempest's brothers matter to her, a lot. They're her entire family.

I know there's a way to put this animosity to bed. But I just can't go there, because of a promise made to a friend to whom I owe my life.

I fucked up, didn't I, Dante? Fuck, Alistair and Gabriel are going to be so fucking angry. And Tempest? What will she think of me?

I'll take Layla's secret to my grave. But that doesn't mean I can't try to put a Band-aid on my relationship with Tempest's brothers.

Even if it's only temporary.

Originally, I'd invited the Black family out to my Hampton's home for dinner. When that got a flat "no", I changed the venue to my penthouse in the city. Gabriel eventually agreed on the condition that *he* host—as if, what, I've got secret ninjas waiting to jump out of my goddamn ceiling to assassinate my in-laws?

But whatever. In any case, here we all are at Gabriel's house.

Gabriel and Alistair stand on one side of the room, occasionally shooting me a dark look. On the other side of the room, Tempest talks quietly with Maeve, who I guess has managed to get away from Charles for the evening.

Suddenly, the door to the living room opens, and Pam steps in with an awkward look on her face.

"Mr. Black, sir," she smiles weakly. "Uh, Mr. *Black* is here."

This should be interesting.

Charles strides in with a deep scowl on his face, which only gets darker when his gaze lands on Maeve.

"You left the house without saying goodbye, sweetheart," he rumbles quietly.

Maeve stiffens as she slips behind Tempest.

"If you had," the older man mutters, eyeing her sharply before clearing his throat, "I would have given you a ride." He exhales as he turns to level a cold look at his grandsons. "Well? What's for dinner?"

Alistair and Gabriel glance at each other before walking over to Charles and me. Tempest shoots me a look before pulling Maeve out of the room and into the adjoining dining room.

"Well, look who decided to grace us with his presence," Alistair growls at his grandfather.

Charles ignores him as he turns to arch a brow at me. "I know why you called for this absurd dinner, Dante."

I smile icily. "And why is that, Charles?"

"Because Vito wants to work together again."

"Well, that depends."

"On?"

My smile drops. "On if you're still working with Massimo and Luciano."

Charles scowls before he can stop himself. I smirk.

"Honeymoon over already?"

He shoots me a look. "Luciano is all over the place. And your cousin…"

"Distant cousin," I mutter.

Charles frowns. "Whatever he is to you, he's a fucking sociopath, and I don't trust him not to shoot me in the back of the goddamn head, much less to respect my business interests."

I lift a shoulder. "Well, in that case, Vito might be interested in—"

"Not so fast," Gabriel growls, stepping between Charles and I and glaring at his grandfather. "Maeve's eighteen now. Which makes her legally an adult."

Charles frowns. "Where are you going with—"

"She's going to be living here now. Not with you."

The room is quiet for a second before Charles begins to laugh. "Is that a fact?"

Gabriel doesn't bat an eye. "It is. I'm *done* pretending I don't see the abject fear in her eyes whenever you're in the same room as her. And to say that you and your gold digger wife are a bad influence on her is a *gross* understatement. It ends now. Maeve moves here to finish high school. After that, she's welcome to continue living here if she goes to school in New York. If not, she can live wherever she chooses."

Rage clouds Charles' eyes.

"That is *not* happening—"

"You might still have a seat at the Crown and Black board-room table..." Alistair hisses.

"A *large* seat!" Charles snaps.

"But don't think for a second we don't know that your empire is burning at the edges," Alistair continues. "You're not a young man anymore, Charles. You've lost friends and alliances. Burned bridges."

Oh, goody. I'm not the only one who's been paying attention.

"So you want to hitch your boat to Vito Barone because your little kingdom is in trouble? Fine," Gabriel mutters. He shoots me a very meaningful, heavy look, before turning back to his grandfather. "But if you want to do that, Maeve moves in here."

And here I thought dinner might get boring.

Charles barks a laugh, turning to me. "Tell Vito I'll be in touch for the two of us to—"

"Their condition applies," I say, turning to nod my chin at Tempest's brothers. "Or there is no deal with Vito."

Charles stares at me, a vein in his temple pulsing. *"Excuse me?!"*

"I'm sure you heard me. Maeve moves in here, or else there's no deal."

Charles sputters and fumes. "You don't have the authority to speak for Vito—"

"Today, I do."

The living room is pin drop silent for a second. Charles glares at me, then his grandsons.

"Fine," he finally snaps. "Fine."

After he strides away, I glance at Gabriel and Alistair. None of us says anything for a moment, but Gabriel nods slightly with his chin.

"You know, I've been meaning to send you both thank you notes for your generous wedding gifts."

Alistair rolls his eyes. "Eat shit, Dante. I didn't get you anything. Neither of us did."

I smile. "Well, I'm sure we could head down to that famous Black family wine cellar and find something to remedy—"

"What the fuck *is* all of this, Dante?" Alistair breaks in. "I mean fucking seriously, what the hell is this dinner you were so desperate for all about? You wanted us to watch you play diplomat and conduct mafia fucking business in *our father's house*? Are you shitting me?"

I exhale slowly. "This isn't about me."

It's about Tempest. And I hate that I can't tell them why this is so important to her. That I want to give her at least *some* semblance of a family with their differences and their clashing pasts put to rest.

"Look, we're family now—"

Gabriel glares at me and Alistair laughs coldly. "Don't remind me."

"And it would mean a lot to your sister if the three of us put the weapons down—"

"Don't talk about Tempest as if you fucking know her," Alistair snarls.

"She's my *wife*, Alistair."

"*Careful*, Dante," he snarls, his teeth bared. "There's already enough evidence with one of my sisters that I could put you in a hole in the ground. Touch the other one and I'll—"

"*Speaking* of evidence," I barrel on, "and despite the fact that I did not receive a wedding present from either you, I'd like to gift both of *you* something. C'mon, ask me what it is."

Silence.

"*What*," Gabriel finally spits. "What is it, Dante?"

"Well…" I turn to smile at Alistair. "The DiBella case you're working on?"

It's a fairly high-profile case. Jimmy DiBella, one of the best hitmen for the Impastato family, a tributary family to the Marchettis, is on trial for, well, *being a hitman.*

"I have a golden bullet that shreds your star witness' testimony."

Alistair's jaw clenches as he gives me a hard look. "Fuck off, Dante."

"That'd be a brutal case to lose. It'd destroy that near perfect record of yours. And I can't imagine Cesare Marchetti would be jumping to put you in charge of more of his billable legal needs if Jimmy goes to prison with you as his defender."

They glance at each other as I bite back a smug smile. They know I'm right.

"What sort of a golden bullet?" Alistair mutters.

"Here." I hand him a thumb drive. "That star witness had an ongoing secret affair with DiBella two years ago."

He tries to hide it, but there's not stopping the way Alistair's jaw clenches at the news.

"Neither of them has ever admitted it, obviously, given that it's *the mafia* and they're both so far in the closet they can't even find the door. But your witness went apeshit on DiBella when Jimmy tried to end things. Trashed his apartment, torched his clothes, smashed up his car. Real psycho shit. DiBella didn't report it, or him, because, well…" I shrug. "The gay thing, not to mention that mafia hitmen tend to prefer not to call the cops for anything."

Alistair stares at me. "There's proof of this?"

I nod at the thumb drive in his hand. "It's all on there. And for *you*, Gabriel, since we don't want you feeling left out…"

I pass him a second thumb drive.

"That drama with the prostitute the media briefly stirred up a year ago, concerning Governor Atkins?"

His shoulders tighten. "Why would I give a shit about Governor Atkins?"

"Dunno," I smile. "But I'm sure the political consulting firm you've had three meetings with might give a *little* bit of a shit about it."

Gabriel stiffens. So does Alistair, who turns and glares at him.

"We were going to talk about that," he hisses.

"It's nothing," Gabriel murmurs back.

"*Any*hoo, those weren't just rumors." I nod my chin at the second thumb drive. "And I think your consulting firm would love to dig into it."

They both drop their gazes to the thumb drives, then raise their eyes back to me suspiciously.

"Why are you doing this?" Alistair growls.

"Because we might not like each other, and I know that's putting things mildly. But I'm Tempest's husband, and you're her brothers. We don't have to be best friends, but can we at least put the fucking guns down? For her?"

They're silent for a second, then Gabriel sighs heavily. "Fuck it. Fine."

"Like you said," Alistair grunts. "We don't have to be best friends." He holds up the thumb drive. "But if this is what you say it is, then... Thank you."

"Guys?" Tempest pokes her head in. "Dinner's ready."

We all step into the dining room, and Gabriel turns to Pam as she sets a tray of food down on the table. "Pam, could you please grab a bottle of the '95 Chateau Margaux? I can open it up here."

"Right away, Mr. Black."

I smirk, glancing at him. "My my, Gabriel. That's an eight-thousand-dollar bottle of wine."

"Yeah, well, happy wedding, you prick."

Again, we're not going to be best friends. But weirdly, the dark cloud over all of this does begin to lift slightly.

…I mean, sipping a glass of obscenely expensive wine doesn't exactly hurt, either.

I can't help but smile when I hear the high-pitched squeal from the other room when Tempest tells Maeve she'll be moving into Gabriel's house. Even Charles seems fine now that he's calmed down.

Pam brings out dinner—perfectly done pork chops with a peach glaze—and we all tuck in. It's no Norman Rockwell scene. It's not all bubbly laughter and witty conversation. But it's not deathly silence and dark looks, either.

I suppose that's what they call "a good start".

Tempest is chatting away with Maeve, but she turns to flash a quick smile at me.

Thank you, she mouths.

I just nod, because if I let myself dwell any deeper on any thoughts about "the time we have left", I'll go insane.

"So then Tempest..." Gabriel chuckles mid-story. "She completely ignores what dad said, and when he's not looking, she takes this whole fucking chocolate cake. Remember, there are like thirty people coming over for her ninth birthday any second. But she takes that fucking cake upstairs—"

Gabriel stops short. His face is pale and growing paler.

"*Fuck,*" he groans, holding his stomach.

He lurches to his feet and awkwardly stumbles to the side, away from the table. Tempest jumps to her feet next to me.

"Gabriel?"

He shakes his head, one hand clawing at the wall next to him. "I'm—I'm fine..."

His face turns ashen before he suddenly twists away and starts to vomit against the wall.

Shit.

Gabriel drops to his knees, still throwing up as Alistair and I run over to him at the same time.

"I've got this," Alistair grunts at me, turning back to his brother. "Hey, bro, let's get you to—"

Alistair's eyes roll back. He suddenly groans and slumps to the ground, just in time to puke all over the floor.

Oh fuck.

I'm aware of Charles dropping to his knees too as I make a beeline for Tempest.

It's the food. Something's in the—

But Tempest and Maeve aren't turning gray. They're not throwing up or falling to the floor. They're just gaping in horror as everyone collapses around them.

"Tempest—"

My legs give out, sending me sprawling to the ground in front of her.

"I—"

My vision blurs.

"Call 911…"

She's screaming my name as I start to vomit. Then my world goes black.

31

DANTE

"I'll stay."

I shake my head, looking up into Tempest's eyes as she sits perched on the edge of my hospital bed. "I'll be sprung within an hour."

A scowl comes over her face. "Says who?"

"The doctors."

"*Which* doctors?" she blurts, her tone suspicious.

I smile. "I'm fine, little hurricane."

Her cheeks flush a little pinker, like they always do when I call her that. Which always makes me want to keep saying it.

"Besides, I think I need to have a chat with your brothers."

We turn to see Alistair and Gabriel, each in their own hospital bed, glaring at us from beyond the glass partition separating my room from theirs.

"I'm a grown woman," Tempest mutters under her breath. "Neither of us needs to explain a thing to them about our…"

Relationship. Say relationship.

"Arrangement."

I grit my teeth a little.

We live together. We share a bed every night. We *fuck* in that bed—and several other places—on a very, *very* regular basis.

We're *married*, for Christ's sake.

But we both stop short of calling this what most people would. Despite how close we've gotten, and opening up to each other, we've both still kept our defenses up a little.

Because we both know this has a time limit, and calling this anything but an "arrangement" hurts too much.

"Tempest, Lorenzo's waiting for you downstairs. Take Maeve with you and head back to my place. I'll meet you there as soon as I get out of here."

She frowns uncertainly. "We're not…I mean, do you think we're in danger—"

"No," I quickly shake my head.

"But Dante, *arsenic* poisoning?"

That's what made the four of us fall down puking all over the place before blacking out. We were fucking *poisoned* by arsenic.

"It can happen with old bottles of wine," I lie, smiling at her.

It wasn't the food. That became obvious because Tempest and Maeve, who ate it, were fine. But they didn't have any wine. It was just Gabriel, Alistair, Charles, and I who did, and ended up in hospital hooked up to IV drips. Even Pam had to get checked out by the paramedics when they arrived at Gabriel's house, because of the tiny sip of the outrageously expensive wine she blushingly admitted she'd snuck for herself.

"You don't think it's…deliberate?"

"No."

Of course I do. But I'm sure as fuck not going to freak her out with that little tidbit right now when she's clearly at her wits' end after everything that's happened tonight. Right now, I just need her to get to my place, where Lorenzo and some more of my men can discreetly watch over her and keep her and Maeve safe.

Tempest sighs and nods. "Okay. I'll grab Maeve from Charles' room downstairs and go find Lorenzo."

"Perfect. I'll see you soon."

She smiles a little, her cheeks blushing as she leans down…

And kisses me.

On the mouth. Tenderly. With her brothers glaring at us through the glass.

Fuck it. My hand comes up to caress her face as I kiss her back a little harder. When she pulls away, her lips are swollen and her face is pink.

"Was that for me?" I growl. "Or them?"

"You. My brothers can mind their own fucking business."

I grin as she turns and sashays out of the room, turning to give me a wink in the doorway before she slips out. After she's gone, I swivel my gaze to Gabriel and Alistair, who both just sit there glaring at me.

Well, guess I'm the one traveling for this meeting.

Being poisoned by arsenic sucks. It fucks with your concentration, your balance, makes your stomach go nuts, and can cause all sorts of mayhem to various organs. Short version, getting up out of bed and making my way to the room next door is the opposite of fun.

I grit my teeth as I step into Alistair and Gabriel's room, pulling my IV drips behind me. I sink into a chair by the window, inhaling deeply as nausea washes over me.

"Thanks for the wine, Gabriel," I grunt. "Think I'll pass next time."

Neither of them laughs. Alistair's brow only furrows deeper at me. "What the fuck was that?" he snarls.

"Arsenic. The doctors said it at least five times, Alistair—"

"With *our sister*, asshole," he snaps.

"Well, Alistair," I smile thinly. "When two adults decide to get married—"

"Fuck off, Dante," he spits. "What you and Tempest have is an obscene business arrangement, nothing more. I'm still looking as hard as I can for a way to cancel it. So don't even joke about being *in love* with her, you fuck."

I don't realize I'm clenching my jaw until it twinges with pain.

"Alistair." Gabriel shoots his brother a warning look. Then he glances at me. "What did Tempest make of all this?"

"I told her old wine bottles can sometimes be tainted with arsenic."

Alister scowls. "You're in the habit of lying to our sister?"

"I'm in the habit of *protecting* her!" I snap.

"Enough!" Gabriel thunders. He glares at his brother, then his gaze swivels to me. "Can we agree to not talk about Tempest right now?"

"Fine," I shrug. Then I peer at him closer. "Where the hell did that bottle come from?"

He exhales. "It was a gift from a client about two months ago."

"*What client.*"

He shakes his head. "Not one who'd want me dead. Margret Worthington."

"The socialite?"

When he nods, I blow air through my lips.

Margret Worthington is an eighty-four-year-old society lady whose father was a telecommunications tycoon. She's used his money to fund hospitals, women's shelters, and orphanages across New York for decades.

The woman is a fucking *saint*.

"I was helping her with some estate planning," Gabriel says. "Her will, how her trusts are structured, how to keep the money flowing to all those charities after her death. That sort of thing." He lifts a brow. "My billable hours were a bit more than perhaps she expected, but I doubt she'd try and kill me over that."

"So someone snuck in," I grunt. "I'm sure you both have enemies. Anyone stick out?"

Alistair rolls his eyes. "I handle some serious fucking criminal cases. There's probably a hundred people on Ryker's Island who'd want me dead. Probably just as many who jerk off fantasizing about shoving a gun down Gabriel's throat."

"Great, thanks for the visual," his brother mutters.

Alistair shrugs. "I'm just saying, the list isn't exactly short. And if we factor in *you* being there"—he points at me—"not to mention Charles, we may as well accuse half the fucking city."

Shit.

I've been assuming this had to do with them. It very well could have been that *I* was the target. Or all three of us. A crazy idea comes to me.

"Do you know anything about Apex Club?"

They both instantly go quiet, and Alistair sits up in his hospital bed a little more, looking at me coldly.

"I'm going to ask you this once and only once, Dante," he growls. "What the fuck do *you* know about Apex?"

"I know you were going to prosecute one of them after what he and some of his buddies did to Tempest and her friend Nina, before he hung himself in a holding cell."

Gabriel starts to struggle out of bed, his teeth bared.

"You had *no* fucking right to dig into that—"

"I didn't dig," I say quietly. "She told me."

Gabriel pauses, staring at me in disbelief. He turns to his brother, then back to me.

"Tempest *told you?*"

I nod. "She did."

Alistair frowns. "If any of Brett's friends wanted us dead, they could have done something years ago."

"I wasn't suggesting that either of you were the target," I growl.

Gabriel arches a curious brow. "You?"

I nod.

"And why exactly would Apex Club consider you an enemy?"

"Because they killed my sister, Claudia," I hiss quietly. "So I've spent the last fifteen years hunting them down and killing them, one-by-one."

The hospital room goes pin-drop silent. Gabriel's looking at me with concern, his brow furrowed. Alistair almost looks like he's holding back a smirk.

"There were seven of them, total," I growl. "In their little club."

"How do you know that?" Gabriel mutters.

I turn to him. "Because I caught number six not very long ago, when he tried to hurt Tempest. He told me."

"And you believed him?" Alistair murmurs.

"People tend to tell the truth when they're getting their *fingers* hacked off, Alistair."

He and Gabriel glance at each other, then back at me.

"Did you do that to him for information, or because he tried to hurt Tempest?"

"Let's just say the information was a nice bonus."

Gabriel curls his lip.

"So, was he right?"

Gabriel frowns and doesn't answer immediately.

"For fuck's sake, Gabriel," I snap. "This is about knowing if anyone else is coming after Tempest!"

He and his brother glance at each other again. When Alistair nods subtly, Gabriel draws in a breath and turns back to me.

"Seven's the number we were told, too."

I scowl. "From the little fuck who hanged himself?"

Alistair nods. "Yep. Brett Sinclair." He all but spits the name. "Good fucking riddance."

This time, he actually does turn his head and spit. I can't say I blame him. But then, something occurs to me, and my eyes narrow.

"Forget his Apex buddies. Would his *family* want either of you—"

"Nope," Gabriel grunts with finality.

I frown. "You seem awfully sure about that."

Alistair smirks. "There's only one Sinclair left, and he sends us a Christmas card every year from one of his several mansions around the world."

My brow arches. "Why the fuck would he do that?"

"After Brett offed himself in the holding cell, the Sinclair family went to shit. His parents got divorced when it turned out Mrs. Sinclair—Jacqueline—had been banging her tennis coach. Grant Sinclair, Brett's dad, took everything and left Jacqueline with *shit*. A few years later, Grant and his new girlfriend died in a car crash and the entire fortune went to Grant's weirdo slacker brother, Chris. I mean this guy was trying to start a fucking kombucha company and then woke up one morning to a dead brother and a bank account worth eight billion dollars. They hated each other, I think, but that was the only family Grant had left. So now Chris sends us Christmas cards, like a macabre thank you note."

I frown. "And the ex-wife? Jacqueline?"

"Also dead," Gabriel sighs. "She managed to hang on a few years by selling off her furs and jewelry. But she ended up broke and was found dead of a drug overdose in some hotel in Vegas a year or two ago."

"Well, shit," I mutter. "We're back at square one."

Alistair eyes me appraisingly. "You really killed six of those fuckers?"

I nod.

"So now they're all dead," he muses quietly. "Tempest know that?"

"She does."

"Good," he growls.

Just then, the door swings open and Lorenzo walks in briskly, a hard look on his face.

"What's going on?" I growl. "Where's—"

"Mrs. Sartorre and Ms. Black are safely on their way to your place, sir, with some of my most trusted men. But you need to see this immediately." He holds up a plastic bag marked "Evidence". "From one of our boys on the NYPD."

He passes the bag to me, and I frown at the cork inside.

"From your house," Lorenzo says to Gabriel. "It's from the bottle."

"Did they test it for—"

I stop cold when I flip the bag over, my eyes locking on the words written by hand, in ink, on the side of the cork.

Even a single lion can bring the savannah to its knees.

You missed one of us.

I'm yanking IV drip lines out of my arm in seconds, whirling to Lorenzo.

"Get me home, *now*."

Then I turn to Gabriel. "I'm sending Maeve with you back to your place, along with ten men, just in case."

Gabriel nods. "And Tempest?"

"I'm taking her out of the city, where she'll be safe."

32

TEMPEST

I love New York City. I was born here, and I've lived here my entire life reveling in the gorgeous chaos of it. That said, getting *out* of it from time to time is great, too.

...Even if that getaway is less "vacation" and more "fleeing clear and present danger".

When we first start to drive to the Hamptons, Dante is incredibly convincing at making it sound like he just needs a break from work, and *that* is why we're headed out there.

Or at least, it would be convincing if I was a complete idiot.

"Old wine bottles don't randomly produce arsenic. I googled it."

His eyes swivel to mine for a second. "Look, this is just a precautionary—"

"Someone tried to kill you!" My heart is pounding. "And my brothers! And your response is for us to just *leave* and—"

"There are ten of my best men watching your brothers, and Maeve, and even your turd of a grandfather."

I frown. "But you don't even like my brothers."

"Well…" His hand slides across the middle column of the Mercedes SUV, his fingers lacing tight with mine. "I kinda like *you*. So, figured I'd keep them safe, too."

My face heats. "Kinda like me, huh?"

"Don't let it go to your head."

I turn away, grinning like an idiot out the passenger window.

"He *is* a real turd of a grandfather, isn't he?"

Dante chuckles as the car accelerates down 495, and the city begins to recede.

THE FIRST FEW days we're out at Dante's house I call my brothers, and Maeve, and Bianca almost daily to check in on them, which is comforting and keeps me from freaking out. Pam, bless her heart, arranges for a courier to cart a giant cooler full of my frozen smoothies out to the Hamptons. She might not be the warm and fuzzy type, but it's sweet of her to do. Especially since she's also dealing with the after-effects of mild arsenic poisoning, after sneaking a little of the wine Gabriel opened up. I think she was also convinced she was going to be fired for that, until my brother assured her he was more concerned about her being okay that about a few sips of wine.

I don't just up and forget that someone tried to poison me and those closest to me. But as the days tick by, being out here starts to feel more and more like a vacation.

Dante and I cook dinner every night. We take walks along the beach—shadowed, of course, by at least three of his men. We watch old movies, lounge around reading, and spend a ridiculous amount of time fucking each other's brains out.

Jesus, I could get used to this.

But a week into living at Dante's sprawling shore house, I'm starting to go a little stir crazy. It's gorgeous out here, but at the same time, I mean, there's only so many walks on the beach you can take.

The weather is crappy on the day I decide to go exploring. Dante's on some work calls in his office, so I start to poke around the several thousand square feet of this house I haven't seen yet.

I meander through the library, the pool house, the *massive* basement wine cellar. I check out guest rooms, sitting rooms, the massive ballroom where he threw our engagement party.

Eventually, I open a door to what appears to be Dante's second home office. It's small, with gorgeous built-in book-shelves and huge picture windows overlooking the Long Island Sound.

It's the kind of home office that makes me want to get my shit together and figure out what the heck I want to be when I grow up so *I* can work out of it.

At least, if I *was* going to grow up.

I'm getting worse. The spells of confusion and dizziness are becoming more frequent. My appetite *sucks*, to the point that I'm basically living off smoothies, water, and the odd cracker.

…And I threw up more blood a few days ago.

I resolutely shove all of that aside.

Dying sucks, but that doesn't mean I have to spend whatever time I have left being miserable. I mean, here I am, living in a mansion, spending my days and nights lounging around like I'm on vacation and having the most mind-blowing sex any woman has ever had with a bona fide sex god.

There are seriously worse ways to spend the last grains of sand in your hourglass.

I slump down into the comfy leather office chair at the desk. For a few minutes, I just swivel idly, looking out the window at the ocean. Then, of course, my curiosity gets the better of me and I start to paw through the desk for no other reason than I'm bored.

There are some financial records, some contractors' receipts for work done on Club Venom. An opened invitation to some gala at The Plaza, and a buyer's information packet on a yacht. Ooh, yacht.

Then, beneath some random papers in the bottom drawer, I find it: a dark wooden box.

Something in the back of my brain tells me to leave it alone. It's not mine, and it's certainly none of my business, and I shouldn't be snooping like this.

So, *obviously*, I pull it out, set it on the desk in front of me, and slowly open the lid.

Instantly, my breath sucks in sharply, a chill zipping down my spine, like I've just seen a ghost.

Layla's smiling face beams up at me from the Polaroid photo, her green eyes shining, her smile wide and welcoming, and her hand raised with her fingers making a peace sign. I wince as my heart clenches sharply.

God, she was so beautiful. And fun, and bubbly. She was the life of every party, without being an attention seeker or making it all about her. Everyone just gravitated toward Layla.

…Including—for reasons I still don't know and that I've been afraid to think about for the last month—Dante.

Dante, who wasn't friends with her, yet brought her to the hospital that day.

Dante, who *married her* in her final minutes, and then completely shut out our entire family.

I swallow thickly as I lift the photo from the box. Beneath it is another Polaroid: Layla again, but this time, she's taking a selfie with her arm around Dante's shoulders.

He's *smiling*.

What the fuck?

There's a handwritten letter from Layla to Dante, addressed to him in Sicily. In it, she talks about being home for the winter holidays from Knightsblood, and about our brothers, and me, and says she hopes Dante is having a good Christmas with the Barone family.

I pull out more Polaroids from the box: pictures of Layla lounging in her dorm room at Knightsblood. One of Dante striking a silly pose in a winter coat, standing on a rock next to the ocean.

One of the two of them, huddled close together.

I feel something stab in my chest.

They don't look like strangers who didn't know each other. They look like best friends.

The stabbing sensation twists sharply.

Not best friends. Closer than that.

I shouldn't have opened this.

I hate that I'm shaking, and I hate that I'm jealous, but I really hate that it looks like Dante and *my own sister* were a hell of a lot more than "strangers". Angrily, my stomach churning, I start to collect everything hurriedly to shove it back in the box. In my haste, I bump the box with my elbow and tips over, dumping the rest of the contents across the desk.

I was hurt before. I felt sick and devastated and jealous beyond belief to see those photos.

...But nothing on earth can prepare me for what I find myself staring down at, there in black and white, on the desk.

———

DANTE LOOKS up from his desk when I come surging into the room. He mutters something into his phone before he hangs up and gets to his feet.

"Whoa, what's going—"

"I want the truth!!" I blurt, shaking as tears stream down my face. My entire body feels like it's wrenching in two, my heart twisting around itself as my stomach ties into knots.

Dante blinks in confusion.

"Tempest—"

"TELL ME!" I scream. "What were you and my sister?!"

He goes still.

"Go ahead!" I yell. "Go ahead and lie! Tell me you didn't even know each other! Tell me you just *happened* to take her to the hospital that night! And fucking *marry* her!!"

Dante's jaw ticks. "It was a complicated situation, Tempest," he growls quietly. "As were the reasons for my actions that horrible day—"

"Complicated because she was fucking *pregnant?!*"

I hurl the ultrasound picture with Layla's name at the top at him. My vision blurs as I start to shake uncontrollably.

"You *motherfucker!!*" I scream again. "You—you—"

"Tempest, listen to—"

"I'm going to be sick." I whirl aimlessly in circles as my breathing comes faster and faster. "This is so fucking…this is *fucked up!*" I wheel on him abruptly. "Is this some sick, twisted fetish of yours?! Fuck one girl and then fuck her little sister, too—"

"I never slept with Layla," Dante chokes through clenched teeth.

"She was fucking *pregnant,* you son of—"

"*NOT. BY. ME!!*"

His voice booms through the room, momentarily stunning me and knocking the air from my lungs. Dante charges around the corner of his desk, and before I can run, he's grabbed me by the wrists and yanked me tight against his chest.

"*Listen to me.*"

"Get your fucking hands off of me!" I scream and sob, tears flowing down my face. "Get away from me! I hate you! I fucking hate—!"

"Your sister, *Tempest!*" Dante roars abruptly, shocking me into silence. His eyes burn into mine, his jaw clenching as a vein pops on his forehead. "Your sister," he chokes a little more quietly, "saved my life, and she was my best, and for a while my *only*, friend."

33

DANTE

Fifteen years ago:

HOPE CAN DIE.

An inch from my toes, the cliff drops to the swirling black waves below. The wind howls in my ears, clawing its way down my back and chilling the cold hard lump knotted in my chest.

They said it would get better, "eventually". Somehow, someday, I'm supposed to "get over" Claudia's death.

No. Some wounds don't heal. Some pain cuts too deep to bleed its way back out again.

My freshman year here at Knightsblood was supposed to be a new start after what happened to my sister. I've even got Carmy here with me. But coming here has only underscored what I've tried to overlook ever since my parents died and Vito took in my sisters and me: we may be living in a house that the mafia built, but we are *not* mafia.

I'm here at Knightsblood because of Vito's influence, power, notoriety, and money. Carmine is, too. But the difference between us is blood. *Every* mafia-connected student at Knightsblood is here because of their parentage.

I'm only here because Vito called in favors, and every day I spend here highlights that even more.

It's not as if Carmine and I don't spend time together. It's just that he's got his own thing going on with other mafia heirs: other students that one day he'll either do business with, or make war on.

That won't be my future, though. So I find myself on the periphery, my soul still ripped into pieces from losing Claudia.

I've tried: God knows I've tried. For her. For myself. For Bianca, of course. For the Barone family, too, after all they've done for us.

But sometimes trying isn't enough. Sometimes, the harder you fight to keep your head above water, the quicker you tire and start to drown.

Interesting choice of words...

I glance down at the ocean beneath me and the cinderblock tied to my ankle. Arrangements have already been made. Bianca will get everything I have, including the letter I wrote to her last night. It's not that I want to leave her alone—in fact, that's the hardest part about going through with this.

It's just that I can't fight anymore.

I don't *want* to fight anymore. I'm tired of it, tired of the endless pain in my heart whenever I think about Claudia and the horrible way she died.

Besides, what am I going to do with my life? Work for Carmine when he takes over as don?

I exhale slowly and tap my toe against the cinderblock.

"Dude…what are you doing?"

My head whips around at the soft, feminine voice. The girl is my age, maybe a year older, with big hazel-green eyes, dark hair, and an elfin chin. Her gaze drops to the cinderblock, and the rope, and the cliff behind me.

I don't answer for a few seconds. I just stand there, studying this curious girl I've never met, but who is probably a fellow student, given the hoodie she's wearing with the university emblem on it.

"Terrible way to do it, incidentally."

"Excuse me?" I growl.

"It's low tide right now, so the water's maybe…eight feet deep?"

I just glare at her.

"If you went *without* the cinderblock, the waves would probably slam you against the cliffs hard enough to knock you out or straight up smash your brains in. Or carry you out further where you could drown properly."

I lift a brow, still silent. This girl is fucking *weird*.

"*But* if you go with the stone, it's going to anchor you. And you're what, six feet?"

"Six-two," I mutter.

"There you go. You'll be tethered by the ankle. And that rope is like a foot and a half long, maybe, so you won't even be underwater. You'll just be stuck there until the tide goes out a little more, and then comes back in. So it'll be slow, and *really* cold. Also, decent chance of breaking your leg on the way down, for what that's worth. I'm just saying."

I can't stop staring at her. "You're kinda weird."

She arches a brow. "Dude, I'm not the one trying to commit suicide by cliff-jumping like some tragic Jane Austen character."

The corners of my mouth curl up slightly.

"What is it?" she prods. "Grades? You get dumped?"

When I don't answer, she shrugs.

"Whatever it is, trust me, it's not that bad. You survived. You're here, and you're alive."

"What's so great about that?" I grunt.

"Umm... Not being dead?"

I smile slightly wider. Weird, but also fun. And interesting, in a curious way.

"I'm Layla, by the way. Layla Black."

"Dante," I growl quietly. "Sartorre."

I look away over the ocean, the call of the abyss getting fainter.

"I wasn't really going to jump."

Layla smirks. "No?"

"Nah. Just taking my pet cinderblock for a walk."

The smirk turns into a grin. "Good. I feel like he could use it. He's looking chonky."

"Bastard just can't say no to cookies."

She grins again, pulling a pack of American Spirit cigarettes —the light blue kind—from her hoodie pocket. "Want one?"

"No way. Those things'll kill you."

She glances significantly at the rock tied to my ankle.

"Touche. Thanks, I'll take one."

We sit in silence about a foot away from the edge of the cliff, quietly smoking and looking out over the black waves. When we're done our cigarettes, I realize the rock is untied from my ankle, and I don't even remember which of us did it.

We stand, and she shakes my hand as if she's just sold me a used car.

"Well, nice to meet you, Dante Sartorre."

"Likewise, Layla Black."

She grins. "Have fun walking your rock."

"Thanks."

She turns and starts to walk away. When she's maybe twenty feet from me, she turns and nods her chin.

"Hey, Dante?"

"Yeah?"

She shrugs. "Don't go over the edge, okay? There's a whole world out there."

Thirteen years ago:

350

SOMETIMES, the darkness and sadness that grips your heart come from something so visceral, it's like a slap in the face. It's impossible to ignore, and it drives you to do reckless, stupid, hopeless things…like stand on cliff edges with cinderblocks tied to your ankle.

Other times, like in Layla's case, that darkness just sort of…*happens*. And there's no telling when, or how hard it'll hit.

Depression is a *motherfucker*.

So is addiction.

The machines looming over Layla's hospital bed beep rhythmically. I grit my teeth so hard it hurts as I stand there looking down at my best friend.

She looks so frail. So weak. Almost lifeless already.

How the fuck did it come to this?

Layla's always said she has an addictive personality. I've seen that clearly over the two years that we've been friends. Cigarettes are the big one. But also guys who should've treated her so much better. And no, it's *not* a jealousy thing on my part, seeing Layla date shitheads who treat her like dirt. It's…protectiveness.

Layla is objectively speaking a very pretty girl, but there's nothing between us. And nobody on campus would assume we *were* an item, because we hang out in private.

Not because either of us is ashamed of the other or anything. It's just that she's got her own world, with her own friends and her brothers Gabriel and Alistair, and I've got mine, with Carmy and Nico, and the other mafia types.

Layla says our platonic relationship is because I remind her of her brothers in different ways. She also says it's because she's my "wish dot com version of Claudia", which feels somehow disrespectful to both her *and* my dead sister, and yet is also hilarious.

Hilarious.

I look down at the shell of a girl lying half-dead in the hospital bed.

No one's laughing anymore. Because Layla's addictive personality finally found its match, after getting bored with cigarettes and terrible boyfriends.

A year ago, Layla found *heroin.*

I will forever hate the day she did.

It's not the first time she's taken too much. I shot her full of adrenaline and drove her to a walk-in clinic when I found her in pretty bad shape once. I've put her into rehab *twice.*

I've almost told her brothers a hundred times. But I haven't, because she's begged me over and over not to. Layla's never wanted her family to know about her demons.

I've wrestled with that ever since I found out about her addiction: telling them and potentially getting her more help, at the cost of losing her friendship. It's a trade I'd be willing to make, for her sake. But she's also not above bringing up that night we met at the cliff, and the way she saved my life.

So I've always kept silent.

Today, I fucking *hate* myself for it.

Things don't look good. Her heart is shot: the surface has become infected. The doctor told me half an hour ago that it would take a miracle for her to see tomorrow, and suggested I start saying my goodbyes.

Layla's eyelids slowly flutter open, and she makes a dry choking sound. I quickly grab the water from the bedside table and bring the straw to her parched lips.

After she swallows, her head sinks back into the pillow, a pained expression on her face. She turns away from me.

"I fucked up, didn't I, Dante?"

When I don't say anything, she glances back at me.

"How bad?"

This time it's me that looks away.

"*Shit*," she murmurs quietly. Tears bead in her eyes as she swallows thickly. "*Fuck*, Alistair and Gabriel are going to be so fucking angry at me for this."

"You can get better," I hiss. "You're not going to—"

"Dante."

Her face is pained as she struggles to lift her hand to mine. I reach for it, grabbing hers and squeezing.

"You're not—"

"I *am*," she croaks, a wry smile on her face. "I can feel it." She looks down, her head slowly shaking side to side. "I'm so sorry."

"Don't be, Layla, just rest. I called a specialist in New York. He's going to be here tomorrow—"

"But I won't be." She looks up at me, her eyes no longer sad, just resigned. "I'm sorry I made you cover up my sins," she whispers.

"It's fine," I grunt. "Don't worry about it."

She sighs. "And my God...*Tempest*. What the fuck is my sister going to think when she learns about this?"

I fight back tears as I grip her hand tighter.

"Dante."

"Yeah."

Layla's face twists into something between a smile and sadness. "There's something else. No one else knows, but I want you to."

She starts to cry.

"I'm pregnant."

Holy. Fuck.

I blink quickly, my breath coming faster.

"It's early," she says quietly, her face twisting in pain. "It's super early..."

I hold her as she cries, cradling her against my chest as she sobs out her pain.

"Jason?" I growl.

She nods against me, and my face turns furious.

Her *dealer*.

Her scumbag, piece of shit dealer who she's also been "sort of dating". He's the motherfucker who led her from cocaine to fucking heroin. And now he's knocked her up just in time for her to overdose.

I'm going to fucking kill him with my bare fucking hands.

Literally.

"Dante, please," she murmurs when I start to shake with rage. "Just…" she exhales. "I want it to be you that tells them. My siblings, I mean. Wait until I'm gone, because I'm way too much of a coward to face them about this myself. But when I'm—"

"What if they never knew."

She looks up at me. "About?"

"About any of it."

She chews on her chapped lower lip, her face gaunt and gray. "How? I mean Alistair and Gabriel are my closest family. They'll be told the second they walk in—"

"What if you had *other, closer* family."

She frowns. "I don't get what you're—"

"What if you married me."

The room is quiet but for the beeping of the machines keeping her alive.

"Ha-ha," she says dryly. "Deathbed jokes. You never cease to surprise me—"

"I'm not joking." I lean closer. "If we were married, I could legally seal off your medical records, even from your siblings."

She smiles wryly. "Heroin use is a felony, Dante," she says quietly, her voice shaking. "I'm already in the system. The hospital was required to report it when I came in—"

"Pregnancy isn't." I grit my teeth. "If you want, I can hide that part."

355

She stares at me, her throat bobbing as her chest with the tubes coming out of it rises and falls.

"Why would you do that?" she croaks.

I hold her hand tighter. "Because you fucking saved me. And I can't save you." I choke out the last words, fury, rage, and sadness burning hot in my chest.

"If they ever do find out, they'll all think it was you that knocked me up."

"Yeah. But they won't find out."

"But *if* they do…"

She's fading out again. Her eyes are losing focus and her pulse is getting weaker.

We're doing this right now.

"They'll hate you," she whispers.

"Then they'll hate me. Just say yes, Layla, and I'll call the hospital chaplain and in-house lawyer right now."

A tear trickles down her cheek as she grips my hand as tightly as she can, which isn't very tightly at all.

"Yes," she chokes out quietly. Then she nods, her eyes closing a little. "Better get that preacher, Dante," she murmurs. "I don't know how much longer you'll have a bride with a pulse."

I'm at the door when she calls my name again. "Oh, and Dante?" She opens her eyes and grins a sleepy smile at me. "Remember: don't go over the edge, okay?"

Twenty minutes later, the documents are signed, and Layla is my wife.

Five minutes after that, I'm a widower.

An hour after *that*, I'm kicking in Jason's front door and committing my first murder—with my bare hands, as promised.

And then I mourn the loss of my best friend, who saved me.

Whom I couldn't save back.

Present:

TEMPEST IS SOBBING by the time I finish telling her everything. She collapses into my arms, clinging to me as she raises her tear-streaked face to mine and kisses me hard.

"You never said anything..." she sobs.

"I promised her," I choke through clenched teeth. "I couldn't break that."

"So why now?"

I look away, my arms circling her tightly.

"Because your sister always used to tell me to not go over the edge. And going one more second without telling you the truth was going to be going over that edge."

Tempest sinks into my arms as I hold her tight: our lips locked, our hearts beating together.

Two toxic souls crashing together.

34

TEMPEST

OUR WEEK in the Hamptons turns into two, and then three. Three weeks in a ten-thousand square foot home on the beach, constantly having the most incredible sex ever?

Pretty sweet.

That said, I do miss my New York life, at times. Gabriel, Alistair, Bianca, and Taylor have all come to visit. And, Pam, bless her, keeps sending those smoothies out like clockwork. Still, it's not the same.

The not-so-sweet part is that Charles has used what happened at the dinner party to go back on his word about Maeve moving in with Gabriel. He's been stalling ever since, blaming the "unsafe atmosphere" around my brothers for not allowing the move to go as promised. Which is obviously complete horseshit.

If my grandfather gives a single shit about his own daughter, it pales in comparison to the shit he gives about power and using her to somehow gain more of it.

Three weeks after we get out here, I'm sitting in the library reading a book when there's a knock on the doorframe.

I grin without even looking up.

"Oh, good, it's the pool boy with my daiquiri and fresh sunscreen."

"I think you're overdressed for a pool."

I giggle as he walks over and plucks the book from my hands, and the fact that he slips a bookmark into it before he tosses it to the side is just...*yeah.*

Chef's kiss.

Dante leans down to kiss me softly. His tongue explores my mouth, his hand tangling in my hair. When he finally pulls away, I'm breathless and *aching* for him.

"What was all that for?" I breathe.

"That," he murmurs, "was me telling you to get dressed. We're going out."

I blink. "I'm sorry, *what?*"

For the last three weeks, we haven't left the grounds of this house at all, with the threat of what happened with the arsenic poisoning hanging over us and all. And now we're going *out?*

Dante smiles a thin, grim smile. My brow furrows.

"Wait, what is it?"

"They found the guy."

My eyes widen. "Seriously?"

He nods. "Ken Freeman. He's a nobody. A rich trust fund drug addict. But his first cousin was Lance Hammond." When my brow furrows, his darkens. "*Lance* was in Apex Club. Ken was hoping to get revenge for his death, I guess."

I shudder, my stomach knotting.

"Oh, and he's dead, by the way."

"Holy shit," I breathe.

"Ken OD'ed on fentanyl-laced cocaine. A concerned neighbor called the cops, and they found arsenic, rubber gloves and chemistry equipment, plus copied keys to Gabriel's back basement door in his apartment. Apparently, your brother lost his keys a few weeks ago for half a day before his dry cleaner found them in one of his trouser pockets."

My head spins. "Wait, so…it's over?"

He grins as he leans down to kiss me. "Yeah, little hurricane," he murmurs. "It's over. So we're going out. Whatever you want to do, we'll—"

"Dancing," I blurt. "I want to go dancing."

That awful night ruined clubs for me. But then Dante happened. The man broke down my walls and pulled me out of my own head, showing me things I'd forgotten that I used to enjoy.

Like dancing at clubs.

Dante arches a brow. "I was thinking dinner at a Michelin spot, or—"

"You said anything," I grin. "I pick dancing. I mean, unless you're scared of sucking at it and—"

I giggle as he kisses me hard. "Get your dancing shoes on."

IF YOU DON'T KNOW, the Hamptons are a total capital-S *Scene*. Manhattan trust fund brats, finance bros, celebrities, heirs to Fortune 500 companies, and the usual socialite crowd. Which is pretty much everything I hate, but it does mean the sleepy little towns that dot the coast of Long Island that together make "The Hamptons" are littered with five-star places for dinner and drinks, and some fantastic dance clubs.

Dante and I—him in gunmetal gray pants and a white shirt with the sleeves rolled up, me in a short black dress that flares out at the hips—end up at the Beachsider. The crowd looks a little less douchey than the usual, and it turns out that Dante knows one of the guys on the door.

"That's Leo," he murmurs in my ear after the guy waves us through the line and inside. "He works security at Venom when he's not here."

I smirk as we step into the steamy heat and neon-tinged darkness. "I wonder if anyone else from Venom will recognize you."

"Doubt it. No one aside from my staff and a few select VIPs know my face. When I'm on the floor at Venom, my mask is always on, just like everyone else."

I turn to eye him. "Do you do that a lot? Browse the scene out on the main floor?"

His lips curl into a smirk and his hand lands on my ass, yanking me close. "Was that your subtle way of asking —*again*, I might add—if I participate in public sex at my own club? You know I don't."

My breath catches as I sink against his chest. "What if it was me?"

A growl rumbles in his throat. "What do you mean?"

"I mean what if it was you and me out on the floor of Venom, with masks on, but nothing else? Would you...*participate* then?"

"Just you and me?"

I nod.

"And if I could gouge the eyes out afterward of every single man who saw you like that?"

I grin. "Sure."

Dante's brow arches. "I'm joking."

"*Are* you?"

Something dangerous flickers in his eyes. "Maybe. If *you* wanted that—"

"I'm not saying I—"

"If it *was*," he growls. "I want you to always be able to explore what you want to explore about yourself."

"Oh, good!" I grin. "So, when we get back to New York, I'd love to explore having three strangers totally bang—"

I gasp as his hand clamps onto my jaw, tilting my face up to his. His eyes burn hotly as they blaze into mine, sending a heated throb through my core.

"*Careful, little hurricane*," he growls.

I tremble. "Of you?"

"Of getting those three strangers put into the uncomfortable position of having their legs and dicks cut off so that they can watch helplessly as I fuck you over the pool of their blood."

Jesus fucking Christ.

Why is that so fucked up and scary, and why does it make me so *wet?*

"There's a chance I have...issues," Dante grunts, his lips curling slightly.

"There's also a chance that was super-hot," I murmur quietly, gazing up at him.

"Let's dance."

Dante leads me onto the floor and into the swirl of undulating, gyrating bodies. We grind together, hot and sweaty in no time—from the music, and the crowd, and the fact that his hands are all over me.

"I'm going to grab a drink!" I yell over the music. "Want anything?"

"Whiskey," he growls into my ear, pulling me against the thick bulge in his pants so I can feel it throbbing against my lower stomach. "Neat."

"So, just in a glass?"

"Or off your skin."

I grin as our eyes lock. Then I slip away and meander my way through the crowd to the bar. I grab Dante's whiskey and an easy vodka soda for myself. I'm turning to go find Dante again when a figure steps in front of me.

"How're we doing tonight?"

The man is tall, with broad shoulders, and yet he looks…*soft*. Pampered. Weak. And *way* too primped and pretty, like he spent more time than anyone else in the club in front of the mirror earlier.

"We're…doing fine?" I smile uncertainly at him.

"Buy you a drink?"

I lift the two in my hands. "I'm good, but thank you. Enjoy your—"

"Hang on."

I stiffen when his hand lands on my hip as I try and move past him.

"We just met, how about we talk for a second at least."

"Let go of me."

The man chuckles. "I like your attitude," he grins. "Feisty."

"Let go of me or you're going to find out *how* feisty, buddy."

He laughs. Suddenly, I jolt, tensing everywhere when he yanks me against his soft body.

"It's loud as fuck in here, gorgeous. Let's go find someplace quiet—"

"I'm not interested. Now *let. Go. Of*—"

He pounces in an instant with a drunken lurch. His hand slides to grab my ass as he drops his face, like he's going to kiss me.

…Which is exactly when something shoves him away with the force of a freight train.

Dante snarls and sends the man flying away from me, tripping over his own feet and landing on the ground. The crowd parts around him as Dante storms over and kicks him hard in the stomach, then drops to his knees astride the man's chest and starts to hit him in the face, over and over.

...There might be something very wrong with me that I find the visual of my husband "defending my honor" against a handsy asshole, with his hands bloodied, *insanely* hot.

A big man dressed in black comes rushing over. I realize he's the same guy who knows Dante—Leo—at the same time that *Leo* realizes the guy dishing out the beating is his at-times boss.

Dante stands and Leo yanks the asshole off the floor by his collar.

"We've got an empty storage room downstairs, Mr. Sartorre," Leo murmurs, glancing at Dante. "If you want me to bring him down there for a little more privacy."

Dante's eyes narrow as he walks up to the bloodied, drunk, douchebag.

"What's your name."

"*Carl!*" The guy sobs through bloody lips. "Please..."

"Carl, that woman you just put your fucking hands on is my *wife.*"

The man goes pale.

"But tonight's your lucky night, *Carl.* You see, I'd rather spend my time *fucking* my wife than breaking every bone in your body. But I will say this."

He grabs Carl's collar and yanks him closer.

"If I ever see you again—here or anywhere else—I'll fucking kill you. Understand?"

Carl nods pathetically.

"Get him the fuck out of here, Leo."

"You got it, Mr. Sartorre."

I rush into Dante's arms as Leo drags a sniveling Carl away.

"Your hands…" I gasp taking them in mine. "Let me get you some ice—"

Instead, Dante suddenly grabs me and yanks me after him as he dives back into the crowd. In the very center of the mass of swirling, grinding humanity, he spins me around quickly and then tugs me back against him. My ass squirms against his bulge, and I whimper softly.

Fuck, he's hard as steel.

His hands skim up and down my sides, teasing the sides of my breasts and grabbing my hips. His cock throbs against my ass, and suddenly, his hand slips under the front hem of my dress.

"*Dante…*"

He just bites down my neck from behind, making me moan as his fingers tease the edge of my panties. They push down lower under the lace, cupping my bare pussy as I start to tremble and shake.

His fingers roll over my clit and then delve deeper, curling as he sinks two thick digits into my eager pussy.

I. Am. *Soaked*.

"You'd better be wet for *me*, not him," he rasps dangerously into my ear, like a knife's edge teasing over tender flesh.

I moan as he starts to finger me hard and fast, his palm grinding against my clit. I turn my head, my eyes locking with his in the neon darkness.

"I'm always wet for you..."

His mouth crushes to mine as his fingers stroke in and out of me. My legs shake and buckle, my body writhing under his touch. His other hand slips between us. Then suddenly there's a tug, and his hand is gripping the back of my dress and yanking it up over my ass.

"*Dante!*" I yelp, my heart hammering as I feel his hand on my bare ass.

Something else presses hotly against my ass, and my eyes bulge.

Holy fuck, is he for real?

Dante's thick, swollen cock slips between my thighs from behind. I can feel him bend his knees, angling his cock up as his hand pulls my panties to the side.

Holy shit. Holy shit. Holy shit...

"Never forget *whose you are.*"

He sinks into me with one powerful thrust. I almost scream before I clamp a hand over my own mouth, Dante's fat cock driving into me from behind.

It's almost too much: too much sensation. Too much danger. Too much risk and adrenaline. But as he keeps fucking me in time to the music, with his hands on my hips and my dress mostly covering us, it just looks like we're dancing extra dirty with each other.

Not a single person who saw us right now would imagine that every inch of this man's cock is rammed deep in my dripping wet pussy.

The beat picks up, and so does his pace. He pounds into me savagely and aggressively, his hands roaming all over my body as I arch my back and push my ass back against him. He cups one of my breasts, pinching the nipple roughly through my dress just as his gorgeous cock sinks balls-deep.

All of it slams together: the crowd, the music, the public nature of this, and the thrill of being caught or seen. And of course, *him*, and his god-like ability to fuck me *exactly* how I need it.

And suddenly I'm shattering for him.

Just as I cry out, Dante grabs a fistful of my hair and twists my face around. His mouth slams to mine, swallowing my moans and cries of pleasure as he fucks into me over and over. I'm still coming when I feel his thick cock swell even more. He sinks deep, and I moan into his mouth when I feel the hot, thick spurts of cum spill into me.

We stay like that, swaying and dancing to the music—lip-to-lip, bodies pressed together, his dick still buried inside of me.

Then we do it all over again.

35

TEMPEST

You could say that what I'm about to do is underhanded, sneaky, and wrong. But I'm choosing to view it through a different lens. This isn't stabbing Dante in the back or meddling with his life.

It's fixing a problem he only has because of me.

I've been thinking about Layla a lot since the truth came out back in the Hamptons, and even more since we got back to New York. The last thing Dante did for her was bury a secret she never wanted any of us to discover. In doing so, he made our whole family hate him and think the worst of him.

Maybe he'll hate *me* for what I'm about to do, but that's fine. I won't be here to feel shitty about it for long. And before I go, I can fix this problem for him.

Dante generally keeps a tight lid on all things Club Venom, and definitely on all things mafia. But the door to his office was open the other night while he was on the phone to someone that I eventually gathered was Vito Barone. Through the open door I heard Dante's side of a conversation about Luciano Amato wanting to shut down Venom, or at least remove Dante as owner, over the situation with Silvio Bonpensiero.

And *that* got me thinking about the firemen's gala we went to, where Renata Bonpensiero was a huge bitch to me. I remembered Dante threatening her back with information he had on her husband working against the interests of his boss, Don Amato.

Dante's conversation with Vito also clued me in that, while he *had* information on Frank Bonpensiero, he wasn't sure about using it quite yet.

I beg to differ.

So the other night, I...*acquired* that information. By which I mean, I might have slunk naked into Dante's office, dropped to my knees and took his cock down my throat. And I *might* have watched him type in his computer password to wake it up again after he'd finished fucking me across his desk.

Again, it's maybe wrong for me to be doing this without even talking to Dante. But this is one thing I can do for him after all he's done for me, not to mention for Layla. I can stop certain people from calling for his removal from Venom.

I take a deep breath as I step out of the Uber in front of the Amato Brothers Funeral Parlor in the Gowanus neighborhood of Brooklyn.

I never thought I'd be a mafia deal negotiator. But, well, here we are.

There's a big guy in a black suit smoking a cigarette by the front door. He eyes me curiously as I walk up to him.

"The Angelino service isn't until tomorrow, miss."

"Oh, I'm not here for that."

He smiles politely. "Well, business inquiries are by appointment only. The website has a way to make—"

"I'm here to see Don Amato."

The man goes quiet, arching a brow at me. Then he eyes me up and down, pulling his jacket open just enough for me to see the gun holstered under his arm.

"I think you need to—"

"I'm not going anywhere until I see Don Amato," I smile. "Trust me, he'll want to meet with me. You can tell him it's Mrs. Sartorre."

The guard quickly sucks down the rest of his cigarette. Then he tosses it aside and stamps it out.

"Wait here."

He slips inside. A minute later, he's back, looking at me with curious interest.

"Come on in."

———

"MY, MY, MY. MRS. SARTORRE..."

Luciano Amato is a large man both vertically and horizontally. He's also *very* well dressed and is somehow not just "pulling off" a pinstripe suit, he's seriously rocking it.

He stands as I'm ushered into his office above the funeral home, which, from what I've heard from my brothers, is notorious for occasionally putting *more than one body* in a casket before burying it.

...If you get my drift.

"Please, have a seat," Don Amato rumbles, gesturing at the chair in front of his desk. "Would you like a drink?"

"No, thank you, Don Amato. Thank you for seeing me."

"Of course. I assume you're here to apologize?"

I smile benignly as I settle in my chair. "For?"

He frowns. "For fucking up my niece's boy's face, and for your prick of a husband putting him in a goddamn coma, that's what."

I clear my throat. "I hear Silvio is awake now."

Luciano grunts. "He is. So, where's this apology?"

"Oh," I smile. "There is no apology. Your niece's son is a giant piece of shit, and if I had it my way, he'd be back in that coma."

Luciano's brows shoot up. He looks half amused, half pissed off as he steeples his hands and studies me from across the desk.

"You got balls, Mrs. Sartorre, I'll give you that," he mutters eventually. "So why don't you tell me why the fuck are you here, then?"

"I'd like to bury the hatchet, so to speak."

I reach into my bag, which the guard at the door already examined, and pull out a stack of printouts from Dante's computer—phone call transcriptions, text message screen-shots, bank statements, and photographs of Frank Bonpen-siero meeting with Kratos Drakos.

I drop the packet on the desk. "You should see this."

Luciano doesn't immediately look down.

"What is this?"

"It's a packet of information concerning—"

"No. *You*, coming here like this. This Dante's idea?"

"No, Mr. Amato," I smile frostily. "It's *mine*."

His eyes finally drop to the pages on the desk. His brow furrows as he pushes aside the top few sheets to land on a printout of a photo of Frank Bonpensiero shaking hands with Kratos Drakos as the large and good-looking Greek guy is literally handing Frank a wad of cash.

Luciano starts to look angrier and angrier as he skims the printouts, until his teeth are flashing and his eyes are drawn to slits.

Slowly, his gaze lifts to me.

"Where'd this shit come from?"

"Let's just say my husband is skilled at collecting information when he wants to."

Luciano smiles grimly. "Apparently so." He drums his fingers on the table before he raises his eyes past me. "PAULIE!" he roars, making me half jump out of my chair. "Paulie! Get in here!"

The door to the office opens, and the big guy from outside steps in. "Yes, Don Amato?"

"Where the fuck is Frank Bonpensiero right now?"

The guy frowns. "Like, right *now* right now? I think he's over in Sheepshead Bay on business."

Luciano leans back in his chair, cracking his knuckles. "Go get him. Bring him here. Oh, and Paulie?" His lips curl. "Clear my schedule for the rest of the day and open up one of the free embalming rooms downstairs, yeah?"

"You got it, boss."

When Paulie leaves, Luciano levels his cold eyes at me. "We're done here, Mrs. Sartorre."

I nod silently, standing and turning to go.

"But you can tell Dante and Vito the next time you see them that my threat regarding Club Venom is off the table. *Capice?*"

I turn and incline my head. "Thank you, Don Amato."

He smirks. "He was smart to marry you, sweetheart. And I don't mean just to keep his little sex club."

I blush as I dip my head again. "Thank you."

36

DANTE

I'D LIKE to think I've accomplished a lot in my life. I conquered depression and my grief for my sister. I founded Club Venom and built the empire I sit atop today. I've hunted demons and brought monsters to their knees.

But tonight, I have a whole new challenge to deal with, one I'm not sure I'll survive: Tempest wants to come to the club.

Not through the back door, to hide out in my office. Through the front, as my wife, my date, and Club Venom guest. Not as Taylor, either. As herself.

At first it was a firm "Oh hell no" from me. But my wife can be...*persuasive*.

My balls are still tingling and my cock is still a little sore from her persuasiveness earlier.

Also, the idea of having her here is growing on me. I mean this *is* my castle, and she's my queen. Obviously, it's not as if either of us is going to be joining in with the "group activities" in the main room. But if Tempest wants to watch?

Why not.

Funny. I never once pictured myself being okay with bringing a woman here whom I was interested in. But here we are.

But before all of that, I'm on the phone in my office, having come to Venom early. Not just any phone call, either.

This might be the most important phone call I've ever had.

"You're sure?" I blurt.

When the guy on the other end answers in the affirmative, I can feel my pulse soar as adrenaline and dopamine flood my system.

Holy shit.

"Yeah, set it up," I grin into the phone. "Make it happen. And —thank you," I murmur quietly. *"Thank you,* Dr. Han."

I'm buzzing as I pour myself a drink and wait for Tempest, who should be here any minute now. I'm practically bouncing up and down as I grin and slam down my drink. Then I glance at the time.

She was supposed to be here five minutes ago.

I make myself a second drink and wait, checking in with some of my people as the evening's festivities get underway. When it's been another twenty minutes and there's still no word from Tempest, I call her.

She doesn't answer.

Half an hour later, she's still not here, hasn't checked in with the front door staff, and isn't answering her phone.

My skin begins to tingle, the hairs on the back of my neck beginning to prickle. I send Tempest my tenth text message of the evening, even though she hasn't replied to or even read a single one of them. My ears ringing, I call her again.

Nothing.

My jaw clenches and I try Lorenzo instead.

"Where are you?"

"Hey, boss," he grunts over speakerphone. "I'm in the car, almost at the Hamptons house. Bianca needed a ride back to the city."

I roll my eyes. "Jesus Christ, Lorenzo." I mean, I know the guy views her as the kid sister he never had, but come on. "She can take an Uber."

He chuckles quietly. "I know. But soon she'll be off touring the world as some prima ballerina, and I won't be able to spoil her anymore."

I sigh. "Okay, just… Let me know when you're back."

"Everything okay, Mr. Sartorre?" he growls, concern in his voice.

"It's fine, Lorenzo," I shake my head. "I can handle it myself. Call me when you get back with Bianca."

I drum my fingers on the desk, ready to call Tempest yet again when suddenly, my phone lights up with a text from her:

TEMPEST:

Come fuck me

I exhale slowly, the knots of worry dropping away from my shoulders.

Someone's feeling a little forward tonight.

ME:

I thought we had plans for Venom

TEMPEST:

Plans have changed. Unless you're not man enough

My brow arches, and I smirk. Someone's feeling *very* forward tonight.

ME:

You're in trouble in twenty minutes

I leave some of my best people in charge of the club and jump in my SUV to speed home. I leave it with the valet and head into the lobby.

…Where suddenly I freeze as I lock eyes with Gabriel and Alistair, who are sitting on the bench against the wall next to the concierge desk, scowling.

"Evening, Mr. Sartorre, sir!" Joey, the front desk guy, smiles at me. "These gentlemen are here to see you."

"We were here *ten fucking minutes ago*," Alistair grunts. "To see our sister, who *also* lives here."

Joey shoots me a sheepish look. "I apologize, Mr. Sartorre. But you know it's building policy that only guests of listed residents be let in. Obviously, I know Mrs. Sartorre is your wife, but we never updated the register with her listed on the penthouse—"

"It's fine, Joey," I smile, shaking my head and turning to frown at the Black brothers. I walk over to them as they stand. "What are you doing here?"

Gabriel frowns. "Tempest texted me that she needed help with something at your place. I got here five minutes ago and was surprised to find this guy"—he elbows Alistair—"already here with the same message from her."

Huh. I get the distinct impression someone whose name starts with "T" and ends with "empest" is playing a game of surprise mediation between her brothers and I. Which *should* piss me off. But fuck it, if that's what she wants, so be it.

Christ, has this women gotten under my skin.

"What is this, a fucking intervention?" Alistair growls.

"It would seem so," I reply.

"Yeah, well, thanks but no thanks," Alistair mutters. He elbows his brother to go. Gabriel stays where he is, and Alistair just shrugs. "Fine. Have fun." He turns, and he's starting to walk away when I just spit it out.

Fuck it. I made a promise, but my future is with Tempest. And that future demands honesty. Besides, Layla always did tell me to not go over the edge, and if I don't tell them the truth and let them keep hating me, that'll be it. *That* will be the edge I fall over.

"She didn't want you to know. Layla, I mean."

Alistair freezes mid-step. Gabriel's face turns to stone.

"What the hell did you just say?" Alistair hisses.

I turn to Joey. "Joey, would you mind…"

He nods. "Of course, Mr. Sartorre." He steps past us and outside to light a cigarette, giving us the lobby to ourselves.

"When I was a freshman at Knightsblood," I murmur quietly, "I was in a dark place. I mean *dark*. Claudia had just died, I had the loss of my parents deaths to think about, plus worrying about Bianca having a future or the proper kind of supervision now that I was away at school..."

I frown and shake my head. "Not telling you about everything that was happening—or had happened—with Layla wasn't meant to hurt you—"

"Bullshit," Alistair snarls. "You stonewalled us just to fuck with—"

"*You?!*" I snap back. "It wasn't ever *about* you, either of you! It was about respecting Layla's last wishes!"

Gabriel's eyes narrow. "Why the fuck would you give a single shit about—"

"Because she was my *best fucking friend*!" I roar. "When I was at my lowest, she brought me out of it. Look, it was never anything more than platonic. We used to joke that she was like Claudia to me, a surrogate big sister."

"Well, she was our *real* sister," Alistair snarls. "And she never once used—"

"Heroin? Wrong. She went to rehab for it twice. The night she died was her fourth overdose."

They both go silent, looking like they're not sure if they should break down or break my face.

"She never wanted you to know because she never wanted you to be disappointed in her. She knew she had her demons," I growl, "and she wanted so badly to beat them before either of you noticed."

Alistair whirls to press his fists to the marble tiled walls of the lobby as he drops his head back and roars a curse.

"Why the marriage?" Gabriel says quietly. "It wasn't to hide the drug use. That went on the record the second she was checked in and tested for narcotics."

When I say nothing, his eyes narrow and he steps toward me. *"Just fucking tell me,"* he hisses.

I bow my head.

"Layla was pregnant."

There's a beat before Alistair suddenly rushes at me. Gabriel grabs him, yanking him back in a tight embrace.

"Easy!" he snaps at his brother.

"I'll fucking kill you!" Alistair roars at me.

I shake my head. *"It wasn't mine.* I've already told you, Layla was like a sister to me. Touching her that way never once crossed my mind." My jaw clenches. "It was her dealer."

Alistair's eyes blaze. I lock mine with his.

"He's dead," I growl quietly, my words heavy with meaning. "And for what it's worth… He didn't go well, or quickly."

Gabriel arches a brow before slowly dipping his chin to me. Which is probably the closest I'm going to get to a "thank you", but I'll take it. I nod back.

Another second or two ticks by before Alistair finally sighs slowly, eying me. "We're not remotely done with this conversation, but should we go up and see what the fuck Tempest wants?"

I smile to myself as I turn and press the elevator button. "Definitely. I'm supposed to be at the club right now. But Lorenzo couldn't swing by to check in because he's on his way to get Bianca."

Gabriel frowns as the elevator door opens. "From my place?"

My head snaps around violently as my eyes narrow on him. "*Excuse me?*"

His brow cocks with some confusion. "Bianca's at my house. I was just there."

"And why the *fuck* is my sister at your house?"

"*Easy,* Dante. She's hanging out with Maeve. They're friends now."

"What?" I snap. "Why the fuck haven't I heard this?"

Alistair snorts. "Probably because Bianca knew you'd throw a shit fit precisely like this if you did."

I grunt, saying nothing as the elevator doors close and we starts to ascend. We're just getting off at my floor when my phone rings.

"Lorenzo," I sigh as I answer. "I don't know if it's miscommunication or Bianca fucking with you, but she's—"

"They got the wrong guy, Mr. Sartorre."

I frown, tensing. "What?"

"Sorry, yeah, I just got in touch with Bianca. She has no idea how that text about her being at your Hamptons house got sent from her phone, but that's not why I'm calling." He clears his throat. "I just got off the phone with my guy at the NYPD. That guy they fingered as the one who put arsenic in your wine?"

"Yeah?" I growl warily.

"They're thinking it's a setup."

My blood turns cold. *"What?!"*

Alistair and Gabriel glance at me with frozen, concerned expressions.

"The guy has a rock-solid alibi for the dates he could have been sneaking into Mr. Black's wine cellar. He was checked into a detox center you can't leave for a week on either side of the night you all got poisoned."

"Shit," I hiss.

"Oh, and there's signs of forced entry on one of his windows. I think it's safe to say someone set the poor bastard up to take a fall. Might even been the same people...or person... who gave him the coke with fentanyl in it."

"Goddammit."

"It gets weirder, boss. They finally got the handwriting analysis back from the cork. It's a woman's handwriting, Mr. Sartorre. Actually, it matches someone on record."

"Who?"

"Ninety-eight percent match with Jacqueline Sinclair."

It suddenly feels as if the world is moving in slow motion as I turn to stare at a confused-looking Alistair and Gabriel. *"The* Jacqueline Sinclair? Brett Sinclair's mom?"

"Wait, what?" Gabriel hisses.

"That's the one, Mr. Sartorre," Lorenzo says.

"But she's *dead*. That's impossible—"

"Dante."

I whirl toward Alistair's cold, warning murmur, and my blood turns to ice when I see where he's pointing: my penthouse door is open a crack.

"Lorenzo," I hiss quietly, my adrenaline suddenly pumping hard. "Get to my place as fast as you fucking can."

I hang up and put the phone in my pocket before I reach into my jacket and pull out my gun. My finger raises to my lips, and I use my toe to ease open the door to my penthouse. I slip inside, with Tempest's brothers right behind me.

Instantly, I stop cold when my eyes land on a cooler with the lid open right inside the door, filled with those damned *smoothies*.

One of them is open and tipped over onto the floor in a disgusting, creamy greenish puddle.

Something is very wrong.

I draw the hammer back on my Glock and move toward the living room, hugging the wall. Suddenly, I stop.

Oh fuck.

Tempest is sitting in a chair on the patio off my living room —bound and gagged.

"Tempest!"

I lurch toward the patio door, when suddenly, I hear a metallic click.

"That's far enough, Dante. Put the gun on the floor and kick it over here. *Now.*"

Holy shit. I know that voice.

384

"What the fuck?!" Gabriel hisses when he comes up behind me. "*Pam?!*"

Gabriel's housekeeper steps out from behind the staircase, aiming a gun at my head.

"I'm *so* glad you could make it, Mr. Sartorre," Jacqueline Sinclair purrs, her lips curling. "I want you to be here to see me exact my revenge."

37

TEMPEST

I'm screaming into the gag as "Pam"—or Jacqueline Sinclair, as I found out half an hour ago when she came over with smoothies for me and then pulled a fucking *gun* on me—shoves Dante and my brothers out onto the patio at gunpoint. For a second, blinded by panic and fear, I lurch to my feet. Instantly, her weapon swivels toward me, her eyes narrowing.

"*Please,*" she hisses. "Give me a reason to pull the trigger, you little cunt."

My eyes dart to Dante. His jaw is clenched, his gaze locked on mine with an intensity that both scares me and fills me with strength.

Sit down, little hurricane, he mouths.

I swallow as I sink back onto the chair, watching as the woman I knew as Pam hustles them all toward three chairs across the patio from me.

This isn't the quiet, somewhat frosty housekeeper who makes me amazing smoothies.

This is the mother of the monster that almost destroyed me.

Part of me is dumbfounded that I never saw who Pam was. Even though Jacqueline and I obviously never met, I mean, she's *Jacqueline Sinclair*. She was a huge name in the New York City socialite scene for years, and her pictures were splashed all over the society news.

But "Pam" looks nothing like that glamorous, cosmetically perfect blonde woman. I remember Gabriel once telling me that after Brett killed himself and his parents divorced, Jacqueline had fallen into drugs and poverty and passed away herself.

Apparently, that last part was slightly exaggerated. But now that I know who she is, you can see glimmers of the old glamorous Jacqueline behind the grayed, harried, old-before-her-time face of "Pam".

"You," she snaps at Alistair. "Tie him up." She nods her chin at Gabriel. "And don't jerk me around. I'm going to be checking when you're done. If it's loose, I use a bullet. Got it?"

Alistair nods silently, kneeling behind Gabriel's chair and tying our brother's hands tight.

"Now him." She nods at Dante. "And don't bullshit me, *Mr. Black.*"

Alistair ties Dante's wrists behind him. When he's done, Jacqueline makes Alistair sit in the third chair, where she ties him up herself. She stands, hefting the gun meditatively and smirking as she walks over to me.

"I've dreamed of this moment, you know," she hisses. "Every night, while I clawed my way back from the gutter. After I inserted myself into your home, and *bowed* to you," she sneers. "Made your fucking bed! Did your laundry! Cooked your *food*!"

She shakes her head, a wild look in her eyes.

"You couldn't just take the fucking money like the rest of those gold-digging little whores who chased after my darling Brett and then cried rape! You couldn't just *take the fucking money*!"

"Because your son was a piece of shit rapist!" Alistair roars behind her.

She whirls, a livid look on her face as she marches over. I scream through the gag as she slams the butt of the gun against my brother's temple, making him groan and jerk back. Blood trickles down the side of his head as he blinks quickly.

"Don't you *dare* talk about my Brett that way!" She screams. "Slandered! Maligned by the press! Driven to hurt himself like that!" She shakes her head, raises the gun, and aims it right between Gabriel's eyes.

I start to scream through the gag. Jacqueline pauses, turning to arch a brow at me.

"Something you'd like to say, bitch?!"

Jacqueline marches over to me, swinging the gun in her hand and making me flinch. Dante roars, his arms bulging as he yanks at his binds. Jacqueline ignores him as she reaches out and yanks the gag from my mouth, allowing me to suck in sweet, clean air.

"Let them go! Please!" I blurt, tears streaming down my face. "You can hurt me if you want! Hurt me for what I drove Brett to!"

"TEMPEST!" Dante roars. "Stop it!"

"Don't talk to her!" Gabriel bellows.

I ignore them both, my eyes leveling with Jacqueline's.

This is a trade I can easily make. She wants someone to kill, to feel like she's avenged her shithead son. *Fine.* That can be me. I can do that. But it's not going to be either of my brothers. And it's *not* going to be the man I love.

I stiffen the second the word even enters my head.

Love.

I love him.

"You want to hurt someone?!" I blurt. "You want to kill for your son?! Then kill me!! Please!"

Jacqueline's brows raise and slowly, the corners of her lips curl up. "Oh, but Tempest," she grins wickedly. "I already have been, for months."

What?

"Do you like your smoothies, hon?" she sneers.

Oh my God.

"They taste just a teensy bit different when you make them yourself?"

Holy fuck.

"I could have just hit you with a car," Jacqueline says coldly, her eyes burning hatred into me. "Or shot you. Or hired someone to beat your face in." She smiles thinly. "But I wanted to make *them* suffer, too, for wanting to take my poor boy to court and ruining his life. I wanted to make them watch you fade away slowly." Her lips curl even more, until her face is a mask of evil. "Your precious Dr. Han would never have tested for it, because, well, who would ever think arsenic when you already show all the signs of methylmalonic acidemia?"

No.

"Tempest!" Alistair yells, his eyes wild. "What the fuck is—"

"She's been dying for the last few months, you idiots," Jacqueline sneers, spinning toward my brothers. "She just hasn't bothered to tell you."

They both yank their gazes past her to me, their faces white.

"Tempest..." Gabriel chokes, shaking his head side to side. "*No.* That's not—"

"The best part, Tempest," Jacqueline continues, "is I've already killed you. I could let you go right now, and there's nothing they'd be able to do to save you. Your organs are starting to shut down. Thrown up any blood recently?"

A single tear starts to trickle down my cheek. Jacqueline spots it and laughs coldly.

"Hmm, that's what I'll do. You can sit there and watch me take away everything you love in this world: your brothers, and your little fake husband. And then I'll let you go. So you can wander aimlessly, like me. So that you can fall into the gutter and scream to nobody who will listen about the injustice that was done to you. And then, Tempest," she hisses, leering close to me. "Then you can fucking *die*."

She whirls, marching over to Dante and my brothers and bringing the gun up.

"Now… Which one do you love the most?"

"Please…" I choke.

"Is it Gabriel?"

She grins as she presses the gun barrel to his forehead.

"NO!"

She laughs. "Or maybe the adopted one?"

"STOP IT!" I scream when she presses the gun to Alistair's temple.

"Or *maybe*," she muses, walking back to Dante, nearest the edge of the rooftop patio. "Maybe it's—"

"GET AWAY FROM HIM!"

The whole scene goes still for a moment. Jacqueline turns her head toward me, smiling coldly. "I think we have a winner."

No.

This isn't happening. Not like this.

I watch, nauseated and horrified, as Jacqueline raises the gun and rests the barrel against Dante's forehead. Then it hits me.

I'm already dead.

There's no saving me.

But I can save him.

I'm not even aware I'm on my feet until I'm running. My hands are tied in front of me, but Jacqueline never bothered with my legs, since she had a gun on me.

That's going to cost her.

She whirls at the last second when she hears my footsteps. But just as her face pales, and she tries to swing the gun toward me, I slam into her as hard as I can. We both scream and go toppling backward, backward, backward....

...And hit the patio railing at waist height.

I hear Dante roaring my name. I feel the lift as I shove Jacqueline backward into midair, then the pull of gravity as I follow her over the railing, forty-odd stories above the streets of New York.

It's okay.

My bill has already been paid. My ticket already punched. And I've always thought the worst part about this whole dying business was that I was going to die slowly.

Looks like it's going to be much faster now.

And besides, I had the time I shared with Dante.

I got to feel love.

And that's a life well lived.

My body follows Jacqueline's over the edge, momentum yanking me down until we both slip over into the abyss.

38

DANTE

It all happens so fucking fast it's like watching a bullet leave a gun.

…But I'm faster.

The split-second Tempest and Jacqueline hit the railing, the ropes at my back finally snap under the strain I've been putting on them. I'm pretty sure I've just dislocated my shoulder, but fuck that.

I'm on my feet a nanosecond later. The rope is still tangled in the chair, so I grab that too as I bolt toward the two women teetering on the edge.

You are not going to die like this, Tempest.

I can save her.

I'm *going to* save her.

Just as they start to slip, I wrap the end of the rope around my wrist and hurl the chair at the planters dotting the side of the patio.

Hey, Dante. Don't go over the edge, okay? There's a whole world out there.

I never did go over the edge again.

But I'm going to now. For Tempest.

I leap over the side of the patio, gravity yanking me down after them. My hand closes around Tempest's ankle, so tight I might rip her goddamn foot off. But I don't let go, even though I'm falling too.

And then, two things happen:

First, the chair catches the planters. The rope goes taut, and if my arm wasn't yanked out of the socket before, it sure as fuck is now. I roar as my arms stretch past their breaking point—one hand holding the rope that's tangled in the chair against the railing above, the other holding Tempest's ankle.

Then the second thing happens. Jacqueline's face is white as she makes one last-ditch reach with her outstretched hand…

…And snags the rope tying Tempest's wrists together.

Shit.

Tempest screams as her arms go too tight from Jacqueline's weight. I see pure searing white pain as *both* arms dislocate from their sockets, agony exploding through every nerve in my body.

But there's *no fucking way* I'm letting go.

Time does pause for a second then, I think: the three of us dangling forty-four stories above the streets of Manhattan. Jacqueline holding to Tempest. Me holding Tempest. The chair holding me.

…The chair that starts to creak *very* loudly a second later.

Tempests screams, her hair whipping wildly in the wind as she looks up at me. Her big hazel-green eyes are terrified as they lock onto mine.

"*I'm not letting go!*" I hiss. "I'm *not. Letting. Go!*"

"Dante!"

I glance up just as the rope gives slightly. Gabriel looks over the edge, frantically grabbing at the rope. The end I'm holding is fraying quickly—more quickly than he can pull the three of us up.

Suddenly, Alistair is there too, grabbing on the rope as well and hauling us up.

"Fuck...*you!*"

My head snaps down just in time to see Jacqueline raise the gun in her hand toward Tempest.

Oh fuck.

Tempest screams as the first shot explodes from the gun. But Jacqueline's spinning in midair, and her shot is way off.

Her next one might not be.

My eyes raise to Gabriel right before he disappears from the edge, and I hope to God he and I are thinking the same thing. A second later, he returns, and indeed he's got the gun I dropped before.

"Shoot her!" I roar.

Gabriels' eyes are wild, his aim all over the place as Alistair keeps slowly pulling us up.

"Gabriel!" I bellow at him. "*Shoot—*"

"I've only shot a fucking gun like twice before!!" he roars back.

Tempest starts to shake violently. My eyes snap back down, widening when I see hers roll back in her head as her mouth begins to froth.

Oh God, no.

She's having a seizure.

She's fucking *dying.*

Suddenly, just as Jacqueline raises her gun, I feel hands grabbing my ankles. The wind slows, and the wild spin of all three of us goes still.

I let go of the rope, feeling the arms around my ankles tighten. I raise my hand as I look back up at Gabriel.

"Drop the gun!"

He stares at me. "*What?!*"

"DROP! IT! TO! ME!"

Time slows to a crawl. I watch as Gabriel lets go, following the gun with my eyes as it slips from his fingers and plummets toward me. The gun hits my hand. My fingers curl around it and I bring it up.

My finger squeezes, and the bullet explodes from the barrel.

Jacqueline's head snaps back, a black and red hole right in the middle of her forehead. Her hand slips from the rope binding Tempest's wrists, and I watch as she drops into space, hurtling away from us.

Tempest is still convulsing.

"Pull us up!!"

Arms tug us back up over the railing until we go tumbling to the patio floor. I lurch over Tempest, ignoring the ripping pain in my shoulders as I cradle her head.

"What the fuck is happening to her!!" Alistair roars as I yank my phone out and unlock it.

"Her kidneys are shutting down."

They both stare at me blankly in horror.

"She's having a fucking seizure because she's dying!" I scream at them both. "My phone!" I jerk my chin at it as I lift Tempest into my arms. "There's a Dr. Han in my contacts. Call him, tell him I say we're doing this *right fucking now*, and that we'll be there as fast as we can. He'll understand."

Gabriel grabs my phone as I lock eyes with Alistair.

"What can I do?" he chokes.

"Drive. Fast. *Now."*

39

TEMPEST

THE FIRST THING I see when I open my eyes is my brothers hovering over me. I frown, blinking away the darkness as I focus on them.

"Not so close, do you both need glasses?" I wrinkle my nose. "Gabriel, seriously. I can smell the fucking French fries on your breath."

The two of them grin widely and exhale.

"How do you feel?"

"I—"

Dante.

I start to jerk to an upright position, but instantly choke on the pain that explodes throughout my abdomen.

"Whoa! Hang on there, T," Alistair grunts, grabbing my shoulders and easing me back down. "You've just had major surgery."

My pulse skips. "Wait, *what*?! Where's Dante?!"

"Just breathe, Tempest," Gabriel murmurs.

"*Where is he?!*"

"He's *fine*," Alistair interjects. "He's here at the hospital, too."

Gabriel smiles and takes my hand as he peers into my eyes. "Yeah, he's fine. How much do you remember?"

I try to force my brain to replay everything that happened on Dante's patio. All I can really remember is falling, and then blacking out.

Shit, I had a seizure.

I close my eyes, exhaling slowly before I open them again.

"I need to tell you both something."

"Tempest, it can wait. We need to talk to you about—"

"Shut up, Alistair," I mutter. "Look, I have something, and it's bad, okay? It's called severe late-onset methylmalonic acidemia—"

"No, you don't," Gabriel smiles quietly at me.

I scowl. "Just shut *up* and let me get this off my chest, okay? I didn't tell either of you, and I feel like shit about it, but I—"

"Tempest, you don't have methyl-acide-whatever."

I glare at Alistair. "Methylmalonic acidemia."

"Okay. Sure. You don't have it."

I blink. "Sorry, *what?*"

"Do you remember the patio?"

I shake my head. "Only bits and pieces," I say quietly as my brain tries to process what they just said. "I'm sorry, did you just say I *don't* have methylmalonic acidemia?"

"Correct. But you *are* working through some serious long-term arsenic poisoning."

Holy shit.

Then, suddenly, I remember.

"Pam..."

"Also known as Jacqueline Sinclair," Gabriel growls viciously. "Tempest, I'm so fucking sorry. That crazy bitch slipped right under my radar. I mean, she was in my fucking *house* with you..."

He looks away, his face pained. Slowly, I inch my hand to his and squeeze it.

"You did think she was dead. And *Pam* looks nothing like the Jacqueline we always saw in the tabloids."

He nods, still looking away. Alistair clears his throat.

"She was slowly poisoning your food. And when you started to lose your appetite, she started feeding you those smoothies. The hospital ran a lab test on them, by the way." He scowls. "That cunt was putting anti-nausea meds in them, too, to make you think they were the only thing you could stomach."

I nod slowly. Anti-nausea meds. *That's* probably why the smoothies tasted different when I tried to replicate them. Then my eyes drop to the hospital gown I'm wearing, and I yank it up over my abdomen. My face pales when I see the bandages on my side.

"What the *fuck*—!"

"*Breathe*, sis," Alistair growls, glancing at Gabriel. "You've had surgery. Think you missed that when we told you earlier."

"For what?!"

"The effects of long-term arsenic poisoning are reversible, mostly. You're going to be on a bunch of meds and vitamins for a month or so to get you back to normal and to kickstart your immune system after the havoc that's been wreaked on it." Alistair frowns. "What *isn't* reversible, and what was adding to the acidosis of your blood and giving you those confusion spells, was that your kidneys were toxifying."

My eyes go wide and a sick feeling pools in my stomach as I look back down to my abdomen—at the gauze and bandages wrapped around it. At the swollen, bruised skin. At the tubes snaking in and out of my veins and the incision site.

Jesus fucking Christ.

"They're both still in there," Gabriel chuckles. "Which I didn't know was how they did it until your procedure. But you've got a new one in there, too."

My eyes snap to his. "Who—?"

"Dante," he smiles.

My mouth falls open. "*What?*"

"He talked to Dr. Han a little while back and had some tests run. Turns out, he's a perfect match. So after we pulled you back onto that roof while you were seizing, Dante called Dr. Han, asked for the operation to be prepped, and we hauled you in."

I stare at my abdomen once again before my head snaps up.

"I want to see him. Now."

Alistair chuckles. "Figured as much—."

"*Now*, Alistair!" I blurt, my heart racing.

"Remember the part where you just had *organ transplant* surgery?" Alistair grunts. But he and Gabriel unlock the wheels of my bed and start to push me and the rack of machines and IVs toward the door.

They wheel me into the hall, where an orderly checks my notes and confirms that I am allowed to be taken into Dante's room. When the door opens, my heart surges when he looks up from where he's talking with Lorenzo and Bianca, the latter of whom squeals and rushes over to me.

"Oh my God, Tempest!" she blurts, squeezing my hand tightly.

I grin at her, but then my eyes swivel right back to Dante. I'm almost bouncing out of my bed as they wheel it next to his. The second we stop moving, I go to claw my way into his bed, but they all stop me with shouts.

"Easy, Tempest!" Gabriel snaps. "For fuck's sake, you're going to kill yours—"

"I need to be *there*," I blurt, pointing at Dante's bed. He looks up and grins as our eyes lock.

"I thought I felt the winds pick up." He turns to my brothers and Lorenzo. "Help her?"

"This is *such* a shit idea," Alistair grunts, but he, Gabriel, and Lorenzo lift me gingerly from my bed and into Dante's.

"Hey, little hurricane," he mumurs quietly.

I turn my head to gaze at him. "You seriously gave me a fucking *kidney?*"

"It's just a loan. I need it back when you're done with it."

I giggle, leaning in to kiss him as best as I can.

"That might not be for a while. Apparently I'm not dying."

"Well, then I guess you just hang on to it."

He grins, leaning in to kiss me again. Just then, the door flies open, and Maeve comes charging in.

"You're okay!" she sobs, shoving past Alistair and Gabriel to hug me tightly, making me wince.

She pulls back to grin at me, wiping a tear away. I frown as my eyes lock onto the bruising around her left one. "Jesus, Maeve!" I blurt. "What the fuck happened to your eye?"

She glances down. "I…it's nothing. I fell."

Gabriel's face hardens to a stony mask as he turns her toward him and peers at her black eye.

"Maeve…" he growls.

"It's really nothing—"

"Thank God you're okay, Tempest!"

We all turn as Charles comes blustering into the room. Instantly, a chill settles over everything as we all look at Maeve's face, then at him.

"What happened to her eye, Charles," Alistair says quietly, his voice ice.

Our grandfather's face darkens for a second before he clears his throat. "What? Nothing. She fell. Didn't you, sweetheart?"

"Fuck this," Gabriel snarls. "No more stalling. No more bull-shit. Maeve, you're moving into my place. Today."

"She *has* a home, Gabriel," Charles mutters.

But my brother just shakes his head. "Not with you anymore she doesn't, you scum-sucking piece of shit."

Charles' nostrils flare as he glares at Gabriel. "*Careful, Gabriel.*"

"Or *what*, Charles?" Alistair snaps. "You'll cause a big scene at a fucking board meeting?"

Alistair scoffs.

"We can't remove you from the board, Charles," Gabriel says pointedly. "But Maeve's moving out of your house. Today. This delay tactic of yours while I'm sure you've been shop-ping her out as a bride-for-cash is fucking *done.* If you put up a stink about it, I will fucking *bury you* in legal motions and criminal complaints, whether Maeve testifies or not."

Our grandfather's face is furious. "You can't *take* my fucking daughter away from—"

"Mr. Black."

Dante's voice is tired. But it still thunders through the room.

"It's time for you to leave."

Charles glares death at him. His hands close to fists. But then, with a snarl, he whirls and storms out of the door.

Maeve bites her lip, looking at each of us in turn before her gaze settles on Gabriel. "I can really move in with you?"

"Definitely."

Everyone stays for another ten minutes or so, then slowly says their goodbyes, promising to check in soon. Dr. Han pokes his nose in, squeezing my hand and telling me my new kidney is doing just fine, and that *I'm* going to be just fine.

Finally, Dante and I are alone, squeezed into the tiny hospital bed.

He turns his head to kiss me slowly, and I grin as I kiss him back.

"I still can't believe you gave me a kidney," I murmur as I lean my head on his shoulder.

"Well, you already have my heart, little hurricane," he says quietly. "Why not a kidney, too?"

We both let that gem of a line hang there for a second before I snort and start laughing, even though it hurts.

"That was a *terrible* joke."

He chuckles as he kisses me again. "Sorry. I'll work on it."

"I'll always love you even if you don't."

Yeah?" He grins as he leans in, his lips brushing mine. "Good, because I'll always love you, too."

EPILOGUE

TEMPEST

Two months later:

My heart is racing as I stand and reach across the desk to shake Dean Keller's hand.

"Thank you so much for seeing me today, ma'am."

She waves off the formality with a grin. "You know, being that I changed one of your diapers once, I think we can stick with Maureen. What do you think?"

I laugh as my face heats. "I think I'm really excited to start."

"Good! Because we're *really* looking forward to seeing you next semester, Tempest."

Back when she was changing one of my diapers, Maureen Keller was one of New York City's top hot-shot attorneys, and good friends with my dad. Now, after leaving private law, she's the Dean of Admissions for Columbia Law School, where she and my dad were students together.

Where I'll be following in his footsteps.

Finally.

Life becomes a bit less singleminded when you realize you're not dying tomorrow. Well, okay, we *all* might die tomorrow, as macabre of a thought that is. But when you're literally ticking days off a calendar until your final breath, it's just one dark tunnel vision.

And then one day, someone shows you a light at the end of that tunnel. Actually, in my case, you get told that *there is no tunnel.* And suddenly, the world opens up.

I'm doing things again I never thought I would. Like I've taken up running for reasons I'm not sure I could even explain, because I actually used to hate running.

I've also started learning to cook, to...*mixed* results, even if Dante puts on an Oscar-worthy performance at whatever I put in front of him, edible or otherwise.

Either way, I'm putting on weight again, which feels fucking *great.*

But another thing I'm doing now that I actually have a future is going back to school.

When what happened to me happened, and when Nina died, I went into recluse mode. I finished high school remotely, and then went on to do most of my undergrad from the comfort of my bedroom behind a laptop screen. My brothers pushed hard for me to apply to the law program at Columbia, which I sort of begrudgingly did but then tossed aside when my diagnosis came in.

Alistair sent it in for me, and then pulled some strings to get me on a sort of "deferred acceptance" list. I spent months feeling guilty that there was probably some other budding young lawyer out there not getting a chance because a dead girl was taking up their spot.

But now, I'm finally taking that shot myself, starting next semester.

After leaving Dean Keller's office on the Columbia campus, I shoot downtown for my appointment with Dr. Han. But first, I make a pit-stop into Magnolia Bakery for a red velvet cupcake, which I know he loves.

Dr. Han was *horrified* when he found out my acidosis was actually arsenic poisoning. Apparently, the man even drafted a letter to the New York Medical Board to ask that his license be revoked for missing it. Mercifully, his wife stopped him before he could jump on the grenade like that.

The misdiagnosis is *not* his fault. I even threatened Alistair with violence if he didn't back off from pushing me for a malpractice lawsuit. I mean the symptoms between what they thought I had and what was actually going on are identical, and who the *hell* would think that they're being poisoned with freaking *arsenic* outside of 1900's London? It'd be like getting diagnosed with "acute stabbing ailment from Jack the Ripper".

So, the cupcakes every time I go in for a post-transplant checkup are my way of telling him we're good.

I still have nightmares from time to time. I still occasionally find myself slipping into the dark places. And I've had some issues with trusting new people recently, after the whole Pam/Jacqueline ordeal. I mean the woman was never my best friend, but she spent almost a *year* smiling into my face as she watched me drink poison.

The night of that ill-fated dinner party, when Dante, Charles, and both of my brothers went to the hospital after Jacqueline had given all the wine glasses a rinse of poison, she even covered her tracks by giving herself a small dose and claiming to have drunk some of the wine, too. The message on the cork she scrawled during the chaos when everyone but Maeve and I were falling sick.

So, yeah, that can throw you off when it comes to opening up to new people. But therapy is awesome, and Alessia, my therapist, is fantastic.

The important thing to remember is, no one is ever "fine". *No one* has it all together without a single crack, or a darkness lurking in their shadows, or a fear dogging their step.

The important thing is, you wake up each day and you make the most of it. And if you find someone who makes you stronger, you hang on to them tight.

And that someone is my next and final stop after my late check-in with Dr. Han.

Lorenzo raises the partition of the Escalade before I even unzip the garment bag, closing me off in the back.

"You sure you don't want to head home first to change, Mrs. Sartorre?" He asks through the intercom.

"Nah, I don't want to be late," I grunt as I kick off my boots and start shimmying out of my black jeans. "You know how the tyrant gets."

Lorenzo chuckles from his side of the partition as I shrug off my cardigan.

"And, Lorenzo, for real, when are we gonna switch to just Tempest?"

"Mrs. Sartorre works just fine for me, ma'am."

I roll my eyes as I peel the rest of my clothes off, blushing at being nude in the back of a moving car, even if the partition is up and the windows are movie-star tinted.

"*Ma'am?* Fucking seriously?"

I yank open the garment bag and grin as heat teases up my neck.

My husband has *fantastic* taste in fashion, I have to say. The dress is gold and slinky, with barely a single thread looping around the back of the neck to keep the whole thing from sliding off. Which wouldn't make that much difference if we're being honest, given that the whole dress is half-see-through.

Which, I suppose, is why it's hanging alongside a pair of *very* racy black lace lingerie meant to be worn under it. The bag also contains a pair of knee-high, lace-up black boots.

He knows me so well.

"How about by summer, Lorenzo? Can we shoot for that for going to a first name basis?"

"Afraid not, Mrs. Sartorre."

I roll my eyes, sighing as I slip the lingerie on and the slinky gown.

"It would be a *great* Christmas present."

There's a pause from the front seat.

"That's a maybe!" I crow, howling with laughter.

I lace up both heeled boots and then reach into the depths of the garment bag for the final touch, just as the car stops.

"We're here…" Lorenzo coughs brusquely. "*Miss.*"

Hey, it's a start.

I pull on my gold and black mask and step out of the car.

"Don't wait up!"

Outside the SUV, I feel my pulse quicken and my core tighten as I look up at the unassuming building with the unassuming dark wood door.

The doorbell is silent out here, along with the rest of the quiet, unassuming side street I'm standing on as a fine mist begins to rain down.

The door opens, and as I step into the dim interior, I shiver as a tall, built man with broad shoulders filling out a shut-up-and-fuck-me tuxedo steps in front of me. His piercing blue eyes eviscerate me, like he's stripping the lace from my body. His chiseled jaw grinds, like he's determining my fate here and now.

He reaches for me, and I feel a pulse throb deep inside of me as his powerful hand grabs my hip possessively and pulls me into him, enveloping me in his clean, slightly spicy scent.

"You know my husband would kill a man for touching me like this."

"Would he?" The man growls, his teeth flashing as he leans in close to me. "Well, I like him already."

"I'm pretty sweet on him myself."

Dante grins as he dips his mouth and sears his lips to mine.

"Ready to go inside?"

"Ready."

"Well then," he turns, and two guards open the next set of doors into the depths of sin, darkness, and desire. "Welcome to Club Venom."

The Venomous Gods series continues with Alistair's story in *Devious Vow.*

Haven't gotten enough of Dante and Tempest?
Get their extra scene here, or type this link into your browser: http://BookHip.com/RTSGDFV

This isn't an epilogue or continuation to *Toxic Love.* But this extra hot "follow-up" story is guaranteed to keep the steam going.

ALSO BY JAGGER COLE

<u>Venomous Gods</u>:

Toxic Love

Devious Vow

Poisonous Kiss

Corrupted Heart

<u>Dark Hearts</u>:

Deviant Hearts

Vicious Hearts

Sinful Hearts

Twisted Hearts

Stolen Hearts

Reckless Hearts

<u>Kings & Villains</u>:

Dark Kingdom

Burned Cinder (Cinder Duet #1)

Empire of Ash (Cinder Duet #2)

The Hunter King (Hunted Duet # 1)

The Hunted Queen (Hunted Duet #2)

Prince of Hate

<u>Savage Heirs</u>:

Savage Heir

Dark Prince

Brutal King

Forbidden Crown

Broken God

Defiant Queen

Bratva's Claim:

Paying The Bratva's Debt

The Bratva's Stolen Bride

Hunted By The Bratva Beast

His Captive Bratva Princess

Owned By The Bratva King

The Bratva's Locked Up Love

The Scaliami Crime Family:

The Hitman's Obsession

The Boss's Temptation

The Bodyguard's Weakness

Power:

Tyrant

Outlaw

Warlord

Standalones:

Broken Lines

Bosshole

Grumpaholic

Stalker of Mine

ABOUT THE AUTHOR

A reader first and foremost, Jagger Cole cut his romance writing teeth penning various steamy fan-fiction stories years ago. After deciding to hang up his writing boots, Jagger worked in advertising pretending to be Don Draper. It worked enough to convince a woman way out of his league to marry him, though, which is a total win.

Now, Dad to two little princesses and King to a Queen, Jagger is thrilled to be back at the keyboard.

When not writing or reading romance books, he can be found woodworking, enjoying good whiskey, and grilling outside - rain or shine.

You can find all of his books at
www.jaggercolewrites.com

f X **⊙**

Made in the USA
Las Vegas, NV
02 November 2024

11028265R00233